Book
of
Nathan

Book of Nathan

A Novel

Curt Weeden and Richard Marek

Oceanview Publishing

LONGBOAT KEY, FLORIDA

Published in the United States of America by Oceanview Publishing,
Longboat Key, Florida
www.oceanviewpub.com

2 4 6 8 10 9 7 5 3 1

PRINTED IN THE UNITED STATES OF AMERICA

For Marti, our children, and grandchildren
—C.W.

To Dalma
—R.M.

Book
of
Nathan

Prologue

There was nothing distinctive about the woman. Her olive skin was commonplace in this part of New Brunswick, New Jersey, where the neighborhood had gone from white to black to brown over the past few decades. Bodegas and front yard statues of Our Lady of Guadalupe left no doubt about present-day demographics. It was an hour short of midnight—the start of the Latino parade to one of two downtown hospitals that fueled their backroom nightshifts with the sweat of Dominicans, Puerto Ricans, and Mexicans. Under ordinary circumstances, watching an Hispanic, forty-something woman walk to a job that paid a notch above minimum wage wouldn't warrant a second look.

Except tonight the circumstances were far from ordinary.

"*Él va a matarme!*" she screamed. "*Él va a matarme!*"

The woman stormed toward me, her arms flailing. A dull light filtering through the iron-barred windows of the Gateway Men's Shelter caught the terror in her eyes.

"*Él va a matarme!*" The woman was a few feet away when the tip of her laced-up oxford jammed into a chunk of sidewalk cement pushed out of place by the root of a half-dead oak tree. She landed hard, her right knee taking most of the punishment. Oblivious to the blood running down her shin, she clawed at my trousers.

"*No dejarlo matarme para! Satisfacer!*"

You can't run a men's shelter in Central Jersey without picking up a little conversational Spanish. I had become all too familiar with *violar, asalter, muerte* since rape, assault, and murder were never more than a few streets away from where I worked. *Va a matarme* wasn't hard to decipher either—*going to kill me* is an inner-city refrain that gets replayed far too often. But even if I hadn't been able to translate, the panic in the lady's eyes was sending the same message.

I knelt at the woman's side and said as gently as I could, "No, senora. *Él no es un asesino.*"

My words weren't enough to stop the woman's shaking. She peered into the darkness and her fear materialized into a giant, grotesque form. The thing that loped toward us wore layers of worn, ripped clothing and a hood that covered most of its face.

"*Él es un hombre sin hogar,*" I explained calmly. "A homeless man, senora. Coming here—to this place." I gestured to the building behind me. The Gateway Men's Shelter—depending on one's perspective, either a Dumpster for losers or the last-chance changing room for those who wanted to claw their way back into the ranks of the socially acceptable.

"*El Dios nos ayuda todos,*" the woman whispered and struggled to her feet. "God help us all," she repeated in broken English. I handed her a handkerchief that she pressed against her knee.

"Him especially." I nodded at the bogeyman.

The creature moved into a pale yellow swath of incandescent light that leaked out the Gateway's window. His hood fell from his head. The lady gasped, made the sign of the cross, and ran into the night, the sound of her footsteps gradually swallowed by the white noise of the city.

Later, I would learn his name. Miklos Petris Zeusenoerdorf. His sallow skin was speckled with bumps and boils—a giant pickle with pimples. His sparse hair grew in patches, the longest strands dangling like brown threads over deformed cauliflower ears. Zeusenoerdorf was huge, but his bulk wasn't muscle. Blobs of fat rippled over his body like sheaves of discolored bubble wrap.

In time, one in-the-know wino would sketch out the man's background. On the street, he was called Zeus and he had just finished a stint at East Jersey State, a lockup that used to be called Rahway Prison.

"You scared the hell out of the lady," I said and took the man's arm.

Zeus grunted out a mix of clicks and groans. It was his own Morse code that I would never quite figure out. I led him toward the Gateway's front door, the portal for so many who had fallen to the bottom of the pile, usually because of addiction, mental illness, or just plain bad luck. Inside, I gave Zeusenoerdorf a closer inspection, and when our eyes locked, a twelve-year-old memory took over with such an intensity that several seconds passed before I could speak.

"You need a place to stay?" I asked him, trying to get past the recollection of that autumn afternoon when I jogged past the Bowery Mission on Manhattan's Lower East Side. I couldn't shake the picture of the twenty-five-year-old woman helping a gaggle of booze-beaten men through the front door of the mission. The woman told me her name and I handed her my heart.

"A place to sleep—do you need somewhere to stay?" I asked, trying to clear the image from my mind. Mercifully, the woman's face faded away but not before she pulled back the curtain to show me more of Miklos Zeusenoerdorf. The man's ugly exterior hid a simple, easily confused, gentle person who had an IQ of an eight year-old and a speech impairment that only made him all the more imperfect.

"A bed?" I asked again. "Do you need a bed?"

A mumbled, unintelligible response that I took as a "yes." I motioned Zeus to sit down and retreated to my office, pretending to look for a Gateway sign-in form. When I was alone, I covered my eyes and drew in a long breath. It had been a long time since I last held my wife, Anne. Yet she still visited me often.

I would see her mostly on those days and nights when I had been kicked hard by a job that came with a paltry paycheck and even less respect. That's when she would remind me why I was here—why I left behind a very different life. The year Anne and I were married, I was an advertising executive on a fast track and my wife was a social worker with the Coalition for the Homeless. When I made senior V.P., which brought me a fat six-figure salary and a load of perks, Anne could have easily given up her long hours and skimpy compensation. But she didn't. Our East Side condo and the summer rental in the Hamptons were far less important to her than the coalition's mobile soup kitchen that kept hundreds of New Yorkers from going hungry. Not often, but sometimes, she'd draft me into the coalition's volunteer core so I could experience what it was like to pull a man out of a gutter and onto his feet. After a night of handing out blankets, underwear, and toiletries, I'd retreat to my day job and try like hell to put my heart into pitching an ad campaign for a new fragrance air freshener or a longer-lasting chewing gum.

For the first few years of marriage, I never really got to know the homeless. Even though Anne made sure that I periodically worked my way down humanity's ladder just long enough to catch the stench of poverty and hopelessness, the exposure came with a light coating. One whiff of despair was enough to send me running back to Madison Avenue.

Eventually, though, I came to understand the passion Anne had for her job. She was a converter; someone with an exceptional ability to transform the wretched. Anne didn't use threats or intimidation. No incantations or banging the holy book. She did it all with her words—and her incredible gray blue eyes that tunneled into the minds and souls of those who had been dumped into America's waste bin.

I scooped together a few sheets of blank paper from beneath a small glass paperweight that usually went unnoticed: *For helping others to help themselves.*

I've never put much stock in awards—but I kept this Coalition for the Homeless memento as a reminder of the special connection Anne had to those nine thousand families in New York City who have no permanent address and no shortage of trouble. If it weren't for my wife, I doubt I would have come to understand what homelessness in America really means. If it weren't for a rare but deadly brain tumor called glioblastoma multiforme that killed Anne, I doubt I would have had the guts to try to do something about the problem.

"Okay," I said, "you're good to go. You've got a bed."

The man cocked his mouth into a smile. Then I noticed he wasn't looking at me at all but was staring through the open door of my office at a barely visible eight-by-ten framed photo.

"My wife," I explained after turning to see what was captivating Zeus. It was as if he knew Anne. "She died. Cancer. A long time ago."

Zeusenoerdorf grunted softly and lowered his head.

"Let me show you where you'll be staying," I said and headed toward the corridor that led to the first-floor resident quarters—a complex of small rooms sparsely furnished with bunk beds, used army lockers, and not much else. The big man pulled himself upright and took an awkward step toward me. As if he didn't have enough problems, Zeus also walked with a limp that put his body slightly off center. When he reached the threshold that divided the Gateway's common area from the resident hallway, Zeus's left foot caught the edge of a small throw rug and he tumbled forward. His shoulder drove into my hip and both of us fell hard to the floor. I disentangled myself and got back on my feet, but

Zeus stayed on his hands and knees. Eyes closed and mouth clinched tight, he braced himself as if expecting the sting of a balled-up fist.

I reached for the man. "It's nothing. An accident. Take my hand."

Zeus was suspicious. The Gateway was filled with men accustomed to punishment and distrustful of those quick to help — so I anticipated his reaction.

"It's all right." I kept my arm extended.

Seconds passed and then Zeus grabbed my wrist. I hauled him from the floor.

Mrrmph.

It was the man's way of saying thanks.

"It's all right," I said again, not disguising the compassion I felt for him.

Again — *Mrrmph.*

I suspected it wasn't something he said that often.

Part I

Chapter 1

Dr. Douglas Kool's moniker fits perfectly with his buttoned-up personality, his thousand dollar suits and an impressive collection of Bruno Maglis. Doug lives and works in Manhattan where high fashion and a suave demeanor resonate like a mellow chord to those roosting at the top tier of society. Good thing. Because Doug's occupation is all about hustling money from the rich and the powerful.

"You can't be serious!" Doug gave me a hard look.

"Totally serious," I replied, at the same time doing a mental rundown on the long list of differences between Doug and me. He was manufactured slick from his hair transplants to his "Doctor" title, courtesy of an honorary degree from the State University of New York. I was a forty-something Joe with a plain vanilla bachelor's degree from Penn State and a retreating hairline. For all our dissimilarities, we had a weird kind of connection that had weathered a dozen years.

Doug adjusted his glasses the way he did when he was super serious. "Bullet, your boy *murdered* Benjamin Kurios!"

I shrugged. "Maybe."

"No, not *maybe*. Two witnesses *saw* Zeupeneltoth—"

"Zeusenoerdorf."

"Whatever. The fact is, your guy used a two-by-four to punch a hole in Kurios's head."

"It wasn't a two-by-four. It was a cross."

"All right, all right," Doug moaned. "So it was a cross. Your boy banged together *two* two-by-fours and then whacked the crap out of the world's most famous Bible thumper."

"He's not my boy," I protested.

"The hell he's not!"

I could have argued, but it would have meant confronting the disconcerting fact that Doug was probably right. In many respects, Zeusenoerdorf *did* belong to me.

Doug glared at me over his nearly finished lunch. "What am I doing here?"

"Eating osso bucco—which I'm paying for."

"Yeah, right," Doug laughed. "If you're paying, then I'm being set up. What do you want?"

Doug Kool might be superficial, but he was far from dumb. He knew I was picking up his tab at Panico's, one of the city's better restaurants, because I needed a favor.

"A meeting with Zeusenoerdorf," I said bluntly. "Face-to-face."

Doug gave a little tug on his tie. "Mission impossible. The man's sitting in an Orlando jail cell."

"I know."

"And even if you could work out a way to talk to him, the bigger question is *why* would you want to bother?"

"Because there's a chance the guy's innocent," I explained. "Zeus could be—"

"Zeus?" Doug interrupted.

"That's what he's called."

Doug puffed his cheeks, shook his head, and motioned for me to continue.

"Look, I know it's a stretch, but it's possible Zeus didn't kill anyone. Maybe he's in custody because he happens to be a little—strange."

"Strange?" Doug cut in. "I think it's safe to say that somebody who pounds the bejeezus out of an evangelist is a few notches beyond strange."

"Being odd doesn't necessarily make the man a murderer."

"Let me get this straight," Doug pressed. "If you can get eye-to-eye with this nutcase, you'll figure out whether he's innocent or guilty. Am I hearing you right?"

It wasn't the easiest case to make, but I was determined to give it my all. I leaned forward so Doug wouldn't lose what I was about to say in the noontime buzz of the busy restaurant.

"There are a couple of things you should know." I spoke with as much sincerity as I could muster. "First, Zeus is slow. Second, he's got a serious speech defect."

Doug grimaced. "I see. The man's not a killer—he's just got a communications defect, right?"

I shrugged. "Could be."

"Good God." Doug waved down a waiter and ordered a cannoli and cappuccino. My wallet groaned.

"I'm not saying he's innocent." I tried the you-may-be-right tactic. "But I'm not totally convinced he's guilty."

Doug took a deep breath. "Can't help yourself, can you?"

"What?"

"Standing up for every loser who falls on his ass."

"Not *every* loser."

"Most. I gotta tell you, you've really found your calling."

"My calling was your lucky day," I reminded my pal. And for a few moments, both of us were spun into the past.

I first met Doug a couple of years after he started with Harris and Gilbarton. H&G was arguably the top fund-raising firm in the nation, and Doug had been hired because he was born and bred rich, which meant he was hardwired to big money. But it wasn't his connections that rocketed him to the top of his firm's talent pool. It was his I-won't-take-no-for-an-answer salesmanship. I figured his annual salary had to be about five times what the Gateway put in my pocket.

Granted, Doug had raw talent, and he might have climbed to the highest rung of his work world without me. But he wouldn't have gotten there so quickly if I hadn't given him a boost. What brought us together was the United Way of America—the charity goliath that H&G had been trying to land as a client for years. The notion that the fund-raising United Way needed help from another fund-raising consulting firm probably would have forever been written off as a bad idea if I hadn't opened the door for Doug.

It happened a few months after Anne died. That was twelve years ago and yet I could easily reconstruct every detail of the Morgan Stanley executive dining room where I was brought in as the dessert-and-coffee performer for ten United Way board members and an H&G representative named Dr. Douglas Kool. H&G, as I would later find out, had volunteered Doug as a pro bono consultant to review my agency's plan for a national United Way public service ad campaign.

I showed up at the Morgan Stanley lunch about the same time I decided to exit the advertising business. I was still on my agency's payroll, but after Anne's funeral, my heart wasn't in the game. That became painfully obvious to the United Way board members who found the crème brulee and cappuccino far more interesting than my story boards. Later that same day, I handed in my resignation.

After my poor Morgan Stanley performance, Doug was invited into the United Way's inner sanctum as a paid consultant. H&G had finally landed one of its most elusive prospects, which might never have happened if it weren't for me.

"It still amazes me that you dumped Madison Avenue," Doug said.

"Every so often, principles trump the pocketbook."

"Principles my ass. You bailed out of New York six months after your wife died. The reason you're running a homeless shelter is your crazy way of paying homage to Anne."

"There are crazier things I could do."

"You've been at this for *twelve years*, Bullet! You've turned your job into a kind of hair shirt memorial to your wife, for God sakes. You don't take vacations. You don't date. Your life is half about running a boardinghouse for lowlifes and half about begging for money to keep the Gateway's lights on."

Harsh and partially true. Granted—Anne had a lot to do with why I first took the job in New Brunswick. I needed to get out of Manhattan, which had become a constant reminder of how much I had lost when cancer killed my wife. I had planned to spend a year or two working with the homeless and then jump back into the business world. That didn't happen. Not solely because of Anne, but because I also became infected with the same convictions that had defined my wife's life until her final day at Sloan-Kettering.

"Speaking of keeping the lights on," I tried moving the conversation in another direction. "Paying the bills would be a lot easier if guys like you could arm-twist the upper crust into using their tax-deductible donations to help the sick, poor, and homeless instead of buying privilege and status."

"Don't start," Doug implored.

I couldn't help myself. It was an old ballad I loved to sing. "You know as well as I do that for every ten-cent donation made to the Gateway, ten dollars goes to some high-end nonprofit that promises to put a contributor in good company or good seats."

"Yeah, yeah," Doug groaned. "So get back to why I'm parked here in Central Jersey. What exactly do you want?"

"A free ride," I answered. "To and from Orlando. Plus room and board."

"What's the point? To spend five minutes with a man who's absolutely, positively guilty! You're in denial, for chrissakes. Two guys saw your man do the deed."

"They didn't actually see what happened. The two college kids who showed up on the scene got there a few minutes after Kurios was attacked."

Doug looked at me in disbelief. "Bullet, what they saw was your guy holding a homemade cross soaked with blood. And they saw Kurios on the street with his skull in pieces. Jesus! What more do you want?"

"To hear Zeus tell me what happened."

Doug leaned back. "You need to give this thing a rest."

"I can't do that—at least not yet."

"You *do* remember who your man, Zeus, exterminated, right?" Doug asked. "Benjamin Kurios. The prince of evangelists."

I didn't need to be reminded of the obvious. The media had been profiling Kurios since the day he died.

"Kurios wasn't just another Joel Osteen, Jim Bakker, or Benny Hinn," said Doug. "He was better than Billy Graham, for God sakes. People followed him like lemmings."

One of those lemmings was Miklos Zeusenoerdorf, who was infatuated with Kurios. He rarely missed a televised sermon and had a complete collection of the evangelist's books on tape. Twice, Zeus saw Kurios live at stadium-sized revival rallies, one at Madison Square Garden and another at the Meadowlands. It was a chance to see Kurios perform for a third time that had taken Zeus to Orlando.

I paused to give my coffee a counterclockwise swirl. Doug and I both looked at my cup like it was trying to tell us something. "Zeus is as gentle as they come."

"If I remember right, you also told me he's nuts."

"I said retarded."

"He's retarded and crazy."

"Even if you're right, he's not a crack-your-head-open kind of crazy."

Doug wasn't buying it. In fact, it seemed the entire country wasn't swallowing it except for me—and a few of the misfits who took up space at the Gateway.

"Here's another fact that may have slipped your mind," Doug said. "The man did a stretch in Rahway."

"Simple theft. He got caught loading a few TVs into a van. It wasn't like he was locked up for murder."

"So stealing televisions isn't a clue your guy has certain antisocial tendencies?"

"A couple of lowlifes paid him to do a half hour of heavy lifting. The cops show up, the bad boys disappear, and Zeus is left holding a forty-six-inch plasma."

"And you actually believe that's what happened."

That's exactly what I believe. "Zeus has, well, he's a man with the mind of a child. If someone tells him to shove a TV into the back of a van, that's what he does. If he gets caught, there's no way he can talk himself out of it."

"And if somebody tells him to whack one of the most magnetic characters to ever set foot on the planet, does he do that too?"

This all was going nowhere. It was time to close the deal—or at least try to. "Let's get back to what I want. Three round-trips to Orlando and three rooms somewhere in the city."

"Three?"

"Three."

"Why?"

"There's a guy named Maurice Tyson who lives at the Gateway. He understands every word Zeus says and that's something no one else can do. So, I need him on board."

"Who's the third?" Doug asked.

I tried not to pause because it was a dead giveaway to my discomfort. But I just couldn't stop myself. "Uh . . . Doc Waters."

"Mother of God!"

"Doc's old news," I said. "The mob can't even remember his name."

"Doc Waters ripped apart the Philadelphia Mafia, for chrissakes.

The mob doesn't forgive and forget. If the man sticks his nose out the door, it's all over. Putting him on a Boeing 757 is sheer insanity."

Point well taken. The New York–Jersey–Philly corridor was loaded with organized crime bosses who had a reputation for long memories. A few years back, Doc Waters kicked the mob where it hurt, which meant retaliation was likely to pay Doc a call. Even so, Doc was an irreplaceable part of my game plan.

"Doc's cousin is chief of corrections for Orange County. Bottom line—he's my foot in the jailhouse door."

"Or a foot in the grave."

"Not negotiable. He's part of the deal."

"You know you're asking for the moon, right? But let's say I work a miracle and muster up three tickets and a place to stay. It'll cost you."

I braced myself. Just because Doug made his livelihood working with charities didn't mean he was charitable. Want him to scratch yours? Be prepared to scratch his.

"You know the name Manny Maglio?"

"The king of strip clubs?"

"Manny likes us to call them gentleman's clubs. He's in the entertainment industry."

Most red-blooded men living in Central Jersey knew about Maglio's Venus de Milo Club in South River. He also had a couple of other nudie operations—one in Queens and the other near Camden.

"So, here's the trade," Doug continued. "Manny's a big-time contributor to United Way."

I gagged on my decaf.

Doug's hands went palms up and did a bad JFK imitation. "Ask not where the money comes from, but what it can do for others."

"Do Manny a favor and he forks over a fat donation?" I guessed.

"Something like that. He's got this niece, Twyla. She's in what you might call show business."

"Show business?"

"Yeah, show business with an erotic twist. She works for one of Maglio's competitors. For spite, according to Manny."

"Nothing like a little lap dancing to really piss off your relatives."

"Seems that Manny promised he'd take care of his niece just days before her dad met with an untimely accident."

"I bet accidents are a big problem for the Maglio family."

"Twyla blamed Manny for not doing enough to protect her dad. So now she's taking it out on her uncle."

"Or taking it off."

Doug gave me a stop sign. "Here's where you come in. Manny wants his niece to go legit—to get a decent job. He's got connections at Universal Studios in Orlando, and he's set her up for an interview. Maglio will do whatever it takes to get Twyla away from the Northeast with all its temptations and bad influences."

"Uh,-oh," I whispered. There was a freight train heading my way.

"She doesn't know that her uncle is working behind the scenes to give her a change of venue. And she can't find out. The lady thinks a cousin of some guy she met at her club set her up with Universal. She also thinks Universal is so hot to recruit her they're sending someone to escort her to Orlando."

I cut Doug off. "Hold it. You had this all figured out, didn't you? You knew I was going to hit you up for a trip to Florida."

"One trip," said Doug. "One trip is what I expected."

"Even so, you knew what I was going to lay on the table."

"Of course," Doug chuckled. "I know you. Like I said, when one of your boys falls on his nose, you're there in a flash. It's in your DNA."

Doug was right. It was all about genetics, and if I had a weird empathy for anyone at the bottom of society's pig pile, then blame Anne. Or maybe even my parents. My old man was a lawyer who went to bat for every scumbag who couldn't afford a dream-team defense. At age eighteen, I had been so indoctrinated with criminal law, I could have passed the New Jersey bar. My mother battled injustice in other ways—mainly by helping poor people find a hot meal, warm blanket, or sometimes a place to get an abortion. When I graduated from Penn State, the expectations were that I would carve out some kind of human-service career. Instead, I fell into a big-salaried ad agency job, which prompted my parents to predict that in time I would find out what was really important. Naturally, they were right.

"Let me make sure I have this straight," I said. "You want me to bring this woman to Orlando. And that's it."

"That's it. She thinks the studio's picking up her expenses for the trip. You get her to Orlando, she walks into the HR office at Universal, and the rest is automatic."

I knew there had to be more. "Why does the niece need hand holding? Why not give her a ticket to Orlando and let her go solo?"

"She's a lot like your Gateway folk," Doug explained. "Her cerebral cortex has a few—kinks."

"In other words, without a chaperone, you're not sure she'd ever make it to Universal Studios."

"I think she'd make it to Orlando. But she could be easily led in a different direction, from what I've been told."

"Which means that somewhere between the airport and Universal, she might decide to further her dancing career," I guessed.

"Something like that."

I took a deep breath. "All right. I'll do it."

"Good." Doug's smile was too wide.

"So when do I meet Twyla Maglio?"

Doug coughed. "Actually it's Twyla Tharp."

Couldn't be, I thought. "Twyla Tharp is a big-time choreographer." I was no dance expert, but Tharp is a hard name to forget, especially when it belongs to a woman who owns a Tony Award and a couple of Emmys.

"Yeah, well Manny's niece has the same handle but different credentials. She changed names when she was twenty-one, probably a smart move since it gets people past their first impression."

Would it matter what a woman called herself if she were wearing pasties and a g-string? But I didn't press the point. "What kind of first impression are we talking about?"

"Twyla's a little on the tawdry side. Manny's niece, I mean—not the Twyla who does Broadway."

"Yeah, I'm getting the picture." It was an IMAX image. I began to back away. "I don't know about this."

Doug reached across the table and gave me a tap on my arm. "Relax. Friends don't let friends drive over a cliff. Trust me—this is no big deal."

Friends? In a sense, this was true. There was an odd but authentic connection between Douglas Kool, Jr., son of a Manhattan real estate magnate, and Richard Bullock, the offspring of a South Jersey couple who thought Karl Marx was just a click short of being a genius.

"A no big deal in your world could be a show stopper in mine."

"Here's what you need to keep in mind," noted Doug. "My world is about people with a ton of money; yours is about derelicts and bums. Occasionally, our two worlds intersect and good things happen." Doug pushed the rest of his cannoli through his smile.

The two-worlds-colliding theory was a stretch, but there was no debating that Doug was all about affluence. He had been nanny-raised in his father's Park Avenue penthouse and shipped off to a high-grade boarding school when he was nine. The right connections and a seven-figure donation got him into Yale. It took another hefty gift to get Doug out of the university with a bachelor's degree. Shortly after graduation, life threw my pal a curve ball. Daddy died and left an estate a tad shy of forty million. Doug's mother, a battery of lawyers, and a couple of mistresses consumed 90 percent of the money, leaving Doug with just under five million. In Manhattan's upper echelons, chickenfeed. Hence, Doug had to find the right kind of socially acceptable job to beef up his net worth.

"You know, you're right," I said after mulling over Doug's statement. "I do hang around with misfits and rejects. But at least I know who I'm dealing with."

"And I don't?"

"You've told me a dozen times that New York is a haven for phonies and pretenders, most of whom can't afford a pot to piss in."

"Exactly!" Doug laughed. "Which is why H&G pays me the big bucks to sort out the fakes and tap the real thing."

Sorting and tapping is exactly how the United Way used Harris & Gilbarton's golden boy. He spent most of his billable hours luring the richest of the rich into the organization's upper echelon of philanthropists. His track record was astounding.

"Let me rephrase what I said a minute ago," Doug said. "I raise the capital and people like you use it to change the world."

"More like, try to change it."

"Whatever."

Yup. That pretty much summed it up. While Doug was milking the moneyed set, I was on the front line flailing away at a menu of social inequities.

"Think I ended up holding the wrong end of the stick, don't you?" I asked.

"Hey, you made your bed. There are a lot of roads that'll take you out of New Brunswick."

"I'm happy doing what I'm doing."

Doug feigned surprise at the comment. Like I hadn't given him this line a dozen times before. He checked his watch.

"Super. Wish I had time to hear more about how happiness means running a men's shelter, but I have a train to catch. Let's review—" It was classic Kool. Every conversation ended with a recap. "If I come through with tickets and rooms for you and your two boys, Twyla tags along. You take a day to do your business with Zeukanintroph—"

"Zeusenoerdorf."

"Whatever you say. Day two is all about taking care of business with Twyla. Third day, you take a morning flight back to Newark. Sound like a plan?"

I nodded. Anything for Zeus.

"Three days and two nights in America's playground. I'm handing you a sweet deal, Bullet. Just make sure Twyla gets to Universal on time."

I paid the Panico's bill and walked Doug a few blocks to the city's ancient train station. We rode the escalator to the platform and waited for the Trenton local. It pulled in fifteen minutes late, which had to irk the hell out of the ever-punctual Doug Kool. But he seldom showed his irritation. That's the way it usually was with my friend. No matter what might be stirring on the inside, there was rarely a mess on the outside. Except once in a while, life finds a way to mar the veneer of even someone as composed as Doug. On this particular day, fate had attached a long piece of Panico's rigatoni on the back of his Versace pants.

"I'll call you," he promised, disappearing into the car. I waved and caught a glimpse of the pasta. I took it as a sign. The deal that had been hatched minutes before was likely to turn sticky for everyone involved.

Chapter 2

If you travel Florida's Interstate 4—the blacktopped, clogged-up, east-west highway that slashes across the Sunshine State's midsection—you might catch a glimpse of the Orange County Jail. But most drivers who pass I-4's exit 79 are oblivious to the walled-in gulag that is partially hidden by an IHOP and a Days Inn.

Of all the strange visitors who have walked into the prison over the years, few could possibly match the weird conga line that barged through the main entrance on a cloudy September afternoon. At point was Twyla Tharp, Manny Maglio's niece. During the Newark-to-Orlando flight, I tried coming up with the right words to describe her. Saucy. Salacious. Sin-sational. They all worked. She had shoulder-length blonde hair that partially hid a pair of oversized triple-hoop earrings. Her gold-plated rope-link bracelet and matching necklace looked more JCPenney than Cartier. Not that it mattered. It wasn't the bling that attracted attention—it was the short skirt and tight, décolleté top that did the job. Twyla stood five six in four-inch spikes and had a well-toned body that I guessed was going on thirty. A master of the tease, she had a raw sexiness that was as powerful as her perfume. And although she would never be invited to a Mensa meeting, I discovered early on that Manny's niece was as street smart as they come.

Behind Twyla was a dark wisp of a man named Maurice Tyson, followed by Doc Waters, an unkempt codger with a wild mop of white hair. I was the rear guard until we fully penetrated the visitation hall, where I moved to the front of the line.

"Need your I.D.s." The guard at the registration desk spoke without ever lifting his eyes from the sports section of the *Orlando Sentinel*.

"I'm Rick Bullock. We have an eleven o'clock to see—"

"You got nothin' until you show me your I.D."

I pulled out my driver's license while Doc and Maurice miraculously found their New Jersey nondriver photo identification cards. The guard gave me what I took to be a semilook of approval, but when it came to Waters and Tyson, he turned suspicious. I could understand why.

Maurice Tyson is as unsightly looking as he is skinny. Born thirty-nine years ago, he never had much going for him other than doling out street drugs for pocket change. Finding a legitimate job isn't easy when you haven't rebraided your dreadlocks for months and are so emaciated you disappear when turned sideways. Although Maurice wasn't what one would call a highly educated man—he and the New Brunswick school system went their separate ways when Tyson finished eighth grade—he had a unique ability to understand Zeus. To me, Miklos Zeusenoerdorf's bizarre muttering was Greek. To Tyson, it was E. B. White.

The guard trained his beady eyes on Doc Waters. With his out-of-control white hair and a badly bent posture, the one-time Rutgers history professor came across as the archetypal mad scientist. Hard to imagine, but at one time, Doc was a respected academic. That was before his gambling habit sent him on a free fall that quite literally landed him in the gutter. The local cops steered Doc to the Gateway and the move probably saved his life. Like Maurice, there was more to Professor Waters than his shaggy exterior. Doc was the Gateway's resident genius—an incredibly bright man with a personality that could be as engaging as it was caustic.

The guard glared at Waters. "Don't I know you?"

Doc answered without hesitation. "Maybe. Were you at last month's Gay Pride meeting?"

"What are you, a wiseass?"

In fact, that's exactly what the professor was. His super intelligence made it easy for him to pop out a snappy comeback any time circumstances warranted. Of course, his wit wasn't worth much when he was plummeting to the bottom. It was during his downward spiral that Doc piled up a steep gambling debt that was ultimately handed over to a Philadelphia gangster for collection. One-liners didn't help much when the mob applied its payment-past-due tactics. First to go were the tips of two fingers on the professor's left hand. A month later, three cracked ribs. Then things got serious. Round three ended up as a cover story in *Philadelphia* magazine. According to Doc, two thugs pulverized his left testicle and promised to do the same to his remaining jewel unless he paid his principal plus interest within two weeks. Instead, the professor told all to the FBI, who pounced on the Mafia bill collector and his enforcers. Doc got fifteen minutes of fame and the mob got furious. Even before *Philadelphia* magazine popularized him as "One Nut Walters," Doc had made his way to the top of organized crime's hit list.

"Wait a minute." The guard studied Doc more closely. "I think I remember who you are."

Manny Maglio's niece suddenly diverted the guard's attention. "My name's Twyla," she announced.

Twyla had been standing behind me, out of the guard's line of sight. When she stepped to the waist-high check-in counter, the guard lost all interest in Professor Waters.

"You're *who?*"

"Twyla Tharp. I'm a dancer." Twyla pushed a business card toward the guard. A full-color, full-figure photo appeared above a few bold, raised letters that spelled out: TWYLA THARP — DANCE PROFESSIONAL.

"You don't say." The guard shifted his gaze from Twyla's business card to her half-buttoned blouse and then to her fake leather micro skirt. "What kind of dancer?"

"A very good dancer."

"Yeah?" The guard couldn't rein in his grin. "Do any private shows?"

Manny Maglio barreled into my brain. Just a mental picture, no words. But I got the message. My job was to keep Twyla on a tight leash that the guard was pulling in a different direction.

I nudged Twyla to the side. The guard's smile vanished and he glared at me as his fantasy evaporated. "Dr. Waters —" I paused to point at my white-haired accomplice, "his uncle is chief of corrections." I upped the volume on chief of corrections just so it was clear that it was the top dog who was opening the door for us. "We've got permission to see Miklos Zeusenoerdorf."

The guard pulled out a computer printout from underneath his newspaper. "You're the people here to see that pervert? Tell you right now — he killed Benjamin Kurios. Been here fifteen years and I can read any asshole who's in here like a book. 'Course even if your pal happens to be innocent, he don't have a chance with the lawyer he's got."

"Lawyer? A public defender?"

"Hell, no. I mean he's got what's walkin' in the door behind ya." The guard looked past me at a rumpled man wearing a discolored yarmulke who darted through the main entrance with as much grace as a Mexican jumping bean. "Yigal Rosenblatt, Esquire," the guard said with obvious distain.

"Looking for Mr. Bullock." The lawyer charged toward me, his words coming out mainly through his nose.

"I'm Bullock."

"Certainly glad to meet you," the attorney replied, pumping my hand. "Certainly glad to meet you."

Yigal Rosenblatt talked with extraordinary speed. But the machine-gun pace of his speech was nothing compared to his herky-jerky mannerisms that had him constantly shifting from one foot to another. Except for a white shirt and a patch of pale skin, Yigal was black from his yarmulke to his scuffed wingtips. The lawyer's beard was dark and unkempt—so was his rumpled suit and unflattering two-toned black tie.

"I didn't know Zeus had a lawyer," I said.

"Oh, we took him on two days ago."

"We?" I asked.

"My firm. Gafstein and Rosenblatt." Yigal lurched left, then right.

"Zeusenoerdorf doesn't have money for a lawyer. Why would a private law firm want this case?"

"Oh, you know." Yigal pointed his eyes to the floor.

"No. I don't know."

"Have to get your name out there," Yigal said. "Chance for exposure. High-profile case and all."

"But if you lose the case—"

"Doesn't matter. We don't care if we win or lose so long as the papers spell our names right." Yigal snorted out what I think was supposed to be a laugh.

"And Zeus wants you to represent him?" I couldn't disguise my astonishment that even a mentally challenged man facing the death penalty would place his fate in the hands of someone like Yigal Rosenblatt.

"Oh, yes. Signed all the papers, which we filed yesterday. Everything's all in order."

"But Zeus can't write his name."

"Had to make a mark. But it's all legal, you know. He's our client right to the end."

End gave me a chill.

"How did you know about me—about us, Mr. Rosenblatt?" I glanced back at Doc, Maurice, and Twyla.

"Standard procedure. Legal counsel gets a notice about all visitor appointments."

The guard grunted his disapproval, but another look at Twyla and his unhappiness with the legal system seemed to disappear.

"Did Zeus tell you what happened, Mr. Rosenblatt?" I asked.

"Oh, yes. We have a signed statement."

"You mean a marked statement."

"Right, right. Had him mark everything important. Even his religious preference."

I blinked. "Zeus has a religious preference?"

"He certainly does. Didn't think he was a Jew, but that's what he is."

"Zeus's *Jewish?*"

"Oh, yes. So he says. That made it very important for us to take the case. You see, I'm Jewish too."

Gosh, really? "I don't think Zeus is Jewish, Mr. Rosenblatt," I stated bluntly.

"Said so himself on a few occasions."

"So you've talked to him?"

"I have."

"And you could understand what Zeus was saying?"

Hesitation. It was the first time since Yigal had walked into the foyer that he stopped moving. "Uh, not everything."

"Yeah, well, that's why we're here." I explained that Maurice Tyson was maybe the only person who could understand Zeus. Anyone else listening to the accused was probably not getting the right story.

"I see." Yigal stroked his beard. "But you understand we transcribed what my client said and then had him read it. After that, he signed the statement with his signa—with his mark."

"Mr. Rosenblatt, Zeus can't read."

"That's not my understanding."

It struck me that Yigal Rosenblatt could easily be one of my Gateway residents.

"What we're going to do is have Maurice talk to Zeus and find out exactly what happened," I said.

Yigal used a stubby finger to scratch his head. "Interesting. We can do that but I'm legal counsel, you know. So, I have to be a party to everything that's said."

I could have argued the right of privacy if there were such a thing in a jail. But I had a full-blown headache. Trying to converse with someone who hopped like a frog on acid would give anyone a migraine. "All right," I agreed and turned to the distracted guard. "We're ready to go in."

"Who's we?" the guard asked.

I gestured to the peculiar group to my rear.

"See that?" the guard pointed to a sign to his left. "Read rule number two."

I got about a third of the way through rule two and wondered why it wasn't rule number one: *Each inmate is permitted a maximum of (3) visitors per session. This total will not exceed (2) adult visitors per session. Children (13) and older will be considered an adult.*

"Can only let two of you in," said the guard.

Yigal started marching in place. "Sounds right. But when the rule says visitors, that doesn't mean counsel. No, it doesn't. We lawyers aren't the same as visitors."

No arguing that point.

"All right, I'll let it go," the guard consented. "So it will be Rosenblatt and two others." He turned to me. "Which two is it gonna be?"

It was an easy decision that came with a potentially bad consequence. Maurice Tyson and I had to be there for obvious reasons. But that would leave Doc Waters and Twyla outside and unsupervised. Although the professor was in his sixties, the way he was studying Manny Maglio's niece, he still had a reservoir of testosterone.

"Look, isn't there some way all of us—"

"Nope," said the guard.

"Well, there is a way," Yigal said. "I have another client here. Beuford Krup. Two of you can visit him. Of course, I'll need to monitor, you understand. So, I'll just go back and forth from one client to another. It can work. Done it before."

"Beuford Krup's yours, too?" the guard asked with an expression that mixed astonishment with disgust.

"Oh, yes."

"You must really be fishin' on the bottom, Esquire."

That pushed me to ask a question I wasn't really sure I wanted answered. "What's Mr. Krup in for?"

"Bestiality. Beuford never met a sheep he didn't want to get to know real well."

"Damn!" I whispered.

"No!" Yigal's shifting became more animated. "Sheep are not part of the complaint. Nothing to do with sheep."

The guard rubbed his chin. "That's right. It wasn't no sheep. It was a mule."

Yigal turned to the Gateway contingent as if we were a jury. "Beuford Krup's innocent. Can't be done. With a mule, I mean. Not without being kicked."

I had heard enough. "Look, it doesn't matter what Beuford did or didn't do as long as he can get us all inside."

"Oh, he can," Yigal assured us. "I have rights as counsel."

The guard looked confused. "All right. But the lady stays outside."

"Why?" I asked.

"Rule seven."

I turned back to the sign.

7. *Proper attire is required at all times. Shoes and shirts must be worn; suggestive clothing: see-through fabrics, halter or tube-type tops, short shorts and miniskirts will not be allowed.*

Twyla's shelf bra pushed her breasts up and practically out of her blouse. Getting past the proper attire roadblock looked like an impossibility until Rosenblatt tossed us a life preserver.

"I have a trench coat," the lawyer revealed. "In my car."

The guard started to resist, but Yigal had already hopscotched his way out the door. A minute later, he was back with a raincoat.

"This will work," he said.

"This is *so* nice of you, Mr. Rosen Bag," Twyla crooned.

"Rosenblatt," the lawyer said. "But you can call me Yigal."

Twyla appeared genuinely moved. "Well, I *love* that name. Yigal. What does it mean?"

Rosenblatt didn't show much facial skin but the little I could make out began to turn red. "He will redeem. In Hebrew, it means he will redeem."

Twyla pulled the lawyer's coat over her hardworking blouse and skirt. "How cute! Do you have a nickname?"

"Oh, no. Just Yigal Rosenblatt. That's my name."

"Well, I'm going to call you Yiggy," Twyla said with a nod that vibrated her chest. "If that's okay with you."

Yigal's flesh went from pink to a brilliant shade of fuchsia. "Well, it's unorthodox. But if you want. Just don't call me that in court."

Chapter 3

"Pick up the phone," a guard instructed after I had parked myself in front of a fourteen-inch TV monitor. I lifted the handset to the right of the television screen and played twenty questions with an unpleasant woman on the other end of the line. "Who was I here to see?" "What was my name?" "What was my connection to the inmate?" And so on.

Once the quiz was over, the TV screen went blank. The delay gave me time to do a more careful survey of the visitor center's high-tech setup. A miniature camera mounted above the monitor in front of me, along with the phone I was still holding, allowed inmates to be seen and heard but only through the wonders of teleconferencing. Any kind of physical intimacy was impossible.

The Orange County Jail Video Visitation Center was crowded with small groups of distressed adults and a few even more anxious-looking children all staring at screens and passing around telephone receivers. The TV-phone setups were lined up in a row with only a small panel separating one station from another.

While Maurice Tyson and I sat waiting for Zeus to pop up on our monitor, Twyla and Doc Waters were one screen away pretending to live by the jailhouse rules. Their TV came to life first, and I leaned around the narrow vertical panel to catch a glimpse of Beuford Krup, who looked like a piece of gristle covered with gray hair.

Twyla grabbed the phone. "Hello, Mr. Cup," she purred and opened her trench coat.

"Krup," was all Beuford said but his expression left no doubt he was already under Twyla's spell.

"How very nice to meet you, Mr. Krap," said Twyla.

Krup had the glassy-eyed stare of a man who might be rethinking whether the back end of a mule wasn't the only place to find pleasure.

I was ready to give Twyla advice about what not to say to Beuford when my own TV monitor sprang to life.

Miklos Petris Zeusenoerdorf, aka Zeus, was born in Copsa Mica, a Romanian town with the reputation as the worst place to live in all of Europe. When the Communists were running the country, the Transylvania air was filled with contaminants from lead-smelting factories and other hazardous pollution-producing plants. Poisonous soot coated everything living and inanimate throughout the town, which became known as the "Black Village."

In Copsa Mica, two out of three kids ended up mentally retarded. With food, water, and air loaded with zinc, lead, and cadmium residue, Zeusenoerdorf never had a chance.

Zeus's mother, Anes-Marie, had just one stroke of good luck in forty grueling years of life. She had a cousin in New Jersey who was sleeping with a bureaucrat high up in the Manhattan District Office of U.S. Citizenship and Immigration Services. That relationship was good enough to spawn a visa for Anes-Marie who moved from a two-room hovel in Romania to a two-room hovel in Jersey City. There, her good fortune took a U-turn. She was diagnosed with colon cancer and did her dying in and out of Newark's University Hospital. Although it was a painful end to a miserable existence, she managed to clear a high hurdle before she took her last breath. Her one and only son was made a full citizen of the U.S. of A.

Zeus became the property of New Jersey's Division of Youth and Family Services. He was shuffled from one residential youth center to another until age eighteen, when he was spun out of the system. After that, it was life on the streets interrupted by a five-year prison stint. Zeusenoerdorf's case file and rap sheet painted him as a lost cause.

"Wha's happenin', bro?" Maurice Tyson greeted the image on the TV screen.

I couldn't hear Zeus's response since Maurice owned the phone. Not that it mattered. As Tyson and Zeus went through some preliminaries, Yigal Rosenblatt was fumbling with a legal pad and pen and trying to flip on a pocket-sized tape recorder. The scene so captivated Maurice that he put the conversation with Zeus on hold.

"Forget the lawyer!" I yelled at Maurice. Easier said than done.

"Pay attention to Zeus! Tell me what he's saying! Everything. Word for word. Understood?"

"Yeah, okay," I had my doubts Maurice grasped the gravity of his assignment. His translation could either put Zeus back on the street or send him to death row.

Maurice leaned toward the small tube-like camera mounted by the TV screen. "So what'd you do, man?"

Zeus's mouth began moving.

After listening for about a minute, Maurice turned to Yigal and me. "This is what he says. He was sleepin' under a pass over—"

"Overpass, is what he means," Yigal interjected. "Not a Passover. I'm sure of it." Rosenblatt did a Lord of the Dance quickstep that I took to be his way of showing disdain for anyone who confused a sacred Jewish observance with a transportation artery.

Maurice shot a look of annoyance at the lawyer. "I'm just tellin' you what he's tellin' me."

"Keep going, Maurice," I said.

Over the next five minutes, Tyson translated Zeus's account of what occurred the night Benjamin Kurios was killed. Around three a.m., Zeus saw a blue sedan following a white van. Both vehicles were traveling fast. When they reached the underpass, the blue car clipped the back end of the van and sent it into a steel stanchion. The crash crushed the midsection of the van with such force its twin rear doors flew open. According to Zeus, Kurios was catapulted out of the van and ended up on the pavement. About the same time the evangelist hit the ground, the blue car did a one-eighty spin and ran into a buttress on the opposite side of the road.

Zeus stopped as if that were the end of the story. I told Maurice to keep the prisoner talking.

"Whoever was drivin' the van—he had a gun," Tyson translated.

"A gun?"

Maurice confirmed what Zeus had said with a nod. I looked at Yigal who seemed more surprised than me by the news.

"Then what?" I asked.

Tyson fed us the next chapter. The van driver was short and stocky. Holding a pistol, he jumped out of the damaged vehicle and rushed toward the not-so-banged-up sedan. He never got past the front fender.

The driver of the blue car was a lot faster and tougher than the man waving his gun. The car driver wrestled the van operator to the pavement and the pistol was kicked to one side.

"That's when Zeus come down from underneath the pass over where he was campin' out for the night," Maurice explained.

"Did he recognize either driver?"

"No."

"If we showed Zeus pictures of the two men—could he identify them?"

Maurice relayed my question and came back with the answer I expected. "He don't think so. The one thing he might remember is the necklace."

Necklace? What necklace?"

"The blue car driver. He was wearin' a chain that had this thing on it."

"What kind of thing?"

"Zeus says it was a circle made out of silver. Had a cross in the middle of it."

"All right. Keep digging, Maurice. Ask Zeus what happened next."

The two drivers were still battling it out when Zeus walked into the van's high beams. His sudden appearance startled the two men, and the fight was over. The man driving the blue car broke free but not before the van driver retrieved his pistol and pulled off two shots.

"Was the other man hit?" I asked.

"Might a been," Maurice interpreted. "Not sure."

"Keep going."

According to Zeus, the driver of the blue car took off in his sedan. Apparently the run-in with a steel column hadn't done any serious damage to the car. The van man was in less of a hurry to leave. He picked up his pistol and walked to the rear of his vehicle. As he leaned over the motionless Benjamin Kurios, Zeus drew closer. Too close. The driver pointed the weapon at Zeus's midsection and pulled the trigger. Nothing but a few clicks. When the man realized the pistol was useless, he dashed for his van and managed to disentangle it from the bridge abutment. The vehicle limped away leaving Zeus and what was left of Kurios in its wake.

I had a million questions and only a few minutes left on the Visitation Center's clock.

"What about the wooden cross?" I asked — the alleged weapon used to beat Benjamin Kurios to death. "It was covered with blood."

"Belonged to Zeus," Maurice communicated the obvious. "He made it."

"Yeah, yeah, I know." Everyone knew about the cross. The media had played it up six ways to Sunday. *Cleric Murdered With Handmade Cross.*

"Zeus says the cops took it," said Tyson.

Of course they took it. It was a prosecutor's dream.

Maurice continued his translation. "What happened was that Zeus leaned over the preacher and the cross got some blood on it."

This was a monumental deviation from statements made by the two college students who stumbled onto the scene while Zeus was still perched over Kurios. The witnesses admitted they didn't actually see Zeus hammering Kurios with the cross, but it was obvious what had happened — wasn't it?

"This is a really important question, Maurice," I said. "Was Kurios dead when Zeus showed up?"

Tyson asked and came back with an answer. "No."

I blinked. "No?"

"No."

"But Kurios was dead when the cops arrived on the scene a few minutes after?"

"That's right."

"So, Zeus was with Kurios before he died."

"Yeah. He seen him pass."

Which must have been one of the most upsetting moments of the homeless man's life.

"Maurice, ask Zeus if Kurios said anything before the police showed up."

Another quick response. "Yes."

I leaned toward the TV screen. "Kurios actually spoke to you, Zeus?"

"Yes." Maurice interpreted.

"You sure about this?"

Another "Yes."

"So what did he say?"

"Father Nathan."

"What?"

"He say, 'Father Nathan,'" Maurice repeated.

"That's it? Just Father Nathan?'"

"He don' remember nothin' else."

Miklos Zeusenoerdorf wasn't into lying, but he was easily confused. Maybe he did hear Kurios mutter something before he died but was the evangelist delirious? Did Zeus mistake what was being said? I tried to formulate my next question but was distracted when I picked up part of Twyla's conversation with Beuford Krup. Something about barnyard animals.

"Tell the truth, Mr. Krap—what's the wildest thing you ever did?" Twyla asked.

I put Zeus on hold and craned my head around the video station divide.

"An ostrich!" Twyla squealed with delight. "Oh, that is *so* naughty!"

"That's it!" I shouted and ordered Yigal to get Twyla off the phone. Then I turned back to my designated cubicle and used Maurice to press Zeus for more details about the necklace worn by the driver of the blue sedan. Zeusenoerdorf came through with a slightly better description of the silver chain and medallion. "Says the round silver thing fell off the necklace durin' the fight," Maurice reported.

I couldn't be certain, but Zeus's verbal sketch seemed to match a picture of a medallion I had seen before. A group of pro-life demonstrators had picketed a Central Jersey abortion clinic earlier in the year. One of the regional newspapers gave the incident a day's worth of coverage, including a sidebar story about the pro-life group that mobilized the protest. I didn't remember the Latin name of the organization, but I recalled the photo of the emblem that was included as part of the story, a silver cross set inside an engraved silver circle.

I was about to push Zeus for more information about Father Nathan when the interview came to an end. Doc, Twyla, and Beuford Krup were trading jokes about llamas when a guard with no sense of humor informed us the Visitor Center wasn't a comedy club. We were told to leave. Immediately.

Twyla waved at the camera. "G'bye, Mr. Krap." The TV went off, and we were ushered out of the center.

"He looked so sad," moaned Twyla.

"Beuford?" Professor Waters asked.

"No. Mr. Zeus."

She was right. Zeus looked unhappier than usual. Worse, I also spotted something else in his droopy eyes. Defeat. It took a lot of years, but it seemed to me like life may have finally ground Zeus down.

"Careful out there," said the same guard we had met in the main lobby a half hour earlier. He motioned to a small but boisterous crowd standing outside the entrance of the center.

"Who are they?" Doc Waters asked.

"They're the real pissed-off fan club of the late Dr. Benjamin Kurios."

I checked out the agitated group of about fifty people—mostly women. They marched in a slow circle about a hundred yards from the entrance to the Visitation Center.

"Those people want your boy's head," the guard went on. The crowd's placards underscored his point.

"Would be nice if they waited until Zeus had a chance to defend himself," I mused.

"Wait until what?" the guard asked. "Until his counselor here tries to get the nutcase off on an insanity plea? If that happens, there'll really be hell to pay."

The way he talked, I knew that given the chance, the guard would join the band of unhappy protesters in a nanosecond. The blood lust for Zeus was becoming an all-American phenomenon.

With Yigal in the lead, we marched out of the Visitation Center into the noisy, banner-waving crowd.

I zeroed in on a woman carrying a three-foot-by-three-foot poster board that read:

GOD'S MESSENGER—BENJAMIN KURIOS
Matthew 5:21

Two young boys stood on either side of the woman. One held up a sign that read:

WHOSOEVER SHALL KILL SHALL BE IN
DANGER OF THE JUDGMENT
Matthew 5:21

The other pumped a placard up and down like he was at a political rally. When the kid gave his arm a rest, I got the message:

THE WAGES OF SIN=*DEATH!*
Romans 6:23

Chapter 4

"Jesus, Doug," I shouted into my cell phone an hour after leaving the Orange County Jail. "Have you seen Manny Maglio's niece? She walks, talks, and dresses like a hooker."

"That's because she is a hooker!"

"Well, why the hell didn't you tell me?" Furious, I walked toward the front office of a nondescript motel called the Wayside. Twyla, Doc Waters, and Maurice Tyson were out of earshot to my rear, seated in a Mitsubishi that I rented in Orlando.

"And get stuck listening to another lecture about how prostitution is anything but a victimless crime?" Doug laughed. "Don't think so."

"No more surprises," I griped. "What else should I know about her?"

"Nothing." Doug's tone was so soothing I knew he had to be lying. "I don't know why you're pissed. Think about it—the woman's trying to find a better life. You're helping her get on the right track. This is what you do, Bullet."

I should have told Doug that hand-holding hookers was not what I did. But it was six o'clock and I was famished. I moved to the main reason I had called.

"Tell me again—isn't the objective of this fiasco to get Twyla a job at Universal?"

"If you get her there, that's what's going to happen—yes."

"Maybe not," I warned. "If she goes into that interview wearing anything close to what she has on now, even Frederick's of Hollywood wouldn't sign her on."

A long wait. "Damnit, there's always something," Doug wheezed. "All right, maybe we can fix the problem. There's a Nordstrom's department store in Orlando—at the Florida Mall. Maglio's in tight with one of Nordstrom's board members. I'll see if I can get this fixed. Figure out a way of getting Twyla to the store before her interview tomorrow afternoon."

"Nordstrom's? What am I, a personal shopper? This isn't part of the deal."

"Yeah, well keep remembering those free plane tickets I got for you," Doug said. "And think of me tonight when you're lounging around that comfortable motel room. You're paying a small price for a boatload of big favors, my friend."

I snapped my cell phone shut and walked into the Wayside's office, where the manager gave me an ice-cold reception. He told me the four rooms reserved in my name by Dr. Kool's secretary were freebies—in-kind donations the Wayside had reluctantly offered to Harris & Gilbarton in lieu of making a cash contribution to one of the charities the firm represented. The manager said he had been told the rooms would be home-away-from-home for a few visiting nonprofit dignitaries. "Instead, I'm forkin' over four rentable rooms for two goddamned nights to a bunch of Yankee yo-yos."

I was tempted to tell the manager he needed a reality check. The $59-a-night Wayside wasn't a place for VIPs. But I kept my mouth shut when he shoved four keys into my hand and jerked his thumb toward the seediest wing of the motel.

I walked back to the car and passed out the keys. Maurice and Doc grabbed a couple of vinyl bags, which they had converted to suitcases, and headed to their respective rooms. Twyla decided to check out the Wayside's murky pool before unpacking her pink and yellow polka-dot carry-on that was still in the trunk. I picked up my beat-up American Tourister at the same time Twyla called my name. She had been at the pool for no more than two minutes but was already carrying on a conversation with a family of four who looked like they belonged at the Wayside.

"Bullet, come over here!"

Mr. Logical, the voice in my head I ignored far too often, screamed don't go there. But I was too tired to come up with an excuse to keep my distance. I trudged to the oversized puddle that the Wayside passed off as a pool.

"This is Conway Kyzwoski and his wife, Ida," Twyla bubbled. "They're from South Carolina."

I flapped my hand and muttered an exhausted hello.

"And these kids are Noah and A-Frame."

"Ephraim," Ida Kyzwoski corrected. "It's from the Bible. The name means fruitful."

Although Ephraim couldn't be more than ten, the way he was studying Twyla Tharp suggested that fruitfulness was in his future.

"Sit down," Conway Kyzwoski ordered. He reached into a brown paper bag and pulled out two plastic cups. "Not supposed to have no beer by the pool but hell's bells, we're at a ree-sort, for God sakes!" Out came a can of Miller Lite.

Twyla pulled me into a moldy folding chair next to an even moldier patio table. I gave in to the forces around me, took the cup of beer, and tried to figure out how Conway could see when one eye pointed left and the other tilted toward the cracked concrete that surrounded the pool.

I was certain I had never seen Conway before, but Ida and her two offspring were another story. No question about it—they were the sign holders I had spotted at the anti-Zeus rally outside the Orange County Jail.

"We come down here from Goose Creek," Conway informed me. He held out a can of Skoal. "Want some?"

"Thanks, but I don't—chew."

"We're here to do God's work," Ida said, studying both Twyla and me. I was sure Ida had seen us at the Visitation Center, but for some reason, she made no mention of it. Instead, she launched into a mini-inquisition. "Why are you in Orlando, Mr. Ballot?"

"Actually, it's Bullock," I corrected. "Rick Bullock."

"But everyone calls him Bullet," said Twyla. "You know, because he shoots straight."

Conway reconfigured the compliment with a snicker. "A straight shooter?"

"Somethin' wrong with that?" Twyla reaction was surprisingly sharp.

It was my first inclination that there was more to Manny Maglio's niece than makeup, a well-proportioned body, and compromised morals. If my wife were still alive, she'd be telling me not to judge Twyla by just her exterior. There could be a lot more to the woman than meets the eye,

Anne would undoubtedly say. It would take a while, but I would come to find out that my wife was absolutely right.

"Still don't know what brings you to Orlando, Mr. Bullet," Ida persisted. I had a feeling she already knew why.

"Business."

Ida blew back my answer with a snort and turned away. She was one of those women you never noticed unless you worked at it. Unlike her husband who was beer bellied and tattooed, Ida was one hundred percent bland. Her hair was short, brown, and flecked with gray. She wore a tan muumuu that covered her pudgy body from neck to toe. If there were anything at all distinctive about her, it was the silver medallion about the size of quarter that dangled from a thin choke necklace. I recognized it immediately—it was identical to the pro-life emblem Zeus claimed the driver of the mysterious blue sedan was wearing.

It was too much of a coincidence. Ida Kyzwoski and a man somehow connected to the murder of Benjamin Kurios both wearing the same necklace? I looked more closely at the inscription engraved on the rim of the silver disk. *Quia Vita*.

"What about you?" Twyla asked Conway in a bedroom voice. "You came here all the way from Goose's Crease?"

"It's Goose Creek," Conway laughed. He leaned forward so he was no more than a foot from Twyla. "Took a few days off from work to be with the family. I'm what they call a mechanical engineer."

"Conway works at Boylin's Garage," Ida clarified. "Like Ephesians says, 'Man must do something useful with his own hands that he may have something to share with those in need.'"

I had my doubts that Conway did his share of sharing.

"You're so lucky to have a daddy who knows about cars, A-Frame," cooed Twyla. Her words lit Conway up like a torch. Ida showed her first hint of uneasiness, squinting first at her husband and then at Manny Maglio's niece.

Conway apparently realized his wife was deciphering the signals. He hoisted his beer can and reluctantly turned his attention to me. "So, what kind of business are you gonna be doin' in Orlando?"

I sucked in a lungful of Florida humidity and gave Conway as little information as possible. "We're here for a meeting."

That might have been the conversation stopper if Twyla hadn't jumped in. "Bullet knows the guy who killed Benjamin Kurios."

Ida made a hand motion that looked to be a combination of the sign of the cross and a swatting of the mosquitoes that were also enjoying the Wayside pool. "I see," she said, showing no surprise.

"We talked to the killer in jail," Twyla boasted. The urge to clamp my hand over her glossy lips was almost uncontrollable.

"Why would you want to do that?" Ida asked me.

I took a tad too long to answer. Twyla kept running with the ball.

"The killer used to live with Bullet in New Jersey," Twyla explained. "And it could be he's not the murderer at all! Wouldn't *that* be something?"

I guessed somewhere between Newark and the Wayside, Maurice and Doc Waters had boiled down my connection to Zeus in a way that Twyla could understand.

"That's not exactly what—"

Ida cut me off. "We *know* who did the killing, Mr. Bullet."

"Well, I'm just here to talk to the suspect."

"Come all the way to Florida to just talk? Why would you do that?"

"To find out for sure if the man's guilty or innocent."

Ida looked at me as if I were insane. Even A-Frame and his brother appeared astonished that anyone would be crazy enough to fiddle with a case that was in the prosecutor's bag. "Holy Father, as You say to us in First Kings, give this man wisdom to know what justice deserves to be administered," she said.

"What?" Twyla asked.

Conway used his beer can to point at his wife. "She's Pentecostal," he explained.

"Oh, I'm sorry," Twyla turned to Ida. "You don't look old enough for the change."

Had Conway announced his wife was dying from rickets, Twyla could not have been more sympathetic.

Ida ignored Twyla and her husband. She had locked on to me and wasn't about to be sidetracked. "Don't be tempted to side with the devil."

"I'll keep that in mind," I promised. "But like I said, I just want to make sure the man sitting in jail actually killed Benjamin Kurios."

Conway ran a dirty fingernail through his two-day-old beard. "What more evidence do y'all want? A couple of kids saw the whole thing."

"Not exactly. No one actually saw Kurios get killed. What they saw was what happened afterward."

"What they saw," Conway interjected, "was your friend carryin' a cross that he'd just used to put a hole in Kurios's head."

Ida's dull eyes turned electric. "Do you believe, Mr. Bullet?"

Oh, oh. This was a classic have-you-stopped-believing-in-Jesus question my missionary friends loved to throw at agnostics like me. It was usually a starter for a philosophical debate, but that's not where I intended to go with Ida Kyzwoski.

"Are you asking if I'm a Christian?"

"Yes, sir."

"Really doesn't matter what you or I believe," I said. "Every human being comes with a twenty percent margin of error."

"What's that supposed to mean?"

"That people aren't smart enough to know a hundred percent of anything. So there's a twenty percent chance that whatever I believe is probably wrong."

Ida was predictably confused.

"You'd be well advised to get back to the Bible," she said.

"I'll consider that."

"And you should stay away from the man who killed Dr. Kurios. Remember Revelation 22:12. 'My reward is with Me to render to every man according to what he has done.' Do something that God will look kindly on. Helping a man who killed somebody who was the Lord's spokesman isn't a step toward heaven."

"I understand." It could have been the Miller Lite or the fact that Ida Kyzwoski was giving me the jitters—whatever, my bladder felt bigger than the Wayside pool. I needed to find a toilet, not God. I took Twyla's arm, threw out some excuse about why we had to leave, and then made a quick exit.

We stopped at the Mitsubishi, picked up our luggage, and headed for our respective rooms. It would have been an opportune time to coach Twyla on what not to say about the Zeus situation. But peeing was more pressing, so I said nothing as she wiggled off with her pink and yellow overnighter in tow. There was another reason I kept my mouth shut. A little part of me didn't want to deflate the woman's excitement over being deputized as part of my Zeusenoerdorf investigation team. After all, when Twyla high-heeled her way into my life, she knew nothing about my truth-finding mission. Now that she was up to her thong in detective work, I sensed she liked being part of something that didn't require a prophylactic. Or was I reading her wrong? The niggling idea that there was more to Twyla than just a voluptuous exterior worked its way back into my head. But it was a thought quickly pushed aside when my brain got an SOS from my panicked sphincter muscle.

Doc, Maurice, Twyla, and I had identical Wayside accommodations—twenty-by-twenty rooms complete with twin beds and bad lighting. We were lined up in a row with Tyson and the professor in the middle and Twyla and me as the bookends. When the team finished unpacking, we reboarded the Mitsubishi and headed for the first inexpensive restaurant I could find. It was after six o'clock and no one had eaten anything since downing a quick snack before our liftoff from Newark. I settled on a pizza joint called My Way or the Pie Way.

After a large pepperoni and a pitcher of beer, I drove back to the Wayside and discovered the occupants in the room to my left, separated by the thinnest of walls, were none other than the Kyzwoskis. For a while, the only noise I heard was A-Frame pounding the hell out of Noah. But in time, the boys' ruckus was out amplified by Conway and Ida.

"Ain't gonna listen to your bullshit about hell and damnation!" Conway screamed. I heard the squeal of the motel room door as Kyzwoski ripped it open.

"You got eyes for her!" Ida yelled back. "You think I'm that stupid! Go ahead and hurt me like you done before! Hurt your family! It's not me or your sons you need worry about. Y'all got God to reckon with!"

I clenched my jaw waiting for Conway to slam the door. He wasn't about to leave without firing a few more shots.

"Woman, you keep on pushin' me and I'll splatter you like duck turd on a rock!"

"Y'all ain't gotta beat me to make me hurt! Your adultery takes care of that!"

"I don't wanna hear it!"

"Matthew 5. But I tell you that anyone who looks at a woman lustfully has already committed adultery with her in his heart!"

Finally, I thought. A passage from the Bible I knew, thanks to an old *Playboy* interview with Jimmy Carter.

"Best thing y'all can do with that Bible of yours is to stick it where even God can't get the sun to shine!"

The Wayside door slammed shut. Through the cheesecloth curtains in my room, I watched Conway clamber into his Dodge Ram flatbed loaded with a white aluminum camper shell. Best I could figure was that this was where A-Frame and his brother were stowed whenever the Kyzwoski family hit the road.

I listened to Ida's whimpering for about a half hour. Then things went quiet. I drifted off into a restless sleep.

At one a.m., I woke in a sweat. At first, I blamed the barely functioning air conditioner for making the room so warm. Then I realized it was something else that sounded an alarm. After yanking on my jeans, loafers, and a tee shirt, I walked outside into a clammy Florida night that was actually cooler than my Wayside quarters. It didn't matter—I was still all perspiration and a few seconds later, I knew why.

Every room was dark except mine and Twyla's. A gusher of My Way or the Pie Way mozzarella bubbled up my esophagus. If Twyla were maimed or worse, I'd be spending the rest of my life running from Manny Maglio and whichever of his associates didn't happen to be doing time. I tapped on Twyla's door. I was hoping for the improbable — that she had fallen asleep before clicking off the twenty-five-watt lightbulb.

Twyla opened the door no more than a foot. "Oh, hi, Bullet." She had cocooned herself in a blanket and her hair was blonde spaghetti gone wild.

"I thought—" I started. "Your light was on and I just wanted to be sure you were okay."

"Ohhh. You're such a sweetheart."

There was enough of an opening for me to catch a glimpse of everything I needed to see. A fifty-dollar bill lay flat on the dilapidated table by the window and a man's foot stuck out from under the top sheet of the bed. Doc Waters? No, this wasn't the kind of refined foot that I assumed Doc might have. It was more simian. Then there was the odor—a mix of Twyla's cheap perfume, cigar smoke, and Valvoline motor oil.

"All right, then," I said. I wasn't sure whether I was feeling relief, confusion or disgust. "Remember, I'm responsible for you while you're in Florida, Twyla. Call me if you get yourself in a fix."

"I will," she promised. "Know what?"

"What?"

"A gotta feeling that you're a real special man."

"Not really."

"Doc told me you were married once," she said. "Your wife died, he said."

"Yes," I replied quietly. "It was a long time ago."

"But I can tell you still love her. After all these years, you haven't forgotten. What it means to really love somebody, I mean."

"Well, I suppose you're right."

"Yeah, I am," Twyla said knowingly. "There's something else. You care about me. I mean, in a good way and all. From what I can tell, you care about lots of people who don't usually get the time of day from just about nobody. See? These are the things that make you special."

It could have been the hot night or the blush making a return visit. My face was warm.

"Well, just be careful," I cautioned.

"I sure will. G'night, Bullet." Twyla blew me a kiss and gently shut the door.

I spotted Conway Kyzwoski's truck parked several spots down from Twyla's room. One of the few lights in the Wayside parking lot illuminated the vehicle and made it easy to read the bumper sticker slapped on the tail end: *God's Messenger: Benjamin Kurios*.

I retreated to my room and tried thinking about tomorrow rather than what was happening in Twyla's room. All that got me was a bad dream.

Chapter 5

"I worked it out." Doug Kool's I-can-do-anything air triggered my gag re-flex. "A woman named Agnes works in women's apparel at Nordstrom's. Ask for her."

It was the morning of my second day in Orlando, and there wasn't a lot to do before delivering Twyla to Universal Studios at three p.m. But the prospect of picking out clothes for Manny Maglio's niece didn't thrill me.

"No charge for whatever goes out the door," Doug explained. "But whoever the hell Agnes is—she gets the final say. Nordstrom's willing to foot the bill—but there's a limit."

"Fine."

"Remember, Bullet, this was your call," my pal reminded me. "You're the one who thinks Twyla should look like Miss Prim."

I didn't appreciate getting blamed instead of stroked for suggesting Twyla needed a makeover. I liked even less the extra day and night I was stuck in Orlando, waltzing around a blood relative of a mob boss.

"So, how'd your little jailhouse confab go?" Doug asked, trying to defuse my aggravation.

The tactic didn't work. I gave Doug an abbreviated account of yes-terday's developments, but my delivery was close to caustic. The saga of the blue car slamming into the white van came out sounding too much like a CSI episode.

"Think your boy's telling the truth?" was Doug's reaction.

"He's not my boy."

"He's a Looney Tune is what he is."

"He's not a liar."

"People who play with half a deck tend to see and hear strange things," Doug reminded me.

"Not the kind of things Zeus talked about yesterday afternoon."

"If you say so," Doug said in a tone that meant *you're an idiot*. "So where do you go from here?"

"I don't know. Thinking about next steps isn't easy when the rest of the morning has to be spent looking for ladies' garments!"

"I feel your pain," Doug said. "Look, maybe I can help with the Zeus situation. There are a few people in Orlando who have a knack for poking around. Could be I might get you a lead on the van that supposedly had a disagreement with a bridge abutment."

Doug and the devil had a lot in common. Take something from Satan and he holds a mortgage on your soul. Take something from Doug and it's an account payable that's going to be collected somewhere down the line. If I accepted his offer of help, I'd be signing an I-owe-you. Still, there was no denying that Douglas was connected to people in all the right—and wrong—places.

"Yeah, okay. See what you can find out."

"Will do. And good luck this morning. Make sure you're at Universal on time this afternoon."

I huffed into the phone.

"Oh, and Bullet, after you and Twyla finish at Universal, give me a call."

Doug's final words perked up my watch-out antennae. "Why?" I croaked. But all I got in return was a dial tone.

AGNES

I ran my eyes up from the stylish nametag to the face of a woman who looked like Miss Vateroli, my first-grade teacher—the Ayatollah Homeni of America's public school system.

"Mr. Bullock?" Agnes had one of those voices that was so husky you couldn't tell whether it was male or female.

"Yes, ma'am." At Hampton Meadows Elementary School, this is when I usually wet my pants. I brought my legs together and squeezed.

"Come with me," she ordered.

I hand-signaled my squad to move forward. The troops paraded single file behind Agnes as she headed toward a semiprivate nook. Bringing up the rear was Yigal Rosenblatt, who had decided to make a day of it with his newfound friends. Apparently, building a defense for Miklos Zeusenoerdorf didn't require a lot of time.

"I've been given instructions to provide you with personal services—" Agnes began but suddenly stopped and gasped for breath when she took in a full view of Manny Maglio's niece. "Oh dear."

"I think someone called you about helping Twyla here with her wardrobe," I said.

"Twyla?" Agnes wheezed. "They told me to expect a Miss Tharp."

"That's right. Twyla Tharp."

"But Twyla Tharp does the Joffrey—the American Ballet Theatre." Agnes began hyperventilating in a refined sort of way.

"This is a different Twyla," I explained. The understatement of the morning.

Agnes's confusion quickly gave way to suspicion. "May I have a word in private?" She led me to a neutral corner. "Mr. Bullock, do you have so much as an iota of fashion sense?"

"I don't think so."

"Your friend—"

I read between the lines and corrected Agnes on the spot. "She's not my friend. She's the niece of someone with a lot of influence. I was asked to chaperone her for a couple of days."

"Do you have any idea of what she's wearing?"

"From what Ms. Tharp told me, it's a liquid metallic tank dress that she ordered from a Ten Thousand Temptations catalogue. I don't know where she got the shoes, though. She calls them centerfold spike heels."

"This isn't a joke, is it?" Agnes asked.

The mere thought of playing a practical joke on someone who was a carbon copy of my first-grade teacher made me shiver. "No."

Agnes studied me carefully. "If this isn't some kind of boorish trick, then we have a great deal of work to do."

"I think you'll find Ms. Tharp to be a very easy customer."

"First, she's hardly a customer. She's paying for nothing, from what I've been told. Second, easy is exactly what she looks like."

I released a low whistle, a tension-releasing habit that got its start thirty-five years ago when my grade school teacher walked into the classroom with a three-foot toilet comet stuck to one of her Red Cross shoes. For that little transgression I got thirty minutes in a corner. I wondered what the penalty might be now.

"This is all extra work for me," Agnes snarled. "If I suspect this is some mean-spirited attempt to humiliate me, you and your friends will be shown the door. Do I make myself clear?"

"You do. This is not a practical joke, I promise."

Agnes marched back to Twyla and yanked her into the women's dressing room. The rest of us milled aimlessly around racks of women's garments for the next hour. Occasionally, we saw Agnes carry several armfuls of clothing in and out of the dressing room. The woman was flushed and one side of her bun had come loose. When she finally brought Twyla back to us, Manny Maglio's niece was still wearing her tank dress with built-in shelf bra.

"I have good news and bad news," Agnes announced.

"There's good news?"

"Some. I found two outfits that will make Ms. Tharp presentable for most kinds of office work. The first is a Donna Morgan bouclé skirt suit. It has a Peter Pan collar with rounded lapels."

Agnes waited for a reaction. Nothing.

"The second is a Kenneth Cole pantsuit. The jacket has a Mandarin collar and button-loop. It's trimmed with printed charmeuse."

Not one of us knew what Agnes was talking about.

"Ms. Tharp and I found it difficult to agree on shoes," Agnes said. "She favors the spiked heel and I tend to be more conformist."

Doc, Yigal, and I inspected Agnes's plain brown flats. We shook our heads in agreement.

"We settled on a pair of Via Spiga pumps," Agnes said. "Plus a very expensive pair of Bruno Magli Doolittles."

"I told Agnes I didn't want the shoes because they remind me of my uncle," Twyla interjected.

"Your uncle?" Doc Waters asked.

"Uncle Manny. Manny Maglio."

"These are Bruno *Magli* Doolittles, not Maglios," Agnes said. "In fact, I'm not familiar with the Maglio line. Is he a designer?"

Twyla looked at Agnes like she was from Zanzibar. "Manny Maglio.

The Mob boss. He's a thief and a murderer. You've heard of him, right, Bullet?"

Doug had warned me that Twyla was never, ever to know I had a connection to Uncle Manny. I tried playing dumb.

"I've heard of him, of course." Then I threw in a lie. "I had no idea you were Mr. Maglio's niece, Twyla."

"Well, I am," she bubbled. "Of course I don't like him much because he's a mean s.o.b. A very mean man."

"Sounds like someone I wouldn't want to meet."

"You wouldn't."

Agnes looked at Doc Waters, hoping a man with a mop of white hair and an unmistakable professorial look might haul her back into the world of the sane. But all Doc did was close his eyes.

"I gather, then, that Mr. Maglio does not make accessories."

"He's been an accessory," Twyla revealed. "Three times, in fact. But they never got the charges to stick."

We needed to move on. "You said you had some bad news, Agnes?"

The woman looked ten years older than when we first met her. The left side of her mouth quivered and her bun had disintegrated into something that looked like a hairy Slinky. "Bad news?"

"Yes, you said there was some bad news." I gave Agnes a worried look. A few more minutes of this nuttiness and she might go over the edge. For her sake and mine, I wanted to get my tribe and me out of Agnes's life as soon as possible.

Yes, there's bad news." The old disagreeable Agnes had returned. "Both Ms. Tharp's suits are going to require alterations." She put her hands on her hips. "Plan to pick them up tomorrow morning."

I sucked in a lungful of purified Nordstrom's air. "That won't do. The reason we're here is for Ms. Tharp to have at least one of those dresses—"

"Suits, Mr. Bullock."

"Regardless, one of those things has to be ready to wear in time for Ms. Tharp to make a meeting at three o'clock this afternoon."

"Quite impossible."

"I can help out, Miss Agnes," Twyla piped up. "I love to sew. My friends tell me I stitch like a bitch."

Agnes may have had the same vision as I did because her knees began to wobble.

"Nothing leaves this store unless our staff does the necessary alterations."

I could see the rigidity setting in. If I didn't act pronto, the woman's rigor mortis could make the entire Nordstrom visit futile.

"Could we talk?" I asked, leading her to the same neutral corner where my waste-management system had nearly broken down more than an hour ago.

"Nordstrom's has a tailor somewhere on the premises?" I inquired.

"We have a seamstress in our department, but she's completely backed up . . ."

I cut her off. "Manny Maglio."

"What?"

"The Manny Maglio that Miss Thorpe was talking about a couple of minutes ago. He's a very dangerous man who has a connection to your store. You don't want to lose your job, do you?"

"Of course not."

"Then we have to make sure Ms. Tharp is dressed in her new wardrobe by two p.m. at the latest."

"Yes, but—"

"There can't be any 'buts.' Somebody has put a boot on Nordstrom's neck. They want Ms. Tharp to show up in the right clothing for an interview she has later today."

Irritation and anger turned Agnes's eyes to little balls of fire. "The garments will be altered, and you can pick them up after lunch," she said quietly. "No earlier than one thirty." She turned her back and vanished behind a rack of Eileen Fisher dresses.

"Thanks!" I said, hoping Agnes might hear me. Even if she happened to, thanks didn't seem to be something that came her way all that often.

Chapter 6

Twyla Tharp pushed a red M&M through her high-glossed lips a few minutes after we left the Florida Mall parking lot. "What exactly is kosher?"

"Food approved under Jewish dietary laws," Doc Waters answered while digging into the bag of candy I had bought earlier in the morning.

"Yigal says he's kosher and Jewish," Twyla said. "I told him I used to be a Catholic and in CYO. But then when the bishop said I was going to hell because of what me and him did, I turned Presbyterian."

There was a long story locked behind Twyla's words, but I was too tired to open the door.

"Yigal says there's no reason why I couldn't go kosher," Twyla continued.

"If anyone could help make that happen, Yigal would be the man," I said.

"Well anyway, thanks for buyin' the M&Ms, Bullet." Twyla leaned across the front seat of the rented Mitsubishi to stroke my right shoulder.

"Yeah, thanks, man," Maurice called out from the backseat. The professor pitched in his own few words of appreciation. It was noon, and after fasting all morning, a couple of handfuls of confectionaries had just made me a minihero. Ironic. Working my tail off to save the life of some social outcast wasn't likely to buy me so much as a tip of the hat.

"Where we going now?" Maurice asked.

"Lunch at Friedman's Restaurant. So go easy on the candy." The older I got, the more I sounded like my mother. If only—

Catherine Manchester Bullock never saw a socially relevant finish line she didn't want to cross. It didn't matter how many hurdles stood in the way. The goal was to get to the end no matter how much energy and personal sacrifice it took. My mother had a supply of grit and determination that made her as tough as she was inspirational.

My parents believed experience was a far better instructor than talk. So, from age ten until I was out of high school, my mother hauled me to a soup kitchen at Camden's Fourth Street Mission. Each Monday and Thursday evening, I helped feed a long line of community castoffs. And although it was my late wife who turned me into a hardcore advocate for the homeless, it was my mother who first opened my eyes to what it was like to be destitute in America.

I still remember the ragged, hungry army that drifted into the mission. First were the women worn down by the ghetto and too many kids. They dragged themselves into the dining hall looking haggard and exhausted. Most ate dead-eyed and sad, oblivious to their whining and screaming offspring doomed by a gene pool and an environment to repeat the fate of their moms.

Next came the surly young men who usually showed up with an attitude that Mrs. Bullock wouldn't let in the front door. They had to leave their boom boxes and swagger outside if they expected a hot meal. Most of the time, my mother got her way plus a reluctant dose of respect.

Last to arrive were the street people—the men and occasional women who smelled as bad as they looked. They hobbled up to the food line mumbling incoherently and scratching lice from their oily hair. In the early years, I was sickened by the grossness and putrid odor. But my mother taught me that mental illness or misfortune didn't justify avoidance or contempt. In time, I traded my fear and loathing for as much understanding and compassion as a teenager could muster.

A hot meal didn't come without a price. After dinner, there was a requisite processional to the chapel where the poorest of the poor sat on wooden benches half listening to a preacher sermonize about the apostles, heaven, and hell. My mother resented the proselytizing, but she was as much a pragmatist as she was an agnostic. She knew it was religion that put the mission in the ghetto. If it weren't there, hunger would take its place. It was a matter of capitalizing on the opportunity and minimizing the downside—another one of life's lessons passed along to her son.

While Mrs. Bullock forced herself to live with the mandatory after-dinner homilies, she wasn't shy about debating religion with the mission's born-again director, a recovering alcoholic who credited his six years of sobriety to Jesus Christ his Savior. They were an odd couple, this man and my mother. For some inexplicable reason, they became close friends who thoroughly enjoyed arguing their polar opposite positions. He never strayed from his religious dogma while my mother plucked the inconsistencies from the Old and New Testaments. But there were also issues that put them on common ground.

Both were incensed by the nation's miserable treatment of the three million homeless men and women who wandered the nation's streets and back alleys. They saw firsthand how poverty and disease walked together. The homeless who rambled into the mission each night weren't just poor, they were sick with tuberculosis, AIDS, malnutrition, infections, and a long list of other ailments. Alcohol, drugs, and mental illness were demons for over half of them; physical disabilities and bad luck plagued the rest.

The director and my mom agreed overpopulation was the root of most of the world's problems. They talked about how the world had to absorb 210,000 new lives every day—and how this extraordinary population growth was stressing the planet. The director was for distributing condoms and tying tubes—but not for abortion. My mother insisted abortion had to be part of the solution. They went back and forth for years, never coming to terms.

My mother died a few months before I met Anne. Had she come to know her future daughter-in-law before a short, agonizing illness pummeled her body and eventually her spirit, she would have closed out her life with a smile. Her baton had been passed. Doug Kool once hinted that I married Anne because she was my mother incarnate, but I know that's not true. There were too many differences between the two women. What I did marry, though, were my mother's ideas and ideals.

Twyla snapped me out of my reverie. "You okay, Bullet?"

"Yeah, I'm fine."

Twyla applied another coat of lip gloss. "Is Friedman's Restaurant kosher?"

"Kosher as they come." Friedman's Nosh & Grill was Yigal Rosenblatt's idea. After Yigal had invited himself to lunch, he confessed to being "religiously constrained"—PC talk meaning he was kosher through and through. Which was why I was now turning into Friedman's parking lot.

Yigal was waiting for us when we stopped in front of the nearly empty diner. Zeus's attorney and Twyla reunited like they hadn't seen each other in months and the happy couple led the way to a round table near the back of the restaurant.

"Yiggy," Twyla purred, studying the menu, "this is all so foreign."

She was right. The bread was *Pas Yisroel* and the meat, *Debraciner*. I had no idea what that meant. Even Yigal was confused. With my head still aching and my body feeling the effects of too little sleep, I was ready for anything that would give me some relief. A glass of an Israeli chardonnay got me moving in the right direction. Next, like everyone else at the table, I ordered a cup of soup.

"What are these things?" Twyla poked at a half dozen round objects bobbing up and down in the broth.

"Matzo balls," Yigal answered. "Definitely. That's what they are. Matzo balls."

"Balls?"

I could feel the conversation degenerating. I asked Yigal to tell us something about the leafy vegetable piled on a serving plate in the middle of the table. It was an unappealing mush that, so far, no one had touched.

Doc Waters picked at the greens. "*Schav*. Some people call it sour grass but it's really sorrel leaf."

"Really?" Yigal looked surprised. "Always wondered what it was. Never knew."

Again, I found myself in awe of Doc's span of knowledge. He was a gentile and yet here he was out-koshering Yigal.

"You think Zeus's story holds up?" Doc asked later over coffee.

"Don't know," I answered. "It could have happened the way he said."

"I'm thinking it's too bizarre a story not to be true. Doesn't matter. The cops are never going to buy it." Doc paused to glance at Yigal who was talking to Twyla. "If this ends up in a courtroom, Zeus is history."

"More than likely."

"The college kids who saw what happened are Zeus's biggest problem."

Not that much of a problem if Zeus could afford a decent legal defense team. The witnesses were two well-oiled Rollins College juniors wandering around the wrong side of town at three in the morning. Dissecting the testimony of a couple of twenty-year-olds who were half in the bag when they bumped into Zeusenoerdorf and Kurios would be a cinch for most defense attorneys. But not for Yigal.

"So what happens now?" Doc asked.

"We drop Twyla off for her job interview, and visit the crime scene."

"The crime scene. Why? Every FBI agent and meter maid within ten miles has probably been over that area."

"Were they looking for evidence that could prove a blue car rammed a white van off the road?"

Doc ran a hand through his hair. "Maybe not."

"Any idea what Kurios was talking about just before he died?"

"Father Nathan?"

I nodded. "Ever hear the name?"

"Never."

Bad news. Doc, usually good for a hypothesis or two, left me dangling.

I paid the bill and walked outside. It was just after one o'clock—time to make a return trip to Nordstrom's. Yigal asked if he could meet us at the department store to continue discussing the Zeusenoerdorf case. The lawyer's ulterior motive, aka Twyla, was sliding seductively into my Mitsubishi and even Maurice chuckled at Yigal's excuse.

I drove to Nordstrom's with Yigal's car in my rearview mirror. When we arrived at the store, I asked for Agnes but was directed to another saleswoman with no nametag. She informed us that Miss Tharp's two suits were finished and so was Agnes—at least for the day. Manny Maglio had a way of inflicting a lot of collateral damage.

The saleslady escorted Twyla to the same changing room where she had been sequestered earlier. A few minutes later, Manny's niece emerged wearing a stylish but still sexy suit with her wild blonde hair pulled back from her face and bunched with a stunning lacquered clip. She looked nothing short of stupendous.

"I don't feel right in these clothes," she carped.

"You look right," I shot back. Maurice and Doc nodded in agreement. Yigal was vibrating like a pile driver.

"You think?" Twyla studied herself in a full-length mirror. "I look so different."

Thank you, Agnes.

We headed for Universal Studios with Yigal still in my wake. The HR and Employee Recruitment office was easy to find—a large building adjacent to a mammoth parking lot.

"According to the interview schedule, Ms. Tharp is to stay with us through five p.m.," a receptionist informed me.

"Okay," I said. That would mean two hours of interviewing. Doug had assured me that Twyla was a shoo-in for a job. Even so, I had this not-so-funny feeling that the more exposure Universal had to Manny's niece, the lower the odds for full-time employment. "Any chance she might be finished before five?"

"All interviews take at least two hours."

"Ms. Tharp is not your usual applicant—"

"Two hours."

Of all the thrill rides and amusements packed into Universal Orlando's one hundred acres, I wondered if anything could quite match the entertainment value of a Twyla Tharp employment interview.

UNIVERSAL: Previous employment?
THARP: Sin City Cabaret, Jersey Dolls, Bare Elegance,
      G-Spot and Jiggles Go-Go.
UNIVERSAL: Convictions?
THARP: Always use a condom.
UNIVERSAL: No, I mean were you ever arrested?
THARP: Only for soliciting, which doesn't really count in Jersey.

And so it would go until the HR specialist happened upon the note clipped to Twyla's file folder: *Applicant preapproved. Recommend placement in back office. No exposure to park guests.*

Since we were free for the next two hours, I told Doc and Maurice that it was time to scout out the spot where Zeus allegedly bludgeoned Benjamin Kurios to death. Yigal thought this was a brilliant idea.

"Wait a minute," I said to Zeusenoerdorf's lawyer. "You haven't been to the crime scene yet?"

"Right now is when we should do it."

I was still shaking my head when Yigal boarded my Mitsubishi and began rattling off directions. A few minutes later, Doc, Maurice, Rosenblatt, and I stepped onto what was an innocuous stretch of roadway that had now become a street of fame. Hundreds of people crowded the strip of asphalt where the most influential evangelist since Jesus had been murdered.

I pointed to the stanchions that supported the multibeam overpass that loomed above us. "Zeus said the white van was driven into one of those poles. The blue car chasing the van supposedly hit another. Look for streaks of paint and check the ground for metal or glass."

We split up.

"Could be something," Doc said, calling me to the street side of a steel column. The metal had been marked with a wide blue swath. The line of paint looked fresh so I used my nail clippers to scrape a few chips into a tissue.

"Keep looking."

For the next few minutes, we worked our way through the flowers and cards piled on the side of the road. When Maurice pulled a half-dollar-sized silver medallion from a crack in the pavement near the steel column, my adrenaline spiked.

"*Quia Vita?*" Doc asked.

"Bingo." It was identical to the emblem I had seen Ida Kyzwoski wearing at the Wayside Motel and the medallion Zeus described during his prison interview.

The professor studied Tyson's discovery. "A lot of people have tramped through this place since Kurios was killed."

The inference went over Yigal's head, but I understood what Doc was saying. The medallion might not belong to the driver of the blue sedan, which meant it didn't necessarily validate Zeus's story.

"The cops had to have searched every inch of this street," Waters added. "If the medallion had been here then—"

"Got jammed in that crack," Maurice explained. "Had to jimmy it out with my pocket knife."

I carefully wrapped the medallion in my handkerchief and put it in my pocket. "I think we have the real thing here, Doc," I said, trying to keep my excitement over Maurice's discovery in check. Whether the medallion would prove to be the first turn of the key in Zeus's jail cell door was unclear.

We took another half hour looking for anything else that might be connected to Kurios's murder, but came up empty. When it was time to head back to Universal, I herded the team toward my rental car. Halfway to the Mitsubishi, a wave of prickly heat rolled up my back. I spotted two Hispanic men who stood out from the somber crowd that had come to pay their respects to Benjamin Kurios. I had a dozen years of watching predators stalk their quarry in the inner city and these men moved like hunters. Maybe it was my imagination, but I had an uncanny feeling I was their prey. The pair got into a nondescript black Toyota Camry. I could only see the three numbers on the car's Florida license plate: 489.

A while later, when we pulled into the Universal parking lot, Twyla came barreling out of the Human Resources office. "Bullet, I got the job! I got the job! Yiggy. Doc. Can you believe it?"

"That's wonderful," I replied, trying to act surprised.

"I start in two weeks!" Twyla cried. "Can you imagine me working right here in Florida? And they said someday I might even get to sew things. Imagine that!"

Yigal wasn't imagining Twyla working a needle and thread, that was for sure. The lawyer was all teeth. He sputtered an offer to help Twyla find a place to stay.

"Oh, thank you, Yiggy."

With Twyla now gainfully employed, I was one night and an early morning flight away from fulfilling my obligations to Doug Kool and the mob. I told my crew to climb into the Mitsubishi because we were heading back to the Wayside for a quick pit stop, and later, a cheap dinner. If Yigal was expecting an invitation to tag along, he didn't get it. There was a limit to how much hyperactivity I could handle in a day. We left the forlorn lawyer vibrating in the parking lot and headed to our motel.

Back at the Wayside, I found the Kyzwoski room vacant. Seemed my least favorite neighbors had checked out. I had parked the Mitsubishi in the spot previously occupied by Conway Kyzwoski's truck-log cabin combo, gave my crew a ten-minute bathroom break, and then marched them two blocks away to one of Florida's five million Waffle House restaurants.

Over dinner, Doc asked to see the *Quia Vita* emblem we found earlier in the day.

Doc pointed to a dark smudge on one side of the medallion after I removed it from my handkerchief. "Looks like blood."

Assuming Doc was right, Maurice's discovery could be more than just a lucky find. If the blood belonged to someone other than Zeus or Kurios, it could support the defendant's claim that there was someone else on the scene the night Benjamin died. Although reluctant to call Yigal Rosenblatt, I needed information only he could give me. The lawyer picked up after the first ring.

"Is there a way we can find out if the cops took any blood samples after they found Kurios's body?"

"Already know the answer. They sent blood to the lab."

"You're certain?"

"They took blood off my client's wooden cross to match it with Kurios's blood. Part of the prosecution's evidence. I know that for a fact."

I didn't hide my skepticism. "You know this for a fact?"

"Yes. And you want to know why?"

I took the bait. "Why?"

"My cousin, Binyamin Saperstein, works at the lab that's doing the blood analysis. In Tampa."

I blinked in disbelief. "Your cousin's doing the lab work for the prosecutor?"

"Some of the work. Binyamin is a chemist."

I could have asked what might happen if Zeus were miraculously handed a not guilty verdict—wouldn't this incestuous family connection spell mistrial? Instead, I gave in to a more pressing question. "Doesn't anyone in your family have a regular Jewish name? You know, like Irving or Mo?"

"My cousins, Yehuda and Zelig live in Miami. My sister's name is Hava."

Question answered.

"Could you ask your cousin, Bin Yahoo, for a favor—"

"Binyamin. It means son of the south."

"Could you ask Binyamin if he could run a test on the medallion we found earlier today?"

"Test?" Yigal's voice took on a seriousness I hadn't heard before. "What kind of test?"

"Doc Waters thinks there's a blood stain on the medallion. If it matches up with Kurios or Zeus—"

"I see where you're going. Yes, Binyamin might do it. It's possible. But—"

Uh-oh. "But what?"

"That kind of test costs money," Yigal said in an uncharacteristically reserved way. "Done this before. Something like four hundred dollars. And if it's done in a day, it could be thirteen hundred. Maybe more."

The mere idea that Yigal's law firm might have to shell out cash on behalf of Miklos Zeusenoerdorf calmed the attorney down faster than a triple dose of Ritalin.

"Can't you fold the cost in with your other legal expenses?" I asked.

"The case is all pro bono," said Yigal. "Good PR, though. But expenses have to be kept low."

I wondered how much "good PR" would come from losing a case that led to a trip to death row for Gafstein and Rosenblatt's most celebrated client.

"What if I get the lab costs covered?" I asked. Whether I could actually deliver the money was as iffy as Twyla's staying celibate for another twenty-four hours. I avoided letting Yigal know that my offer to come through with a bag of cash was a little on the soft side.

"Oh, that would be good."

"I'll work on getting the money," I said. "You pick up the medallion at the motel before we leave for the airport tomorrow morning. Get cousin Bin to start working on this fast. And tell him to do this on the sly."

I closed out my phone call and finished my Waffle House dinner. A few minutes later, Twyla, Doc, Maurice, and I were back in our respective Wayside rooms. I tried watching a *Seinfeld* rerun, but it gave me a headache. Around midnight, I heard a car roll into the Wayside parking lot. If it weren't for my insomnia, I probably wouldn't have looked outside. But since sleep wasn't an option, I had nothing better to do.

The car was in an unlit parking area maybe two football fields from my room. Even at that distance, there was something familiar about the vehicle. I pulled on a pair of jeans and stepped outside to get a closer look. When I cruised by Twyla's room, I learned everything I needed to know about the mystery car and its driver.

"You okay?" I asked Manny Maglio's niece after she answered the door.

"Oh, yeah, Bullet," Twyla said. "I'm super."

Twyla was wrapped in a sheet and her hair was so disheveled that she looked like a blonde Chia Pet. Sitting atop her head as proudly as a Miss Universe crown was a black yarmulke.

"You want to be careful, Twyla," I said. Whatever the hell that meant.

"Oh, I will. I will."

"Okay then," I gave her a wave.

Twyla shut the door and I headed toward my room warning my mind not to broadcast pictures of Yigal cross-examining Maglio's niece. I opened my door, but before stepping inside, I heard the drone of a car engine. A black Toyota, headlights off, had its nose pointed directly at me. It was too dark to see who was inside, but a visual wasn't necessary. The Camry turned and pulled away, the light from the Wayside's neon road sign catching the rear license plate: 489.

Chapter 7

Dawn arrived without the sun. If the thick cloud cover over Orlando wasn't depressing enough for the surly manager of the Wayside Motel, I did nothing to brighten his day.

"We're checking out," I announced.

"None too soon." The manager scooped up the four room keys I slapped on the counter.

"By the way, what happened to the family in the room next to mine?"

The manager scowled. "Kyzwoski. Freakin' rednecks. Got into such a screamin' domestic I nearly had to call the cops."

Tell me about it.

"Had them idiots to deal with and you four freeloaders as well. Don't want to find no damage to any of them rooms you've been usin'!"

"No damage," I assured him.

"Damn Doug Kool," he muttered. "Him and his smart charity means more business bullshit. Cost me four rentable rooms. Next time, I'll know better."

"You're supposed to give 'til it hurts."

"Let me give you some news, my friend. I'm through helpin' lowlifes and anybody and any organization that deals with 'em. God-damned charity isn't worth shit!"

"That's the spirit."

I walked out the Wayside office door and into Yigal Rosenblatt. For the sake of appearances, he had vacated Twyla's room sometime before dawn and was now back on the premises looking a little less animated than usual.

"Don't lose it," I said after handing him the *Quia Vita* medallion.

"I won't," the lawyer promised. "Bringing it to Binyamin this morning."

"Good."

With a long separation from Twyla imminent, Yigal hopped in half circles while I loaded the Mitsubishi. A minute later, we were battling Orlando's morning traffic on the way to the National rental car return lot. At the Continental ticket counter, I put a little distance between my traveling companions and me and dialed Doug on my cell.

"Remember I said I owed you one?" he opened. I told the Harris & Gilbarton golden boy to speak up. A thousand screaming, mouse-eared kids made phone talk nearly impossible. "I want you to know I'm delivering!" he yelled.

"Delivering what?"

"Not what—who. Ever hear of Arthur Silverstein?"

"The billionaire?"

"One and the same."

"What about him?"

"He and Benjamin Kurios were close."

"Kurios?" I asked. Something didn't make sense. "Silverstein's Jewish, right? Why would he have anything to do with a Christian evangelist?"

"Why don't you ask him?"

"What the hell are you talking about?"

"Look, I know Silverstein. Know him well enough to have turned him into one of United Way's top contributors."

"So?"

"So I talked to him yesterday and told him about your conversation with Zeus."

How could I not be impressed? In some ways, Doug was one of the most superficial people I knew. He had always been a fund-raising gun who would hire out to the highest bidder. Still, his ability to connect with some of the most affluent people in the country was mind boggling.

"Silverstein invested in a lot of Kurios's operations," Doug continued. "He's interested in helping you figure out if Zeumanikof—or whatever the hell his name is—actually murdered the preacher."

This was sounding too good to be true. "You're talking about *the* Arthur Silverstein?"

"Yeah, the investment banker Silverstein. He's thinking about bankrolling you."

"Bankrolling me?" I felt a shred of suspicion, but it was wiped away by the thought of how my Zeus campaign could use more cash. "Why?"

"I didn't read his mind. He wants to lend a hand, which in Silverstein language means cutting you a check."

"Are there strings attached?"

"You know everything I know."

"You're a lucky man, Doug," I said. "I was going to put the arm on you to hit Manny Maglio up to cover a few of my expenses."

"What expenses?"

I didn't have to tell Doug about the bloodstained medallion and Yigal's cousin Binyamin. But I did. Seemed to be the right thing to do since he was opening the door to a billionaire.

"The kind of money you need is chump change for Silverstein," said Doug and he went on to drop the other shoe. "Listen, there's a little something extra we need you to do."

I should have hung up and run. Instead, I stood still.

"Manny Maglio wants Twyla in safe hands for another few days. For a week, actually—until she can make the move to Orlando, and start her job. He doesn't think she should go back to her apartment. Too many temptations and whatnot."

If shock and awe hadn't overwhelmed me, I might have taken some pleasure in picturing Twyla performing a whatnot or two. "You're not telling me—"

"Look, Bullet, I'm out there working for you. I got you money. I threw you a few bones all free of charge. The only thing you have to do is keep an eye on Twyla for what—maybe five or six days."

"Five or six— How am I supposed to do that when I'm in New Brunswick, and she's God knows where?"

"That's the thing," Doug practically sang. "She's going to be in New Brunswick with you!"

Last night's meal danced in my intestines. "Absolutely not!"

"Manny's got her a room at the New Brunswick Hyatt, which, if I recall, is only a few blocks from your Get-Away. All you have to do is check on her once and a while."

"Doug, apparently you don't know Manny's niece. Think nympho-maniac who charges by the hour."

"That's the point. She needs to go into withdrawal before she heads south. This is all about salvaging a life, Bullet. That's what you do."

That's what I tried to do. I had my successes, but my best intentions and skills sometimes didn't fit with the person who needed salvaging.

"Even if I went along with this, Twyla isn't going to trade her apartment for a hotel room," I said, hoping Doug wouldn't remind me she made that kind of trade every time she took on a client.

"She's already out—she just doesn't know it. As we speak, she's probably getting a phone call and a lot of bad news."

Curiosity got the best of me. "How'd you pull that off?"

"Not me. Manny. He owns the property management company that handles the house she rents. It's being fumigated. For real, I mean. The damn thing is wrapped up in plastic and they're pumping it full of poison."

I wondered if there was any politician in the country who could make things happen like Manny Maglio. Or Arthur Silverstein.

"Twyla won't be able to get her stuff out of the house for days. She'll be getting a 'so sorry' and an all-expense-paid vacation at the Hyatt plus money for a new wardrobe. Jesus, Rick. She just won the lottery!"

I stayed on the phone a couple of minutes more, but whatever else Doug said never made it past my left ear. I hung up and walked back to the seating area where Doc and Maurice were looking wide-eyed at Twyla.

"Fleas!" she screamed. "Oh, my God! Fleas!"

The hysterics went on for five more minutes until we boarded our flight.

"Bullet, this is terrible," Twyla sobbed. "I hate fleas. And the whole friggin' house is infatuated with them things."

I sighed. "Infested."

"That too," she went on crying. "They're in my clothes, my shoes, and my makeup. God—they're in everything!"

I gritted my teeth. What I wanted to do was to untie the truth and let it fill the Continental terminal. "It's temporary, Twyla. By next week, you'll be back in Florida."

"That's true," Doc chimed in. "And while you're in New Brunswick, we can take very good care of you."

There was a subliminal message weaving its way through the professor's comment, and I didn't like it.

"Thanks for being such a friend, Doc," Twyla said. She ran her hand up and down the professor's forearm the same way I used to tickle my poodle's belly to make its back legs twitch. Then she turned and stroked Tyson's cheek. "And you, Maurice." Then it was my turn. She looked me right in my lying, no-good eyes.

"And you, Bullet. Especially you."

My smile disappeared when I saw the two Hispanics who had been on my tail for the past twenty-four hours. Their dress was business casual but the cleaned-up look didn't fool me. I locked eyes with one of the men and that sent them scurrying away from the ticket area and out the main terminal doors. Left behind was a Nike sports bag resting against a self-serve ticket kiosk. When the second Hispanic pulled a cell phone from his belt holster and began punching the dial pad, my instincts took over.

"Run!" I screamed.

I bulldozed Twyla, Doc, and Maurice away from the kiosk. Five seconds later, a blast ripped apart fifty feet of Continental Airlines's ticket counter.

Part II

Chapter 8

Thirty minutes after three pounds of C-4 plastique exploded inside Florida's busiest airport, the FBI and Homeland Security ordered an immediate lock down. For the next four hours, teams of investigators interviewed over two hundred passengers and workers who were in the terminal at the time of the explosion. Twyla, Doc, Maurice, and I were among the first to be hauled into a makeshift interrogation room. Five hours later, we were given the okay to board a Newark-bound Delta MD-88—one of the first flights to leave the just reopened airport.

"You sure you seen those two guys?" Maurice asked. He was seated next to Twyla one row behind the professor and me.

"I saw them." Not that it mattered. My story about two Hispanics and a Nike bag didn't stack up with what thirty other witnesses saw—a man in his late twenties of "Middle Eastern descent" who bolted just before Continental's ticketing operations were blown apart. The feds wasted no time in issuing a warrant for the suspect.

"There were a lot of Latinos in the terminal when the bomb went off," Doc reminded me. "Maybe what you saw was—coincidental."

"It wasn't a coincidence."

"But how do you know?" Twyla asked.

Twelve years of working with men who were never far from trouble taught me the body language of guilt. I knew who was responsible for the disaster, and it wasn't difficult to figure out how he did it. Eleven percent of America's homeless are ex-military, and more than a few spent time at the Gateway. I couldn't remember how often I had played posttraumatic stress counselor—how many hours I had spent listening to a soldier or Marine describe what happened to his leg or arm after a run-in with a roadside bomb. Most of them had an expert knowledge of IED technology. Disassemble a cell phone, attach one of its wires to a detonator, and when you're ready, dial the cell number and close the electrical circuit. Not hard to do, and the results were usually catastrophic.

"No matter who blew the place up, the fact is you saved our collective asses," the professor said to me. "If you hadn't told us to run, they'd be scraping us off the floor."

I ignored the compliment. "I'm stepping on somebody's toes, Doc, and that somebody wants me out of the picture."

"Why?" Doc asked. "I don't mean to insult you, Bullet, but what makes you think you're that important or dangerous?"

"Best guess is Zeus. If I find out he's innocent, that means someone else gets nailed for Benjamin Kurios's murder. Somebody wants Zeus convicted and me off the case."

Sheer exhaustion and the lingering shock effect of what had happened at the Continental terminal stifled conversation. Not much was said during the remainder of the flight or the drive from Newark Airport to New Brunswick.

Then more bad news. The Hyatt Regency, which Doug Kool told me would be Twyla's home away from home for the next week, was booked solid when I showed up at one thirty a.m. It took another half hour to find Manny's niece a room at a Route 18 motel about seven miles from downtown.

At eight thirty the next morning, I picked up Doc and Maurice and drove north toward Arthur Silverstein's estate. A headache and a high-pitched ringing in my ears were reminders of last night's close call. About an hour later, my Buick Century's eight-year-old, 110,000-mile engine was wheezing and bucking along a two-lane road more suited to chauffeur-driven limos that hauled the likes of Jacqueline Mars, Steve Forbes, and Diamond Jim Brady. Bad as the car's internal combustion troubles were, Maurice's internal problems were worse. He had picked the backseat for our trip to Silverstein's mansion, which put the professor in front with me. Estimated time of arrival was ten minutes when Maurice stuck his head out the rear window and spewed the half-digested remains of a McDonald's breakfast over a lot of expensive landscaping.

"Damnit, Maurice!" I swore.

"The fun's just starting," Doc predicted. "Know anything about the brain's vomit center?"

"This isn't the time, Doc," I growled.

"Once the center clicks into gear, it's stays on. At least for a while. You might want to pull over."

I navigated my Buick on to the shoulder of the tree-lined road. Maurice scrambled out of the car just as my cell phone went off.

"Yigal?" I asked, trying to decipher the voice coming through the static.

"Just calling about last night. Wanted to make sure Twyla is all right. And the rest of you too."

"We're fine. What about the blood test? Did you hear from your cousin?"

"Binyamin just called me."

"And?"

"He knows whose blood is on the medallion."

"Whose blood is it? Zeusenoerdorf's?"

"No. Not my client."

I wasn't in the mood to play twenty questions—not with Maurice continuing to heave into a neatly trimmed hedge and Doc deciding to play mechanic with the engine of my already-distressed Buick. "Then whose, Yigal!"

"Juan Perez. That's whose blood it is."

"Who's Juan Perez?"

"The dead man the police found in Kissimmee."

I drew a long breath. "Yigal, help me out here."

"My cousin Binyamin was working on the medallion. That's when another blood sample showed up at the lab."

"And the second sample belonged to Juan Perez?" I interjected just to be sure I was traveling in the same direction as Yigal.

"Yes. An accident victim. Real bad accident. Needed a DNA test to prove it was Perez, and the lab asked Binyamin to do the analysis."

"So Benny Yomin happened to be working on the *Quia Vita* medallion and noticed that the blood sample matched the one taken from Perez?" I wanted absolute confirmation.

"Yes. That's what Binyamin said."

I tried to understand what Yigal was telling me. I was close to certain the medallion was the same silver disk Zeus had seen the night Kurios died. But what was the connection to a dead man named Perez? "Yigal, where did they find Perez's body?"

"Near Lake Tohopekaliga in Kissimmee. The car he was driving caught fire. He was inside."

I took a wild stab. "A blue car?"

"Yes. That's what my connections said."

"Paint!" I said, my excitement mounting. By sheer luck, we might have just discovered who was behind the wheel of the sedan that had forced the white van off the road. "Is there any paint left on the outside of the car?"

"Yes there is," replied Yigal. "Not all of it burned off. Saw pictures. One door still had paint. Blue paint."

"Listen to me." I wanted the lawyer's full attention if that were possible. "Is there a way you could get one of your connections to scrape some that paint off the door?"

"I can try. I know a few people in Kissimmee."

"A few chips of paint," I cut in. "See if you can make that happen."

"I can do that," Yigal said, then picked up an old refrain. "But we owe Binyamin his money. Thirteen hundred dollars."

"Yeah, I remember," I said. "I'm good for it." At least I thought I was, thanks to my questionable decision to give insider information to Arthur Silverstein. "Let's get back to Juan Perez. If you can deliver paint samples from Perez's car, I'll try to find somebody who can tell us if the paint matches the chips we scraped off the underpass piling where Kurios was killed."

"Morty Margolis can do that."

"What?"

"He's my partner's brother-in-law. Does that kind of lab work for the FBI."

Astounding, I thought. For all his weirdness, Yigal Rosenblatt did have important connections. "Let me get this straight. This guy, Margolis—he could tell us if the two paint samples came from the same van?"

Yigal paused. I could feel him about to lay an egg that could mean nothing but trouble. "Yes, he could. But I would have to talk to him. Face-to-face would probably work."

"Face-to-face," I mumbled and then gritted my teeth. "And where does Morty do business?"

"Weehawken."

"Weehawken? Like Weehawken, New Jersey?"

"That's where he works."

"So. You want to come all the way from Florida to New Jersey just to talk to Margolis?"

Pause. "That would be good. I don't mind driving. Cheaper than flying. At Gafstein and Rosenblatt, we keep expenses down."

I knew Yigal had a two-word ulterior motive for making the trip: Twyla Tharp. Even so, I decided not to bury the suggestion. "If you get paint off Juan Perez's car, then we'll talk."

I ended the phone call about the same time Doc closed the hood of my Century. "Besides a filthy air filter, looks like a tip-in problem," he said. I was only half paying attention, partly because I have little interest in cars, but mostly because I was still sorting through what I had just heard from Yigal. The possibility that Juan Perez could be connected to the Benjamin Kurios murder, not to mention the two Hispanics who bombed the Continental terminal, made my Buick's engine malfunction seem insignificant.

"You got a 3.1 liter engine in this thing," Doc went on. "Time for a new vacuum hose elbow for your PCV system. I gave it a temporary fix, but you're going to be bucking and stalling again in no time, unless you get this thing to a mechanic."

"I'll take care of it."

"Want to know how I figured out what was wrong?"

It was pointless to say "not really" because nothing was going to stop Doc. He held up a rag. "You use this to wipe your windshield?"

"Yeah."

"From the looks of it, it gets a workout."

"When the temperature hits forty degrees or so, fog builds up inside the windshield. The damn defroster doesn't do what it's supposed to."

"There you go," said Doc with a smile. "It's all about knowing what clues to look for and figuring out what they mean. A Buick Century with a defroster problem and an engine that idles rough or stalls usually add up to a faulty vacuum hose."

Doc didn't explain how a history professor knew more about cars than General Motors. He was an enigma and it was best to leave it at that. My malfunctioning defroster did remind me, though, that Doc had an incredible ability to problem solve—except when it came to extricating himself from his own self-made troubles. While I had long admired Doc's logic, I had no idea I'd be using it as a life preserver in the days ahead.

A few minutes later, we were on the road again. My Buick purred its way to the front of an iron gate that blocked the main drive leading to the interior of the investment banker's spread. I pressed a red button on a squawk box attached to one of the two impressive stone columns that loomed like sentinels on either side of the drive. A raspy voice leaked through the speaker, and after I delivered the right answers, the gate swung open and I navigated my Buick into a mini-Versailles. The Silverstein grounds were enclosed by a perfectly trimmed six-foot hedge and a lethal-looking electric fence. Doug Kool would tell me later that Silverstein had purchased enough electronic surveillance devices to monitor nearly every inch of the sprawling estate. For added protection, he employed a squad of security personnel to patrol the place.

En route to the main house, there was nothing but spectacular scenery. Every tree, shrub, and blade of grass appeared to be in top-notch shape. If the flora scored high, Silverstein's home was off the charts. We circled around a colossal fountain and parked in front of a tier of steps that could have been the walk-up to the Lincoln Memorial. The four-story mansion was by far the most imposing private residence I had ever seen. Doc pulled himself from the Buick, took a long look at the building, and blew out a whistle. My sentiments exactly. Even the bedraggled Maurice Tyson was obviously impressed.

We were greeted at the door by Arthur Silverstein's aide-de-camp who introduced himself as Abraham Arcontius. Thanks to an earlier phone conversation with Doug, I recognized the man the second he came into view. He had a long, narrow nose and his ears were so freakishly big they resembled feelers. According to Doug, Arcontius's physical appearance was as strange as his personality.

"You're Bullock?" Arcontius asked.

"I am."

Arcontius leered at Doc and Maurice. "We weren't told you'd be bringing company."

"Mr. Silverstein wants information about the Benjamin Kurios murder investigation," I explained. "I brought along my—associates to help spell out some of the details." The exaggeration seemed to suit Maurice just fine, a dose of importance making him beam.

"Come this way." Arcontius didn't walk, he slithered.

Doug called Arcontius "a composite guy—part chief of staff, part appointment secretary, and part butler." There were, he told me, those who claimed Arcontius pulled Arthur Silverstein's strings while others said he was an indentured servant who had given many years of his life trying to please his master without ever succeeding. My own take was that he was just plain nasty all the way from the tip of his balding head to his polished oxfords.

"Mr. Bullock is here to see you," Arcontius announced as we entered a two-story chamber with as much warmth as the New York Public Library reading room. The walls were all dark wood but barely visible behind shelves and shelves of books. A monstrously large desk in one corner of the room ruled over the other lesser pieces of furniture. Behind the desk hung a larger-than-life oil painting of a young blonde woman wearing a red dress and a smile more forced than genuine. The lady in the portrait was not as well endowed as Twyla and was perfectly groomed and dressed. But there were startling similarities—high cheekbones, the shape of the mouth and, particularly, the eyes.

A short man wearing a dark suit and striped bow tie stood as we walked into the room.

"Ah, yes." Arthur Silverstein held a cigar in one stubby hand and greeted me with the other. "Welcome, Mr. Bullock."

I shook hands with a five-foot-five-inch man who resembled a shrunken Winston Churchill.

Arcontius jerked his head toward Maurice and Doc. "These two accompanied Mr. Bullock—unexpectedly."

I introduced the two men by name.

"I see. Abraham, would you show Mr. Bullock's companions to the sitting room?" It was clearly an order couched as a question. The banker turned to me. "Would you be interested in a short tour of my home, Mr. Bullock?"

Without waiting for a response, Silverstein led me to the grand foyer. We began ambling through corridors that would have made a Ritz-Carlton proud.

"I understand you had a narrow escape yesterday." Silverstein said as we walked.

"Very narrow."

Silverstein had a low, strong voice that didn't match his diminutive size. He sounded more like a billionaire than he looked. "I've often thought about how vulnerable we are to chance—to circumstances and events that we don't control. When fate treats us badly, it's sad indeed. But of course, there are times when our own reckless behavior puts us at risk. When that happens and the consequences are unpleasant, well, we have no one or nothing to blame other than ourselves."

I was trying to sort out whether Silverstein was being philosophical or sending me a warning, when the billionaire motioned to an array of paintings displayed on the corridor wall.

"Do you enjoy art?" he asked.

"*National Geographic* covers. French postcards. That sort of thing."

Silverstein found no humor in the comment. He stopped in front of a picture that gave star billing to two men—one lying naked on a pile of logs and a second standing over him holding a knife.

"Are you familiar with this work?" Arthur asked. "It's quite well known."

"Afraid not."

"It's a Marc Chagall. Called *The Sacrifice of Isaac*. Do you know the story?"

I pleaded ignorance.

"It's from the Bible—Book of Genesis. God decides to test Abraham's allegiance by telling him to sacrifice his son, Isaac. This is the scene on Mount Moriah where Abraham agreed to go along with God's wishes."

"Why?" I asked and silently answered my own question. *Because the father was a religious fanatic.*

"Abraham was committed to carrying out God's will without question—in other words, he proved himself worthy of God's trust. Consequently, he became the father of all of us. Jew. Christian. Muslim. We're all Abraham's children."

Abraham wasn't the kind of man I wanted anywhere near my family tree. "Asking someone to sacrifice his child seems a little extreme, doesn't it?"

"There are times when a personal sacrifice must be made for the greater good. No matter how difficult that sacrifice might be."

While I tried to fathom what he had just said, Silverstein resumed the tour. "The white-haired gentleman you brought with you," Silverstein asked. "Is he the same Professor Waters who once taught at Rutgers?"

I nodded. Silverstein pulled the cigar from his mouth and grimaced. Doc's testicle-squashing misfortune had a predictable cause-and-effect impact on all men regardless of their income.

"As I recall, he's as brilliant as he is misguided," Silverstein noted. "No matter what shape or form it comes in, I respect intelligence. Always have."

"When it comes to figuring things out, there's no one smarter than the professor."

"Good. That's a quality that should prove quite helpful, shouldn't it?"

We continued our stroll past more art and artifacts. There was no further mention of what was hanging on the walls or perched on pedestals. Instead, Silverstein shifted his attention to the business of the moment.

"So, tell me about Miklos Zeusenoerdorf."

I cannot recall one other occasion where someone other than me pronounced Zeus's name correctly.

"He says he's innocent—claims he didn't kill Benjamin Kurios."

"I see." Silverstein thought a few seconds before continuing. "And what's your opinion? Is he innocent?"

"Could be that he's just a poor slob with a low IQ who stumbled into something that wasn't his doing."

Silverstein shook his head. "Public opinion doesn't seem to line up with that possibility. Quite the contrary. Most seem to think Mr. Zeusenoerdorf is, indeed, a cold-blooded killer."

I glanced at the short man. "And what about you?"

Silverstein smiled. "I never accept probability as certainty. That's why I'm interested in assisting you, Mr. Bullock."

"Assisting me?"

"You and your—team—have a connection to Mr. Zeusenoerdorf that no one else seems to have. I'm anxious to learn what you already know and what else you're able to find out about Kurios's death."

Silverstein stopped, put his cigar-free hand into his suit jacket pocket, and pulled out a letter-sized envelope.

"This is to retain your services as a—let's call you a private investigator. I have two ten thousand dollar checks in here that I want you to have. The first is made payable to your men's shelter, which I understand can accept tax-deductible donations. The second is made out to you—consider it an advance."

"But—"

"For other reasonable expenses, just let Mr. Arcontius know and we'll reimburse you over and above your retainer."

This didn't smell right. It was the kind of thing that ended up as a page-one story in the *New Brunswick News Tribune* laced with words like "under-the-table payoffs" and "indictment."

Silverstein read my anxiety. "Don't worry, Mr. Bullock. I've gone through all the necessary channels to make sure this is legitimate. One of my legal staff contacted your board chairman and verified that your employment contract doesn't exclude you from working on the side."

It was all too neatly packaged. I tried protesting again, but it was wasted energy. Silverstein had already moved on.

"What did you find out when you visited Mr. Zeusenoerdorf in Orlando?"

I fed Silverstein just some of what happened in Florida, including news about the *Quia Vita* medallion discovery. But I didn't mention what Zeus claimed were Kurios's last words—Father Nathan. And I left out cousin Binyamin's report that the blood on the silver medallion belonged to a dead man named Juan Perez. Time and trust—not a few thousand dollars—was what it would take to buy full disclosure.

"How much do you know about my involvement with Benjamin Kurios?" asked Silverstein.

Why did I think this was more of a bear trap than a simple question?

I picked my words carefully. "From what I've read and what a few people have told me, you were a major donor to his religious movement."

"More of an investor in Benjamin than his movement," Silverstein amended. "And I am sure you know my reputation when it comes to making prudent investments."

Next to Warren Buffett, there was no one who could throw the Wall Street dice better than Arthur Silverstein. The tycoon was best known for being a hedge fund genius, but in recent years he'd become what *Fortune* called a "natural resource speculator." He had untold land-holdings around the world—especially in Latin America, where he owned mineral and oil rights in Mexico, Guatemala, Venezuela, and Brazil.

"Each time I spend money on an opportunity, I look for—make that expect—a return on that investment. My financial involvement with Benjamin was no different from other commitments I've made. His un-timely death meant I ended up with less of a payoff than I anticipated. That displeases me."

"Uh-huh." I didn't get the connection between laying millions of bucks down on a stock and dumping a like amount on an evangelist. But what I did get was an unmistakable message that this was a short man who got piqued when he was shortchanged.

"You see, Mr. Bullock, I believed in Benjamin Kurios."

"But he was a Christian evangelist. And you're a Jew." I couldn't help myself. It just came out.

"As was Christ."

"Well, then, you're—you're a Jew for Jesus."

"Not in the way you might think. I believe that Jesus of Nazareth was as mortal as you are," Silverstein explained. "He was a Jew who was extraordinarily charismatic and perhaps a little on the egocentric side. Benjamin Kurios had the same qualities."

We had made a long, winding trip through the innards of the Sil-verstein castle and were now back in Arthur's library.

"So you invested money in Kurios—"

"I did and for good reason. You see, Benjamin had a unique abil-ity to influence the masses. So much so that he could change their be-liefs and even their behavior. I believe you were once in the advertising business?"

I wasn't surprised that Silverstein had done his homework. I guessed that somewhere in his office there was a dossier marked RICK BULLOCK put together by Silverstein's security personnel.

"I left the ad world a long time ago."

"Still, I think you know what I'm talking about. It's quite a challenge, is it not, to get adults to change the way they think to the extent that they change their behavior?"

Just when I thought I was in Silverstein's intellectual wind stream, he veered off. "Are you familiar with the *Book of Nathan?*"

The question rattled me. Before the jailhouse interview with Zeus, the only connection I had with a Nathan was a Coney Island hotdog stand and an ex-con I once hired to clean the Gateway gutters. Now Nathan was coming at me from two directions—Zeusenoerdorf's mysterious Father Nathan and Silverstein's book. Could there be a link between the two? That didn't seem probable, but it wasn't something I was about to rule out.

I answered Silverstein's question. "No."

"Really?" Silverstein looked at me square in the face. "I find that rather surprising."

"I don't get to read a lot."

"It's one of the so-called missing books of the Bible."

I told Silverstein that the Bible—like fine art—was not one of my strong suits. I couldn't begin to tell him which books were in the Bible, never mind those that were missing. Silverstein gave me another suspicious glance and opened a drawer in his desk. "I think this might interest you." He slid a typewritten page across the desk. The heading read: MISSING BOOKS OF THE BIBLE.

MISSING BOOKS OF THE BIBLE

Missing Book	Biblical Reference
Acts of Abijah	2 Chronicles 13:22
Prophecy of Ahijah	2 Chronicles 9:29
Epistle to Ephesians	Ephesians 3:3
Book of the Covenant	Exodus 24:7
Prophecies of Enoch	Jude 1:14

Book of Gad	1 Chronicles 29:29
Book of Jasher	Joshua 10:13; Samuel 1:18
Book of Jehu	2 Chronicles 20:34
Epistle to Laodiceans	Colossians 4:16
Visions of Iddo	2 Chronicles 9:29
Manner of the Kingdom	1 Samuel 10:25
Epistle of Paul to the Corinthians	1 Corinthians 5:9
Book of Nathan	1 Chronicles 9:29
Book of Shemaiah	2 Chronicles 12:15
Book of Samuel	1 Chronicles 29:29
Saying of the Seers	2 Chronicles 33:19
Book of the Acts of Solomon	1 Kings 11:41
Acts of Uzziah	2 Chronicles 26:22
Book of the Wars of the Lord	Numbers 21:14

"We know from the books that are in the Bible that there are many others that were excluded," Silverstein said. "Check the Biblical references on the right side of the page."

"What does this have to do with Miklos Zeusenoerdorf?" I asked.

He ignored the question. "What's fascinating to me is that many of the books some think were misplaced or lost were intentionally left out. The Hebrew Bible was an especially fluid document that changed from one generation to the next. Not only were there translation errors along the way, but it seems certain editorial prerogatives were taken."

I gave up trying to figure out where Silverstein was leading me and went with the flow. "So the *Book of Nathan* ended up on the cutting room floor because some rabbi, priest, or monk decided the Bible was too long?"

"Or too controversial, provocative, or dangerous. Of course, the omission of a few books seems quite justified. The apocryphal books such as Tobit, Judith, and the Maccabbees, for example. They're so religiously insignificant that they've been removed from the list."

Silverstein was so far over my head that I could do nothing but sound stupid. "So the Bible is really God's *Reader's Digest*. A lot got left out when the final condensed edition got published."

Surprisingly, he seemed to like the analogy. "You're not far off.

There are a few credible scholars who think the Bible is actually only thirty-five percent complete."

I tried again to bring the conversation back to the main point. "Why all this interest in the *Book of Nathan*? Why not—" I ran down the left-hand side of Silverstein's sheet "—the *Book of Jasher* or the *Book of Jehu*?"

"Some of the missing books such as Jasher for instance, have been located and translated. But a small number of the books on the list I gave you have eluded us."

"*Nathan* being one of them?"

"Yes."

I took another stab. "And Benjamin Kurios had a connection to the *Book of Nathan*?"

Silverstein gave me a wary look. "Quite right. Benjamin was going to use his revival meeting in Orlando to talk about the book."

It was the same Citrus Bowl spectacular that had lured Miklos Zeusenoerdorf to Orlando. "Kurios would have had an audience of— what—seventy thousand people?" I asked.

"Actually, a far larger audience than those sitting in the bleachers. Benjamin had negotiated a live TV broadcast on the FOX network. In fact, all the media seemed ready to give the event extensive coverage."

"Why?"

"Because Benjamin was going to read excerpts from the *Book of Nathan*."

"Kurios told you that?"

Silverstein settled into a high-back leather chair behind his desk. "Since I was among Benjamin's most generous financial supporters, he and I were quite close. Shortly before he died, he confirmed something I had suspected for a long time—that he had been given a translated edition of the *Book of Nathan*."

The connection between Kurios's last words and a recently discovered book of the Bible was getting a lot tighter. "How'd he get it?"

Silverstein's steely eyes dissected me. I felt like I was plugged into a human lie detector. "Benjamin was smart. He worked hard to bring the right people into his fold. Henri Le Campion, for instance. Ever hear of him?"

"No."

"He was one of our great modern archaeologists and linguists," Silverstein said. "Also happened to be a genius when it came to computers. Died of a heart attack just after his sixty-fifth birthday—only a couple of weeks before Benjamin was killed."

Strange how the Grim Reaper was never too far behind the *Book of Nathan*, I thought. Kurios, maybe even the driver of the blue sedan—both dead. And Zeus might be next if I didn't beat him to the finish line.

Silverstein propped up his short body. "Several years ago, Henri found the *Nathan* scrolls in a cave not far from Jerusalem. It should have made more news than the Dead Sea Scrolls discovery in 1947. But that didn't happen."

"Why not?"

"Because for reasons we'll never know, Henri was fanatically attached to Benjamin. He carbon dated the scrolls to validate their authenticity, and then spent years translating the *Book of Nathan*. At every turn, he kept Benjamin informed of his progress."

"And when he finished the translation—"

"He converted an English version to an encrypted computer disk. Well, partly encrypted, to be more accurate. The actual translated text requires a translation code or key. But Le Campion's preamble doesn't. It's mostly Henri's own discourse that he uses to blow his own horn—he was a notorious chest beater."

"An old man's ego trip," I mused, momentarily forgetting I was in the company of an old man whose ego was bigger than his house.

"Benjamin let me read a few verses that Le Campion had folded into his preamble. They were Henri's way of teasing one into wanting access to the full text."

"How teased were you?"

"Considerably. I was taken by what I read. As mentioned, the second part of the disk is the coded translation of the full *Book of Nathan*. Very sophisticated work, according to Benjamin. Try to download or decipher part two without a computer conversion key and the entire text is scrambled into an omelet of meaningless words and phrases."

"What about the original scrolls?"

"Hidden," Silverstein replied.

"Hidden?"

"Henri was an eccentric. More than likely, he found a safe place for the scrolls somewhere near Jerusalem. But it's doubtful we'll find much of anything until we locate the disk."

"Because the coded part of the disk includes the English translation and directions to Henri's hiding place," I guessed, enthralled by what lay ahead.

"You're right," Silverstein confirmed. "Supposedly the directions to the scrolls are encrypted along with the complete translation of the book."

Since Silverstein had not invited me to sit, I was still on my feet separated from the billionaire by his desk. I felt appropriately inferior. "Since you bankrolled a lot of Kurios's operations, you must have some idea of what the book says," I conjectured.

Silverstein puffed himself up. "Shortly before Benjamin died, he predicted that the *Book of Nathan* would prove to be the most important document of our time. He was betting his credibility on what's in that book."

I had no idea why Silverstein was giving me so much information. No matter. I wanted more. "You pumped a lot of money into Kurios's operations. Why wouldn't he tell you what was in the book?"

Silverstein gave me another ocular MRI. "A promise."

"A promise?"

"A promise Benjamin made to Le Campion. You see, Henri demanded secrecy. He didn't want the book's contents disclosed to anyone until Benjamin could orchestrate an event where it would get worldwide attention."

"The Citrus Bowl revival."

"Exactly."

"And Kurios was so honor bound that he wouldn't even talk to his inner circle?"

Silverstein paused to relight his cigar.

"Apparently so."

"He kept you totally in the dark about the *Book of Nathan*?"

"Not totally."

I had perfected my interrogation skills quizzing homeless men. The right information doesn't fall into your lap. It's all about knowing what questions to ask. "So, Kurios did slip you some information?"

"Information might not be the right word," corrected Silverstein in a surprisingly matter-of-fact tone. "More like a hint, actually. Benjamin inferred that the book would resolve one of the most divisive issues mankind has ever had to deal with."

My skin tingled. I tried not to show my excitement, but it bubbled into my next question. "Did he tell you what that issue happened to be?"

"Not directly, since that would have broken his pledge to Henri. But he did leave a trail of large crumbs."

"And?"

Silverstein used another pause to keep me in suspense. "It seems the *Book of Nathan* includes God's definition of when life begins."

Now it was my turn to blink. "Excuse me?"

"You've heard of ensoulment?"

"The point in time when the soul enters the body?"

"Yes. It's at the core of an age-old debate."

"You mean the dividing line between the pro-lifers and the pro-choicers?"

"Exactly," Silverstein confirmed. "The Bible as it currently exists isn't clear on ensoulment. Is it something that happens at conception? Three months into a pregnancy? At birth? According to Benjamin, the *Book of Nathan* answers the question and finally settles the contentious argument about abortion."

I pictured my parents listening to this conversation. The last thing they needed to judge the legitimacy of an abortion was a religious text. To them, an abortion was far more acceptable than irresponsible or accidental reproduction, and there wasn't a scripture ever written that would have changed their minds. I wondered if Silverstein knew I shared many of my parent's thoughts. I wasn't one to march around preaching the importance of protecting a woman's right to choose, but if pressed, I'd be quick to argue that a decision to abort or go full term should be based more on common sense than religious hoopla. I would usually toss in a caveat—that abortion is a lousy type of birth control that unfairly penalizes women more so than men. But these were the views of an agnostic that I had learned a long time ago ran counter to America's religious mainstream. To the vast majority of people, the *Book of Nathan*'s definition of ensoulment would be *big* news—so big that I was still skeptical.

"Out of nowhere, a missing book turns up and just like that, the abortion debate is over?" I asked. "No matter what the *Book of Nathan* says, a lot of people will blow off the message."

"Exactly what Henri feared." The banker leaned forward until his biceps pressed against the surface of the desk. With just his head and shoulders exposed, he looked like a talking bust. "Which is why he wanted Dr. Kurios to be the messenger."

"Could Kurios have pulled it off?"

Silverstein blew out a cloud of smoke. "We'll never know, will we?"

"Nope," I concurred. "Of course, if the missing computer disk is found, somebody might take another shot at making the book public."

"That's a possibility."

"Which I assume is why you want the disk."

"Let's just say it would be a way to recoup some of my investment in Benjamin's good work."

I was getting a better sense of Silverstein's determination. It had little to do with educating mankind. "And if you did get the disk?" I asked.

"Depends."

"On what?"

"On a careful review of Le Campion's translation."

"In other words, if the *Book of Nathan* lines up with your point of view about—what did you call it?—ensoulment, then you might look for another Benjamin Kurios to spread the word." Even I was surprised by the bluntness of my words.

"Something like that."

"So, what is your point of view?" I asked, not expecting—and not getting—much of a response.

Silverstein turned his chair until he had a sideways view of the woman captured in oil on canvas. He locked on to the painting for several seconds and then stood up, walked around his desk, and positioned himself in front of me. "Let's get back to Mr. Zeusenoerdorf. I think he may know more about the missing disk than he's admitted."

"So, what you want me to do is grill Zeusenoerdorf about the *Book of Nathan*. Whether he actually killed Kurios is secondary."

"More information about the disk may prove helpful to Mr. Zeusenoerdorf."

"I want you to know that I'm in this to figure out if Zeus is innocent or guilty. The only reason I'd dig around for the disk is to find out what happened in Orlando."

"Whatever your motivation, keep our business relationship in mind," Silverstein advised. "If you learn anything about the disk, I'll expect you to notify me before you talk to anyone else."

Silverstein had put me in his pocket without my knowing what happened. No wonder the man was a billionaire. "And if I should forget?"

The short man glowered. "That would be a serious misjudgment. There would be consequences."

I was tempted to tell the little man that a dozen years at the Gateway had made me immune to threats. But I didn't want to risk cutting the cord to someone who had the connections and resources that could help Zeusenoerdorf. "Okay, I hear what you're saying."

"I'm pleased that you do," Silverstein guided me toward the library door. Halfway across the room, I put on the brakes.

"Who else might want Benjamin dead?" I asked. "Or maybe another way of asking the same question—who else might want the *Book of Nathan* disk?"

Arthur surprised me with a fast comeback. "*Quia Vita.*"

"*Quia Vita?*"

"Yes."

"The medallion we found not far from where Kurios was killed—that *Quia Vita?*"

"Yes."

"The medallion might have no connection to what happened to Kurios," I proposed. "We found it in a gutter. Anyone could have lost the thing."

"That's possible," Silverstein conceded. He walked back behind his desk and ground out what was left of his cigar, glancing once again at the painting of the young woman. "On the other hand, the medallion might be pointing you—us—in a very important direction. What we know for certain is that *Quia Vita* has its reasons to be concerned about what's in the *Book of Nathan.*"

"Isn't *Quia Vita* an ultra pro-life group?"

Silverstein nodded.

"Wouldn't that put them in the same corner as Kurios? I'm guessing Benjamin was against abortion since he was as Christian as they come."

"Check his writings and sermons," Silverstein suggested. "He was more flexible on that issue than *Quia Vita* would have liked him to be."

"Meaning what? Kurios might have endorsed abortion if the procedure were done before the soul showed up in a fetus?"

"He might have. Yes."

"So, your hypothesis is that since *Quia Vita* couldn't be sure about what was on the disk, they didn't want Kurios to go public with the *Book of Nathan*."

"A more logical theory is that Mr. Zeusenoerdorf murdered Benjamin," replied Silverstein. "But if there were to be a line-up of other suspects, I would move *Quia Vita* to the front."

"Would *Quia Vita* have actually killed Kurios in an attempt to get the computer disk?"

Silverstein raised his eyebrows. "Considering what's at stake, anything's possible."

"You know, your line of reasoning points to another suspect," I noted.

"Who might that be?"

"You."

Silverstein jaw tightened and he straightened his slightly hunched back. I could feel what he wanted to say—that I was nothing but a low-end homeless shelter director who had the audacity to get in the face of a billionaire. But Silverstein buried his irritation behind a chuckle that told me he had high hopes that I could shake out some useful information from Miklos Zeusenoerdorf. "I'll grant you that I want to see what's on Le Campion's disk," he said, "but if that doesn't happen, so be it. I'll write the whole business off as an investment that didn't work out. The disk is far more consequential to *Quia Vita*. It may contain information that could jeopardize its existence."

"I know nothing about *Quia Vita*, Mr. Silverstein." It was a fact I was sure he already knew. "I have no connections to the organization at all."

"But you do have connections to Mr. Zeusenoerdorf." Silverstein pulled out another cigar, clipped its end, and fired it up. "Perhaps you should pay him another visit. Ask him specifically about the disk. Dig as deep as you can."

Talking to Zeus again wasn't such a bad idea, except it would mean making another trip to Orlando. And since Doug had Twyla and me attached at the hip, that wasn't going to happen. I said I would give the suggestion careful consideration.

"Be sure to stay in touch," Silverstein ordered just as Abraham Arcontius appeared. After a quick handshake, I was back in the foyer of Silverstein's mansion. Doc and Maurice were waiting for me at the front door.

"One question," I fired at Arcontius while he was busy herding us outside. "The painting in the library. Who's the woman?"

Arcontius's beetle-like face told me what he really wanted to say was "none of your damn business." But he decided to spit out an answer. "Ruth Silverstein—Mr. Silverstein's late daughter."

Chapter 9

"Want a historical factoid to help pass the time?" Doc Waters called out from the back of my Buick.

"All right." Like it or not, it was trivia time.

"Arcontius was a Catholic bishop."

"Yeah, right." I cranked my head to catch a glimpse of the white-haired genius behind me. Doc had been relegated to my car's rear seat for the return trip to New Brunswick, while Maurice got in front. The passenger shuffle was all about keeping Maurice's motion-sensitive gut under control.

"I'm not talking about the worm who polishes Arthur Silverstein's boots," Waters clarified.

"That should make a billion Catholics feel better."

"Somewhere around the eighth or ninth century, there was a French bishop named Arcontius. He went nose-to-nose with a mob that had some issues with the church and ended up getting clubbed to death. Because he stood up for the boys in Rome, Arcontius was made a saint."

"Fascinating," I said, intrigued. "The guy we just met must come from a different bloodline. Because I guarantee you—sainthood isn't in Abraham Arcontius's future."

In my rearview mirror, I saw the Doc nod.

"Change of subject," I said. "What did you and Arcontius talk about while Silverstein was marching me around his mansion?"

"Absolutely nothing. Arcontius dumped Maurice and me in a room next to the library. Never saw him again until he threw us out."

"When Arcontius first brought us into Silverstein's library, did you notice the painting behind Arthur's desk?"

"The one you asked him about?"

"Yeah, the picture of Silverstein's daughter. Know anything about her?"

Doc grinned. He knew everything. "Absolutely. It was a big story twenty, thirty years ago. His daughter was an addict who overdosed in some lower Manhattan dive. The tabloids had a field day speculating on whether it was an accident or whether she deliberately killed herself. Anyway, the kid's death unhinged Arthur's wife and she spent the next year or so in and out of a psych ward. You probably know the rest of the story—Mrs. Silverstein jumped off the Queensboro Bridge."

Coupling pity with Silverstein didn't come easy. "This is going to sound weird," I said, "but Twyla looks like Arthur's daughter."

The professor laughed. "Promise to have me around when you tell Silverstein that his kid has been reincarnated as a lap dancer."

I wanted more of Doc's input, but my curiosity was cut short by my cell phone. It was Doug Kool returning a call I had placed earlier in the day.

"Holy Christ," Doug said. "You nearly got your ass blown off. Talk about bad luck. Getting mixed up in a damn terrorist attack."

"It wasn't a terrorist attack. I think the bomb was meant for me."

"What? Are you nuts? Don't you watch TV, for God sakes? It was some Islamic fundamentalist idiot who blew the place up. Besides, who'd want you dead?"

"I'm trying to figure that out," I answered. "And by the way, I don't watch TV because I'm too busy keeping both eyes on Twyla Tharp."

Doug went quiet for a time, probably thinking about the possibility of how an attack on me might also damage Manny Maglio's niece. "Listen, I don't want Twyla getting hurt, Bullet. Not a scratch. Jesus, that's all I need is to have her banged up. And I'm not talking about the usual way she gets banged up."

"Try not to worry too much about me," I said sarcastically. "I called you earlier because I need a favor."

"You're going to squeeze me again?"

"You're going to get squeezed as long as I have to play den mother to your big donor's relative. You stuck me with Twyla, and my guess is you knew from the start this was going to be a long-term deal. Well, here's a bulletin. I'm teetering on the edge of saying 'so long' to Manny's niece."

I listened to Doug take a long breath. "Don't even think about rocking the boat. Maglio's contribution will put the United Way over the top this year. All I'm asking is that you keep Twyla in check. You owe it to me."

I knew enough about Doug's business to grasp the seriousness of the situation. In his world, it was about making the numbers. If the United Way missed its annual fund-raising goal, then it would be bye-bye to the Harris & Gilbarton contract. And God forbid my friend should have to go bottom-fishing for work. He might even end up managing a homeless shelter.

"I don't owe you anything!" I argued. "When we flew back from Orlando, we were even steven. If you want me to continue playing nursemaid, you're going to lend your old friend a hand."

The man who rarely lost his cool was working harder than usual to keep himself under control. "All right. What do you want?"

"Two things. First, I want a rundown on Arthur Silverstein's daughter."

"Ruth Silverstein? She's ancient history."

"Doesn't matter. I want to know what happened to her. What really happened."

"She was a screwed-up druggie," said Doug. "Went over the edge and OD'd. Not a lot more to know."

There was a hint of hesitancy in my friend's voice. Maybe Doug was just confounded about my interest in Silverstein's kid. Or maybe he was privy to information that wasn't supposed to come out.

"I want the story behind the story."

"What's this all about, Bullet?"

"I don't have to answer that." Which was a good thing since I couldn't come up with an intelligent response. It was about the way Silverstein connected with the painting in his library.

"All right, all right," Doug gave up. "I'll see what I can do. So what else?"

"*Quia Vita.*"

"*Quia Vita?* What about it?"

"Let me save us both some time. Don't start with the 'I don't know the organization.' You're wired to every nonprofit operation in New York."

"All I know is that *Quia Vita* plays nothing but hardball. And the woman who runs it—"

"What woman?"

"Judith Russet. She's a Mack truck. I'm telling you—don't get involved."

"I'm not looking for a one-on-one with the lady," I said. "I'm trying to find out whether *Quia Vita* had a connection to Benjamin Kurios."

"Listen, don't go there." Doug's voice rose. "You're completely over the edge. Until now, it's been a harmless game of Clue. But you start messing with *Quia Vita*'s top dog and you're up against a pit bull."

"You want me to watch Twyla or not?"

"Jesus."

"So what's it going to be? *Quia Vita* or Manny's niece dropped on your doorstep?"

Doug cogitated. "*Quia Vita* holds a meeting in Manhattan each month. Don't ask how I know—I just do."

"What kind of meeting?"

"I'm not sure. It's not a group that broadcasts its agenda. If I remember right, they meet the third Friday of every month."

"That's tomorrow night," I said more to myself than to Doug. "Where does this crowd get together?"

"You need to hear what I'm saying. Don't mess with these people!"

"Where?"

Doug sighed. "Always the same place. The Grand Hyatt."

"Midtown? At Grand Central Station?"

"Yeah."

"You don't have any idea what goes on at these meetings?"

"They're recruiting sessions. *Quia Vita* rounds up pro-lifers with deep pockets from around the country and brings them to Manhattan. It's an invitation-only deal."

I wasn't planning on taking the next step. It just happened. "Get me in, Doug."

"In where?"

"The meeting tomorrow night."

"Are you nuts?"

"Finagle a couple of invitations."

"I won't do that," Doug said flatly.

"Too bad. I'll put Twyla on the train in the morning. She should be at your office in time for lunch."

"I can't believe this," Doug grunted and snorted for a time. Then he came through. "All right. There's this Hyatt sales rep who handles the *Quia Via* account. I've thrown her some business over the years. Maybe she could open the door. I don't know—it's a long shot."

"Get her to cough up a couple of invitations. Doc Waters will be coming with me."

"What?"

"Doc has his faults, but he has a way of solving puzzles. I want him at my side."

Doug wasted more time trying to convince me my idea was sheer insanity. I wouldn't bend. All arrows were pointing to *Quia Vita* and I needed as much insight about the organization as possible. Climbing into the belly of an extremist group would be dicey, but doing nothing was more dangerous. The two men who tried and failed to exterminate me were probably regrouping. Staying ahead of their next bomb meant moving fast and taking a few necessary risks.

I dropped Doc and Maurice at the Gateway and drove to a car wash on Route 1. The seven dollar super-clean cycle and a two dollar vanilla deodorizer strip were no match for the odor Maurice had left in my Buick. A half hour later, I was back in my office and found two Post-It messages slapped on my phone.

Pick up Twylie Thorp at four thirty, call Middlesex County Admin. Office.

Call Figgy Rosenblatter

The first call was answered by Twyla's probation officer who explained that Manny's niece had been referred to an occupational counselor. Middlesex County was trying to find something Twyla could use to make a living other than her vagina. Apparently Twyla mentioned that she had already been offered a job at Universal Orlando, but the bureaucrats brushed that off as wishful thinking. I could have validated Twyla's story but that would have just put her back in my custody sooner than four thirty. So, I left things the way they were and placed my second call to Yigal Rosenblatt.

"Got paint from the car that burned," Yigal proclaimed. "I'm ready to bring it to New Jersey."

"Yigal, this guy you know in Weehawken—"

"Morty Margolis is his name. He's my partner's brother-in-law. Remember?"

"I remember. The point is, it would be a waste of time for you to drive all the way from Florida to Jersey if this guy Margolis can't or won't give us a hand."

"Oh, he'll help," Yigal insisted. "Not a waste of time."

I pictured the drool rolling out of Yigal's mouth. The thought of touching base with Twyla before doing business with Morty Margolis was putting a little extra buzz in the already overly stimulated lawyer.

"So, when will you be here?" I asked.

"Leaving now."

"Now? You're going to drive all night?"

"Be there in the morning."

Was there any more powerful motivating force than a man's testosterone? Nothing came to mind.

"Something else," Yigal added.

"Go ahead," I said.

"The guy driving the blue car that was burned—"

"Juan Perez?"

"Juan Perez was who he was. Nothing much left of him because of the fire."

"We know all that," I interjected. "What's the point?"

"My uncle plays golf with a Kissimmee detective. I have connections, you know."

"So you've told me. Go on."

"Perez was from Caracas. Visiting a cousin in Orlando."

"Caracas, Venezuela?"

"That's where he was from. "

"What else?"

"Venezuelan police says he's a mercenary."

"You mean like a gun for hire?"

"That's what he was, is what I was told."

I mentally translated. A South American hit man comes to the U.S., chases a van with Benjamin Kurios stuck in the back. He runs the van off the road and into a bridge abutment, gets into a fistfight with the van's driver, and then ends up charbroiled in a one-vehicle crash. I could just hear Yigal using this cockamamie story in front of a jury. Zeus might as well place an order for his last meal now.

"What else do you know about Perez? Is he connected to any other Venezuelans in Orlando?"

Coincidence can only go so far. The two fee-for-service assassins who had tried to kill me were probably working for whomever had hired Perez. The threat level just went up a notch.

"Didn't hear about anybody else from Venezuela," Yigal said.

"If something else comes up about Perez, let me know," I told Yigal.

"Okay. Will be there in the morning. Staying at the Hyatt."

"The Hyatt? The New Brunswick Hyatt?"

"Yes, that's where I'll be."

And that's where I would be registering Twyla in about two hours. I gathered Manny's niece had slipped Zeus's lawyer this information.

"You can find a cheaper room on Route One."

"Gafstein and Rosenblatt can afford a good hotel."

"Yigal—" I began with such a moralistic tone of voice that I could almost hear Rosenblatt drifting away.

"Have to leave." End of conversation.

I cursed Doug and spent the next hour and a half catching up on office work. Then I made the short drive to the Middlesex County administrative offices where I found Twyla standing outside with her parole officer.

"Five minutes late," the officer said.

"Sorry."

Twyla bounded into the car.

"You run the men's shelter in town, right?" the officer asked.

"Yup."

"That place is full of drunks, hopheads, perverts, and thieves."

I shrugged. "Can't deny that."

"Uh-huh. Well, I was told you're on the up-and-up. That you wouldn't do nothin' to, shall we say, complicate Miss Tharp's probation."

I faked a smile. "Nope—I try not to complicate."

The woman chewed on her lower lip. "I also heard you got friends in low places. But they're not the kind of friends I want Miss Tharp associating with. *Capeesh?*"

"Well, let's not call them friends. But I *capeesh* all the same." I put my Buick in drive, leaving Twyla's parole officer at the curb.

A few minutes later, we pulled up to the Hyatt Regency. I escorted Twyla to the registration desk where I ran into the hotel's general manager, Robert Gonzales, known to most of New Brunswick as Four Putt. Since he had arrived in the city five years ago, Gonzales and I had played in a dozen charity golf outings, some of which included Manny Maglio. I learned early on how the hotel's top executive earned his nickname.

Gonzales pulled me into a corner. "Look, Bullet, I want nothin' to do with this."

"With what?"

"With her." Four Putt jerked his head at Twyla who was now the center of the universe for the hotel's two male registration clerks. "Maglio's people told me they needed a room and I came through. But they didn't tell me who it was for. I don't want nobody in the 'business' stayin' here!"

I tried putting some spin on a bad situation. "It's just for a few days."

Four Putt wasn't buying. "Damnit. You remember what's across the street? Johnson & Johnson's worldwide headquarters, is what. Those guys find out I got a hooker on board and my career's shot."

Actually, Four Putt's career had been pretty much put on hold when Hyatt's management sent him to New Brunswick. Word was that his performance had not been stellar at two previous properties.

"Why are you unloading on me?" I complained. "You played golf with the devil and for that little bit of bad judgment, you've got no choice but to give his niece a room and a king-sized bed."

"His niece." Four Putt gasped. "Jeez, I didn't know it was his niece."

Uh-oh. "That's classified information you didn't hear from me," I said. "As a matter of fact, if word gets out that you know about the blood connection between Twyla Tharp and your golfing buddy, you'll be teeing up in hell."

Four Putt threw back a confused stare. "Twyla Tharp? She picks a Broadway choreographer for her alias?"

"Not an alias. She changed her name a few years ago," I explained. "She's a dancer."

Four Putt slapped his head with one of his large, hairy mitts. "What she is—is a prostitute."

"Who's looking to make a career change."

"Jeez, this could really do it to me. A damn streetwalker of all things."

"I feel your pain. And since we're talking about people of ill repute, there's a lawyer who'll be checking in tomorrow."

"So what?"

"Give him a room as far away as possible from wherever you're stashing Twyla."

"Oh, my God," Four Putt whispered. "What's going on?"

"So far, nothing. And I need your help to make sure things stay that way."

Chapter 10

Yigal Rosenblatt showed up at the Gateway around noon, looking more disheveled than ever. The first words out of his mouth told me that the long drive from Orlando to New Brunswick had done nothing to dampen his caffeinated personality.

"Here they are—I have them here," Yigal announced between bounces. He held up a legal-sized manila envelope and tore it open. Three scraps of metal each about the size of a silver dollar fell onto a coffee table—one of the newer furnishings in the Gateway's common room. All three metal pieces were painted blue on one side.

"You're positive these came from the burned-out car?"

"That's where they came from. Had them cut out of the door."

"Your partner's brother-in-law—"

"Morty Margolis."

"We can rely on him?" I deliberately let my skepticism eke out.

"Called him yesterday. Says he'll do what he can."

I gave Yigal as earnest a look as was feasible. "Look, I don't know whether these paint chips and the paint samples we scraped off the stanchion in Orlando add up to evidence or just two handfuls of junk. But what I do know is that your partner's brother-in-law is the man we'll be relying on to give us the answer."

"That's what he'll do."

"Remember—whatever Margolis finds or doesn't find could either set Zeus free or put him in the electric chair."

"Maybe I could say hello to Twyla," Yigal suggested. "Before I go to Weehawken to see Morty Margolis."

A one-track mind knows no detour.

"Business first." My cell phone saved Yigal from a protracted sermon.

"This is Abraham Arcontius." Silverstein's assistant had a voice that matched his reptilian look. Sound hissed through his distended throat like steam from a vent.

"Something I can do for you?"

"We understand you'll be attending the *Quia Vita* meeting tonight."

It took me two seconds to figure out how Silverstein and company knew I would be at the Grand Hyatt. Doug Kool.

"That's the plan," I admitted.

"We want a full report tomorrow."

"No one said anything about daily briefings."

"Please be at Mr. Silverstein's estate tomorrow, Mr. Bullock."

"With all due respect, I'm not on call. If you want to schedule a meeting, that's fine. But I need more lead time if you expect me to show up."

"Perhaps you don't quite get what's going on here," Arcontius said.

"Educate me."

"We're giving you a chance to show us what you're really up to."

"What the hell are you talking about?"

"That's something we can discuss tomorrow."

My dislike for Arcontius was growing like a cancer. "Look, I had a couple of checks stuffed into my pocket as payment for feeding your boss information. I wasn't comfortable taking the money in the first place and now I'm thirty seconds away from mailing them back."

Arcontius wasn't rattled. "The money is incidental. There are bigger issues on the table."

"The only issue I'm aware of is a man who might be getting the shaft in Florida."

"If that's the case, you'll be here tomorrow, and you'll tell us whatever you learn at the meeting tonight."

"Us?"

"A collective us. The Silverstein team is extensive."

In my line of work, it's not uncommon to run into disagreeable, distrustful, and dislikeable people. Arcontius bundled up all these undesirable qualities into one slimy package. He used Silverstein's power base to pump up his own importance. When I didn't roll over on command, the man wasn't happy.

"Anything that happens tonight can be summed up in a phone

call," I said. "I don't expect to walk away with any big news. Remind Silverstein I'm starting at the low end of a learning curve. The reason I'm going to the *Quia Vita* meeting is to get a better handle on the organization. End of story."

"Mr. Bullock, I don't think I'm making myself clear. We want you at the Silverstein estate tomorrow. A phone call won't do it. There are things we need to discuss face-to-face. Don't push aside a chance to play by our rules. Because if you do, you'll deeply regret it."

"Define 'deeply regret.'"

"*Occasio aegre offertur, facile amittitur.*"

"What?"

"It's a Latin saying. It means: 'Opportunity is offered with difficulty but lost with ease.' I know you'll show up tomorrow."

The Grand Hyatt has a lot in common with Yigal Rosenblatt. With over 1,300 guest rooms and 55,000 feet of "function space," the place is in a perpetual state of hyperactivity. When Doc Waters and I walked into the lobby around six p.m., it was 100 percent bedlam.

We checked the hotel TV monitors for meeting information but there was nothing posted for *Quia Vita*. Doug Kool had instructed me to go to the front desk and ask for an account manager named Jane. She would meet us in the lobby.

After a five-minute wait, a middle-aged woman appeared with an outstretched hand pointed at Doc's stomach. "Mr. Bullock?"

I took the mistake as a compliment. I had dressed the professor in a blue suit left over from an Episcopal Church rummage sale and a white shirt a size too small for Doc. With the conservative tie pulled from a box of clothing donated by Goodwill, Doc came across sort of corporate.

"Ah, if only I were." Doc sounded as suave as he looked. "My name is Professor Waters and it is a distinct pleasure to make your acquaintance."

Jane loved every word. "Dr. Kool told me you were interested in booking a meeting with us in a month or two."

This was the cover Doug had told me to use. Doc and I were looking for meeting space for a fictional religious higher-education association. Jane had been told we were deeply committed pro-lifers who knew about *Quia Vita* but didn't have the kind of bank accounts that would get us an invite to one of the group's monthly sessions. In consideration for the business Doug brought to the Hyatt, Jane agreed to provide back row seats for his two friends.

"I'm so pleased you could be here tonight," she gushed. "The room configuration you're interested in is exactly the setup we use for Ms. Russet."

"Judith Russet?"

"Oh, yes. She's truly a hero, isn't she? I'm so privileged to be in her service."

Doc lifted his thick white eyebrows. "How wonderful that you're a member."

"A member of *Quia Vita*, of course. But not the Order of Visio Dei—the group that's meeting here tonight. As I'm sure you know, it's a membership category open only to those who have both the resources and the will to share God's vision in a very special way."

"We have the will, but we're short when it comes to the money," I said sadly.

Jane looked to the floor. "I do have a confession to make. I didn't tell Ms. Russet that you were financially unqualified."

"Oh?"

"I hope you don't mind. I'm in charge of putting together the attendee roster for each meeting—I do that on my own time, of course. As a *Quia Vita* volunteer."

"Of course," said Doc.

"I thought it would be easier all around just to include your names as potential Visio Dei members. It would be awkward if Ms. Russet were to find out that you don't meet the monetary threshold for membership. Could I impose upon you to—"

"We're so honored you'd even think to put us on the invitation list," Doc interrupted. "We'd never put you in a compromising position, Jane." He grinned at her conspiratorially.

"You're very kind—both of you."

"It's you who's so kind, Jane," Doc said. "Tell me, how is it that you became involved with *Quia Vita*?"

My early warning light switched on.

"It was God's calling," Jane rolled out a pat answer to a question she had probably been asked innumerable times. "I believe so strongly in the sanctity of life."

"Ah, yes, I understand." Doc brought his hand to his chin the way only academics are able to do. "And I imagine you find comfort and guidance in the Bible for your beliefs,"

"I do, Dr. Waters. I certainly do."

"Doc—" I tried to interrupt.

The professor pretended I didn't exist. "How mysterious it is that the Bible never mentions abortion, don't you think, Jane?"

"Well, I—"

"Sometimes I wonder if Aristotle were right. I'm sure you recollect his theory."

Jane's plaster smile cracked. "Well, I—"

"Granted, Aristotle was a little pagan in his approach. But think about how much less conflict we'd have if everyone agreed with him. That a male fetus doesn't take on a soul until forty days after conception. Or that a woman has no soul until after ninety days of gestation."

"Oh, well . . . I can't . . . well, I mean, I just don't believe . . ."

I barged in before Doc could continue. "The professor can sometimes play devil's advocate."

Plugging the devil into my comment didn't sit well with Jane. An uncontrollable shudder rattled her Hyatt nametag.

"I suppose it's my way of testing just how firm one is when it comes to his or her pro-life position," Doc explained. "This is not a movement that should be corrupted by those who aren't knowledgeable about all aspects of the abortion issue. Wouldn't you say so, Jane?"

"Well, I . . . It's just that I believe God switches on the soul once a person is conceived."

"Ah, if we could only locate, feel, smell, touch, weigh, or measure a soul. We could then be certain. But it's the uncertainty of it all. Perhaps that's why for much of its history, Christianity thought ensoulment didn't happen during the ninety days after conception and religious leaders were more tolerant of abortion."

Jane looked appalled. "That can't be—"

"Of course there are others who think that the soul doesn't show up until we have at least some sense of awareness. Do you know what the first sign of awareness is?"

"Well, no, I—"

"Pain. And a fetus is not developed enough to feel pain until around one hundred twenty days after conception."

"Oh, no, Professor Waters," Jane pushed back. "That can't be. The *Silent Scream* shows a baby in terrible pain. And it was only twelve weeks old."

I watched Doc's face redden. According to the professor, the anti-abortion movie, *Silent Scream*, set the high bar in raping science.

"We must be so careful of our credibility," said Doc. He was straining to control himself. "A fetus simply cannot register pain at twelve weeks."

"But the baby was frantic just before it was aborted."

"A reflex response, my dear, that has to do with the movement of the uterus. Do you recall the late Dr. Carl Sagan?"

The woman nodded.

"He said we really don't become persons until we can think, and that doesn't happen until the cerebral cortex starts functioning. It takes six months in the womb before the cortex gets fired up. So during the first two trimesters of pregnancy, Dr. Sagan—the good Lord rest his soul—would tell you the fetus is not really a person."

Jane gasped.

"Such a difficult issue," Doc muttered. "When does personhood begin? Who's right and who's wrong? Will we ever have a decisive answer?"

"I—" Jane worked hard to put a few words together. "It's a matter of faith, Professor."

"Yes. But it is also a matter of law and—if you happen to be a woman—often a matter of choice."

If devil topped the list of the words Jane least wanted to hear, choice was a close second. "I don't remember meeting any pro-lifer who talks the way you do," she said.

"Professor Waters is an eminent scholar in the field," I said, trying to do some quick repair work. "He forces us all to strengthen our arguments and moral commitments. Which is why he will truly make his mark on *Quia Vita*."

"I shall make every effort to do so," Doc promised.

Chapter 11

Judith Russet was a washboard of pasty white flab under a crown of gray hair cut so short that it resembled a bathing cap. A quick once-over and you might think *Quia Vita*'s executive director was soft as cotton candy.

As we were about to discover, not true.

According to plan, Doc and I were the last to be seated at *Quia Vita*'s Visio Dei meeting. Just before we had slipped into the back of the room, I let the professor have it for climbing all over Jane. Doc had given me a halfhearted reassurance that he'd behave and, with reservation, I decided not to put him on a train back to New Brunswick.

Judith Russet arrived two minutes late and began the meeting with an apology. A weather-delayed flight from Chicago.

"Life," she opened, "is under attack." A LCD projector blasted an eight-by-eight-foot screen with words that exploded like incendiary bombs: *abortion, euthanasia, doctor-assisted suicide, reproductive and genetic technologies, cloning, infanticide, eugenics, population control.*

"You—" Russet let the word hang in the air until she surveyed all fifty-plus attendees seated in the room. "You are here because you have been chosen to be life's guardians. Nothing you ever do will be more important."

For the next twenty minutes, Russet delivered a message that cut into the small group like a cleaver. Every sentence came out as a shriek. Doc was breathing hard and his face was flushed.

"Over one point three million children in the United States are killed by an abortionist each year. Most of these immoral procedures are not done in hospitals. They're carried out in over four hundred death chambers ironically called health clinics."

A split-screen video followed. On one side, a woman cried into the camera. On the other side, a slow zoom-in on a bottled fetus. "I went into the bathroom and passed the placenta," the woman said between sobs. "When I looked in the toilet, I saw my baby — its perfectly formed hands, the little fingers — " Russet took over. "This is a woman who used to be pro-choice. A woman who chose to kill her baby seven weeks after becoming pregnant."

Russet went on for another fifteen minutes mixing words with PowerPoint slides and two more video clips. Once the room had been properly worked over, she stepped in front of the podium.

"I'm here today speaking on behalf of millions of unborn children. I hope you can hear their voices. What they are asking you to do — what they're begging you to do — is to enlist in the highest echelon of *Quia Vita* — the Order of Visio Dei. Why? Because when it comes to waging war against the unjust and immoral slaughter of children, we need Visio Dei if we have any hope of winning."

Russet made a slow journey through the room.

"Let's be clear about what's going on. Abortion equates to premeditated murder. Most abortions carried out in the United States are a grotesque means of birth control — less than five percent are performed because the fetus is diagnosed as abnormal or because the mother's health is at risk. And less than one percent of abortions are performed because of rape or incest. That means more than nine out of ten abortions are willful homicides that shouldn't be classified as anything but murder in the first degree."

Russet continued prowling. "Does it bother you?" The question was rhetorical but still got a lot of heads bobbing. "Just how troubled are you? Troubled enough so you feel it in the pit of your stomach? Troubled enough to want to cry for the four thousand babies who will be massacred in the U.S. today — or the one hundred twenty-six thousand children worldwide who in the next twenty-four hours will be cut out of the womb and tossed away like garbage?"

Russet inched her way toward the back of the room, pausing to make eye contact with each guest. When she reached our table, Doc caught her stare and his face instantly twisted into a look of disgust. The rotund woman was caught short by the expression and briefly stumbled over her next line. When Russet shifted her attention to me, she got back on track although I could sense her confusion.

"I want to tell you something," she said, heading back to the podium.

"*Quia Vita* and everything our organization stands for may soon come under attack like never before. Over the next few weeks and months, you may be hearing new arguments that will be shoved in your face—arguments abortionists will undoubtedly use to justify their butchery."

A murmur worked its way through the room. Whatever the new arguments might be, they stirred the crowd. I thought back to Arthur Silverstein's comment that the *Book of Nathan* could shake *Quia Vita*'s core. Maybe Russet knew about the missing book—knew what it said about ensoulment. It was all conjecture on my part, but convinced me I needed to know a lot more about Russet and her organization.

"Visio Dei is reserved for those who are in a position to do more than just talk about stopping abortionists," she said. "It is open to people like you who have the resources to fund the battle to protect the unborn. The question is—do you have the determination to use some of those resources to fight for life? Because if you do, then you'll pledge yourself to Visio Dei. It won't be cheap and it won't be easy."

Russet let the group ponder the picture she had painted. Then she opened the floor for questions. A few hands went up, and soon there was discussion about the responsibilities and price tag for a Visio Dei membership. The *Quia Vita* CEO distributed a handsome folder stuffed with brochures and leaflets. One insert explained the financial hurdle that needed to be cleared if one were to make it into the top tier of the organization. While there were different ways to join the club (tithing, living trust, property transfers), it would take a minimum of $7,500 a year to remain a member in good standing.

An hour into the meeting, Russet unfolded a note that had been left on the podium. Had she arrived for the meeting on time, she probably would have read the message earlier. The way she glared at Doc and me after scanning the note, I was relieved she had waited.

The crowd split in two. Half surrounded Russet and half headed for a roll-in table loaded with desserts, coffee, tea, and an assortment of after-dinner liqueurs.

The commotion made it easy for Doc and me to slip out. We took a few steps into the adjacent hallway before Russet rumbled through the doorway.

"Follow me," she ordered. There was no salutation—just a requirement. We trailed the woman into a small room two doors down from where the prospective Visio Dei members were stuffing themselves with cream puffs and petit fours. Jane, the Hyatt group account manager, was alone in the room.

"Do you know these men?" Russet asked.

"Yes, ma'am," Jane said. "Well, not really, ma'am."

"Not really is the right answer," Russet snapped. "You're the gatekeeper to Visio Dei. I trusted you to make sure only the right people get into the meetings. And you let us down. You opened the door to two men whose mission is to stop us from defending the unborn."

"But they're pro-life," Jane said. "That's what I was told. They're pro-life."

Russet approached her like a demon from hell. "Told by whom?"

Jane could have mentioned Douglas Kool, but she didn't cave, mainly because she was crying so hard she had lost the power of speech.

"I want to make it clear to you what you've done," Russet said, three inches from Jane's face. "You let these two steal information—information they can twist and warp in a way that could prevent hundreds or thousands of babies from being born."

"But, I—"

"I want you to leave," Russet demanded. "Now!"

Jane tried to muffle her hysterics with a hanky the size of a credit card and then dashed out the door.

Russet turned to Doc and me.

"I know who you are."

"And we know who you are," I said calmly.

"You got lucky, Mr. Bullock. Lucky I didn't get the message about you and your friend here until minutes before the meeting ended. Had I known, I'd have exposed you to the others in the room. And I can assure you, it would have been a most unpleasant experience."

My curiosity plowed through my fury. Who sent the note that tipped Russet off? Who gave us away? It certainly wasn't Jane. Best guess was that Doug had slipped the information to Silverstein who, in turn, made contact with Russet. But it didn't make sense that the billionaire would let *Quia Vita* know two interlopers had penetrated its defenses. Which brought me back to Doug. There was no good reason to think he ratted me out on purpose, but my friend was notorious for his loose lips.

"Why are you here?" Russet asked.

"Fact finding."

"And I know the facts you're looking for. You're checking out just how deep *Quia Vita*'s pockets are. Well, I'm happy to give you that information. All you have to know is that we have sufficient funds to pay for whatever God tells us we need to purchase."

"Enough funds to buy some common sense?" Doc asked.

"I'm not going to stand here and wallow in your insults."

Doc returned fire. "Why not? We spent an hour wallowing in your pro-life twaddle."

"Pardon me?"

Here we go I thought.

The professor stretched out his arms to make sure he had Russet's attention. "Where do you find all these people who have more money than brains?"

"What each of them has is a soul. Something you appear to be lacking."

"The world has its share of fanatics. You happen to be one of them and so be it. What turns me purple are the people who sit there and soak up your drivel as if it were nectar."

Russet was unflappable. "The nectar you're talking about has another name. The truth."

"Half truths, at best. You let people think there's no difference between a single-cell zygote and a six-year-old kid."

"That single-cell zygote has forty-six chromosomes and everything it needs to grow into that six-year-old child. You seem to have forgotten your biology. The only difference between a zygote and a baby is a trip down the birth canal."

"Crap. That single-cell zygote also has the same DNA makeup as a hair follicle. Hello, Ms. Russet. We're in Dolly the Sheep's world. We're a whisker away from taking a strand of your short, gray hair and turning it into a living, breathing thing."

"Your immorality astounds me, professor," said Russet. There was a reverberation in her words that reminded me of a volcano about to spout. Disgusted, she began working on me. "What about you, Mr. Bullock? Are you as determined to kill babies as your friend?"

I wasn't here to get into a firefight over abortion. I knew my take on the issue would only fan Russet's flames, so I picked my words carefully.

What I wanted to say was that *Quia Vita* should spend more time in my world where squalor, alcoholism, drug addiction, and penury make for a lousy bassinette. I never castigated a woman who didn't want a child born into such a morass. I didn't find fault with a mother who ended an unwanted pregnancy because she had already produced too many kids who were pulling her into inescapable destitution. No one could sell me on the idea that the end product of rape or incest should be allowed to go full term. In my opinion, trying to pin down whether an abortion was appropriate or immoral three minutes after conception or three months down the line was much less important than figuring out how to stop people from conceiving by accident or stupidity. That's what I could have said. Instead: "Given your religious beliefs, I can understand why you feel strongly about—"

"You don't understand anything about me," Russet charged. "What I understand is that both of you are here to inflict as much damage as you can on my organization."

Doc threw a counterpunch. "Like you inflict guilt and shame on innocent women?"

"Make sure you hear me," said Russet. "I know what you both want. Coming here hasn't helped you. Not in the least. All that you accomplished tonight is to prove to me how disgusting each of you are."

"If someone like you finds me disgusting, then I've been paid the ultimate compliment," Doc roared.

It wasn't a knockout blow, but it put the woman back on her heels. For the first time, I spotted something behind Russet's iron-plate exterior. Sensitivity.

"You're truly cursed," she said to the professor.

"Cursed because I want you off the back of any woman who has the right to decide whether to continue or end a pregnancy? I don't think so."

Russet stormed out of the room. "*Liberate te ex Inferis!*" she called back to us.

"Advice you might want to heed yourself!" Doc yelled after her. "Oh, and if we should meet again, *da mihi sis crustum Etruscum cum omnibus in eo!*"

I waited until Russet had disappeared. "I thought we agreed this wasn't the time or place to get into an argument," I said to the professor.

"Couldn't help myself. Sorry."

"What was the Latin shouting match about?"

"She told me to save myself from hell," Doc translated.

"What was your comeback?"

"The only Latin phrase I could remember. Bring me a pizza with everything on it."

Chapter 12

"Enough bitching!" Doug snapped. "You were the one who wanted me to dig for whatever I could find about Silverstein's daughter!"

"You could have done your digging without telling Silverstein I was going to Judith Russet's meeting last night," I yelled into the phone. It was nine a.m. and I was as exhausted as I was irritable.

"I didn't tell him," Doug said.

"Give me a break."

"Look, I never talked to Arthur. He wasn't in. I spent a half hour with Abraham Arcontius yanking out as much information as I could about Ruth Silverstein. Your name happened to come up."

"Which is when you told Arcontius I'd be infiltrating Russet's party."

"What if I did? I tried to smooth things over between you and Silverstein. Arcontius says Arthur's not sure he can trust you, and I wanted to put a little polish on your credibility. The old man thinks you've got a hidden agenda—that you're out to do more than save Zeusipath's ass."

I can't explain why I called Doug a friend. We weren't bonded by trust, that's for sure. Whatever commitment or promise Doug made usually came peppered with loopholes. Even so, I knew if I were really in trouble, Doug would be one of the first to hold out his hand.

"Just remember," Doug went on, "if Arthur gets word I was asking about his kid because you wanted me to, then you and I both have a problem."

I already had one problem—Twyla Tharp. I didn't need another. I let my friend continue talking.

"Nailing down Ruth Silverstein's history wasn't easy. When I was on the phone with Arcontius, I fed him a fairytale about an auditor who was looking into an endowment Arthur set up with one of the charities he supports."

"Keep going."

"The endowment is restricted—it can only be used to fund the kind of medical and health care programs that could have prevented Ruth's death or improved her treatment. I said the auditor wanted evidence the endowment was being used properly and that meant we had to revisit Ruth's medical records."

I could almost see Arcontius's pencil-thin eyebrows cocking up like a minitent. "He fell for that load?"

"You forget who's on my end of the phone. There's nobody better at selling fiction as reality."

I couldn't debate that point. After all, Doug was a professional fundraiser, and being able to invent a storyline for any occasion was what made him so good at his profession. "Doesn't sound like it took much pressure to convince Arcontius to dive into Ruth's archives," I said.

"You're wrong. I had to kick him to get him to put in a couple of hours of search and find. He said that if he was going to do me a favor, he wanted something in return."

"That's when you rolled over and told him where I'd be last night."

"It wasn't like that," Doug insisted. "Arcontius has orders from Silverstein to watch you. You never told me you signed a contract to keep the old man in the know about what's happening with the Kurios murder investigation."

"There's no contract. Go on."

"Arcontius said he needed a rough idea of your schedule so he could get Silverstein off his back in case the old man wanted an update on what you were up to."

Who had manipulated whom? Doug had tugged information out of Arcontius, who had played Dr. Kool like a viola.

"That's when you opened up about what Doc and I were planning to do last night."

"Yeah, I did," Doug confessed. "But Silverstein has no connection to Russet or *Quia Vita*. Never has. Never will. So, I didn't think talking about your Hyatt adventure was any big deal."

"I was ambushed—that's the big deal," I fumed. "Russet got word that a couple of uninvited guests named Waters and Bullock were in the room. Who could have clued her in, Doug?"

"Not Silverstein or anyone connected to him."

"Yeah, well then that leaves only you. Did you tell anyone besides Arcontius where I was going to be last night?"

There was a long interlude. Too long. "No."

"Who did you tell?" I screeched.

"All right, all right. A couple of my staff people helped make the arrangements with Jane. You met her, right?"

Apparently, Doug didn't know Russet had forced Jane to take a long walk on a short professional plank. If the woman hadn't slit her wrists by now, she was probably on her way to the local unemployment office.

"That's great, Doug. A couple of your staffers talk to a couple of pals who talk to who knows who and suddenly, Doc and I are getting bushwhacked by the wicked witch of the west."

Doug was through getting beat up. He moved our discussion in a different direction. "But the good news is that I got what you wanted about Ruth Silverstein. Want me to fax it over to you?"

"Yes."

"I'll even throw in some press clips and a few other papers I dug out of my own files," he added. I took the offer as a kind of peace offering. "Just don't let anyone know any of this stuff came from me."

"Uh-huh." Typical Kool strategy. Put a little salve on the wound and hope the injured party stops crying.

"So what's your next step?" Doug asked.

"Like I'm going to tell you."

"You have a meeting at Arthur's estate this morning, right?"

Good God! My life was stark naked. "According to your friend, Arcontius, I do."

"He's not my friend. But he has the old man's ear. Arcontius can turn Arthur against you, Bullet. Don't let that happen. Silverstein's not somebody you want on your wrong side. He's a powerful man."

"And he's a king-sized donor to United Way."

"That too."

My donated Hewlett-Packard fax machine churned out the multi-page document sent from Harris & Gilbarton's New York office a few minutes after I finished screaming at Doug. I was flipping through pages marked PERSONAL AND CONFIDENTIAL, when Yigal Rosenblatt and Twyla Tharp showed up at nine thirty. Zeus's lawyer was a little less frenzied than usual. I wrote it off as a postcoital letdown. Twyla, on the other hand, looked ready for more.

"Should have something in a day or two," Yigal informed me. "That's what Morty Margolis said."

Yesterday, Yigal had made a late afternoon trip to Jersey City, after I warned him that Twyla would be indisposed until a deal had been cut with the brother-in-law of Yigal's law partner.

"Good," I commended the lawyer. "So now you can head back to Orlando. Call me when Morty finishes his work."

"Oh, Yiggy," Twyla whined. "You're not leaving so soon?"

"Maybe not so soon. No need to rush home."

I concocted an excuse to pull Yigal aside. It was time for a heart-to-heart.

"Here's the deal," I began. Yigal must have known what was coming because he began bouncing up and down like a yo-yo. "You need a time out—from Twyla."

If there were any doubt Yigal was up to his hairy chin with Manny Maglio's niece, it was blown away by the painful expression that twisted his face.

"The thing is, you're getting distracted. I need you focused. Your client needs you focused. Remember your client?" Yigal's eyes were getting misty, so I lightened up. "Look, when the Zeus situation gets resolved and when Twyla starts her job in Florida—"

"Oh, yes," Yigal interrupted. "Oh, yes."

"For now, though, you have to remember we could be on to something that could prove Zeus had nothing to do with the Kurios killing."

"Yes—we could be on to something."

"Right. So, I'm asking you to get back to Orlando. It's important. Somebody has to stay close to Zeus."

Yigal said nothing, but I thought I saw him nod. It was tough to be sure.

"There's something else." I wanted to lay it on the line the same way my mother sat me down when I was in the ninth grade. 'You're known by the company you keep,' was all I heard for weeks after she caught me in a compromising position with Lucy Klabesodel, my high school's Miss Easy. "Twyla has an unusual assortment of relatives—the kind that could make a lawyer's life miserable."

"Not to worry. Misery doesn't bother us at Gafstein & Rosenblatt."

"There's also Twyla's dancing career and various side jobs. These kinds of things can complicate a man's life."

"I understand that."

"And you know she's not Jewish, right?"

Yigal snapped back to reality. Twyla's religious standing was obviously more of a concern than her participation in the world's oldest profession. "Have to work on that."

"Work on it in Florida. Will you do that?"

Yigal mumbled something that sounded like okay and then hopped back to Twyla. She greeted him with a hug and a smile. Probably just bought-and-paid-for affection, I thought. But when I studied her more closely, it occurred to me she was giving the lawyer more than money could buy.

I had an hour to kill before my meeting with Arthur Silverstein. I took the twelve pages Doug had faxed me and retreated to the Rutgers Club, about a mile from the Gateway. The club was a roost for Rutgers University faculty, staff, and a few locals recognized as "good citizens" by the school. I knew but didn't care that my access to the quiet oasis wasn't about my citizenship, but about how I kept homeless shelter riffraff off the campus lawn.

The faxes included press releases about Ruth Silverstein that sugarcoated her short life and questionable death. They had been churned out by Silverstein's public relations agency. A cup of coffee later, I was into some private correspondence Doug had pulled from his own confidential files. Although I was left feeling Ruth's life story was a couple of chapters short, Doug's information painted Arthur Silverstein's kid in vivid colors.

Ruth was born to parents who were not quite billionaires at the time of her arrival. She was a spoiled brat from birth and sometime around her Bat Mitzvah, matured into a classic rich bitch whose irresponsibility made life dismal for everyone including herself. At age fourteen, Daddy's little girl was shipped off to a private school in upstate New York. Her infrequent visits home usually coincided with her mother's trips to an expensive rehabilitation retreat—aka psych ward. Nothing I read proved Ruth was responsible for her mother's craziness. On the other hand, she seemed to have been the kind of unpleasant, ungrateful daughter who might inspire a mother to take a nosedive off the Queensboro Bridge.

One of the pages Doug sent me was as mystifying as it was intriguing—a copy of a juvenile arrest record that had somehow been smuggled out of a youth agency office in Manhattan. According to the report, Ruth was a drug dealer's dream come true before she hit seventeen. She notched a slew of misdemeanors on her Coach suede belt, but Daddy was always there to shoo the consequences away. There was, however, one felony charge that must have been tough to keep under wraps. Just before her eighteenth birthday, Ruth burned down a Long Beach Island shore house after the owner's daughter stole the affection of one of Ms. Silverstein's boyfriends. Nothing in the report explained how Ruth walked away from that one, although I'd lived long enough to know what a pile of cash can do to the justice system.

The largest question mark was how Ruth died. According to a clip from the obit page of the *Newark Star Ledger,* the girl succumbed to an "undisclosed illness" at Overlook Hospital in Summit. The tabloids interviewed a few of Ruth's friends and put together a convincing case that it was drugs that did Arthur's daughter in. However, the media may have gotten it wrong. The death certificate and a physician's notation that Arcontius had faxed to Doug listed the official cause of death as: iochia followed by acute ischemia and cardiac arrest. I had no idea what *that* meant so I phoned one of my MD friends who worked a few blocks away from the Rutgers Club at St. Peter's Medical Center.

"Blood problem," he told me.

"Not a drug overdose?"

"Not according to what you just read," he said. "Of course, medical reports and death certificates have a reputation for leaving out a lot of patient information."

"So this says Ruth Silverstein died from—"

"She bled to death."

•   •   •

I wasn't intimidated by Arthur Silverstein and even less so by his right-hand man. But I was curious about how much more information I could coax out of the billionaire. So I made the morning drive to the Bedminster mansion just as Arcontius had demanded.

I drove to the front of Silverstein's home and was greeted by Arcontius and an Asian man the size of a sumo wrestler. "This way," the Asian grunted without so much as a hint of an accent. I was led through the main foyer, past Silverstein's library, and into a modest-sized office at the back of the residence.

"Sit down, Mr. Bullock," Arcontius instructed and pointed to a wooden chair. With a shove, the Asian hulk encouraged me to do what I was told.

"Thank you, Mr. Dong," Arcontius said, then motioned the man out of the room.

"The strong, silent type," I commented.

"An accurate description. Of course, Thaddeus has other qualities as well."

"Thaddeus? Thaddeus Dong?"

"It isn't Mr. Dong's odd name or lack of manners you should be concerned about. It's his penchant for solving problems with a heavy hand."

"Okay," I muttered. Of course, it was not okay. Thanks to Manny Maglio, I already had enough thugs in my life.

Silverstein's aide-de-camp leaned toward me, his spike nose pointed directly at my heart. "Do you have the CD?" he asked.

"What?"

"The computer disk. Do you have it?"

I looked behind me thinking Arcontius had to be talking to someone else. Nope.

"Is it me or is it you who's in the wrong meeting?" I asked.

"Tell me about the CD."

"I don't know what you're talking about. Maybe you forgot why you asked me to show up today. Your boss wants a blow-by-blow of last night's *Quia Vita* meeting."

"We know about last night's meeting. What we want is the CD?"

"You know about last night's meeting? What exactly do you know about it? Oh, and here's another one you can answer—where's Silverstein?"

"He's not coming. An unexpected business problem. Mr. Silverstein asked that I act in his stead. Tell me about the CD."

I wasn't happy. I'd wasted gas and time hauling my Buick from New Brunswick to the hills of Somerset County. Plus I had an accumulated sleep debt that was making me cranky.

"You couldn't have picked up the damn phone and rescheduled the meeting?"

"Mr. Silverstein sends his apologies. Did you forget the arrangement, Mr. Bullock?"

"What arrangement?"

"Mr. Silverstein instructed you to work through me."

That's not exactly how I recalled the deal. To be truthful, though, I had stopped listening when Arthur plunked two ten thousand dollar checks in my paw.

"So, let me ask you again. What about the CD?"

"I'll tell you what happened last night. But what I can't tell you is anything about a CD."

"Perhaps you missed what I said. We know what happened last night."

I decided to toss Arcontius a cryptic question or two as a defense.

"Last night's meeting. How do you know what happened?"

"That's not information we need to disclose."

"Really? Well, then there's no point in wasting any more of your time or mine."

Arcontius took a different tack. "When you and Mr. Silverstein met, you had a conversation about the *Book of Nathan*."

I drawled out a "So?"

"You were told Benjamin Kurios would be going public with the *Book of Nathan* at his revival meeting in Orlando."

"You're right—that's what I was told."

"And Mr. Silverstein mentioned the book's text had been transcribed onto an encrypted CD that Dr. Kurios had with him the night he died—a CD that's now missing."

Dealing with Arcontius was like swimming in pond scum. If I

couldn't have face time with Silverstein, then I wanted out of the pond. Continuing this little dance with Silverstein's lieutenant was as pointless as it was frustrating. I was about to end the morning meeting when the snake unwound his skinny frame and leaned over his desk.

"Let's not stretch this lunacy out any longer," Arcontius said. "Yesterday afternoon, we received a message telling us the *Book of Nathan* disk is for sale."

This was news I didn't expect. My interest in making a quick escape vanished. Whoever was shopping the stolen disk had to have something to do with the Benjamin Kurios murder. As much as I wanted to get out of Arcontius's office and take a shower, I stayed put.

"Does the price include delivery and tax?"

"I'm so pleased you're enjoying yourself," Arcontius grumbled. "Good humor is hard to come by when you're facing the prospect of paying five million dollars for a computer disk."

"Five million—" Arthur Silverstein had piqued my curiosity with his story about the *Book of Nathan* disk. But there's nothing like a multi-million dollar price tag to really perk up one's interest.

"Very clever marketing deal. The nonencrypted first part of Le Campion's disk gets sent to us in installments. Five separate e-mail attachments. If we like what we see, each installment costs us five hundred thousand, which we wire to an offshore account. Five installments. Two point five million. Once all the earnest money is sent, we're told where we can pick up the actual disk—provided, of course, we cough up another two point five million."

Shades of my Madison Avenue days. Use the big tease to lure in a buyer.

"Here's where I think we are," Arcontius went on. "You went to the *Quia Vita* meeting last night to see how much money was in the room because maybe—just maybe—the people connected to *Quia Vita*'s Order of Visio Dei could come up with more than the five million you want from Silverstein. In other words, I smell the start of a bidding war. Am I heading in the right direction?"

"You're walking backward. I don't have the CD."

"We both know better. Let me guess what happened in Orlando on that fateful night. Your man, Mr. Zellendickol—

"Zeusenoerdorf. And he's not my man."

"Regardless. He did indeed kill Benjamin. Then he stole the disk and handed it off to some other homeless bottom dweller who eventually delivered the CD to you."

"I'm not the guy with the CD."

"Then I think you probably know who has it," said Arcontius. "However, let's go with the remote possibility that you're telling the truth."

"Welcome to the world of reality."

"It would be a healthy decision on your part to prove to Mr. Silverstein and me that you don't have the disk and you don't know who does."

"How do I do that?"

"Mr. Silverstein and I would like you to press Mr. Zeus— to press your homeless friend to tell us what he knows about the disk. If he helps us find it along with the person or persons trying to sell it, your chances of staying in Mr. Silverstein's good graces go much higher."

I wasn't about to let Arcontius know Zeus never mentioned a CD. Of course, to my knowledge, he was never asked. And unless Zeus was confronted with a specific question, he rarely contributed.

"Could be that by now, your CD has been copied," I noted.

"Again, my compliments if you're acting. But I think you know as well as I do that half the disk is coded to permanently corrupt itself if any attempt is made to copy its contents."

I was no computer whiz kid, but even I could appreciate Le Campion's genius. I fished for more information. "If the book's translation is encrypted, figuring out what's on the disk is going to be next to impossible."

Arcontius sighed. "The text requires a translation key—a key Benjamin had on his computer, which, you might be interested to know, we've managed to acquire. We believe *Quia Vita* also has the know-how to decode the disk if it's ever located."

"Sounds like it might be worth it for Silverstein to pay five million to make sure *Quia Vita* doesn't get the disk."

Arcontius gave me a hard look. "I'm sure you'd like me to agree and hand over a check. Well, we're not quite there yet, Mr. Bullock. For the time being, let's just say we're considering the request."

Arcontius's well was just about dry. Time to push for a close. "Where do we go from here?"

"That's largely up to you. Get back to me within the next twenty-four hours. Either admit you have the disk or tell us when you'll be making another trip to Orlando. And we want to discuss lowering the price. Five million is too steep."

I fought off the urge to squeeze Arcontius's rope-like neck. "You want me to jump through your hoop by this time tomorrow."

"It's in your best interest."

"And if I don't?"

Arcontius flicked out his tongue and ran it across his thin lips. "Then we'll know you can't or won't do much to solve our problem."

"And what would that mean?"

"Terminating your consulting agreement."

"You know what? I'm not happy about this Abraham-in-the-middle arrangement. Whatever I have to say from here on will be to Arthur Silverstein."

Arcontius showed his teeth, a cross between a smile and a sneer. "If you want to talk, you'll do it through me. That's the way Mr. Silverstein wants it."

"And if I don't?"

"Then Mr. Dong gets involved. He's very good at ensuring the only people who enter Mr. Silverstein's world do so through the chief of staff's door."

I remembered Doug's explanation of Arcontius's blurry role in the Silverstein organization. "I see."

"I hope you do," Arcontius said. He pressed an intercom button on his phone and Dong appeared. "Show him out," Arcontius instructed.

The sumo wrestler gripped my arm and hoisted me to my feet.

"Mr. Bullock," Arcontius called as I was being pushed into the mansion's foyer. "Tomorrow. Don't disappoint me."

Chapter 13

Saturday night's eleven o'clock news opened with new developments in the Orlando Airport bombing investigation. The FBI announced it was holding a twenty-five-year-old Jordanian graduate student as a "person of interest." Witnesses had spotted the man leaving the airport minutes after the Continental ticket counter had been decimated. The suspect was a member of a Tampa mosque that had been under surveillance by the feds because of its "radical Islamic teachings."

It was a relatively quiet weekend night at the Gateway. One of my men was in the lockup on a drunk-and-disorderly charge and another was getting stitches at a downtown health clinic after a run-in with six Rutgers students. Doc Waters was helping me do a final nose count before we closed the Gateway doors for the night. That's when Four Putt Gonzales from the Hyatt called.

"This thing is outta control," he wailed. "Way outta control. You gotta get down here, Bullet. Right now."

I figured whatever was bothering him must have something to do with Twyla. Four Putt told me to meet him in the Hyatt parking garage in a half hour. It was a pleasant enough night so I invited the professor to join me for the fifteen-minute walk to the hotel.

The first level of the hotel's multideck garage was dimly lit and it took me a couple of minutes to spot Four Putt's vintage Ford Crown Victoria. Gonzales was as good at restoring old cars as he was bad at playing golf.

I introduced Four Putt to the professor, which turned out to be unnecessary since the two were acquainted.

"What's going on?" I asked.

Four Putt opened the Ford's front door. The dome light ignited and

I saw several cardboard boxes crammed into the backseat. "I got more of these in the trunk!" Four Putt said.

"More what?"

"These." He pulled a box out of the car and dropped it on the cement floor of the parking deck. Four Putt leaned over to open the carton. "I don't want her here, Bullet! You told me there wasn't gonna be no problems, right? Then I find out that not only is she in the business, she's doin' business!"

The last time I saw Four Putt this animated was when he hooked a new Titleist into a water hazard. "I don't know what the hell you're talking about," I said.

Four Putt stopped clawing at the top of the box. "Two goons show up earlier tonight, drag me out here, and tell me this shit belongs to Twyla Tharp. Said the stuff can't stay in her apartment because it's full of fleas—some of which are probably hitchhiking their way into my damn hotel."

I glanced at Doc. The professor looked as confused as I did.

Four Putt finally ripped open the top of the carton and straightened. "There." He pointed at dozens of silver balls each about an inch and a half in diameter.

Doc lifted one of the small globes out of the box. "Amazing! I haven't seen these since I was in China."

"First, I thought they were ball bearings, for chrissakes," said Four Putt. "Felt like an idiot."

"They're Ben Wa balls," Doc explained.

Four Putt threw up his hands. "Jesus, Bullet. She's gonna be selling these out of a room on the third floor."

The professor lifted two balls from the box. "Premium grade. Hollow with a small weight inside. Insert two of these in the vagina and it's magic time."

I did another quick inspection of the Crown Victoria's interior. "These couldn't all be Ben Was," I said, all the while trying to remember the last time I had seen the things. It was when I was a freshman in college and Tracy Glivitz gave me tutoring lessons on everything erotic. She said her pair of Ben Was never delivered an orgasm. Not once. We ended up using them as marbles.

"You want to know what's in them other boxes? Clitoral stimulators. Vibrating panties. In the trunk I got strap-ons and six different kinds of dildos. She's sellin' every kind of sex toy you can dream up. Outta my hotel."

"All right, relax, Four Putt. How do you know she's going retail with these things?"

"The guys who made the drop told me she called and wanted this stuff delivered here. She's gonna turn her room into a goddamned triple X storefront."

Even before I fell into my job at the Gateway, I learned how easy it is to misread people. Twyla was more than just an exotic dancer and an occasional hooker. She was also an entrepreneur. I was starting to really like this woman.

"What's that?" I pointed to a four-foot gold pole lying across the Ford's back seat.

Four Putt pulled the rod from the car and held it like a shepherd's staff. "A collapsible stripper's pole. A few twists and it grows to ten feet. Screw it between the top of a door frame and the floor and start grindin'."

Four Putt dropped the pole next to the Ben Was.

"So what do you want from me?" I asked. "You know who we're dealing with."

"That's the point—I know who we're—" The look on my face stopped Four Putt midsentence.

"What? What is it?" he asked.

Sixty yards from where we were standing, a man walked under one of the parking deck's dull overhead lights. I couldn't make out his face but I recognized the thick gold chain and the tan shirt. It was one of the Hispanics I had seen at the Orlando Airport and earlier at the Benjamin Kurios murder site.

"Get down!" I shouted and pushed Doc behind the Ford's driver's-side door Four Putt had left open.

The Hyatt manager was too bewildered to move. "What?" he shouted at the same time the gunman fired six shots at the car. One bullet caught Four Putt in the left thigh sending him to the cement floor just behind the professor and me. Four Putt tried screaming, but shock and pain tied his vocal chords in a knot.

The Hispanic's hard-soled shoes clacked toward us. The man moved at a steady pace, obviously not in a hurry since he had to know that we weren't going anywhere. He fired five more shots. One pinged off the Crown Vic's door and the others went wild.

"Doc," I whispered, "we've got to distract the bastard." I picked up two fistfuls of balls and jammed them into Doc's hands "Follow my lead."

I faked a move that made it look like I was going to sprint to the hotel entrance. Two more rounds shattered the Ford's driver's-side window. That's when I roared, "Maurice, hold your fire. Don't waste a shot until you see him."

The footsteps stopped. I heard a shuffling sound, probably the Hispanic dodging behind one of the cars lined up on the deck.

Doc looked at me like I was insane. "Maurice isn't here—he's back at the Gateway," he said softly.

"The asshole out there doesn't know that." I reached into the Ben Wa box and picked up the only ammunition we had at our disposal. "When I give you the word, throw as many of these as you can, then run like hell."

Doc turned to his rear. Four Putt was writhing on the ground, both hands clamped on his left leg. "What about him?" Doc asked.

"Whoever's out there isn't after Four Putt. He's after me."

Doc put his mouth close to my ear. "Hold on. I think I can buy us a few seconds." The professor glanced at the hotel entrance, which was two hundred unprotected feet away.

The heavy footsteps had come to an abrupt stop. The Hispanic was now probably no more than ten parked cars from us. "You better talk fast."

"Our boy's using a Beretta M9 pistol. I caught a glimpse."

This would usually be the time to pause and marvel at Doc's encyclopedic mind. Right now, I needed an explanation about why I should care what kind of firearm was aimed at me. "And how's that supposed to help us?"

"The pistol has a fifteen-shot clip. He's used thirteen and he's fast on the trigger. Unless he's changed the magazine—and I don't think he has—there are two rounds left in the gun. Two more shots and he'll have to reload. That'll take a few seconds."

Doc was brilliant but he was also a lousy gambler, and now he was placing a bet that could get both of us killed. Like it or not, though, my chips were lined up next to his. Time to role the dice.

I tossed a half dozen Ben Was at a Toyota Camry parked diagonally across from Four Putt's Ford. "Maurice, pin him down! Pin him down," I yelled.

The Hispanic took the bait. He stepped from behind a Chevy Suburban and fired twice at the Camry. And then a click.

Before the gunman's empty magazine hit the parking deck floor, Doc and I stepped to the side of the Crown Victoria's front door and pelted the Hispanic with metal buckshot. Instinctively, the man raised his right forearm to protect himself from the broadside attack. The loaded clip fell out of his hand.

Doc sprinted to the door that led to the hotel's main reception area. I was heading in the same direction when I glanced back at the Hispanic. He was kneeling on the floor, one hand on his ammo clip and the other pressed against his right eye. One of our Ben Was had done some unexpected damage.

I could have easily made it to the Hyatt entrance. But I didn't. The man who had tried to kill me twice was on the ground, and I had an opening. It was time to end this thing. Grabbing Twyla's stripper pole, I charged the Hispanic as he pushed a fresh load into his Beretta. He hoisted the pistol, but his right eye was swollen shut, and he didn't see the rod before it landed with a thwack on the bridge of his nose. The man fell back, a gusher of blood turning the lower half of his face red. The Beretta flew across the deck and came to a stop under a Cadillac Escalade.

I pulled the pole over my head and took aim. The next swing would be an ax-like blow across the man's knees. I wanted him alive, incapacitated, and able to answer a lot of questions. The Hispanic was dazed but not disoriented enough to stay still as the pole began its downward arc. Instinctively, he rolled to one side and the rod hit nothing but concrete.

"*Hijo de puta!*" the man gurgled, blood pouring into his mouth. Defying the damage to his face, he scrambled to his feet and dodged behind a row of cars. I chased him as he raced through the gated parking deck entrance and headed toward a black sedan. Even with his injuries,

the Hispanic was agile. He was twenty feet ahead of me when he reached
the car and pulled open the front passenger-side door. I sent the pole flying, a gold javelin that speared the man's ribcage just before the driver
yanked him into the sedan. I recognized the man behind the wheel. It
was the other Hispanic I had described to the FBI after the Orlando
Airport catastrophe.

The car sped off and I circled back to the wounded Four Putt Gonzales who was still on his back, clasping his bloodied leg. I unlatched
my belt and turned it into a makeshift tourniquet just as Doc reappeared.

"Called 911," the professor said.

Four Putt suddenly found his voice. "Oh, shit! Pick up them balls.
Pick up them balls."

"Worry about your leg, not your balls," Doc suggested.

Four Putt's eyes widened with panic. "Listen, this thing could ruin
us. Ruin us. Don't let the cops find no Ben Was. And get that other sex
shit out of my car! The shooting's gonna be some kid doin' target practice with a stolen pistol."

I could practically read Four Putt's mind. The Hyatt was booked a
year in advance for weddings, Bar Mitzvahs, and Quinceañera fiestas.
Bullets plus blood could equal cancellations. Enough of those and Four
Putt would be doing the night shift at one of the rooms-by-the-hour, no-
tell motels on Route 1.

"Go along with this, Bullet." Four Putt insisted. "You and Manny
Maglio stuck me with Twyla Tharp, for chrissakes. You owe me one."

I told Doc to start collecting balls while I moved boxes of sex para-
phernalia from Four Putt's car to a nearby hotel van. As we worked, the
wail of police sirens grew louder, gradually drowning out the Hyatt
manager's cries of pain. Or was it despair?

Chapter 14

High noon on a gloomy Sunday in New Brunswick. I was power walking my way along George Street trying to shake off the events of the past fourteen hours. Four Putt Gonzales was in Robert Wood Johnson Hospital nursing a nasty leg wound. The cops were running a trace on the Beretta they recovered from under the Escalade. Good luck. The pistol's serial number had been filed off, and I remembered the Hispanic was wearing surgical gloves. Fingerprints were out of the question.

Four Putt was sticking with his story that last night's incident was a byproduct of some juvenile delinquent whose vandalism got out of control. The police lightly grilled Doc and me about what happened. We crossed our fingers and played Four Putt's song. What got a couple of detectives scratching their heads was the trail of blood that streaked the parking deck and front driveway of the hotel. The kid doing the shooting must have cut himself, Doc surmised. The detectives bought the improbable story mainly because—like Four Putt—they wanted to downplay the event. Anything other than an out-of-control adolescent fiddling with a handgun he just happened to have found might poison New Brunswick's renaissance.

I was walking back to the Gateway when my cell rang.

"Mr. Bullock?"

I pulled up short.

"We need to talk," Judith Russet said. "I'll be in Princeton this afternoon. You're only a short drive away so I suggest we meet. It's important. Shall we say three o'clock?"

Being told where I should be and what time I should get there was getting aggravating. "Why?"

"It concerns the *Book of Nathan*."

Russet knew the magic words. "All right," I said. "Where will I find you?"

"Do you know the Nassau Club?"

I forced out a "no." People from the Gateway—whether residents or staff—don't do Princeton. Russet rattled off directions and added a postscript.

"Do not bring Professor Waters. It's imperative you come alone."

I headed back to the shelter, checking my watch. I had missed Abraham Arcontius's twenty-four-hour deadline for scraping up information about the missing disk and/or about making plans to revisit Orlando. Arthur Silverstein's aide-de-camp was surely working up a list of ways to make my life miserable.

Yigal Rosenblatt was at the front door when I arrived at the Gateway. "I set it up," was his greeting.

Once again, Yigal surprised me. Earlier in the day, I had asked him if any of his "connections" could arrange a jailhouse phone call with Miklos Zeusenoerdorf. The odds for coupling Zeus with a telephone were slim, yet Yigal had come through. There was a lot more to this perpetual motion machine than I first thought.

"When?"

"A half hour from now." Yigal sounded pleased with himself, as well he should. Thirty minutes later, with Yigal and Maurice at my side, I placed the call to the Orange County Jail.

"Remember, Maurice," I said, "don't spice up what Zeus is saying. Give it to us word for word. Understood?"

"Yes."

I pushed the speakerphone button on the donated phone in my office. Zeus's voice came through as a string of grunts and mumbles.

Maurice translated. "He's been havin' a lot of bad dreams. About God."

"Listen, Zeus—" I shouted at the phone. It was wasted breath. Zeusenoerdorf kept on blathering.

"Says God thinks Zeus did take out the preacher," said Maurice. The quasi admission of guilt stopped the translator in his tracks. He went from interpreting to castigating. "Ah, shit, Zeus. Why'd you do that for, man?"

Intervention time.

"Zeus, you didn't kill Benjamin Kurios." I screamed. "This whole God-in-your-dreams business is a figment of your imagination. You didn't kill anyone. And remember this, if you're convicted for what happened to Kurios, that means the real murderer goes free."

Not once in the past had I told Zeus flat out that he was innocent. Actually, I still wasn't fully convinced he was. But with only ten minutes of phone time left, I didn't need Zeus beating himself up.

"He says, okay," Maurice reported. "But he wants to know what a fig-a-ment is."

I held back a scream. "Forget the figment. Right now, I need you to think back to the night Benjamin Kurios died. Do you remember seeing a computer disk?"

"What's a computer disk, he wants to know," Maurice translated.

"A disk, you know, like a DVD." Watching movie rentals on a donated DVD was one of life's highlights at the Gateway.

Maurice passed on Zeusenoerdorf's answer. "He says, yeah."

"You saw a disk?"

"No. He took the disk."

"What?"

"He took what you said," Maurice repeated.

I was stunned. "You took the disk?"

"Zeus says he thought it was a music CD," Maurice explained. "Had a lot of words on it. One started with the letter N like on his Nelly album."

Thanks to Zeus and a boom box, I had learned more than I ever wanted to know about Nelly, the rap artist who sang classics like "Ride Wit Me" and "Pimp Juice." Leave it to Zeus to presume that any CD with an N on it had to be a hip-hop recording.

"What did you do with it?" I shouted at the phone.

Maurice's translation followed a run of grunts. "He shoved it under a rock."

I took a deep breath. "Let's see if I have this right," I said. "After a car sideswipes a van and after Benjamin Kurios ends up on the pavement and after two guys try to tear each other's throats out, you find a CD and decide to hide it under a rock?"

Maurice replied, "He says that's right."

I closed my eyes. "Why didn't you say something about this before?"

Maurice jerked his head at Yigal . "He told his lawyer, Figgy."

"What?" I glared at Yigal who was doing a rain dance around the speakerphone.

"Very hard to understand," Yigal said. "Couldn't figure out what he was saying."

Back to the phone. "Zeus, the cops went over the crime scene dozens of times. They would have found the CD even it were under a rock. Are you sure about this?"

A rattle of sounds. "He's sure."

It was possible. Granted, few humans would have given top priority to hiding a CD after stumbling across a man whose head had just been pulverized. But this was Zeus, whose neurotransmitters worked in mysterious ways. Maybe I was wrong about the crime-scene investigation. I remembered seeing a lot of rock and chunks of cement under or near the bridge overpass. Nothing weighing more than half a pound appeared to have been moved.

I strained to come up with the right question. "Did you see anybody take the CD? Did anybody even go near the rock where you hid the disk?"

A burst of sound followed. "He didn't see nobody else. After he hid the disk, he went back to help the preacher."

"How long before the cops showed up?"

"Probably ten minutes. But that's a guess, he says."

"Could someone have taken the disk from under the rock during those ten minutes?"

"He don't know. He don't think so."

"What about the two college kids? Could they have walked off with the disk?"

Maurice listened to Zeus jabber for a few seconds. "He don't think the boys got close enough to get the CD. But he's not sure about that either."

I was out of steam. "All right, Zeus. Anything else we should talk about?"

"Yes," Maurice said.

"What?"

Hesitation and then a short spurt of noise. "He wants to know if you really think he didn't kill the preacher."

"I think we're going to find out who killed Benjamin Kurios," I replied. It was a far less definitive statement than I had handed to Zeus earlier. In fact, the response was so slippery and lawyer-like that Yigal stopped his jiggling long enough to give me a look of admiration.

For a couple of reasons, I didn't phone Abraham Arcontius to tell him about Zeus's bombshell and offer up a mea culpa for missing his "deliver-or-else" deadline. First, I loathed the thought of having to deal with—never mind apologize to—the piece of scum. Second, I had a hard time thinking about Silverstein's lieutenant when I was thirty minutes away from meeting a woman who probably could squash Arcontius like a cockroach.

My Buick started coughing as soon as it entered Princeton Borough. I reminded the car if it broke down in a town where the per capita income was higher than my Gateway annual budget, it was one phone call away from a donation to the National Kidney Foundation. The Buick straightened out and got me to where we needed to be: 6 Mercer Street, only a few clicks from the heart of Princeton Borough.

"You're here to see—?" asked a man who sounded as stuffy as he looked.

"Judith Russet."

"Ah, yes. Please wait in the reading room. I'll notify Ms. Russet you've arrived."

I parked myself in a leather chair and surveyed the six other men taking up space in a large corner room of the Nassau Club. The men were all old and in various stages of sleep. Two were snoring, one appeared dead. I had this creepy feeling the Grim Reaper was among the Nassau Club's most frequent visitors.

"A lovely room, don't you think?"

The voice came from behind me but I didn't need a visual to know who had arrived.

"In fact, the whole house is exquisite. A physician named Samuel Miller lived here a long time ago. His residence became a private club back in 1889."

"Interesting," was my witty response.

"I'm not a member but one of *Quia Vita's* donors is," Judith Russet said. "He makes arrangements for me to use the club when I'm in Princeton."

I got the message. Russet rubbed noses with people of influence. "Good to have friends in high places."

"That's something you should keep in mind. We have a private room downstairs. This way."

We walked to the lower level of the Nassau Club and into a room barely large enough for a round table and four chairs.

"Let me get right to the point," Russet said even before I was seated and the door soundly shut. "I'm going to give you some confidential information and then I'm going to offer you some advice. I hope you listen very carefully."

"That's why I'm here."

"Before I start, you need to know your Friday night stunt was despicable. I just wanted to make that perfectly clear before anything else is said."

"Go on."

"There are two possibilities," Russet continued. She had put herself in a chair cattycorner to mine so she was at my eye level. "Possibility number one is that you're a crook—a purveyor of stolen goods. The second possibility is that you're an ignorant fool."

"I'm moved that you hold me in such high regard."

"Regardless of which possibility happens to be correct, I want you to know where *Quia Vita* stands. Before I do that, let me make sure we're both on the same page."

Russet opened her purse, took out a sheet of paper, and slid it across the table. I read the sentences marked with a yellow highlighter:

> We concur that the *Book of Nathan* and the *Book of Jehu* scrolls are authentic. Regrettably, only a small portion of the *Book of Jehu* can be salvaged, but the entire contents of the *Book of Nathan* are intact. In answer to your question about the accuracy of the translation regarding personhood—yes, we are positive the Aramaic to English conversion is correct. *The Book of Nathan* is clear about the definition of personhood.

I guessed what Russet was showing me was a passage from a message written by Henri Le Campion that *Quia Vita* had managed to intercept. It was becoming more and more obvious why the *Book of Nathan* was on the market for five million dollars.

"It may surprise you," Russet said, "that we've known for years Henri Le Campion found the *Nathan* and *Jehu* scrolls in a cave seventy miles from Jerusalem."

"It might surprise you that I'm not surprised." Which was true. I didn't know a lot about *Quia Vita* but had learned enough to know the organization had big money and a long reach. If Arthur Silverstein had good intelligence about the *Book of Nathan*, it was safe to assume *Quia Vita* had it also.

Russet redeposited the sheet of paper into her purse. "You're one of a very few people who know about the *Book of Nathan* and the *Book of Jehu* discoveries."

Russet waited for a response. I didn't cooperate.

"It was common knowledge that Henri Le Campion was an avid Benjamin Kurios follower. Actually, that's an understatement. Let's call him a fanatical follower. We learned from an informant that when Le Campion told Kurios about his discovery, Kurios agreed to bankroll a lot of tests, including carbon-14 dating. The tests proved the animal-skin scrolls that Le Campion found are genuine."

"You seem to know a lot about went on between Le Campion and Kurios."

"We monitored Kurios for years. We were aware that he was in regular contact with Le Campion, but even so we knew very little about the scrolls. Then, for some unexplained reason, Le Campion got careless. He sent an open e-mail to Kurios. The hard copy I just showed you is a printout of part of that note. Not long after we found out that one of the scrolls included a definition of personhood, we learned Kurios was planning to go public with the English translation of the *Book of Nathan* at his Orlando meeting."

"His revival. Would have been interesting."

Russet reacted sharply. "Revival suggests that Kurios's spectacle was to be a religious event. Hardly the case. Benjamin Kurios was more showman than a man of God. Orlando would have been a circus with the *Book of Nathan* as its main act."

Russet stood, her flabby body unfolding like an accordion. "We don't have all the specifics, but we suspect Kurios was planning to tell the world that personhood doesn't begin at the moment of conception. If he were to make that kind of announcement, the implications to *Quia Vita*, of course, are clear."

"Put you out of business, would it?" The question wasn't intended to be impertinent even though it came out sounding that way. I was genuinely curious about whether a pro-life advocacy group could survive if there were Biblical evidence that one of its core beliefs was bogus.

"You underestimate our commitment to do God's work," Russet growled. "Whatever lies Kurios might try to sell to the public would never have stopped us from doing what we know is right."

"How do you know you're doing God's work?" I asked. Again, I wasn't trying to antagonize Russet. I was trying to get a better feel for how people like her became so convinced they were correct.

"Don't test my faith."

"Isn't faith what we're talking about here?" I argued. "Seems to me that when faith turns fanatical—"

"Protecting the unborn is hardly fanatical, Mr. Bullock!"

"From where I sit, a fanatic is somebody who doesn't leave a little wiggle room when it comes to believing in things that can't be proven. There's not a lot of hard evidence about when personhood comes into play or when it doesn't. Which means you could be right—or you may be wrong."

"We're not wrong." Russet's words were fierce. "And I will tell you that if the *Book of Nathan* is contrary to what we know is right, then you can be certain the translation from Aramaic to English is inaccurate. In fact, Benjamin Kurios might have had the translation altered so it would serve his own purposes."

That brought back my confusion about just where Kurios stood on the abortion issue. I had Googled a list of articles about the evangelist and found Kurios had walked the murky middle ground whenever the topic surfaced. Kurios had been the king of caveats and qualifiers.

"Maybe you read Kurios wrong. Maybe he was pro-life all along."

"Benjamin Kurios was pro Benjamin Kurios. A first-class opportunist. He'd take any position on anything if he thought it would be advantageous to him."

"And one of those anythings was the *Book of Nathan*."

"Exactly."

"Still, since you don't know what the book says about personhood and abortion, it might not be out of step with *Quia Vita*'s point of view."

"If that were the case, Kurios would have come to us to promote his so-called revival," Russet replied. "That didn't happen. Draw your own conclusion. We did. Now let's talk about Le Campion's CD."

"I thought that's what we've been doing."

"We want the disk."

"I already figured that out."

"We're willing to discuss terms as long as we can verify that the disk is for real. And the deal needs to include the translation key that will allow us to decode the text."

"What makes you think I have the CD?"

"Stop running in circles," said Russet. "We have every reason to believe you're trying to extort five million from *Quia Vita* in exchange for giving up Le Campion's disk."

This was the time to lay the truth on the line. But Russet didn't give me an opening.

"Just for the record, we received your e-mail. Very clever the way you used a relay and routing system to hide your Internet address."

Whoever took the disk from Zeusenoerdorf's hiding place was no fool. Coming up with the technology needed to keep a billionaire and an organization with deep pockets in the dark was impressive.

"How will this work?" I asked, figuring it would be worth squeezing Russet for more details before convincing her I didn't have the disk.

"Reluctantly—very reluctantly—we accept your terms. You'll break up Le Campion's preamble to the book's translation and e-mail us a few pages at a time. For each e-mail attachment we receive, we'll pay you a portion of the preliminary two point five million if we consider the notes to be legitimate and of any real value."

The more I learned about the *Book of Nathan*, the more curious I became. But far more intriguing to me was Henri's introduction to the translated disk. It had to be a masterpiece of seduction, luring both Silverstein and Russet. Whoever had walked off with Le Campion's disk was chopping up the preamble into expensive little pieces. It was one elaborate, pricey, and ingenious tease.

"Assuming we buy the full set of Le Campion's introductory notes, we'll consider paying you a second two point five million for the full encrypted translation of the book."

Russet went quiet, waiting for a reaction. I was too engrossed with my own thoughts to answer.

"Do we have a deal?" Russet asked after several seconds. "If so, we need instructions on how to wire the money to your Cayman Island account."

"No, we don't have a deal," I answered. "And I'll tell you why. I can't deliver something I don't have."

Russet tilted back in her seat and scrutinized me carefully. "The game continues, does it? This is a play for time, isn't it? So you can move the bid higher. Well, here's some advice: don't go there. Our patience is already threadbare."

"You're making an assumption that I'm a common crook," I said. "But supposing I'm just a disinterested third party. Somebody who's been sucked into this deal by accident?"

"If that's the case, you'll need to be very careful."

"Why?"

"Because you'd be worthless. And to some, worthless people are expendable, particularly when they've been made privy to sensitive information."

I knew all about worthless people. It didn't take sensitive information to make most of them expendable.

"There are those who'll do whatever it takes to protect their beliefs," Russet went on. "Some are convinced that selective violence is appropriate if it's a means to a justifiable end. You're cruising into dangerous waters."

I got it. But the notion of sailing into a storm wasn't enough to ward off a change in strategy. Instead of taking another stab at convincing Russet I wasn't auctioning the *Book of Nathan* disk, I just shut up. Being falsely accused had its advantages. After all, I now had plenty of new information. For the time being, I decided to let Russet continue thinking I was behind the theft and sale of Le Campion's CD.

"*Quia Vita* wants to bring this to closure," Russet said. "I expect to hear from you tomorrow. Any delay beyond that would be ill-advised."

I watched Russet's bowling-ball body disappear through the room's narrow doorway. I let a few minutes pass before ungluing myself from my chair and making my way to the back door of the Nassau Club. En route, I passed four ancient men playing cribbage. They all looked near death, but I had a nagging feeling I'd be paying a visit to the pearly gates long before they would.

Chapter 15

A shallow, muddy stretch of the Raritan River is the divide between a suburb called Highland Park and New Brunswick.

"Holy shit."

I shot Maurice a look of disapproval. He knew I had a thing about public profanity.

"Sorry," Maurice apologized. "But over there—I think that's the—" He stared into a thick Monday morning fog that lifted off the Raritan and made the Albany Street Bridge all but disappear.

I followed Maurice's eyes and got my first glimpse of a phallic-looking vehicle penetrating the dense wall of Monday morning river mist.

I couldn't stifle my own oath. "What the hell is that?"

"I'll tell you what it is. It's the Wienermobile."

For some mysterious reason, Maurice was an expert on one of America's most imaginative marketing inventions—the Oscar Mayer Wienermobile. I, on the other hand, knew nothing about the traveling hotdog and bun. Maurice gave me a quick tutorial while we hurried across Albany Street, a main drag that ran through the heart of New Brunswick. Until this unexpected diversion, we had been on our way to the Hyatt Hotel hoping to locate Yigal, whom I figured had to be taking full advantage of Twyla's free room.

"Oh," Maurice gasped again as a gargantuan vehicle rolled into full view, a trail of dark gray smoke spewing out its back end.

"Oh, oh, oh," Maurice mumbled, grabbed me by my arm and began running toward the disabled conveyance. We were a bun length away when two men who may not have been old enough to buy beer climbed out.

"Damn." one of the men yelled and kicked the rear passenger-side tire.

The other man was less distressed. He turned to Maurice and me who were now at his side.

"Name's Frank," he said and stuck a hand at my belt buckle.

I wondered if the kid was putting me on. "Frank?"

"Yup."

"Whatever you say."

"The junk heap's been givin' us trouble the last couple of days," Frank explained.

Maurice blinked a few times. "Is this . . . is this the Wienermobile?"

"This thing?" Frank slapped the broken-down bun. "Nah. This is the Dubensko Kielbasavan."

"But it looks like—" Maurice moaned.

"Yeah, I know—like the Wienermobile," Frank broke in. "Get that all the time. Dubensko Polish Meat Products ripped off the idea and built this piece of crap to advertise its all-beef sausages. Oscar Mayer ain't happy about it but so far that hasn't kept this fat piece of kielbasa from travelin' all over Jersey."

Maurice was too crestfallen to continue talking. I took up the slack. "So what happens now?" I asked with a gesture to the dormant sausage.

"Well, we can't drive it no more until it's fixed. Know where we could park the thing?"

I tried to find another sane-looking soul who might come up with a suggestion. Even though it was nine thirty in the morning and we were standing on one of New Brunswick's busiest thoroughfares, there wasn't a human in sight except Maurice.

"Albany Street's fairly flat," I observed. "Might be able to push it back toward the river."

Frank cranked his head to the side. "Sweet. So we push the kielbasa backward into that side street over there." He pointed to a road that ran parallel with the river. "Right?"

"Sounds like a plan."

"How about holdin' up traffic?" Frank proposed to both Maurice and me. "You know, until we get on the side street."

"Will we get a whistle?" Maurice asked.

The last time I recalled feeling I was in such a state of unreality was when I smoked hemp. "What are you talking about, Maurice?"

"A whistle. The guys who drive the Oscar Mayer Wienermobile give away whistles that look like wieners. What about you? Got any whistles?"

Frank turned to Maurice. "Yeah, man, we got whistles. Shaped like small sausages and ours come in different colors. Give you a handful if you want."

The revelation snapped Maurice out of his momentary depression. The Kielbasavan might not be the Wienermobile, but toss in a few whistles and it was close enough.

A couple of minutes later, Frank, Maurice, and I were waving off inbound traffic while cranky driver number two jockeyed the Kielbasavan backward until it reached a side road called Johnson Drive.

"This here road goes to that place, right?" Frank pointed to a gleaming white tower connected to a series of angular buildings resting on acres of manicured grass.

"Seems to, yup," I replied. To be honest, I had never before set foot on the road that led to the office complex.

"So what is it?"

"Johnson & Johnson."

"The baby powder company?"

"That's the one."

Frank seemed impressed. "This where they make the powder?"

I was about to explain that this was Johnson & Johnson's headquarters that made nothing but a lot of managers very, very comfortable.

"They make tampons," said Maurice, drawing this odd bit of knowledge from his undersized memory bank.

"Really?" Frank was on the verge of pressing Maurice for more information when a city cop pulled alongside the Kielbasavan.

"Get this thing out of the middle of the freakin' road," he yelled.

Driver number two turned off the Kielbasavan's engine and threw the key at the cop. The kid clearly had a problem with authority figures. "You want this thing off the freakin' road? Then you move it!"

The cop barreled out of his car. "Watch your smart-ass mouth, boy!"

"Whoa!" Frank stepped between the two hotheads. "We're not

lookin' for no trouble, Officer. We got a blown engine and this here thing can't be moved until we get a tow."

The cop was too busy staring down the second sausage driver to hear much of what Frank was saying. The eyeball-to-eyeball standoff might have gone on for some time had it not been for another New Brunswick PD patrol car that had worked its way through a tangle of vehicles, choking Albany Street to a standstill.

"Christ Almighty," a cop with stripes on his arm shouted at the patrolman. "What the hell are you doin'? You let the city get tied up in knots because of this? I want this street clear—now!" He waved his arms at the snarled traffic. Cars and trucks were either stopped cold or slowing to check out the drama unfolding on the corner of Albany Street and Johnson Drive.

"All right, goddamnit," the junior cop relented. "I'll call in a tow."

"Tow my ass," the senior cop shouted back. "That'll take another half hour. The road's packed all the way to Edison. Since your car's practically up the butt end of this thing, push the wiener or whatever the hell it is down Johnson Drive."

"It's not a wiener," Frank broke in. "It's a Dubensko kielbasa." Both cops gave Frank a killer look.

The junior cop stormed to his city-owned Chevy, rammed it into gear, and slid the front bumper and hood under the back end of the Kielbasavan's elongated bun. A perfect fit.

"One of you boys get behind the wheel and steer," the junior cop screeched at the two kielbasa drivers. Frank took up the passenger seat and driver two slipped behind the wheel. Once the Kielbasavan's transmission was in neutral, junior cop gave the vehicle a whack and it made a slow turn onto Johnson Drive.

"Where we goin'?" the driver with an attitude shouted at the senior cop who was now jogging alongside the kielbasa.

The cop pointed to Johnson & Johnson's main entrance. "The driveway up ahead. Turn left and park it there."

Junior cop gave the kielbasa enough momentum to navigate the turn into J&J's property. The maneuver worked perfectly. The sausage and bun came to a stop about the same time a Johnson & Johnson security guard arrived on the scene.

"What are you doin'? the guard screamed. "What are you doin'? What are you doin'?"

The Kielbasavan had inserted itself into Johnson & Johnson's sanctuary and the guard knew it was a nonconsensual act. No unauthorized vehicles were allowed to breach the boundaries of the corporation's worldwide headquarters.

"This here is staying put until we get a tow," the senior cop informed the guard.

"That's not gonna happen!"

"It's already happened, bozo."

What little authority the guard had was fading fast. "Who said you could do this? Who said?"

Frank pointed to me. "This man told us to take the side street and—"

The guard cut off the explanation. "You," he roared and glowered at me. "Who the hell are you?"

"Just trying to help," I explained. My mantra. As Doug said, "It's what you do. If I weren't planning to be cremated, the words would be etched on my tombstone."

"This can't happen!" the guard insisted and unholstered a walkie-talkie to beep someone higher up the security chain. "They said to get it off the property!" he said a few seconds later, repeating an executive order from somewhere deep inside J&J's command center.

Whoever they were did nothing to intimidate the cop with the stripes. "It's not goin' back onto that goddamn street!" he bellowed back.

The guard squawked into his radio one more time, but was clearly getting no help. Johnson & Johnson's red-faced sentinel was on his own and the way he was sweating, dealing with a kielbasa wasn't in his job description.

"All right, all right!" the guard sputtered. "But you can't leave it blocking the whole damn driveway."

"You got a better suggestion, genius?" the senior cop asked.

"Pull it up more."

The junior cop stuck his head out the driver's-side window of the squad car. "What's pull it up more supposed to mean?"

"More. You know, more."

"Idiot." The senior cop pointed a finger at the hot-tempered kielbasa driver. "You, steer the thing over there!" He waved at the sixteen-floor tower that housed Johnson & Johnson's executive brain trust.

The guard glanced at the gleaming white building. "Oh, good God, not—" Nothing was more sacred on the corporate grounds than the white spear that was the cerebral cortex for the world's largest diversified healthcare business. The security officer turned to the senior cop and used his wide eyes to beg for mercy.

But it was too late. The junior cop bumped the mobile and it moved forward along a ribbon of asphalt that wound its way through twenty acres of perfect landscape. The kielbasa might have ended up in front of the corporation's main entrance had it not been for the now totally panicked guard who sprinted alongside the Kielbasavan screaming at the driver doing the steering. When the guard realized it was going to take more than words to keep a disaster from turning into a catastrophe, he ran a few yards in front of the Kielbasavan. Then he made an abrupt about-face, planted his feet, stretched out his arms, and turned himself into a human barricade.

"Ah, shit," the driver with an attitude yelled, and yanked the steering wheel hard to the left. The Kielbasavan missed hitting the guard but the maneuver sent the vehicle down a steep curved drive that led to an underground garage. The kielbasa plummeted toward the entrance to the subsurface executive parking lot.

"What the hell?" the junior cop cried out.

"Mother of God," the guard croaked.

The driver with an attitude pounded the kielbasa's brake pedal, but the van kept skidding down the drive. He yanked the emergency brake lever and jammed the transmission into reverse. The metal-mashing sounds that followed were ear piercing. But the noise was mellow compared to the resonance of steel and fiberglass being mashed against the driveway's stone wall.

"Sonofabitch." roared the driver. The Kielbasavan had traveled halfway down the drive that was the only way in or out of the garage. The back tip of the sausage was flattened against one side of the driveway and the vehicle cab was flush against the opposite wall.

"What the hell have you done?" the security guard wailed.

The senior police officer quickly grasped the extent of the tie-up and assaulted the junior cop with a minute's worth of profanity. Junior cop didn't seem at all upended by the incident and, in fact, looked as amused as Maurice Tyson.

"Back that thing out of there!" yelled the guard.

The sausage driver retracted the mobile's sunroof. "Hey, jerkhead. The freakin' transmission's shot, man. So're the damn brakes."

The sweaty guard swallowed and made the sign of the cross.

The driver with an attitude added more bad news. "The only thing that's keepin' this thing from rollin' the rest of the way down and takin' out the garage door is a piss pot of brake fluid that's leakin' out fast!"

"But you have to back it out!" the guard implored. He was near tears.

"Mr. Guard," Frank called out through the opening in the kielbasa's roof. "The Kielbasavan can only go one way and that's down! We need something to stick under the front wheels before the brakes let go altogether."

"What?"

The senior cop grabbed the guard by his shoulder and told him to radio for help. "Somebody needs to open the garage doors and throw a chuck under them wheels!"

The guard was more comfortable taking orders than solving problems—particularly a problem that was blockading the transportation artery used by the corporation's most powerful men and women. He turned to me once he finished talking to a J&J garage attendant. "Seventy cars down there and now not one of 'em can get out. See what you done?"

Before I could complain I was being falsely accused, the executive garage door rolled up and a husky man with a crew cut walked out carrying a ten-foot piece of lumber.

"That's a six-by-six," the senior cop said knowingly. "Should do the trick."

The garage attendant kicked the beam under the Kielbasavan's front tires and the angry driver lifted his foot from the brake pedal. Then he and Frank made an emergency exit through the small opening in the kielbasa's roof.

"I'm puttin' a call in for a wrecker," the senior cop said to the guard.

"You know who owns those cars parked down there?" the guard asked anyone who'd listen. "I'll tell you who owns 'em. The people who can fire my ass, that's who. That garage is filled with Beamers, Lexuses, and Jags, for chrissakes. And not one of 'em can get out because—" The guard turned to the two young men hauling themselves off the Kielbasavan's roof and onto the ledge of the driveway wall. "Because of this—this bratwurst."

"It's actually a kielbasa, sir," Frank said and got back such a vicious stare that he and his colleague loped away from the driveway and headed toward Johnson & Johnson's prized piece of outdoor artwork, Henry Moore's *Mother and Child.*

"All of yous—clear out," the security guard shouted at the small crowd that by now had lined the sidewall of the executive garage driveway to get an interior view of the Kielbasavan through its open roof.

I told Maurice the show was over. He agreed to leave the premises but only after hustling two kielbasa whistles from Frank.

The New York metro TV outlets had a field day with footage of Dubensko's Kielbasavan stuck in one of Johnson & Johnson's most guarded orifices. According to news reports, things got worse shortly after Maurice and I left the scene to continue searching for Yigal and Twyla . About the time we found the happy couple downing café lattes at a nearby Starbucks, the Kielbasavan's gas tank ruptured. A hazmat team was called in to handle the fuel spill and all attempts to dislodge the kielbasa from the executive garage driveway were put on hold. When a pair of heavy-duty wreckers were given the go-ahead to extract the sausage, workers discovered that any yanking and pulling would cause serious damage to the stone walls bordering each side of the driveway. It was at that point a J&J heavyweight made an executive decision to bring in a crane to hoist the Kielbasavan up and away from the garage entrance. That meant waiting until morning before the luxury cars trapped in the garage could be given their freedom. Finding a crane, it seemed, was not that simple—even for a corporation with seventy billion dollars in assets.

"The trials and tribulations of the captains of capitalism," Doc chuckled as he and a dozen other Gateway residents watched NBC's eleven o'clock news broadcast on our only TV. Seeing some of the city's royalty—and in New Brunswick that definitely included J&J's brass—get royally screwed proved to be top-notch evening entertainment.

Then the anchorman reported Johnson & Johnson was arranging

a limousine pickup for every executive whose car was stuck in the underground garage. The mood went sour. Doc said, "Still, an embarrassment to the company."

"You think?" I asked. It seemed to me the corporation had turned a serious transportation problem into a minor inconvenience.

"Letterman's going to be working this for the next month and a half," the professor prophesized. "Somebody sticks a sausage where it doesn't belong and it's a manna from heaven for every comedian in America."

Doc's humor didn't register with Yigal, who was spending his last night in New Brunswick before returning to Florida. The lawyer was preoccupied with Twyla—one of the few women ever to get past the Gateway's front door. A half hour earlier, I had spotted Manny's niece taking an evening walk and hauled her into the shelter before she found a way to violate her parole. In a few minutes, I'd be taking her back to the Hyatt. For the moment, Twyla was tantalizing Yigal and every other Gateway resident.

"Know what I love, Bullet?" Twyla asked.

"What?"

"Sausages. I love them thick, long sausages."

Why wasn't I surprised?

I shifted gears. "It's getting late. We need to get back to the hotel." Sequestering Twyla with a bunch of sex-starved men had its risks—but an even bigger peril would have been to let her loose on her own. I didn't want her wandering into any compromising situations with Yigal, Doc, or anyone else who might raise Maglio's ire. Plus, there was the matter of the two Hispanic thugs still wandering the streets. Thanks to Twyla's stripper pole, one was down for what could be a long count. The second, however, was still in good health and probably a bad mood. I wasn't sure what his next step might be, but hurting, harassing, or even kidnapping Twyla as a way of getting to me could be an option. Until I could deposit Manny's niece in a safe place, I would do what I could to keep her protected.

"That sausage truck got stuck right across from the hotel, didn't it, Bullet?" Twyla asked. Only Albany Street separated the Hyatt from Johnson & Johnson's executive garage. "I really would love to see the sausage. Just a quick look. Can we, please Bullet?"

Yigal jumped on the idea. "Yes, we should. Good idea."

I checked my watch. Eleven thirty. I didn't have the fortitude to beat off another crazy proposal. The prospect of wandering through downtown New Brunswick at this time of night put me on edge. But since Central Jersey's newest attraction was luring a horde of curiosity seekers, I figured there had to be a few midnight spectators who would give us cover. Besides, I wasn't about to let a couple of would-be assassins dictate every move I wanted to make. I piled Twyla, Yigal, and Doc into my car and drove to the Hyatt.

After parking the Buick only a few spaces from where Four Putt Gonzales had been shot in the leg, we headed toward Albany Street. We were on the sidewalk bordering Johnson & Johnson's campus when Doc grabbed my arm. "That truck—I've seen it before," he said, pointing to a nondescript pickup that made a right turn on a street that ran behind the Hyatt.

"Looks like eight million other trucks," I said.

"It had an out-of-state plate," Doc noted. "I can't place where I saw it, but—"

An impatient Twyla pulled on the professor's arm. "It's just a truck, Doc. Come on. Let's go." She dragged Doc ahead, Yigal and I trailing.

Johnson & Johnson's property was designed by I. M. Pei to be a seamless part of New Brunswick. The corporate headquarters' grassy perimeter rolls up to city sidewalks without any kind of barrier. Except for bums and inebriated college students, pedestrians are rarely discouraged from wandering around the property. On this particular evening, there was a group of spectators lined up along one side of the garage driveway to get a late-night look at the disabled Kielbasavan.

"No security," Professor Waters observed. I caught a quiver of uncertainty in his voice.

As usual, Doc was right. We showed up midway through a shift change of Johnson & Johnson's security guard. Five minutes earlier or later and we probably wouldn't have gotten within fifty yards of the garage entrance. Now there was no one to stop us or about two dozen other Dubensko Kielbasavan fans from pressing ourselves against the driveway wall and gawking at the immovable sausage and bun. Twyla began stroking the meat product replica in a way that made Yigal's knees go weak. At the same time, Doc noticed a man standing behind the large *Mother & Child* sculpture that stood between us and J&J's front entrance.

"The thing in his hand," Doc whispered to me. "It's either a video camera or a weapon."

The distant, dark form shifted to the right. The man was too tall and heavyset to be either of the Hispanics who had been chasing me since my visit to Orlando. The pale light filtering out from J&J's headquarters lobby caught the object in the man's hand.

"It's a camera," I said. "No big deal. He's taking pictures of the kielbasa."

Doc shook his head. "It's not the kielbasa he's videoing. It's us."

"Well, then maybe he wants a few candids of Twyla—"

"He's been pointing that camera at you, me, and Yigal since we got here."

I doubted there was anything sinister about the mysterious figure. Still, a logical plan would be to blend in with the small crowd, wait for the next security team to arrive, and then get escorted across the street to the Hyatt. But aggravation overrode logic. I was tired of being followed, intimidated, photographed, bombed, and shot at. I was through boxing with shadows. It was time to go on the offensive, so I called Doc and Yigal into a huddle. "Let's go talk to Mr. Candid Camera."

The professor glanced over his shoulder at the heavyset man dressed in a lightweight jacket and baseball cap. "That isn't a good idea, Bullet."

"Maybe not, but it's what I'm going to do. I could use a little backup just in case."

"You know, you're right—he's probably here to take a little footage he can send as a video clip to his friends," said Doc, looking for a way out.

"If he's a regular Joe, he won't mind my striking up a conversation. But if he isn't—"

"He could make a run for it," Yigal predicted.

"Good point. If he does, here's what we'll do. Yigal, you and Doc approach him from either side and I'll come at him straight on."

Doc pulled at his hair. "This could turn out bad, you know."

"Couldn't be much worse than a few pounds of C-4 blowing up in your face or fifteen rounds of ammo coming your way," I said. "Look, you're probably right, Doc. Chances are he's nothing more than some slob fooling around with his camcorder. Let's go find out."

"I'm telling you, I have a bad feeling."

No more discussion. I ordered Yigal to take the right flank and Doc the left.

"What if he does run?" Yigal wanted to know.

"I don't know. Chase him."

Yigal bounced off on a path wide right of the large Henry Moore sculpture. I nudged Doc on a course heading to the left of the mystery man and I strode directly toward the target.

As we approached, the man backpedaled toward Johnson & Johnson's front door. When we moved closer, he turned and ran full tilt into Yigal's zone. His mistake. Panicked, the lawyer exploded into a super storm of out-of-control energy. Yigal's arms flapped, his legs pumped, and his head wagged so ferociously that his yarmulke took off like a Frisbee.

"Yigal!" It occurred to me the man in our crosshairs might actually be a nobody who thought he was a whisker away from being mugged. Being responsible for someone else's heart attack was something I didn't need.

"Yigal!" I screamed again.

Yigal was in a frenzy, whirling his body around like a mini-tornado. Camera Man cut his sprint to a crawl.

"Yigal! Get out of his way!"

My screaming had no impact on the lawyer, but it flustered Camera Man. He lowered his head and launched a full-speed assault on the lawyer, catching Yigal with his shoulder and driving him into J&J's manicured turf. Zeusenoerdorf's attorney was pudgy and out of shape so he was easy to put down. But he had a Weebles-like quality that had him back on his feet in a second. Whether it was deliberate or another impulsive act of lunacy, Yigal took off after Camera Man.

With the lawyer flailing away only a few feet behind him, Camera Man had little choice but to head toward the driveway that led to J&J's underground executive parking lot.

Yigal kept charging, arms flapping and head gyrating. He was nearly on top of the man when the two reached the yellow tape that cordoned off the entrance to the garage.

From the distance, it was impossible to tell if Camera Man was pushed by Yigal or whether he slipped on the layer of absorbent material that had been shoveled onto the pavement by the hazmat team. Whatever, the man tumbled through the tape and slid face-first down the driveway. Yigal also fell hard but managed to keep himself from plummeting toward the Kielbasavan.

I was too far away to get a close-up view of what happened next. According to Twyla, the man with the video camera rolled under the Kielbasavan's chassis. Still skidding, he slammed into the six-by-six beam wedged beneath the mobile's front wheels. The force of the impact dislodged the wood and the Dubensko motorized sausage broke loose.

Unfortunately for Camera Man, his descent was slightly faster than the kielbasa's start-up speed. He banged into the closed door of the garage an instant before the Kielbasavan hit the entryway, catching Camera Man with the tip of its twenty-five-foot bun.

Twyla and the other Kielbasavan admirers erupted with a chorus of gasps and screams. Doc and I raced to the edge of the driveway, hopping over Yigal who was seated on the ground brushing debris from a gash on his right arm. We half ran, half slid to what was left of the J&J garage entrance, ending up on either side of Camera Man. The lower half of his body had been pulverized by the Kielbasavan—his mangled legs stuck under the front wheels. Blood gushed from a jagged tear in his neck.

"Damn," I shouted at Doc. "His artery's been cut."

"Got to stop the bleeding," the professor said, and like magic, a cotton blouse fell from the sky. Doc quickly turned the woman's shirt into a compress and jammed it against the man's neck. I looked up and spotted Twyla hovering over the wall wearing nothing but a skimpy bra.

A half dozen men joined Doc and me at the lower end of the garage driveway. They tried pushing the Kielbasavan uphill a foot or two, but the vehicle didn't move.

"Not good," Doc muttered. "He's trapped."

"Check his skull," I ordered. The injured man's baseball cap had slipped forward and the visor covered his forehead and eyes. Trickles of blood leaked from under the sweatband.

Doc gently removed the man's hat and then pulled back with a start.

"My God," the professor whispered.

"What?"

"It's . . . It's Conway Kyzwoski!"

Chapter 16

"Conway." I shouted.

Kyzwoski was bleeding out fast and his voice was feeble. Doc and I had our ears to his face doing our best to decipher what he was saying.

"They're . . . They're after you."

"Me?"

Kyzwoski nodded.

"You've been following me—videotaping me?"

Kyzwoski coughed. "Yeah."

"But why?"

"Somebody wants somethin' you got—computer disk."

I wasn't sure what to ask next. Kyzwoski's gaunt look told me time was running out for him. "How'd you get mixed up in this? You didn't even know who I was until we met at the Wayside Motel."

"No. They sent me and Ida to Florida to follow you."

I grabbed him by one of his blood-soaked shoulders. "Who sent you? *Quia Vita*? Judith Russet?"

Kyzwoski had enough left to answer. "No."

"Who?"

Kyzwoski didn't respond. Instead he gurgled out a few more words. "Get you on tape . . . after Florida, that's all I was supposed to do . . . never wanted to hurt you . . . others got paid to do that."

"What others?"

Conway reached for my arm. "Listen . . . about my boys . . . Ephraim and Noah—"

"Great kids," I lied. "Conway, I need to know what's going on. If Russet didn't hire you, then who—"

"Don' want the boys to know 'bout this . . . mean a lot if you could make sure—"

The man was dying. What was I supposed to say? "I'll do what I can."

Kyzwoski tightened his grip on my arm. "Somethin' else. Tell my wife . . . I did my work for Jesus."

"I will if I see her," I promised. "Now tell me who you're working for. Who's after me, Conway?"

"Occasio—" The word was barely a whisper.

I leaned closer to Kyzwoski's bloodied ear. "I don't understand."

"Tell Ida that I done the things they asked. *Occasio aegre offertur . . . facile amittitur.*"

Conway Kyzwoski drew a deep breath. His last.

Yigal, Doc, Twyla, and I could have told the small army of cops the truth—that Kyzwoski had been hired to track me like a rabbit and accidentally died on the job. Instead, the three of us made a pact to let the authorities think we had no previous ties to the man. Making claims that Kyzwoski was actually a henchman for some mysterious group that had its sights on me would either convince investigators I was totally insane—or spin me into an eddy of interviews with one cop after another. It was a risky decision to keep the truth buried—but I wanted time to help Zeus, not to do coffee and doughnuts at the local precinct house.

"What the hell was some halfwit backwoods hick from South Carolina doing in New Brunswick at midnight, for chrissakes?" asked the same senior cop who had hassled the two sausage drivers earlier in the day.

"Same thing as us other halfwits," Doc piped up. "Getting a close-up look at Dubensko's kielbasa."

Twyla, Doc, Yigal, and I were questioned separately, each of us sticking to our story. None of us mentioned that Kyzwoski had been carrying a palm-sized video camera which I had tucked away in my jacket pocket moments after Conway died.

Just as Kyzwoski was being carted off to the morgue, the cops located his Dodge Ram pickup parked outside the Hyatt in a space reserved for Hertz rental cars. As Doc refused to let me forget, it was the same truck the professor had spotted earlier in the evening.

Shortly before one a.m., I dropped Twyla at the Hyatt and then Doc and I drove to the emergency room at the Robert Wood Johnson

University Hospital. We found an exhausted-looking resident attending to Yigal, who was seated on a gurney.

"Any problems?" I asked the doctor.

"Twelve stitches in his arm. He'll be hurting for a day or so."

"Yeah, but he'll be okay, right?"

The resident stared at the professor who was talking to Yigal. "Hey, isn't that One Nut Waters?"

"Just a look-alike. What about Rosenblatt?"

"Who?"

"The guy you just stitched up," I reminded the resident.

"Oh, yeah, yeah. He'll be okay. Says he's a lawyer so he'll probably sue the shit out of whoever made him bleed."

"Nah, I don't think so." Not even a competent lawyer could squeeze a dime out of the late Conway Kyzwoski.

A few strokes shy of two a.m., Yigal was patched up and ready to leave the hospital emergency room. "Be careful," I said to both Zeus's lawyer and Doc Waters.

"Don't worry about us," replied Yigal. "Worry about yourself."

Doc agreed. The professor looked more at ease than I could re-member. And I knew why. For years, he had been a mob target who wore the most-likely-to-be-assassinated crown. Now, for some unfathomable reason, I had become the prey of choice.

Part III

Chapter 17

Tuesday noon. New Brunswick was awash in scarlet and black. It was the start of another academic year and Rutgers' colors were as much a harbinger of fall as the turning of hardwood leaves or the squadrons of southbound birds. Students flooded the streets and the old city reverberated with an injection of youthful energy.

The downtown McDonald's buzzed with the college set and the usual blue-collar fast-food junkies. Doug and I sat in one corner of the restaurant looking like two lumps in an otherwise well-blended lower income batter. I dabbled with my grilled chicken sandwich, trying not to show my irritation. The last time we shared a meal, I was the one who shelled out good money for a decent Italian spread—dessert included. Now it was Doug's turn to pick up the tab and here I was working on a five-buck combo. Life isn't fair.

"Great news," Doug said between mouthfuls of his Big Mac. We were down to the reason he had taken the 10:40 a.m. New Jersey Transit to New Brunswick.

Doug's news really was great—Universal Studios was ready for Twyla Tharp. But naturally there was a hitch. Manny Maglio wanted me to escort his niece to Florida for a second time.

"Are you insane?" I shouted.

"Hear me out," Doug said in his usual unexcited way. "Maglio will pay for your time and expenses."

"Sorry. Once was enough."

Doug squeezed his lips into a thin line. "Think about your situation. Somebody hired a backwoods, Polish nutcase to ride you like a fly on a turd."

I grimaced. "You paint a beautiful picture. But the answer's still no."

"Remember the little movie what's his face Kazakny made?"

How could I forget? I had replayed the footage stored in Conway Kyzwoski's video camera a dozen times. There was nothing compromising about what Conway had recorded, but the fact he had been logging my day-to-day routine put me back on my heels.

"The guy was filming your life story for a bunch of fanatics," Doug said.

"Can't argue that. And he did it like a pro. Never had a clue he was on my trail."

"He's from South Carolina, for godsakes. Next to tracking possums and weasels, you were child's play."

"Yeah, well, think about this: Conway's being shipped back to Goose Creek in a body bag, so I don't need Maglio's protective services. But thanks for the offer."

"Don't be so damned naïve." Doug's brow wrinkled a trumped-up look of concern. "Think about what's going on, Bullet. We're not just talking about some wacko chasing you with a camera. You've already had two close calls, right? If the word gets out that Manny's your guardian angel, you won't have to run around wearing Kevlar twenty four seven."

Score one for Doug. He knew how to sweeten a deal. "So I take care of Twyla and Manny takes care of me."

"That's how it works."

"And once I deliver Twyla to Florida—"

"Look," Doug said, wiping a drop of McDonald's secret sauce from the corner of his mouth, "putting a little distance between you and the Gateway for a few days isn't such a bad idea. Maybe things will sort themselves out if you take a short leave of absence."

"Why me?" I asked. "Maglio has the money to hire any Tom, Dick, or Luigi he wants to haul Twyla back to Orlando."

"True. But Manny likes what you've done with her. Twyla's morphing into the kind of person Manny thinks she should be. You've got her cleaned up, dressed decently, and she hasn't been turning tricks. Bottom line? He trusts you."

I didn't bother to toss in a couple of minor corrections. Apparently Manny's intelligence network didn't know about the Wayside fee-for-service exchange between Twyla and the late Conway Kyzwoski. Then there was Yigal Rosenblatt.

"It's just a couple more days." If Doug weren't concerned about wrinkling the crease in his Gucci suit, he might have gotten on his knees. "Go to Florida, drop Twyla off in Orlando, and you're back in Jersey in a flash. Want to take another day or two for some R&R? Manny will pick up the tab."

I could see right through my long-time friend. "And what do you get out of this?"

"The satisfaction of helping a young lady turn her life around."

"Yeah, and a fat bonus for getting Maglio to come through with his megadollar pledge to the United Way."

"Why do you love to make things difficult?" Doug used one of those premoistened towelettes to clean his fingers. "What else do I need to do to make this happen?"

I was ready. "You're the point person for the United Way's national donor recognition dinner, right? The big deal on Ellis Island scheduled for this coming Saturday night."

Doug burped. The fat grams he had just consumed suddenly weren't sitting right. "So what?"

"And at the dinner, who will United Way be honoring as the donor of the year?"

Doug's answer was barely audible. "Arthur Silverstein." The billionaire banker wasn't exactly Bill Gates, but he was on the radar screen as a very rich American who once in a while tossed a load of appreciated stock at a nonprofit or two, including the United Way. Since he was old, Doug probably wanted him in the spotlight while he still had a pulse. That might spell b-e-q-u-e-s-t, which could mean really big money once Silverstein checked out.

"I want in."

"What?"

"I want my name on the invitation list."

"Bullet, this is an orgasmic event for the United Way. Understand? It's a heavy-duty fundraiser. Tables go from fifteen thousand dollars to fifty thousand each. No offense, but it's not your kind of crowd."

"You asked what it would take to close the deal and I'm telling you," I said. "I want to be at that dinner."

Doug drew a long breath. "So, if I get you a seat, we're square? Orlando gets to see you and Twyla a second time?"

"Seats—not seat. There are a couple of other people who need to be on the guest list."

"No way."

"Two more passes or we're done talking."

"For whom?"

"Doc Waters," I said softly and watched Doug's eyes double in size. "What?"

"The professor's smart, a good conversationalist, and can charm the bling off your high rollers."

"Waters is the Mob's Salman Rushdie. Jesus. Besides, he looks like a sheep dog."

"I'll clean him up," I pledged.

Doug threw up his hands. "Of all the people you could bring to the black-tie dinner of the year, why pick Waters?"

"I have my reasons."

"Not good enough."

"Good enough to get me to bring Manny's niece back to Florida."

Doug threw his napkin on his tray. "Who else?"

"The same guy I brought to Florida, when you forced me to hand-hold Twyla. Maurice Tyson."

"You're out of your mind. This is not a soirée for bums. Think about what you're asking me to do."

I thought about Doc and Maurice waltzing with a cross-section of America's Who's Who and conceded that Doug had a point. "All right," I said. "Add both of them to the waitstaff."

Doug pushed himself forward, his silk tie dangerously close to a pair of uneaten fries. "What's this all about anyway?"

"I'm looking for something."

"What?"

"The truth."

Doug grimaced. "Listen, if you want me to put you and your two loose cannons on Ellis Island, then I need to know why. Even if it means giving up Maglio's donation to the United Way, I can't risk flushing hundreds of United Way's biggest check writers down the toilet."

Doug was a man facing a couple of bad options and was closing in on picking the worst of the two. Maybe I had pushed him to the limit.

"All I want is another one-on-one talk with Silverstein," I confided. "That's it."

"So make an appointment to meet with him, for godsakes."

"Won't work. I can't get past Arcontius."

Doug knew what kind of monumental roadblock Arcontius could be, so he didn't waste time suggesting there might be other ways to leapfrog Silverstein's chief of staff. "Did you ever consider there's a reason why so few people ever get to see Arthur in person?"

"I saw him," I reminded Doug.

"Yes, you did, and I was surprised as hell he met with you. It wouldn't have happened if he weren't so interested in the Benjamin Kurios case."

"He's got a problem meeting people?"

"It's a bigger problem than that. Silverstein's got something called Lewy body dementia. It isn't pretty. He flips back and forth from being lucid to being delusional."

"The man was perfectly sane when I met with him."

"Then you got him on a good day. From what I've been told, he spends a lot of time chasing ghosts—especially his dead daughter. When he's not nuts, Arthur hits the bottle and hits it hard. Can't blame the poor bastard. There's no way he's going to bounce back."

This didn't sound like the Arthur Silverstein who had given me a walking tour of his mansion. "All I can tell you is he wasn't crazy and he wasn't drunk when I was with him."

"My source tells me that's a rarity. Which is why I get diarrhea wondering if Arthur will either be too whacked out or too sloshed to show up at his own testimonial. The United Way made the call to put him in the spotlight knowing this will probably be his last public appearance. It's one hell of a gamble."

If Doug was looking for someone to commiserate with, he was in bad company. I had too many problems of my own. "You're telling me Arcontius and some others high up in Silverstein's organization are keeping him boxed up because he's—"

"Old, unpredictable, delusional, and a boozer. That sew it up for you?"

"Not enough to back me off from trying to meet with him again."

"Why? Even if you could get to him, what's so important about looking him in the eye?"

"He stuffed twenty grand in my pocket and thinks he bought himself a slave. I intend to renegotiate the deal, but that won't happen if Arcontius keeps fending me off."

Doug switched on his please-don't-do-this face. "Can't you handle this some other way? You could end up screwing me and the entire United Way organization."

"Won't happen. Arcontius knows Doc Waters and Maurice Tyson—met them when we paid Silverstein a visit. If he spots two residents from the Gateway working the Ellis Island crowd, Arcontius is going to be distracted just long enough for me to get to Silverstein."

Doug sighed. "Seven hundred fifty people will be at that dinner. Seven hundred fifty very rich people!"

"Yeah, yeah. I get the point."

"And you've read stories about how Silverstein is ninety percent recluse—and that was before he started falling off the deep end. He'll hole up somewhere until it's time to make a cameo appearance. Even if Arcontius isn't there to protect him, sneaking into Arthur's world won't be easy."

"I'll find a way."

"I want a guarantee the two oddities you want to bring with you won't cause a problem."

"Sounds reasonable."

"This is no joke, Bullet. I don't want them wandering around on their own. Give me a flat-out promise the nutty professor and the other idiot won't hassle anyone at the dinner."

"Hassle" was a broad term that came with a lot of leeway. "Done."

"All right, then. So, you need to get Twyla on the road by—"

I held up my right hand. "The bargaining's not over."

"What?"

"One more thing."

Doug blinked. "God in heaven."

"The doctor at Overlook Hospital who was the attending the night Arthur Silverstein's kid died."

"What about him?"

"I want to know if he's alive. If he is, I need you to contact him and get him to agree to a phone call or a visit."

"How the hell am I supposed to make this happen?"

"Use the same kind of line you threw at Arcontius," I proposed. "The Ruth Silverstein Trust is under review. The directors are revisiting the funding guidelines so donations made by the trust go toward solving the medical problems that messed up Arthur's daughter. You've asked me to call the doc for a short interview to get his recommendations."

"But why do you want to talk to this guy?" Doug moaned. "What's the point?"

I didn't have a convincing answer, only that I was working on a hunch that wouldn't go away. Ruth Silverstein's portrait kept popping out of my memory bank, and the sketchy medical records that Doug had faxed to my office were nudging me toward the doctor. Then there was Doug's comment about Silverstein's obsession with his dead daughter. Maybe someone familiar with the family's medical history could help me understand if I were onto something or just chasing my tail.

"Those are my terms," I said.

"All this because that lunatic in an Orlando jail cell has turned you into Inspector Clouseau."

"He's not a lunatic. Do we have a deal?"

Doug got up and emptied his tray into a waste bin. "Yeah, but so help me, if you turn that dinner into a fiasco—"

"Not to worry," I said as Doug trudged out the door.

My GE phone and answering machine were leftovers from a juvenile diabetes silent auction. Like a few other items that hadn't drawn a bid, the equipment needed a home. The gifts were appreciated, but never got much use. Residents weren't allowed to make outgoing calls unless I gave them the okay, and incoming calls were rare—at least they were until about three hours after my lunch with Doug.

Five messages were stored in the answering machine when I drifted into my office around four o'clock. Three were from Abraham Arcontius who asked, then demanded, and then commanded that I call him. I was now long past due in getting back to Silverstein's scrawny sentry who wasn't accustomed to being ignored. Finding ways to aggravate Arcontius was a pleasure, which is why I didn't dial his number.

The fourth message was from Judith Russet who also insisted I call her. Unlike Arcontius, her voice was level, but intense, which told me she had something important on her mind. Yigal Rosenblatt left the fifth message that ended with a callback number. Twyla's room at the Hyatt, where Yigal was apparently spending his last day and night in New Brunswick before heading south to Florida. I called him first.

"Morty Margolis just called," Yigal proclaimed.

"And?"

"The paint samples matched."

"He's sure?"

"Yes, he is."

Morty Margolis's lab results would probably never hold up in court. Nevertheless, the information still might help save Zeus's hide. The burned-out sedan the cops found in Kissimmee was the same car Zeus saw the night it ran a white van off the road and into an Orlando bridge abutment. Juan Perez, the well-cooked Venezuelan discovered inside the car, was probably one of the men who battled it out under the overpass where Benjamin Kurios died.

I finished with Yigal and dialed Russet.

"What didn't you understand when we met in Princeton?" Russet asked. "If you value your safety, give us the computer disk."

I came back with a counterpunch. "I'll tell you what I value. I value not having some fanatic turn into my shadow."

"What are you talking about?"

"One of your *Quia Vita* faithful. The man you paid to keep me in his video camera viewfinder."

Russet hesitated. It wasn't a long pause but long enough to tell me I had struck a vein. "As I said, I don't know—"

"People who have a foot in the grave don't tend to lie. A couple of Conway Kyzwoski's last words were Quia and Vita."

"Kyzwoski? I had nothing to do with Mr. Kyzwoski."

"But your organization did?"

"As difficult as this may be for you to grasp, I'm trying to do you a favor. So let me be as clear as I can. Kyzwoski wasn't directly connected to *Quia Vita*. But he was involved with a pro-life fringe element that is extremely dangerous—a fringe group that's not happy with what you're up to."

Trying to make sure a homeless man accused of murder got a fair shake is what I was up to. That fact seemed to have been buried under the misimpression that I was hawking Henri Le Campion's computer disk. Of course, I could have done more to let the "fringes" know I didn't belong at the top of their hate list. But proving that I was being wrongly accused would mean an end to the information people like Russet and Arcontius were feeding to me. Information that could prove weighty enough to convince the law enforcement community to apologize to Zeusenoerdorf for his wrongful detention.

"What do you know about a Venezuelan named Juan Perez?" I asked.

"Damnit, Bullock. You're not getting it. You've stepped over the line, and now you're in deep trouble. So much so that your life may be in jeopardy."

"I do get it. Who's Juan Perez?"

"I don't know anyone named Juan Perez," said Russet and I believed her.

I jumped to a different question. "Who's involved with this ultra-radical fringe group you're talking about?"

"That's not something I'm going to discuss. Just know that your problem isn't *Quia Vita*."

"Maybe my problem's with the Order of Visio Dei. Isn't that the dangerous fringe group you're talking about?"

Russet laughed. "Hardly. Visio Dei is a part of *Quia Vita*. A very important and morally sound part of our organization."

"At the Visio Dei meeting the other night, you warned that *Quia Vita* was going to be challenged like never before," I reminded her.

"If it falls into the wrong hands, the *Book of Nathan* disk might be used to discredit us. We need Visio Dei's financial help to beat back those attacks. We're not signing up thugs to help us do battle."

"Juan Perez was a thug. Seems he was paid to steal the *Book of Nathan* disk and apparently Benjamin Kurios got killed in the process. You're telling me none of Visio Dei's money was used to buy Perez's time and services?"

That stopped Russet for a few seconds. When she resumed, her tone was sharper than ever. "Visio Dei's members are decent people. If you knew them, you'd realize what you're saying is not only absurd but insulting."

"You want Le Campion's disk, but you're worried it might end up someplace else. Besides *Quia Vita*, who do you think has made an offer for the CD?"

"You, of all people, know the answer."

"Do I?"

"I told you—auctioning off the disk would be a mistake. Possibly even a lethal one. By playing *Quia Vita* against another party, you've infuriated a lot of people."

I decided to lay down my cards. All of them. "Time out. I don't have the disk. I never did. If I've led you to believe otherwise, it's because I'm trying to help a poor schmuck locked up in an Orlando cell block."

Dead silence. Then: "I don't believe you."

"I can understand why you wouldn't. Truth is, I've been leading you on."

"Why?"

"Like I said—to get as much information as possible that could help Miklos Zeusenoerdorf."

Russet chewed on what I said. "Are you telling me you know absolutely nothing about the disk?"

Since Russet had given me a lot more information than I'd expected, I had an odd urge to reciprocate. "I know a little. The disk was found beneath an overpass where Kurios was killed."

"Who found it? Who has it?" Russet was breathless.

"I'm not going to say anything more until you tell me who's on the fringe in the pro-life world."

"I want to remind you that even if you're telling the truth, there are those who think it's you who's brokering the sale of the *Book of Nathan*. As long as that disk is in play, your life is in danger. If you work with us—cooperate fully with us—*Quia Vita* can help you locate the CD. We have a large and influential constituency."

"Some of those constituents could be over-the-edge extremists who'd love to see me cremated. So thanks, but no thanks."

Judith Russet growled—actually growled. "Think about the benefit of joining forces, Mr. Bullock. Then think about what will happen to you if you don't."

I tried to sort out whether Russet was handing me an opportunity or sending me a warning. Maybe she was sincere. The events of the last few days proved I could use backup and a lot of it. Then again, maybe she was telling me that if I didn't get in line with her organization, she'd unleash holy hell. Either way, I wasn't going to board her train. *Quia Vita* and its fuzzy "fringes" still came with a label that read "danger."

Just after six, the phone rang again. Thinking it might be Arcontius, I let the answering machine collect the call. When I heard Doug's voice, I picked up.

"You're in," he said.

"Meaning what?"

"You have a seat at the Silverstein testimonial dinner."

"And?"

"And what?"

"What about Doc Waters and Maurice Tyson?"

Doug coughed out the news like a piece of gristle. "They'll be working as bus boys. Remember—if either of them gets out of line, the United Way's going to feed me my family jewels."

"Beats the crap you usually eat."

"Hilarious. By the way, everyone on the island wears a tux. That includes the worker bees. So get a couple for One Nut Waters and Mike Tyson."

"Maurice. It's Maurice Tyson."

"He still has to wear a tux."

"That could be a budgetary problem."

"Why aren't I surprised? Call Hinkle's in Edison. They owe me a favor."

"No charge?"

I could practically hear Doug compressing his lips. "I'll put a call in to Hinkle. I can't believe how much I do for you."

"Or to me," I said. "What about Ruth Silverstein's doc?"

"His name is Meseck. I'm working on him."

"Thank you."

"You're not welcome. By the way, Maglio wants Twyla on her way to Florida by Friday."

"Friday? Are you nuts? I can't move her until Sunday—the day after the Ellis Island dinner."

"Not good enough. She has to be in Florida by Friday. If she isn't, plan on moving to Bosnia."

"I've got a job, for godsakes. I need to find a stand-in and I've got to—"

"I've done my bit," Doug broke in. "Now do yours. Oh, yeah, something else. Maglio wants to see you tomorrow afternoon. Any time before five at his office in Edison."

"Not a chance." I wasn't about to consort with an organized crime icon unless such a meeting came with a monstrous payoff.

Doug understood what kind of carrot he needed to wave in front of my nose. "Manny has something to tell you in person. He wouldn't give me any specifics. Only that it's very important and it's not about Twyla. Something to do with what happened at the Orlando airport and the New Brunswick Hyatt."

Chapter 18

Manny Maglio ran his seedy empire from a four-room office tacked on to Climax—a stucco, windowless nudie bar that fronted on one of Edison's busiest streets. At two in the afternoon, there were only a few vehicles in the parking lot—mostly pickups and a couple of beat-up sedans. I pulled my Buick to the rear of the building and looked for a back door employee entrance.

I had tried calling Maglio earlier in the day, thinking I could take care of business via the phone. Maglio's assistant, who sounded like Marilyn Monroe with asthma, told me her boss had to see me in person. So here I was, face-to-face with a guard the size of the Statue of Liberty who conducted a full-body pat down before he let me through the door.

Maglio's office was surprisingly conservative. Dark paneling dotted with framed certificates and awards from the Chamber of Commerce, Rotary Club, Knights of Columbus, and United Way. I expected calendars with naked women and lamps that looked like sex organs. Instead, there were pictures of a dark-haired woman in her fifties and two girls, each a little on the heavy side, who looked to be in their teens.

The woman who had answered the phone earlier in the day walked into the room. She didn't fit my mental profile of a porno king's personal assistant. The lady was plump, unattractive, and chewed gum with a vengeance. She told me Maglio was handling a situation in another part of the building and should be finished shortly. I wondered what the situation looked like and which parts were being handled.

Maglio charged into his office a few minutes later. Twyla's uncle was fifty pounds overweight and wore what little hair he had in a shaggy dark semicircle around a gleaming pink dome. His gray suit was wrinkled and a pair of half-rim glasses hung by a black cord around his neck. In a lineup, he'd be the last person picked as a mob boss and first as a CPA.

"Sorry." Maglio was breathing heavily and the collar of his white shirt looked damp. "Wednesday's when we audition. Every man's fantasy, right? Twenty women takin' their clothes off."

Maglio gulped down a quarter can of Red Bull, licked his puffy lips, and plopped into a high-back leather desk chair.

"Here's the thing," he went on. "I'd pay nineteen of them broads to keep their clothes on."

I threw back a smile, but I sensed Maglio wasn't trolling for laughs. He was looking for commiseration. "Hard job," I said.

"It's a bitch, is what. I got places from Tampa to Boston, and it's the same shit all over. Not enough talent. Top of that, you got cops lookin' up your ass twenty four seven."

"Has to be tough."

"Tough? You don't wanna know. The thing of it is, I'm runnin' an entertainment business, is all. Like Disney, MGM, or Universal, for chrissakes. But think I get respect for givin' the public what it wants? Not a chance."

I had opened up a wound, and Maglio was bleeding self-pity. I nodded to the framed photo of the woman and two teenage girls. "At least your family appreciates what you do."

"Them? They could give a crap what I do as long as I pay the bills and stay outta the news."

I doubted he was exaggerating. Mrs. Maglio and her two spoiled offspring were probably sitting comfortably a safe distance from Edison, where friends and neighbors pretended Mr. Maglio was just another run-of-the-mill businessman. "You wanted to see me?"

"Yeah," Maglio said and shifted his large buttocks the way people do when they either have hemorrhoids or are about to dive into an awkward conversation. "The thing is, I can't use the phone when I wanna talk private. Which is why I had to set up this here meetin'. I got more people tapping me than a hooker on Saturday night."

Maglio would know.

"I couldn't figure how to handle this exactly," Maglio continued. "So, I thought I'd lay it out to you. Man to man and all that shit."

Wife and daughters excluded, how many people had ever seen Maglio looking this ill at ease? Those who had were probably parked under a headstone.

"The thing is, the two hit men who got the contract—"

Maglio's chunky assistant broke into the room. "Baltimore's on the phone. Pasties never showed up."

"Jesus, Mildred, can't you see I'm in a meetin' here?"

Mildred? The emperor of smut and God knows what else had an assistant named Mildred?

"It's Wednesday, remember?" the lady croaked. "You know, Wednesday. Cop night?"

"See, this is what I gotta deal with," Maglio said, his face tight with stress. "This dancer, Bambi—she's got nipples as big as manhole covers. Every Wednesday, Baltimore sends in its inspectors, right? If Bambi doesn't have them things covered, I get fined. Know how many times I had to pay off that goddamned city just because they don't make pasties the size of paper plates?"

I checked my watch. "About why you wanted to see me—"

"Oh, yeah. Well the thing is, I din't know nothin' about the contract until the two a-holes blew up the airport terminal in Orlando." Maglio's eyes pointed to the floor as he talked.

"What contract?"

Maglio talked over my question. "Ten or fifteen years ago, this wouldn't-a happened. I mean, everybody knew where the lines were and you din't cross 'em."

I had no idea where Maglio was heading but wherever it was, he was taking the long way around.

"Let me make sure I have this right," I said. "Two men were hired to set off a bomb—"

Maglio shook his head. "No, no! Nobody told 'em to bomb nothin'. See, that's the thing. Most of the people ya hire today are worth shit."

"But the two are hit men, right?"

Manny nodded. "Imports. That's the thing these days. Bring a couple of illegals in for a hit and then ship 'em out when the job's over. Trouble is, you never know what these bastards are gonna do."

The cloud was slowly lifting. The Hispanics brought in to take care of business had used a bulldozer to squash a gnat. Decimating the Continental ticket counter was a case of overkill that still missed the target. So what about the incident that turned the Hyatt parking deck into a shooting gallery?" I asked Maglio.

"Yeah, yeah, I know. Jesus, can you believe it?" Manny took a deep breath and whistled. "They said Four Putt Gonzales wasn't supposed to get popped. An accident. But that don't matter. The thing of it is, they put a bullet in somebody I know. Even worse, they did it on my turf!"

Two uncontrollable, incompetent wild men were on the loose and at least one of them was still healthy enough to do more damage. Find out who hired the Hispanics and maybe there was a way of calling off the dogs. "Who put out the contract?" I asked.

"Yeah, well the thing is, I didn't have nothin' to do with that. It was the Orlando family." Maglio waved his left hand like he was wiping a countertop. "No, no, that's not right. Orlando was fine until the Philly boys moved south. It's them bastards from Philadelphia, who don't give a squat about nothin' or nobody."

Maglio seemed to be drifting toward a discourse on the ethical erosion of America's organized crime movement. Not what I wanted to hear. "You know the Hispanics almost took out your niece."

Maglio dabbed his brow. "I know. I know. Jesus—my brother must be floppin' around in his coffin. I'm supposed to be his kid's guardian, for chrissakes."

"So how does this thing get fixed?"

Maglio pulled at his collar. "It's done. Taken care of. That's what I wanted to tell you."

"What?"

"The two Latin guys are finished. The contract's off the table. It's over."

Maglio had a reputation for being the alpha boss among the mob set. Although he looked more like a government bureaucrat than a gangster, he obviously had underworld pull. "Going to tell me how you worked this out?"

"Me and the old Philly family reached an understanding. That's all you need to know. 'Cept that I wouldn't be doin' this if it wasn't for my brother's crazy daughter. I don' want her getting' whacked, which is why I got this whole thing put back in the drawer."

Maglio began fumbling with some papers on his desk that I took as a signal that the meeting was over. But I wasn't about to leave until a couple of other issues were resolved.

"There's a kid in jail who's charged with the Orlando airport bombing," I said.

"The Arab?"

"He needs to be released."

"It'll happen," Maglio promised. "Give it a day or so. The cops are gonna try coverin' their asses before the kid files a wrongful detention lawsuit."

It sounded like Maglio knew a lot about wrongful detention.

"What about Juan Perez?"

"Who?"

"Perez. The Venezuelan who was lit on fire in Orlando."

Maglio gave me a blank stare. "Don't know nothin' about a Venezuelan. The contract was with a couple of Dominicans."

Now it was my turn to look puzzled. I thought for sure there was a connection between the man Zeus had seen behind the wheel of the mysterious blue sedan and the two murder-for-hire thugs. Maybe not.

Maglio's assistant made another uninvited appearance. "Crystal's on the line."

"Mildred, for godsakes."

The woman yawned. "Needs a doctor in Atlanta. She's got the clap."

Maglio brushed a few beads of sweat from his upper lip. "Give me a couple a minutes, will ya?"

"You're gonna have to pay for the office visit," Mildred warned. "And the penicillin."

"See, this is what I go through," Maglio said once we were alone again. "The thing of it is, it's always like this. Never stops. Never."

I leaned forward trying to capture Maglio's full attention. "You know I'm watching out for your niece until she starts work at Universal in Orlando, right?"

"Yeah, and I really appreciate it. Doin' a hell of a job."

"Twyla's with me a lot," I said. "You know that, don't you?"

"Yeah. Which is good. It's a good thing."

"Neither one of us wants her hurt."

Maglio spread his arms. "I told ya it's all over. The contract's been pulled, and there ain't gonna be nobody screwin' with nobody no more."

"Glad to hear that," I said. "But what I don't understand is why a couple of Dominicans would want me dead."

Maglio looked at me like I was from Uranus. "Who said they wanted you dead?"

"What?"

"Are you dense or somethin'? The target was always that snitch bastard, One Nut Waters. If he didn't clamp himself on you like a jockstrap, there wouldn't be no problem. He'd be dead and you'd be helpin' my niece get a new start in Florida."

I felt a rush of relief—or was it stupidity? The Hispanic assassins had nothing to do with the Kurios case or the *Book of Nathan*. It was sheer happenstance that Twyla, Maurice, Four Putt Gonzales, and I had been hanging around with a man who years ago had kicked the mob in the groin. When Doc made an unexpected appearance in Orlando, he apparently jogged the memory of a few Philly gangsters who had taken up retirement in the area. The bloodbath that followed was all about payback and it was a miracle I was still alive.

"Why didn't you ask Doc Waters to come here?" I asked. "You could have told all this to his face."

"The guy's been runnin' scared for years. Think he'd come here knowin' I was connected?"

Mildred reappeared carrying two sheets of paper that she slapped on Maglio's desk. They were legal-looking documents with a few words marked by a yellow highlighter: lewd acts, exposure of genitalia, cease and desist.

"Besides," Maglio said and pushed the papers aside, "I wouldn't want that piece of garbage stinkin' up my place. So, you go back and tell that fart I saved his ass and the one nut he's got left. You be sure an' tell him that."

Chapter 19

A thin layer of smog caught the early rays of Thursday's sun and turned the Jersey horizon into a painter's palette. It was six thirty a.m. and I was too exhausted to catch the irony of how the coupling of Mother Nature and air pollution could produce something so beautiful. Thanks to Doug Kool and Manny Maglio, the only contemplation I could handle was where to find a strong cup of coffee and a newspaper. I was about to take another unexpected trip to Florida, and that impending reality along with yesterday's meeting with Maglio had put me in a stupor.

I walked three blocks to a convenience store and bought a large Brazilian Brew plus a *New York Times*. Maglio's people had wasted no time. The front-page headline read:

FOUND SHOT IN CAMDEN, NJ
Dominican Drug Dealers
Linked to Orlando Bombing

The paper reported that each man had been killed execution-style, a single bullet through the back of the skull. An anonymous phone call had led police to the murder scene—the caller also claiming the two men were responsible for the Orlando airport disaster. Traces of C-4 were found in the trunk of the car. An unnamed FBI spokesman said the explosive had characteristics that matched samples taken from the Continental terminal blast. Asked if the Jordanian graduate student being held in connection with the airport bombing would be released, the FBI said authorities were checking to determine if there were any connection between the student and the Dominicans.

At seven o'clock, I was back at the Gateway and Yigal Rosenblatt drove to the front entrance exactly as planned. If it weren't for an interest in talking to Conway Kyzwoski's wife, I would never have balled myself up in the backseat of the lawyer's Ford Taurus. A nonstop flight out of Newark would have been the logical way to transport Twyla to Florida. But since Zeus's lawyer was reluctantly returning to Orlando, and since widow Kyzwoski lived in a town close to the Route 95 interstate, I hitched a ride with Yigal and Twyla, who was half asleep in the front passenger seat. Twelve hours later, we were cruising into South Carolina.

"Take the next exit," I told Yigal after we'd traveled about a hundred miles through the Palmetto State. "Follow the signs to Goose Creek."

"Why are we stopping here?" Twyla asked. I knew she was fixated on Universal Studios, and anything that sidetracked us from getting to Orlando would make her unhappy.

"Goose Creek's where Conway Kyzwoski lives—or used to live," I said.

"Oh, God, poor Conway," moaned Twyla with a kind of sadness that comes from losing one's pet dog, an intimate friend—or a client.

"This won't take long. I have a few questions for Kyzwoski's wife."

"So sorry for her." It looked like Twyla had pushed the rewind on her mental TiVo and was playing back that memorable moment when she met Conway's wife at the Wayside Motel. "Lost her husband and all. Glad she's got the Bible thing going. She's got plenty of faith, which is what you need if your spouse gets run over by a sausage."

"Very religious woman," Yigal reminded Twyla and me. "Faith will help her heal even if she's not Jewish."

My memory flashed a picture of the bland-looking Ida spouting scripture in her muumuu just as Yigal hooked left off of a main east-west highway and onto a backwoods road.

"Pull in here," I said, pointing to a dirt parking lot in front of a run-down shack that housed the Pringletown Video and Bait Shop. Yigal braked to a stop, and I ventured into the shabby store hoping to find someone who could tell me where we were and where Goose Creek happened to be.

The shop was empty except for a puny woman wearing an apron who sat behind an antique cash register.

"Happen to know where I can find the Paradise Mobile Estates?" I asked. "It's a trailer park in Goose Creek."

The lady's agate eyes scanned me from top to bottom. "Get back on

I-26, head east, and you'll see signs for Goose Creek. The trailer park's on the main road not far off from Sonic."

"Thanks." I bought a pack of Twizzlers as a way of showing my gratitude.

The woman wagged her finger at me. "You're the one who was on TV. Talkin' about your wiener, wasn't you?"

There are certain inalienable rights that come with being anonymous and that suits me just fine. So, when an ABC news team had asked me for a couple of comments about the Kielbasavan incident, it never occurred to me that my remarks would be beamed coast to coast. But they were and I unwittingly became an icon of stupidity even in the backwaters of America.

"It wasn't my wiener," I said softly. "It was actually a kielbasa."

"A what?"

"Never mind."

"So if it wasn't your wiener, why was you talkin' about it?"

"I made a mistake," I admitted. "I should have kept my mouth shut."

"If it weren't your wiener, that's what you should-a done."

I buried the urge to throw the old lady into the Pringletown night crawler bin, barged out of the shop, and climbed into Yigal's Taurus.

Fifteen minutes later, we spotted the sign: PARADISE MOBILE ESTATES: A FRIENDLY PLACE FOR FRIENDLY PEOPLE. Yigal turned left and we surveyed rows of doublewides, all of which were alike except for the piles of junk in front of each.

"Excuse me," I said to a kid who looked no more than thirteen, but sauntered around like a punk twice his age. "Do you know where the Kyzwoskis live?"

The South Carolina sun had long gone and the kid's dark skin blended into the night.

"Waccha want Ephraim for?"

"You know A-Frame?" Twyla squealed and turned on the car's dome light. "Where's his house, honey?"

With Twyla's torso fully illuminated, the kid's temperament turned. It's hard to look surly when you're wearing a smile that travels from one pierced ear to the other. Without lifting his eyes from Twyla's chest, the kid gave us directions to the Kyzwoski residence.

Yigal rolled through Paradise Mobile Estates searching for a white trailer with a partially dismantled Buick in the front yard. Recalling that Conway was an auto repairman, I guessed the remains of the car had to be a legacy to the late Mr. Kyzwoski. When we found the place, I told Yigal and Twyla to stay in the Taurus while I conferred with Kyzwoski's widow. The last thing I needed was a confrontation between Twyla and Mrs. K. who, I remembered, was a woman scorned.

I maneuvered my way around piles of litter and knocked on the Kyzwoski door. A-Frame's brother, Noah, answered, skittered away, and returned with Ida who looked as happy to see me as a repo man.

"I'm sorry to bother you, Mrs. Kyzwoski," I opened. "My name is Rick Bullock. We met in Orlando—"

"I know who you are."

"Well, I wanted to stop by—and, uh, well, I'm very sorry about your loss."

"You din't come all the way here to tell me that."

"I was driving to Florida and happened to notice Goose Creek wasn't that far out of the way—"

"What is it you want?"

While I was struggling to fabricate a reason that wouldn't get the Kyzwoski door slammed in my face, Ephraim scooted up to the front door on a battered bicycle.

"Ain't you the one that got my pappy kilt?" he asked. He wore a stained tee-shirt that bulged at the beltline—Conway's kid, all right.

"No," I said. "There was an accident and I just happened to be there when your father died."

"Yeah, well, mama says pappy got kilt 'cause of you."

What I wanted to scream back was: *If your redneck pappy hadn't been shadowing me, he'd still be spitting tobacco and making home brew.* But instead I turned my attention back to Ida.

"If I could have just a moment, Mrs. Kyzwoski," I said. "Without the children, I mean."

Ida whacked the two boys away, then pushed open a ripped screen door and nodded me into her home. What was supposed to be the living room was a trash heap except for two adornments. First, a frosted acrylic crucifix was standing tall on a shabby end table. It was lit from the inside and its multicolor glow gave the cross a kind of disco look. The second was a large color print of Jesus and a host of angels caught up in a swirl of white clouds. A tiny spotlight tacked to the ceiling made the picture sparkle.

I couldn't help but feel a tad sorry for the late Conway Kyzwoski. His living quarters had been a shrine and his wife was having a love affair with another man. Maybe Kyzwoski shelled out a few dollars for some extramarital attention now and then because he couldn't find what he needed at home. What chance would a mortal have when competing with the Son of God?

Ida motioned to an upholstered chair that had long ago lost most of its stuffing.

"You know I was with Conway when he died," I began.

"I do."

"He said some things before he passed away." Passed away were not words that went with Conway Kyzwoski. Croaked would have been more fitting.

Ida's hard shell started to crack. "Like what?"

"Well, at the end, he said he didn't want the boys to know what really happened in New Brunswick."

"Go on."

"He wanted me to tell you something, too."

Ida bit her lip, sensing that whatever was coming next was the real reason I was sitting in her living room.

"He said I should tell you he wasn't as religious as you are, but he still did his work for Jesus."

I saw tears well up in Ida's eyes. My words hit home.

"How much do you know about what my husband was doing in New Jersey?"

"Not much. All Conway told me was that he was working for a pro-life group." That wasn't exactly Kyzwoski's message, but when coupled with information from Judith Russet, it rang true.

"So did y'all tell that to the police?"

"No."

"Why not?"

"I don't know," I answered honestly. "I guess because it could have stirred up a lot of questions. As far as the police are concerned, Conway's death was an accident. But there's more to it than that, isn't there?"

"For a change, he was trying to do the right thing." Two lines of tears traveled south.

"By following me? Taking pictures of everything I did? Everywhere I went?"

"He did it because Arita Almiras asked me to help. I was the one who talked Conway into spying on you. It was me who got him involved with Almiras."

Bewilderment didn't even come close to describing my reaction. Who the hell was Arita Almiras? "I'm sorry, Mrs. Kyzwoski, I'm lost."

Ida shifted in her seat. She wore the same style muumuu that she had on when I first saw her at the Wayside. "Proverbs says that he who so committeth adultery destroyeth his soul. Did y'all ever hear that?"

"No, ma'am. I don't think so."

"Conway committed adultery. Any number of times far as I can tell."

At least once, I thought, recalling Conway's hairy foot protruding from Twyla's bed at the Wayside Motel.

"What I did was to push him into a corner," Ida went on. "Like he said, he din't believe the same way I did. Even so, I told him if he was to stay with me and the boys, he had to do penance. That's when I made him do the extra work with Almiras."

"The extra work—was it for *Quia Vita*?"

"No. *Quia Vita* wasn't why Conway went to New Jersey."

"Visio Dei?"

"The rich part of *Quia Vita*? Never had nothin' to do with them, and I know they wouldn't be bothered with people like me or Conway."

"So it was this Arita Almiras who asked your husband to follow me?"

"Had to take time off from work to do it," said Ida. "But Conway went along with what Almiras wanted 'cause I forced him to. My husband wasn't all bad, in spite of what most people think."

I have no idea what turned the Kyzwoski living room into a confessional. Ida's insides were suddenly spilling out, and I was sitting in a bug-infested chair taking it all in like a priest. "How is it that you're connected to Almiras?"

"Shouldn't be sayin' much about this. But it seems Almiras isn't what he's made out to be. The dark places of the earth are full of the habitations of cruelty. Psalm 74."

"Could we go back a step or two? Why is this Almiras interested in me in the first place?"

"Got something he wants," Ida explained. "Some kind of computer disk. Conway's job was to take pictures of you wherever you went and send 'em to one of Almiras's assistants. Then the others searched places where you might-a hid the disk."

Manny Maglio had taken care of two men who had tried twice to walk over me as a way of getting to Doc Waters. Conway Kyzwoski had been tracking me since my memorable stay at the Wayside Motel. Now Ida gave me the unnerving news that there were others picking through my personals. "Others?"

"You need to understand Almiras wants that disk bad. That's why it wasn't just Conway who was workin' on you."

I was having trouble getting my head around her words. "Help me understand what's going on."

Ida drew a deep breath. "There's another group that's different than *Quia Vita*. A lot different."

"You belong to this other group?"

Ida nodded.

"And Arita Almiras?"

"He heads it up."

"When you say the groups are different. How so?"

Ida took time to phrase an answer. "Almiras is more about action and less about talk."

"I see," I said, not seeing anything. Action could cover a lot of territory, including hospitals and autopsy rooms. How much danger was I in?

"The Almiras Society is what it's called."

"Go on."

"The society does things *Quia Vita* doesn't."

I was starting to understand. The society sounded like an extremist faction that broke away from Judith Russet's crowd. A clique made up of those who weren't big on discussion but high on disruption. "Things like what?"

"Puttin' abortionist names on the Internet. Makin' sure neighbors know if they got a baby killer livin' on their street. Things like that."

"The woman who runs *Quia Vita*—"

"Russet."

"What does she know about the Almiras Society?"

"From what I hear, she tries not to know much," said Ida. "Probably don't ask a lot of questions because Arita Almiras isn't someone you want to offend."

I couldn't picture Russet worried about offending anyone. "You think she's afraid of this Almiras?"

"Most people are."

If Russet were afraid of Almiras then this had to be one menacing fanatic. "I'd like to meet Arita Almiras. How would I find him?"

"Don't know."

"You don't know? But he runs the organization you belong to."

"It's not the kind of society where we elect officers and have meetings. We're connected by what we believe—about savin' babies. Far as I know, most of us in the society have never seen Almiras."

Seemed impossible until I remembered the wizard in *The Wizard of Oz*. Intimidating until Toto pulled back the curtain. What I needed to do was find the Almiras Society's home base and then part the drapes. Exposing Almiras might be the only way to keep him from nipping at my heels—or chewing off my head.

"Do you know what he looks like?"

"No. He has a couple of assistants. They're the ones who send us information about special assignments."

"What kind of assignments?"

"Usually ones the society pays for."

"Did you get paid for your trip to the Wayside Motel in Orlando?"

"Conrad probably already told you about all that," Ida incorrectly guessed. "Yes, we got paid—but not much."

"Why were you sent there?"

"To watch you. At the time, it was me who was working for the society—not Conway. When he got tangled up with the woman you was with—well, that got things off track."

A flash of anger and sorrow wrinkled Ida's face.

"How could Almiras possibly know we'd be at the Wayside Motel?" I asked, not expecting Ida would answer. She didn't need to. I was beginning to unravel the mystery on my own.

"Don't know. We just do what we're told. Once you left the motel, my orders were to follow you as long as you was in Orlando."

"Did you?"

"Not right off. Got interrupted for a time after Conway and me had a disagreement of sorts."

I said nothing about how the Kyzwoski disagreement had cost me part of a night's sleep at the Wayside. "After you checked out of the motel, you tracked me down."

"Caught up with y'all at the jail when you was meetin' with Dr. Kurios's killer. But you was on your own a lot of the time before then. Almiras was unhappy about that from what I was told."

"And after Orlando?"

Ida's remorse choked her up momentarily. Her feelings for Conway obviously still ran deep. "That's when I convinced the society to use Conway to keep tabs on what you was up to."

"You didn't go with him to New Jersey?"

"Stayed here with the kids. Conway drove his truck up north, and did his work with a video camera the society gave him."

Ida's expression told me she was about finished. "Thank you for being so honest, Mrs. Kyzwoski," I said.

"Tellin' you all this 'cause of what happened to Conway. I think he done a lot of things that ain't right. I want to make up for whatever he done that's wrong. Plus, you didn't tell the police why Conway was in New Jersey. So, I owe you somethin'."

"I understand."

Ida hoisted herself out of her chair. "Don't think you do, Mr. Bullock. Understand, I mean. That's as much as I can say right now."

"Well, thank you, ma'am." I followed Ida to the torn screen door. "Just one more thing. Arita Almiras—I never heard a name like that before."

"It isn't the man's real name. Arita and Almiras are angels. Don't know what Arita means but Almiras is supposed to be the angel who's the master of bein' invisible."

"Thanks again for giving me your time," I said with sincerity. "I hope I have an opportunity to meet Mr. Almiras. He and I have a lot to talk about."

"If you get the chance, you shouldn't let it pass. It's what the society's motto says."

"Motto?"

"In Christ's language, it goes: *Occasio aegre offertur, facile amittitur.*"

I spun around. "What did you say?"

"*Occasio aegre offertur, facile amittitur.* Means an opportunity is offered with difficulty but lost with ease. Ever hear that before?"

"Yes." A bolt of electricity ran up my spine. "Yes, I have."

Chapter 20

Ten minutes after leaving Paradise Mobile Estates, we were lost again. Yigal pulled into a run-down, two-pump gas station hoping a grease-coated attendant might get us back on course.

I rolled down my back window. "Which way to Charleston Airport?"

The attendant said nothing.

"The airport," I repeated. "How do we get there?"

The attendant moved closer to the car and looked inside. When one of the station's floodlights gave the man a decent peek at Twyla, he blurted out directions through a mostly toothless grin.

"Thanks," I said, and Yigal started pulling away.

"Hold it!" the attendant yelled. He was still holding the passenger-side door handle.

"Something we can do for you?" I asked.

"Wasn't you on TV? That wiener thing—"

It was more than I could take. I shrugged off the attendant, shut the car window, and told Yigal to head for the airport. Fast.

"You're famous, you know," Yigal informed me.

"You are, Bullet!" Twyla chimed in. "Isn't it something what a sausage can do?"

Yigal nodded in agreement and asked, "Why the airport?"

I could have told Yigal that the conversation with Ida had given me new coordinates in my search for who really killed Benjamin Kurios. But I said nothing that might lead to a long, protracted discussion.

"I need a favor," I said to Yigal.

"Okay."

"I have to get back to New Brunswick. Unexpected Gateway business."

"You're not goin' to Florida?" Twyla squealed. I couldn't tell if she was disappointed or elated.

I gave her a reassuring pat on her shoulder and kept on talking to Yigal. "If I can get a flight out of Charleston tonight, I'm going to leave Twyla in your hands."

Yigal's eyes twinkled. I knew he was picturing one hundred and one things his hands could do, some of which were illegal in South Carolina.

"Listen," I implored. "This is very important. If I bail out, I want you to promise me you'll finish the drive to Orlando. No side trips. No distractions."

"I can do that," Yigal said with far too much enthusiasm. "Yes, I can."

I turned to Twyla. "Try to understand something. I'm on the line here. You have to be in Orlando tomorrow and ready to start work on Monday."

"I know. I'm so excited!"

I leaned forward and breathed into Yigal's ear. "This is all on your shoulders. Can I count on you?"

"Yes, you can."

In the deep recess of my exhausted brain, I heard Manny Maglio growl. I recoiled into the backseat. "On second thought, this isn't a good idea." A flight from Charleston to New Jersey tonight would give me all day tomorrow and Saturday to chase the leads I had picked up in Ida's trailer. On the other hand, riding another six hours in the rear of Yigal's car, pulling an overnight in Orlando, and depositing Twyla in a safe location would keep Maglio off my back. I was five seconds from telling Yigal to forget the airport when Twyla said, "Getting the job at Universal is the best thing that ever happened to me. Nothing's going to stop me from starting work on time. Nothing."

There was a zeal in her voice that pushed me into saying, "All right."

Fifteen minutes later, I was standing at the Delta counter listening to an agent tell me that if I cleared security without a hitch, I might make an 8:49 that would get me to Newark with a stopover in Atlanta. I took the ticket and phoned Yigal that the flight was a done deal.

I had no trouble with security until one of the TSA workers yelled, "Hey, mister! Didn't I see you on TV?"

I raced toward the Delta gate.

A half-hour flight delay and a long limo ride from LaGuardia to New Brunswick put me in bed at three a.m. My alarm woke me at eight thirty and after a quick shower and a cup of coffee, I was on the phone. First call was to Yigal whose cell dumped me into his voice mail. I tried the lawyer's office and got a recorded message informing me that Gafstein & Rosenblatt wouldn't open until nine. My anxiety began to spike.

The next call was to *Quia Vita*'s Manhattan office. A receptionist gave me the usual runaround. Judith Russet was tied up.

"Tell her Rick Bullock's on the line." The receptionist put me on hold, but not for long. Russet picked up, her icy tone laced with fury.

"Proud of yourself?" she asked.

"What?"

"I'll give you this. After our last conversation, I started thinking maybe you didn't have the disk. I should have known better. From the start, this was about more than extorting a few million dollars, wasn't it? It was about playing me for a fool."

I huffed out half a word, but Russet rolled on.

"No more games. We want confirmation the money made it to your account."

"What money?" A meaningless question since I already had the answer. Whoever was selling Le Campion's disk wasn't treading water. The auction for the *Book of Nathan* CD was apparently over. *Quia Vita* had cast the winning bid and was about to acquire the motive for Benjamin Kurios's murder.

"Come on, Bullock," Russet shot back. "There's no point in keeping up this ridiculous pretense. We did what you asked. Sent five transfers of five hundred thousand dollars for each of five installments of Le Campion's notes you emailed us. There's a total of two point five million sitting in your Cayman Island account."

"When did you wire the money?"

"We're done with the first half of our arrangement. You got your asking price. Give us the disk and we'll make our final payment."

Both Abraham Arcontius and Russet had spelled out how the deal was to be done. So, I wasn't surprised by what I was hearing—only surprised by how fast the sale was being transacted. "I don't have a Cayman Island account."

"For the love of God, you're a millionaire! And we're ready to double what we've already paid you. What more do you want? Give us the CD. If it's the real thing, you get another two point five million."

"Don't wire another dime. Not until you hear what I have to say."

"When you're finished with your charade, let me know."

"I told you before—I don't have the damn disk. I never did."

Russet came through with such force that my phone seemed to vibrate. "You're still trying to convince me you're the crusading public defender? You are who you are. A low-life extortionist!"

"I have nothing to extort with," I yelled. "My only interest in the disk is how it might help a homeless man."

My rejoinder brought Russet back from her boiling point. "And the only thing I'm interested in is the *Book of Nathan* disk. Your little campaign for justice means nothing to me."

"I don't believe that. Didn't from the first time I talked to you. You're not the type to let an innocent man get the ax."

"You're using the man who killed Benjamin Kurios as a cover, which makes what you're doing even more disgusting."

"Goddamnit. I don't have the *Book of Nathan* disk. And I doubt Miklos Zeusenoerdorf ever killed anybody."

"This conversation is over."

And it almost was until I threw back two words that kept Russet from slamming down the phone.

"Arita Almiras."

Russet said nothing, but I could hear a slight wheeze.

"That's why I called you this morning. To ask you about Almiras. Some way, somehow, I think he's connected to the Kurios murder."

I heard a mix of surprise, confusion, and maybe even a sprig of concern. "You're moving into very, very perilous territory."

"That's territory I've been calling home for some time. Look, if Almiras is responsible for what happened to Kurios, then Zeusenoerdorf is taking a hit for something he didn't do. I'm ready to go to the police, but before that happens I thought you and I should talk."

"We'll talk only if you prove to me you have nothing to do with the *Book of Nathan*."

"How am I supposed to do that? I can't prove I don't have something that I've never had. Look, maybe you should do a character check. I'm not the money type."

"We already did that."

I was getting more of a once-over than a pole dancer at one of Maglio's strip clubs. "Then you should know I'm telling you the truth."

I could hear Russet take a deep breath—or maybe it was a sigh of resignation. "What do you want to know about Almiras?"

"He runs something called the Almiras Society. It's connected to *Quia Vita*, isn't it?"

"No," she stated emphatically. "It's a stand-alone group with no ties to my organization. None whatsoever."

"Isn't it true most members of that society are also *Quia Vita* members?"

"I have no idea."

"I think you do. I just talked to a woman who wears both hats. She's *Quia Vita* and she's Almiras Society, which says to me that you're blood relatives. So if the Almiras crowd gets implicated in the Kurios killing, *Quia Vita's* going to be answering a lot of questions."

I could almost feel Russet leaning into the phone. "I don't know Arita Almiras. In fact, I don't know anyone who knows his real identity. But this much is known—he has powerful connections and access to money. He's someone who could do you considerable harm."

Russet wasn't just warning me to watch my step with Almiras, she was confirming my theory that the man could do damage to *Quia Vita* if he were exposed. "Suppose Almiras and company get charged with banging the brains out of this country's favorite evangelist?" I asked. "What happens to your organization when it gets roped into that kind of investigation?"

Russet came back with an unexpected disclosure. "If Almiras had anything to do with Benjamin's death, then he most likely would own Le Campion's disk. That's not the case."

"How do you know?"

"Because we think he's one of the people who's been trying to buy the CD."

This came as a surprise. I thought there were just two potential buyers—Silverstein and *Quia Vita*. If Russet were right, there was a third horse in the race. "You were bidding against Almiras for the book?"

"It doesn't matter. We're the first to put a down payment on the CD. Now we have exclusive rights. Another two point five million and the disk is ours."

Russet's right-to-life convictions were so rock hard that she had tunnel vision. But she was also smart. Too smart not to consider the possibility *Quia Vita* was being conned. "How do you know Le Campion's notes haven't been sold for two point five million a pop to anyone else looking to buy the *Book of Nathan*?"

"The notes themselves have value," she answered. "For that reason, it's possible others may have bought them. But the notes have little credibility without the book's text to back them up. The text is encrypted and can't be duplicated. Which means only one buyer walks away with the prize and that buyer is *Quia Vita*."

"How can you be sure?"

"The seller appears to be more sympathetic to our cause than others who have an interest in the *Book of Nathan*."

There were probably other guarantees plugged into the deal *Quia Vita* cut for the purchase of the full text. Whatever those were, Russet was convinced she was about to become the owner of Henri Le Campion's translation. "When are you supposed to get the disk?"

Russet hesitated. She had already dispensed more information than I thought I could extract in a phone call. "That's not something I'm going to discuss."

"I told you—I don't want the disk. I want whoever is milking you for five million bucks. Whoever that is probably owns the foot that I need to kick down Miklos Zeusenoerdorf's jailhouse door."

"Sorry. I can't take this any further."

I had only one more card to play, but it was my high trump. "Let's make a deal. You give me the specifics about when and where you're going to pick up the disk and I tell you who Arita Almiras is."

Russet went silent. Then: "There's no way you could know—"

I hadn't planned to put the spotlight on my theory so soon. However, as someone recently reminded me, opportunity is lost with ease. "Arita Almiras is Abraham Arcontius."

"That's impossible!" Russet shouted.

"I'm not one hundred percent sure," I admitted. "But I've enough evidence to make a pretty strong case."

There was an uncharacteristic rattle in Russet's voice. "You don't understand—Arcontius doesn't have anything to do with the Almiras Society."

"Why? Because he's Arthur Silverstein's trusted sidekick?"

"That's not the—"

"He's a mole," I interrupted. "The fox in Silverstein's chicken coop. Think about it. Arcontius intercepts information sent to Silverstein by his pro-choice friends and then uses it to map out his own society's game plan."

Russet said nothing, apparently weighing my words. When she resumed the conversation, her words were missing their usual sharp edge. "What are you planning to do—expose him?"

"I want Miklos Zeusenoerdorf freed," I said. "If Arcontius gets outted in the process, so be it."

Russet took a deep breath. "I'll call you later this morning. There are people I need to talk to before we continue."

Chapter 21

While waiting for my second conversation of the day with Judith Russet, I called Yigal Rosenblatt's cell and was bounced into the lawyer's voice mailbox—again. I left a message reminding him that if Twyla wasn't gainfully employed by Universal Orlando on Monday at nine a.m., he would be learning a lot about radical reconstructive surgery.

Shortly before noon, Russet was back on the phone. What I heard was a woman who sounded like she had her moxie extracted.

"We can't have you publicly exposing Arcontius. So we're willing to negotiate."

"Why the change of heart?"

"Because Arcontius isn't Arita Almiras."

There was no uncertainty in Russet's statement. "Really? And you know that because—"

"Because Abraham has been working undercover for years. Not for the Almiras Society. For *Quia Vita*."

This I didn't expect. It was one of those unanticipated lightning bolts that frazzle pre-conceived ideas. "He works for you?"

"Yes."

"I'll be goddamned!" Of course! It was Arcontius who sent the note to Russet the night Doc and I crept into her Visio Dei meeting. Doug had told Arcontius we'd be infiltrating the session and he fed that information to Russet.

"Out of the blue you call me up and blow Arcontius's cover," I said. "Why?"

"Because you're on the verge of pulling him out of the closet. The right kind of detective work will prove that Arcontius is actually a *Quia Vita* operative. If that were to happen, our organization could be greatly compromised."

Compromised was an understatement, I thought. Ruined was more accurate.

"In a week, maybe two, Abraham's going to leave his position," Russet continued. I figured it was information that was supposed to make me feel better about keeping quiet. No reason to talk about a little espionage if the secret agent was no longer on the job.

"You mean he's going to quit? Just because you say so?"

"It will be a medical leave of absence," Russet explained. "Abraham will be sick for a few weeks and later on, he'll tender his resignation. For health reasons."

I wondered what kind of trumped-up illness Arcontius was about to contract or whether *Quia Vita* would make the slimy rat bastard sick for real. "You'll miss your deep-cover spy."

"Abraham hasn't been as effective as he once was. It could be his age or maybe he's just tired."

"Or maybe he's been wearing three hats instead of two."

"Meaning what?"

"How certain are you that Abe isn't running the Almiras Society? What if he's been skimming the cream from his undercover exploits and feeding it to the Almiras crowd. All *Quia Vita* has been getting the last couple of years is low-fat milk."

"That's ridiculous." I heard little conviction.

"Is it? Look, Silverstein thinks Arcontius works for him. You think Abraham works for you. But didn't it ever occur to you that Abe could be pushing his own agenda?"

"Out of the question."

"You know the man. Doesn't he think your organization is too soft? Hasn't he been on your case to turn *Quia Vita* into a more militant organization?"

It was pure supposition. I took Russet's silence as a "yes."

"Ida Kyzwoski told me the Almiras Society has connections to big money. Well, supposing Arcontius found a way to tap into some of Silverstein's fortune. Would a billionaire miss a few million? Done the right way, maybe not."

"You're reaching," charged Russet.

"Possibly. But I think I'm cozying up to the truth. Abraham Arcontius. Almiras Society. Same initials. Same man."

"Arcontius is our problem," said Judith. "We'll handle him. What we're asking you to do is to keep all of this to yourself."

"And in exchange, you'll do what?"

"Give you what you said you wanted. Information about when and where the *Book of Nathan* disk is to be handed over to us."

I reacted too quickly, which made it obvious I had been anticipating Russet's offer. "I'll think about it. But first, I need you to answer a question. Le Campion's notes that you bought for two point five million—did they tell you anything about the *Book of Nathan*'s take on abortion?"

Russet held back an answer. She was trying to figure out where I was heading. "Henri interpreted certain parts of the book. But until we see the translated text firsthand, we won't know how accurate his notes are."

"But whatever he put in his notes got your attention."

"Our conclusions are likely to be different from Henri's. Like I said—we won't know that until we get the disk and use the translation key to pull apart the encrypted text."

"Henri's conclusions—what are they?"

"I'm not getting into that." Russet punched out her words like bullets.

Maybe a little provocation would keep the dialogue alive. "I take that to mean Henri found something in the book that won't sit well with the pro-life world."

"Le Campion's notes aren't explicit."

"Explicit enough to convince *Quia Vita* to buy those notes and the *Book of Nathan* translation for five million. Not a bad investment if the disk turns out to be bad news for your organization. Buy it, then bury it."

I could feel Russet's irritation boil into anger. I knew she wanted to tell me to go to hell, which is where she thought I was destined to end up anyway. But I had picked at a scab that caused an automatic defensive reaction.

"If you think the book dismisses ensoulment, you're wrong."

"Interesting," I said. "Then Le Campion's notes must have told you when ensoulment actually starts."

Russet was getting increasingly careful with her words. "In a way."

"And?"

"His notes are ours. We're not about to give you or anyone else free access to that information."

"Here's what I think. If the notes back up *Quia Vita*'s position that ensoulment begins at conception, then you're probably already planning a national information campaign that can be launched when you get the disk. If the notes say otherwise, you can't wait to throw Henri's translation in the furnace."

It was another stick in Russet's eye and it poked out a few words she probably should have kept to herself. "Ensoulment is a process, not something that's switched on at conception. At least that's the way Henri Le Campion interprets the *Book of Nathan*."

"You can't be ecstatic over that bit of news," I said. "After Mr. Sperm does his thing to Ms. Egg, whatever's created is soulless."

"We're created with a receptacle, Bullock. According to LeCampion's interpretation of the book, what we put into that receptacle determines the level of ensoulment. That's as much as I'm going to tell you."

"Fascinating," I replied. And actually it was fascinating, although hardly intriguing enough to justify killing a man or even coughing up five million bucks. "So, where does that leave you and *Quia Vita*? If we're conceived with a receptacle and not a soul, that sort of weakens your pro-life argument, doesn't it?"

"It doesn't change the fact that personhood starts at conception."

"You can be a person without a soul?"

"Yes. People are created with the capacity to become ensouled. That capacity is what defines personhood and personhood begins at conception."

"Unless the *Book of Nathan* also blows that assumption apart."

"Speculating on what's in the book and what isn't doesn't deal with the matter at hand," said Russet. "What we need right now is your word that you'll keep the information you have about Arcontius confidential."

"How do you know I'll keep whatever promise I make?"

"I told you before, we're quite good at learning as much as we can about the people who can help us—or hurt us."

I recalled Conway Kyzwoski's video production featuring Rick Bullock. "You and a lot of other people."

"Of course, as trustworthy as we think you are, we still need insurance that you won't create—a problem for us."

"Insurance?"

"We have information about your involvement with Manuel Maglio. Pictures of you entering and leaving his office in Edison. Copies of checks you received from one of his holding companies. Spending time at a place called Climax isn't likely to further your career."

Russet apparently didn't understand that managing a men's shelter isn't on par with running IBM. A few Polaroids of a visit to an Edison nudie bar would hardly be enough to get me fired. A payment or two from Manny Maglio might be a different story—but my board of directors would most likely let me off that hook as well because it's a lot easier to forgive a transgression than to go through the agony of hiring a new shelter director. Even though Russet's threat meant nothing, I was rankled by the tactic she was using.

"Is blackmail something *Quia Vita* does often or just on special occasions?" I asked, trying to keep the reins on my anger. "And by the way, Maglio's money was reimbursement for travel expenses."

"That doesn't matter," Russet said. "Just understand we have what it takes to damage your reputation." I picked up an undercurrent of embarrassment that I took to mean the *Quia Vita* chief wished she weren't wading in this kind of muck. "Everything stays under wraps as long as you stay quiet about Arcontius."

"This intimidation nonsense isn't just demeaning to you and *Quia Vita*, it's totally pointless," I said heatedly. "I gave you my word and if you've really done your homework, you know I don't back off a promise. Now tell me when and where you'll be picking up the CD."

Russet didn't waste time. "We're supposed to get delivery of the *Book of Nathan* disk tomorrow night. It's to be given to two of our Visio Dei officers."

"Who's going to make the delivery? The thief who took the disk?"

"No. A middleman named Osman Seleucus. Once we're in contact with Seleucus, we'll be told when and how to send a second two point five million to the Cayman Islands."

The news came as a setback. I had hoped there wouldn't be an intermediary involved. "Osman Seleucus—what do you know about him?"

"Nothing. He's probably just a hired hand."

"What about your two Visio Dei people who'll be picking up the disk? How will Seleucus recognize them?"

"As part of the deal, we posted their names and pictures on our main Web site. That was done earlier today—their photos are the last entries on a page we use to honor our volunteer leaders."

It was becoming more apparent that whoever was selling Le Campion's CD was both smart and crafty. "How will you let me know when the disk gets handed over?"

"One of our people will call you on your cell phone. You're to keep your distance until the transaction is finished. After that, you can follow Mr. Seleucus or take whatever action you want as long as you don't implicate *Quia Vita*."

"Where's all this going to happen?"

The answer was matter-of-fact to Judith Russet and staggering to me. "Ellis Island."

"Ellis Island?"

"Yes. Tomorrow night."

"There's a testimonial dinner for Arthur Silverstein tomorrow night. At the Registry Hall on Ellis Island."

"Which is where Osman Seleucus is to turn over the *Book of Nathan* disk."

Chapter 22

Noon. My Manny Maglio apprehension needle was about to cross into the panic zone when Yigal Rosenblatt finally called. Yes, he made it to Orlando. Yes, Twyla was fine. And—oh, by the way—"she's staying at my place."

I wondered what the lawyer's nest must look like. It couldn't be pretty—not if the interior design were as out-of-kilter as Zeusenoerdorf's defense attorney.

"You're going to get Twyla to Universal Studios on Monday," I reminded Yigal.

"I will."

"Before nine a.m."

"I'll drive her there," Yigal assured me.

"And for the rest of the weekend, stay low. Maybe hang out at your place."

"Okay," he said too quickly.

"And turn your damn cell on. I tried reaching you all morning. No answer."

The lawyer pledged to keep his phone at the ready. Apparently it had been turned off last night and for most of the morning. Seems Twyla and Yigal decided to sleep late. I didn't ask for details. Better not to know.

"If there's a problem, call me."

"I'll call."

"It's important. If anything smells funny, get on the phone."

"I can do that."

"I should be reachable all weekend. Except maybe tomorrow night. I'm not sure what the cell reception is like on Ellis Island."

Yigal's reaction was uncharacteristically slow. "Ellis Island?"

"Yeah, tomorrow night."

"Why Ellis Island?" Yigal's tone was even and deliberate. I could feel his sense of concern.

"Going fishing," I answered. "I'll call Sunday and let you know if I got lucky."

After I disconnected, the change in Yigal's tone of voice nagged at me. Maybe there was more going on underneath the hopped-up attorney's exterior than I thought.

Doug called just after lunch. "You in Orlando yet?"

"Getting there," I said, trying to sound farther away than in my office, which was just an hour southwest of the Hudson River.

"What do you mean, 'getting there?' Didn't you fly? I told you Manny was good for the tickets."

"We're driving."

Doug instantly sounded concerned. "What does 'we're' mean?"

"Remember Yigal Rosenblatt—Zeus's lawyer?"

"Yeah, I remember. What's going on, Bullet?"

"Nothing," I replied just a tad too easily. My lie needed some pumping up. "Yigal had to drive back to Orlando, so Twyla and I hitched a ride. We left yesterday, spent last night in Savannah, and now we're closing in on Orlando. Let Manny know we're saving him all kinds of money—maybe he'll up his United Way pledge."

"Why do I think there's more to this story?" asked Doug who could smell a fabrication a mile away.

"Relax. Twyla will be parked in Orlando tonight, and I'll be on a plane back to New Jersey first thing in the morning. I have a car service lined up to get Twyla to work on Monday."

"Just don't screw this up."

"I won't if you won't," I told my pal. "Which brings us to Doc Waters and Maurice Tyson. You're sure they're on the worker list for tomorrow night's dinner?"

"They're on the list," said Doug. "Be in Jersey City by five o'clock tomorrow afternoon. And remember to get to Hinkle's and pick up a couple of tuxedos for your pals. You'll never know how many strings I had to pull to make this happen."

"And you'll never know what it's like to handhold Manny Maglio's promiscuous niece."

"Cry me a river. Listen, there's one wrinkle—" He stopped.

Uh-oh. "Wrinkle's a naughty word, Doug."

"It's a small thing."

I braced myself. "What small thing?"

"The doctor you wanted to talk to—the guy at Overlook Hospital in Jersey who worked on Ruth Silverstein."

"What about him?"

"Roger Meseck's his name and he's heading out of town."

"Where's he going?"

"He and his wife are driving to Baltimore later today for a medical conference and a long weekend with their daughter and grandson. So, you're going have to put off contacting him until he gets home."

"Dammit," I muttered.

"Did my best. The man isn't going to be around."

"You talked to him in person?"

"Called him at his house."

"You have his number?"

The hesitation that followed told me Doug knew he had stepped into quicksand. "Don't hassle the guy, Bullet."

"Any time you're ready. Make sure you include the area code."

Dr. Roger Meseck answered his phone a half hour before he and his wife were to leave. I managed to convince him "it would really be helpful to those of us working on the Ruth Silverstein Trust" if he could make a quick stop and meet me at the East Brunswick Hilton just off exit 9 of the Jersey Turnpike. An hour later, the Mesecks' Jaguar pulled to a stop in front of the hotel.

"Oh, my God," Mrs. Meseck squealed. "You were on TV. The kielbasa thing."

It was now as obvious as Mrs. Meseck's facelift that I had become branded for life. As soon as I ended my campaign to save Zeus, the Dubensko Polish Meat Products Company and I would have a little chat about a multimillion dollar endorsement deal.

"We're going to one of Roger's dreary meetings," Mrs. Meseck informed me as if I had known her half my life. "I'll be visiting with my grandson, David, while Roger is doing who knows what."

I smiled as politely as I could. "Sounds like a plan."

"But here's the thing," Mrs. Meseck continued. "Little David saw the Kielbasavan on television, Mr. Bullock. He simply adores it."

"It's easy to love," I concurred.

"I have Davey's cap in the backseat of our car. Would you be a dear and sign the brim? And you know what would be really special? Could you draw a little picture of a kielbasa under your name?"

If I didn't want answers from Roger Meseck, I would have written a couple of words on Little Davey's hat that would have gotten the kid expelled from kindergarten.

"Dr. Meseck, I have a question about Arthur Silverstein's daughter," I said after handing the autographed hat to the doctor's wife complete with a turd-like rendition of a sausage.

"Yes, Dr. Kool mentioned you're updating the giving guidelines for Ruth's charitable trust?"

"That and we're also trying to put together a few words for Arthur's testimonial dinner. You know about the Ellis Island event?"

"We weren't invited," the doctor said. "I don't support the United Way. It's too socialistic, and they give money to causes we think are left of center."

Like a men's homeless shelter? It would have been fun to poke at Dr. Meseck's philosophy of life, but there was a more pressing issue.

"I gather Ruth Silverstein died from severe blood loss," I said.

"I don't understand. What's this got to do with the trust or the testimonial?"

"We've heard all kinds of rumors about Ruth—her life and how she died. For purposes of the trust's records, we want to reaffirm the facts. As for tomorrow night's testimonial, we want to make sure nothing is said about Ruth that will set off more rumors."

"I see," said Dr. Meseck. "Well, you know those of us in the medical field keep patient information confidential. That's particularly true when it comes to rich patients." Both the doctor and his wife giggled.

"I realize that. But this has to do with a patient who died a long time ago. Maybe you could give me just a little more information without mentioning Ruth Silverstein's name. You know—in consideration for—" I jerked my head toward Davey's cap that Mrs. Meseck was cradling like the Hope Diamond.

"Well, perhaps—"

"If a young woman came to you today with the symptoms you ran across those many years ago—"

"Almost any medical student could peg what would be wrong, Mr. Bullock. Even back then, it wasn't much of a challenge."

"Really?"

"The patient in question was admitted in nineteen seventy, as I recall. So, the problem was far more apparent in those days."

"Those days?"

"Yes. Before the Roe vs. Wade case. When illegal abortions were common."

"So, Ruth—so, the patient had a botched abortion."

"Not at all unusual," the doctor stated. "Not back then, at least."

"Would the medical records and cause of death certificate say anything about abortion?"

"Not specifically. But anyone with a basic medical background could look at those records and make an educated guess."

"Did—did Arthur Silverstein know?"

The doctor glanced at his wife who was busy stuffing Davey's hat into a plastic bag. I could see a flash of concern in his eyes and I could read the question running through his well-educated head: what's the point of doling out more answers since I've already snagged an autographed cap?

"Yes," Dr. Meseck said softly. "I told him."

"Yet he never went public with what actually happened. He let the world think his daughter died of a drug overdose."

"Her blood work was positive for cocaine."

"But cocaine didn't kill her."

A spark of trepidation lit up Meseck's eyes. "There was no autopsy."

I didn't want the doctor thinking this was some kind of American Medical Association sting. So, I tried lessening his concern. "The medical records were sealed except for the copy passed along to Arthur."

"And a copy that apparently found its way to the trust files."

"Yes," I concurred without really knowing if that were true or whether Doug had managed to pilfer the records some other way. "But this was all kept confidential and that's not going to change. It's just curious Arthur wouldn't counter the impression his child died of an overdose."

"Actually, Mr. Silverstein never commented openly about his daughter's death. I remember talking to him when he was sitting shiva. He said it was best to say as little as possible about how and why Ruth died. And he asked me to be discreet about what happened to her."

I wondered if Silverstein used the word "discreet" at the same time he pushed a few thousand bucks into Dr. Meseck's pocket. "But when you talked to the press, you inferred Ruth OD'd."

"I didn't infer. I just didn't contradict the media speculation. It was common knowledge Ruth was a drug user. She had a couple of arrests. So, it was a logical assumption that Ruth couldn't handle her habit."

Logical assumptions and the truth didn't always line up. Ask Miklos Zeusenoerdorf. The logical assumption was that he used a wooden cross to beat Benjamin Kurios to death.

"Arthur Silverstein knew what actually happened," I said to Meseck. "Somebody ripped open his kid in a back alley. He doesn't seem to be the kind of man who would forgo tracking down whoever killed his daughter."

"People like Arthur forgo very little," Meseck said with a shrug that told me he had more information at his disposal. "Anyway, Ruth's death turned Arthur into an avid pro-choice supporter. It's common knowledge he puts a lot of money and time into making sure abortions don't revert back to coat hangers and lye douches."

"Do you know which organizations he—?"

He stood abruptly. "I'm afraid we must be on our way."

I thanked the Mesecks and fired a few more questions as they folded themselves into their Jaguar XK. "Do you remember Mr. Silverstein's reaction when you explained Ruth's cause of death?"

Surprisingly, Meseck was forthcoming. "Indeed. Arthur's wife had been institutionalized a couple of years earlier—"

"Yes, that's well documented."

"So he was pretty much on his own when his daughter was brought into the E.R."

"It must have been very difficult for him."

"Very. His money meant nothing that night. It was blood, not dollars, we needed to save his daughter."

I didn't hide my puzzlement. "Blood?"

"Ruth had a rare blood type. I'm not sure she would have pulled through even if we could have found a compatible donor. Anyway, we just didn't have time to—"

"What about her father?" I broke in.

"Arthur wasn't a match. And his other child was an infant—too young to be a donor."

I hadn't expected Meseck to deliver any jaw-dropping surprises— only to confirm the suspicions I had about Silverstein and his daughter. This news was a lightning bolt.

"Other child?" I asked through the driver's-side window of the Jag. "I've read and heard a lot about Arthur Silverstein. I thought he had only one child."

Meseck gave me a look that told me the wrong information had just leaked out. "I shouldn't have mentioned that," he said.

"But you did. There's another child?

"It was a product of—shall we say—an indiscretion," he said. "And this is not something you ever heard from me. Do we understand each other?"

"We do. I assume Silverstein never openly acknowledged that he had two children."

"I was told by a third party that Arthur paid the boy's mother a handsome sum for child support and more money for her silence."

"Do you know the boy's name? Any information about where he was brought up?"

"No," Meseck said, "And frankly, I gave you much more information than was warranted even if you did sign my grandson's cap."

Chapter 23

Saturday was as close to nirvana as New Jersey ever gets. No smog. Seventy-two degrees. Low humidity. All signs pointed to ideal conditions for Douglas Kool's Ellis Island nighttime extravaganza.

After breakfast, I dialed Yigal's cell. No answer. Figuring the lawyer was once again cross-examining Twyla, I distracted myself with Gateway office work until noon. Then I drove Doc and Maurice to Hinkle's Black Tie in Edison, dropped them off, and circled back to the office.

I took a few minutes to pull up the *Quia Vita* Web site and memorize the faces of the two Visio Dei members who would be picking up the *Book of Nathan* disk from the mysterious Osman Seleucus. They were the last photos on a Web page titled TRIBUTES AND RECOGNITION subtitled FOR MERITORIOUS SERVICE.

At four o'clock, I was straightening my black bow tie, adjusting a new two-color cummerbund, and picking the lint off my tux jacket. I knew Doc and Maurice had returned to the Gateway—Hinkle had reluctantly agreed to drive the pair back to New Brunswick, after dressing them in donated formal wear. I told my assistant to track them down while I navigated my Buick to the Gateway's front entrance. Five minutes later, Doc and Maurice appeared looking like Ralph Lauren's worst nightmare.

"What the hell—"

"Get what you pay for," the professor noted with a shrug.

"Good God."

"Hinkle has problems with your United Way friend," Doc explained. "Said he was ambushed into donating the tuxedos but he'd be goddamned if he was going to fork over labor costs for alternations."

Doc's pants were too short and his coat at least a size too large. He wore a blue and silver paisley vest that hung over his pot belly like a skirt.

Maurice's white wing tip shirt gaped open just below his bright red-striped bowtie. Both men wore scuffed brown loafers and tan socks.

What I was looking at was beyond bad taste. My boys were going to send Doug into shock. I checked my watch—four fifteen. Too late to make any clothing adjustments since the ferry to Ellis Island was leaving at five thirty.

I drove through light traffic on the turnpike to exit 14B and followed signs to Liberty State Park. While the State of New Jersey and the feds put a boatload of money into revitalizing the waterfront near Ellis Island and the Statue of Liberty, they spent nothing on upgrading the convoluted roadway that led to the park. We jostled over potholes and torn-up cobblestones before reaching a cordoned-off stretch of road near the ferry terminal that served as the reserve parking area for those with invitations to the United Way dinner.

"Over there—that's Figgy's car!" Maurice pointed to a Ford Taurus that had stopped short of the guarded entryway to the VIP parking lot.

One of the side effects of using mind-altering drugs is an occasional hallucination. When Maurice says he sees things, it's usually because he's slipped into momentary delirium. So, if he claims he spotted Alicia Keys driving a sanitation truck in New Brunswick or Barack Obama selling chickpea falafels in Manhattan, you learn to take these things skeptically. Since it was impossible that Yigal Rosenblatt was within a thousand miles of Liberty State Park, I didn't even think about cranking my head to check the car Maurice was looking at.

"It is Figgy," Maurice repeated.

"You know, I think he's right," Doc said.

The starched collar on my After Six tuxedo shirt suddenly became tight. I braked my Buick and my eyes followed Maurice's index finger that was aimed dead center at the Taurus.

I did a U-turn and navigated my way to Yigal's car.

"Yigal. I screamed. "What—"

The lawyer opened the door and flapped his arms. "I had to come back. No choice. No choice at all."

"But why? Why?"

Twyla scrambled out of the passenger side. "It was something, Bullet," she said excitedly. "And if it wasn't for Yiggy—"

"What the hell are you talking about?" I could practically feel Manny Maglio's garlic breath on the back of my neck.

"Followed us to the house," Yigal chattered. "They broke in."

"Who broke in?"

"Two men. Don't know who they were." Yigal massaged a lump on his forehead with his right hand.

This made no sense. Maglio had eliminated the two Hispanic hit men as a threat. Besides, even when they were still breathing, the pair had no interest in Yigal and Twyla—just Doc Waters. Even Arita Almiras wasn't a likely suspect. Ida Kyzwoski had sounded a warning about the Almiras Society and how it had enlisted more than just her late husband to keep tabs on me. But I was the target, not Zeusenoerdorf's lawyer and the niece of a mob boss. "What did they want?" I asked Yigal, suspicion oozing through the question.

"Told me to back off, is what they said."

"Back off? Back off from what?"

"Kurios case. Said Zeus was guilty and I should let things be."

Twyla jumped in. "Thank God for Yiggy, Bullet. Those two guys might of killed us both."

"You saw them?" I asked.

"It happened outside the house," she explained. "I never saw nobody, but as soon as Yiggy came inside, he told me to pack my suitcase. We took off and didn't stop once on the way here except for going to the bathroom and to buy mascara."

The fishy odor of Yigal's story was getting stronger, but there wasn't time to probe. "Why didn't you call?" I asked the lawyer. "You were supposed to call. Remember?"

"Smashed my cell phone, is what they did," Yigal claimed, "Totally destroyed it."

"Did you ever hear of a pay phone?"

"Had to get here as soon as we could. Orlando's not safe. Nowhere's safe." Yigal's yarmulke flew off. Twyla retrieved the cap from the pavement and handed it to the attorney with a starry-eyed look reserved only for those who are gaga in love.

I pulled Yigal to one side and pressed hard on his shoulders. His vibrating stopped long enough for me to look him in the eyes. "You listen to me. I don't know what's happening here, but you put me in a really bad place. The first thing in the morning, you're flying back to Orlando with Twyla. Then you're going to live up to your promise to get her to Universal Studios by nine a.m. on Monday. Understood?"

I released my grip on the lawyer who began gyrating again. "Oh, I do. I understand."

"Park your car over there," I ordered and waved at a mostly empty visitor lot. "Until I say otherwise, stay out of sight."

I ordered Doc and Maurice back into my Buick and headed for the VIP parking area. It was already crowded with limos and expensive cars. Dozens of workers were loading flowers and other provisions onto two large boats. The first was a bulky Circle Line ferry ironically named *Miss Gateway* that the United Way had booked to carry a small army of workers and a few supplies that hadn't already been trucked in from Liberty Park over a narrow bridge to the 27-acre island. The second was a spectacular, 110-foot yacht christened *Resolution* that would be transporting guests to and from the island. Doug had told me earlier the *Resolution* was big enough to accommodate 150 passengers for a stand-up reception. The yacht would make two or three trips from Jersey to Ellis Island during the early evening. An even larger luxury vessel was shuttling guests from Battery Park in Manhattan.

I greeted Doug who was making nice to a couple of early birds about to board the *Resolution*. "Can I have a word?" I took Doug by the arm, guided him to the passenger side of the Buick and suggested he peek through the window. When he saw what Hinkle had done to Doc and Maurice, he groaned.

"They can't show up on the island looking like that!"

"They're busboys. They don't need to look like they stepped out of GQ."

"What they look like is a couple of clowns," Doug wailed. "Send 'em home."

I shook my head. "Not going to happen. I lived up to my end of the bargain and now it's your turn. If you want to butt heads, go a couple of rounds with your pal, Hinkle."

"Look, people are paying up to fifty thousand dollars a table for this goddamned dinner."

"And the two men in the car are going to clear the dishes."

The hard edge to my words convinced Doug it was useless to continuing pressing.

"Dammit." he swore. "You're one royal pain in the ass."

Doug waved at a middle-aged man who was all muscle and sweat. "This is Albert Martone. He's the catering supervisor. Handles the boats, Ellis Island, the whole nine yards."

Martone gave me a damp handshake. Doug explained the unanticipated problem and told the catering manager the two men sitting in my Buick were busboys who had to be added to the work crew for the evening.

Martone looked through the rear window. "Them?"

"I know, I know. But we need to get them in the lineup, Albert. It's very important."

"They have to wear decent looking tuxedos," Martone said. "Don't matter if they're scooping shit. Gotta be dressed right. I gotta reputation, for chrissakes!"

"You have extra tuxedos on hand, right?" asked Doug. "For emergencies?"

"I'm adding this to the damn bill," Martone threatened.

"That's fine, Albert. That's okay. I understand. Really, I do."

"Get 'em on board the ferry. When they land, I want 'em to go straight to the wardrobe trailer. One of my people will try to turn them into something passable."

I asked Martone if I could have a few words with Doc and Maurice first.

"Make it fast," the catering chief snapped back.

I climbed back into the Buick.

"What's your job?" I asked.

"Huh?"

"Your job. What are you supposed to do tonight?"

When dealing with anyone from the Gateway, testing for retention was crucial.

"Corner Abraham Arcontius," Doc responded. "Long enough for you to connect with Arthur Silverstein."

"Right. And you'll do this how?"

"Arcontius knows us. He saw Maurice and me at Silverstein's place. Running into us on the island will shock the hell out of him. While he's off balance, we're going to engage the worm in a conversation about ci-vility."

"He's smart enough to figure out your being on the island isn't a co-incidence," I reminded Doc. "If he gets too suspicious, he's going to skit-ter."

"No he won't," Maurice promised, sounding like a man who wasn't a neophyte when it came to culling a target out of a crowd and keeping him bottled up.

"I need at least ten minutes with Silverstein with no interruptions," I said.

"Consider it done," Doc assured me.

Martone rapped on the window. The catering manager was getting jittery.

"Quite a freakin' pair," Martone muttered as Doc and Maurice waddled their way toward *Miss Gateway*.

"You don't know the half of it."

Whether it was a stroke of genius or a flash of idiocy is debatable. But there was no weighing the upsides or downsides of the idea before it came flying out of my mouth.

"Fortunately the other two aren't quite as wacky," I said to the cater-ing director.

I could feel Martone's stare burning into me. "What other two?"

"The other couple who'll be working on the island. Doug Kool—" I paused and gave Martone a confused look. "Doug did tell you, right?"

"No, he didn't tell me!"

"Well, we have to get them to the island."

"What are they? They with the models?"

"Models?"

"The models! You know, the goddamned people Kool hired to walk around dressed up like goddamned immigrants."

I remembered Doug telling me he'd recruited a New York talent placement agency to put together a group of models who would show off eighteenth- and early nineteenth-century garb at the Ellis Island dinner. When it came to special events, Doug was king.

"Yeah," I said. "One's supposed to wear a Jewish outfit and the other is—" I stopped short of plugging in turn-of-the-century hooker. "Uh, she's good to go in just about anything on the rack."

Martone looked leery. "The Jew—what is he? A Hasidic? We could probably use a Hasidic. Is he a Hasidic?"

"No," I assured Martone. "He's a run-of-the-mill Jew."

"Can he pass for a Hasidic?"

"Absolutely."

Martone produced two clip-on red tags, which he stuffed in my tux jacket pocket. "Tell 'em to put these on. You got ten minutes to get the both of them on the ferry. And that's it for favors. Damn Kool needs a kick in the ass."

"Couldn't agree more," I said and jumped into my Buick, picked up Twyla and Yigal, then made the return trip to the pier. There was still time to back off my impromptu strategy of shipping them to Ellis Island. Plan B would be to leave them sitting landside at the ferry terminal for several hours until the United Way dinner ended. Not a good choice given Yigal's unpredictable and so far unexplainable actions. Better to have both of them closer to me and confined to a small spit of land surrounded on all sides by water.

"These red tags will get you on the boat and on the island," I informed the pair. "When you get off the ferry, look for a wardrobe trailer. Twyla, pick out something ethnic and put it on."

Twyla looked perplexed. "Who makes ethnic, Bullet?" Then a flash of anticipation. "Wait a minute—is it Louis Vuitton? Oh my God, is it?"

I rubbed my head. "Ask Yigal," I suggested. "He knows ethnic."

Did he ever.

Chapter 24

Arthur Silverstein was last to board the *Resolution*. The pint-sized king of the investment world gave a wave of his cigar to a small crowd of admirers and was quickly whisked to a stateroom on the main deck. According to Doug, this was the modus operandi for Silverstein at any event he attended. The billionaire was not one to mingle with the masses. If things went according to plan, the United Way's guest of honor would remain incognito until called to Ellis Island's Great Hall to make a few pithy remarks put together by his PR staff. Then he would slip back into obscurity.

As the *Resolution* left its Liberty State Park mooring, a seven-piece band played "Anchors Aweigh," the first of a long run of up-tempo selections. Most of the rich and famous had already found the three open bars strategically scattered about the main deck. One man, however, seemed completely uninterested in the premium brand liquors and assorted hot and cold hors d'oeuvres. It was Abraham Arcontius, who stood guard only a few feet in front of the door to Arthur Silverstein's cabin.

A few minutes into the short cruise across New York Harbor, the Asian leviathan named Thaddeus Dong sidled up to Arcontius. Since he was only a couple of inches shorter than the Empire State Building, Dong had an eagle's eye view of the crowd and it wasn't long before I was on his radar screen. He whispered something to Arcontius, which sent Silverstein's right-hand man slithering toward me.

"You have a problem returning phone calls," Arcontius said. He didn't seem at all surprised to see me, which probably meant Doug had let him know I was on the guest list.

"I lost your number."

Arcontius's pointy ears turned red. "But not my Internet address, which brings us to the reason you're here. I assume you got confirmation that we made the installment payments. We moved two point five million to your account."

I pretended to study the New York skyline trying to decipher what I was hearing. My last conversation with Judith Russet left me thinking Arcontius was no longer in *Quia Vita*'s inner circle. If that were true, why had he been informed about the organization's multimillion dollar payment for Le Campion's notes? I needed to bring all this into sharper focus, and the only way to make that happen was to pump Arcontius.

"Two point five million is a lot of money," I said.

"We can put this deal to bed before we get to Ellis Island," said Arcontius. "Give me the disk and I'll BlackBerry instructions to have the additional two million wired to your account."

"Two million?" I asked. My confusion must have come off sounding sarcastic because Arcontinus's face knotted into a scowl.

"Don't go there. You agreed to cut the price for the second payment by five hundred thousand. No more bargaining. Stick with the deal you agreed to."

It was like pulling away gauze. Arcontius wasn't fronting for *Quia Vita*. He was representing another buyer. Arthur Silverstein? The Almiras Society? I couldn't be sure. What I did know was whoever stole the disk had discovered a way to rake in millions. *Quia Vita* and another shopper had each put two point five million on the table to get a peek at Le Campion's nonencrypted notes. *Quia Vita* was willing to double down in exchange for the full translation of the *Book of Nathan*, but Arcontius was coming in $500,000 short. That meant *Quia Vita* was probably about to become the rightful owner of Le Campion's CD with Arcontius and company left holding an empty bag.

I hoped I could shake more information out of the weasel. "What we had was an agreement in principle." Whatever that meant.

"I'm finished doing this dance," said Arcontius. "The total package is four point five million. Period. We owe you another two million. You're going to take the second payment and you're going to hand over the goddamned disk."

"Before we take this any further, there are a couple of other issues we have to talk about," I said.

Even when he wasn't angry, Arcontius looked like a constipated Jiminy Cricket with a skin condition. Now that he was irate, his pointed head turned fuchsia—I could practically see steam blowing out his elongated ears. "Let me be clear about something. You're a nauseating thief. You'd be making a mistake if you didn't settle this now."

I straightened my bow tie, turned my back on the Statue of Liberty, and looked Arcontius right in his ball bearing-like eyes. "This isn't about more money. Just a couple of questions that need answers."

Arcontius gave me a look that could melt steel. "What questions?"

"Questions about Arita Almiras and the Almiras Society."

What followed was a long interlude of silence. Arcontius pushed back from the *Resolution*'s deck rail. Then he gave a slight finger wave to Thaddeus Dong. The Asian giant was still parked by Silverstein's cabin. It took him only a few steps to make his way across the deck.

Arcontius tilted his head toward the Asian. "You remember my associate, Mr. Dong."

"He's hard to forget."

"Do you know what the Chinese word, Dong, means?"

"Not a clue."

"Historian," replied Arcontius. "And it fits Mr. Dong perfectly. He has a long memory when it comes to people who cross us. He helps us remember to even the score if people don't live up to their commitments. Do you get what I'm telling you?"

"Sort of. But with all due respect to Mr. Dong, we still need to chat about Arita Almiras."

"Your inquiring mind has a way of pulling you into a tar pit, Mr. Bullock."

I nodded. "It's a curse."

"You'd be advised to take your money and walk away."

"Not until you tell me what you know about the Almiras Society."

The onboard band was finishing "New York, New York" when Arcontius resumed the discussion. "Tell me—does your line of questioning have something to do with Mr. Zeusenoerdorf?"

"It does."

"I'm surprised. I thought your quest for justice would evaporate once you turned millionaire."

"I'm full of surprises."

"Yes, I'm beginning to see that," Arcontius said. "Very well. We'll talk. But this is a conversation that has to be private."

My alarm bell sounded. "Okay."

Arcontius pointed to a door. "The lower deck." A moment later, we were walking down a steep stairway that led to a section of the yacht that was all engine and storage. Apparently, Arcontius knew the *Resolution* from bow to stern. I recalled Doug telling me that the anal Arcontius always paved the way for Silverstein, which meant he probably conducted an on-site inspection of the yacht days ago.

"Dong!" Arcontius looked up to the giant who was still at the top of the stairs. "Make sure we're not interrupted." The Asian shut the metal door at the top of the stairway. I pictured Dong standing outside, looking like Mr. Clean on a bad day. No one would be getting past Arcontius's henchman until the guard dog was told to stand down.

Arcontius led the way through a door that put us in an open-air area tucked under the main deck. A pair of Yamaha WaveRunners and other small watercraft were stowed and locked in place behind a complicated launch-and-retrieval system. Arcontius waltzed me around until I was standing with my back against two thick cables that passed as a railing. Aside from those strands of twisted metal, there was nothing between me and the brackish water of New York Harbor.

"What do you know about Arita Almiras?" Arcontius asked.

I raised my voice so I could be heard over the rumble of the ship's engines. "I'm the one with the questions. Let's start over. What do you know about Arita Almiras?"

"Enough to assure you that it's a name you would be better off forgetting."

"There's a man named Conway Kyzwoski who did his share of remembering before he died."

It was as if Arcontius knew what I was going to say before I said it. "Kyzwoski," he whispered, "and what did he tell you?"

"According to Conway, I'm looking at Arita Almiras," I lied. "Apparently, you're the major domo for an organization called the Almiras Society. Given different circumstances, what Kyzwoski had to say wouldn't mean a thing to me. But then Conway added that the society was connected to the Benjamin Kurios murder. He also said your organization had attached itself to me like a tick to a dog."

"I've heard of Mr. Kyzwoski," Arcontius conceded. "And I know something about the Almiras Society. But that's as far as it goes."

"Really? Because according to Judith Russet, you know a lot about the society." I was getting accustomed to stretching the truth.

This Arcontius had not expected. He looked like he had just been hit by the *Resolution*'s anchor. The possibility that the head of *Quia Vita* had openly linked Arcontius with the Almiras Society caught him off guard. "What did Russet tell you?"

I dodged the question. "How long have you been a pro-life fox in Silverstein's pro-choice chicken coop?"

Arcontius did his best to hold himself together. Difficult to do when the verbal bullets were finding their target. "A very serious accusation, Mr. Bullock."

"It is," I agreed. "And one you don't want Silverstein to hear. Which is why you've kept me away from him."

"Keeping rubbish away from Silverstein's door is my job."

"*Occasio aegre offertur, facile amittitur.*"

Arcontius winced. "Excuse me?"

"It was your parting shot the last time we were together," I reminded him. "Opportunity is offered with difficulty but lost with ease. A little more than coincidence that it's also the Almira Society motto, don't you think?"

The pile of evidence had grown too high. Arcontius stopped talking, pushed back his tuxedo jacket and dislodged a Colt .38 snub-nosed pistol from its shoulder holster.

He waved the weapon at my midsection. "This is to make sure I have your full attention."

"I listen better without a muzzle stuck in my belly."

"Apparently you think that you can blackmail me into coughing up another five hundred thousand dollars for Le Campion's disk. Well, you're a fool."

"I told you, I'm not looking for money. I'm looking for a guarantee you're not going to send another Conway Kyzwoski my way with a video camera or a bullet. And there's something else."

"What?"

"Shoot me and you can forget about the *Book of Nathan* disk. You'll never see it."

The possibility of losing the disk outweighed what I knew Arcontius longed to do. He reholstered his pistol but kept his jacket pulled back.

"Interesting," mused Arcontius. "It's the first time you admitted you have the disk."

It wasn't actually an admission—but I understood how Arcontius might have come to the conclusion I was marketing Le Campion's disk. I figured this wasn't the time to set him straight. "Since we're into confessions, explain why your society has had me in its crosshairs ever since Kurios was killed."

"We put you under surveillance not long after your man Zeusenoerdorf was picked up on a murder charge," Arcontius acknowledged.

"Zeusenoerdorf's not my man."

Arcontius disregarded the correction. "No one was instructed to take you out—just to follow you and recover the disk. We work hard to minimize loss of life unless we feel it's absolutely essential to our cause."

It was a roundabout confession, but good enough for me. Arcontius had just admitted he was the Almiras Society's alpha dog.

"Why was it absolutely essential to kill Benjamin Kurios?"

"The society had nothing to do with Benjamin's murder."

"What does that mean? You didn't beat Kurios to death personally but hired someone to take care of it?"

Arcontius kept talking as if wanting to set the record straight. "I'll tell you what happened to Kurios."

"I'm listening."

"The society had been keeping an eye on Benjamin after we learned Le Campion sent him the *Book of Nathan* disk. We were waiting for the right opportunity to work out—how should I put it?—a change in ownership."

Arcontius stopped, possibly reconsidering his offer to give me details about how Kurios died. "So, on a dark and rainy night, you pulled Benjamin out of his hotel and beat the shit out of him," I said.

His face reddened. "We had nothing to do with abducting Benjamin. But one of our people saw him when he was forced into a van with a little help from a tire iron. When the van took off, our man stayed on its tail."

"It was your boy who was driving the blue sedan Zeusenoerdorf saw—the car that ran the van off the road."

"Yes."

"Juan Perez."

Arcontius was unruffled. "Mr. Perez was an experienced investigator."

"He was a Venezuelan mercenary."

Arcontius raised an eyebrow, telling me he was surprised about how much information I had scraped together.

"We imported Perez because we needed someone with his skill set."

"Skill set?"

"Most of the members of our society are not trained to handle high-risk situations. I suppose you already know we recruited Perez from one of Silverstein's security teams in Caracas."

"Seems Silverstein's employees like wearing two hats." I wondered how Silverstein could be so successful and yet be so myopic. The old man had made billions, but couldn't spot a double-cross if he tripped over one.

"Perez did so for many years," Arcontius confirmed. "He wasn't just muscle, he was also observant. Perez spotted something important the night Benjamin was beaten."

"The *Book of Nathan* disk," I guessed.

"Yes. The van driver took the disk from Benjamin and put it in his pocket just before he took off."

"Then what?"

"It was early in the morning and there was no traffic. We had no idea where the van was heading—where Benjamin and the disk might end up. When Perez cell phoned to let me know what was going on, I ordered him to stop the van."

"Your guy uses his car to slam the van into the bridge piling and out pops Benjamin Kurios."

"I assume Mr. Zeusenoerdorf gave you those details. As he also probably told you, Perez ran his car into an abutment. The two drivers ended up in hand-to-hand combat, which is when the disk fell out of the van driver's pocket and landed not far from Benjamin, who by that time was nearly dead."

I knew Arcontius's story could be bogus. But his description of what happened the night Kurios died matched Zeus's jailhouse testimony.

"During the fight, Perez's neck chain and *Quia Vita* emblem got ripped off," I said.

"Yes," Arcontius grumbled, showing his distain for his man's carelessness. Or was it the way Perez wore his affiliation to Judith Russet's organization around his neck? From my talk with Ida Kyzwoski, I had learned that most Almiras Society members were also connected to *Quia Vita*. Maybe Arcontius resented Perez for not getting his organizational priorities straight. After all, it was the Almiras Society that was paying the Venezuelan to tail Kurios.

"Then Zeusenoerdorf arrives."

"Carrying a heavy piece of lumber."

"It was a cross," I plugged in the correction.

Arcontius took a couple of steps to the side, his skinny frame between me and the door to the interior of the yacht. "So it was. The street fight ended. Perez headed back to his car, but was shot twice by the van driver."

"Which is why Perez didn't or couldn't pick up the disk."

Arcontius sighed. "Exactly. He drove a few miles from the scene before he bled to death. Fortunately, there were other society members in Orlando who we called in to clean up the mess. We removed the bullets from the corpse then burned the car and body. A rainy night and a careless driver. Just another accident."

"Ever ask yourself why the van driver didn't circle back and pick up the disk?"

"Until you put the disk up for sale, we thought that's just what the van driver had done. Now we think the man either panicked when he saw Zeusenoerdorf or was too disoriented because of his fight with Perez. Are we finished?"

"No," I said. "There's a man in prison about to be convicted for a crime he didn't commit. You know Zeusenoerdorf didn't kill Kurios."

On the deck above, Sousa's "Stars and Stripes Forever" overrode the whir of the yacht engines. The *Resolution* was making a slow semicircle around the east side of the Statue of Liberty's twelve-acre island.

"Our job is to fight a war," Arcontius said. "And as in any war, there's always collateral damage. Zeusenoerdorf falls in that category."

"He could be executed for something he didn't do."

Arcontius shrugged. "Sacrificing one life to keep millions of children from being butchered is a price worth paying."

"Depends on whose life is on the line, doesn't it?"

"Well, mine isn't."

Arcontius was growing tired of my interrogation. With time running short, I took a chance. "Where'd you come up with the money to pay for the disk?"

"You figure it out."

I already had. Arcontius certainly wasn't using *Quia Vita* money, and it was doubtful the Almiras Society had millions at its disposal.

"You filtered out a few crumbs from Silverstein's bank account to finance this deal. It couldn't have been that difficult to siphon four or five million bucks from a pot that's worth billions—especially when the pot belongs to a man who's crazy one minute and drunk the next."

Arcontius blinked. This was another revelation that was unexpected. "Very few people know about Silverstein's condition."

"The list is getting longer. Silverstein's dementia made it easy for you to pick his pocket."

"Not so easy," said Arcontius, his voice rattled by irritation and anger. "Dementia with Lewy body is an unpredictable condition. Arthur can be cogent in the morning and a lunatic in the afternoon."

"How hard could it be? If your boss wasn't hallucinating, he was drunk."

The inference that milking Silverstein for a small fortune was simple clearly aggravated Arcontius. "How we're financing this deal is not your concern."

"Maybe I don't want to do business with the Almiras Society. Maybe I'd rather talk Arthur into shelling out the full two point five million second payment. He hired me to find the CD in the first place."

"Maybe you need to think about what you're saying," warned Arcontius. "Maybe you should consider what will happen if you don't come through with the disk."

I didn't need to consider—I knew what Arcontius would do if Le Campion's transcription didn't land in his pocket. "I told you—if you take me out, the disk is history."

Arcontius tugged at his jacket to remind me he was armed. "Just to be clear—we'd rather the disk rot in obscurity than risk having it used by anyone who's pro-choice."

I let the sound of the *Resolution's* hull cutting through New York Harbor fill a few moments while I pretended to ponder what Arcontius had said. I was getting accustomed to ducking threats and intimidation. Even handguns had lost most of their shock value. Running a men's shelter has a way of hardening the body and soul to these kinds of things. Still, I wanted Arcontius to think his tactics were giving me second thoughts.

"All right," I said at last. "Pay up and the disk is yours."

Arcontius retrieved his BlackBerry from his jacket pocket. "Hand it over and I'll activate the transfer to your account. I assume you have some way of validating the receipt of funds?"

"Contrary to public opinion, people who run homeless shelters aren't all idiots," I said. "The disk isn't on me—or this yacht, for that matter."

Arcontius pursed his thin lips. "More games?"

"Osman Seleucus," I said quietly.

"Who?"

Arcontius gave me a blank look that reconfirmed he had not been brought into *Quia Vita's* plan to acquire the stolen disk.

"Somebody who'll be helping out tonight," I explained. "When we get to Ellis Island."

"An accomplice?"

"Safety in numbers."

"Seleucus has the disk?"

I ignored the question. "Later on tonight, I'll tell you where we'll make the exchange. Give me your cell number."

Arcontius took a gold fountain pen from his jacket pocket and scribbled on the back of a business card. "Just so you know, Dong will be with me."

Hardly a surprise. The pair were pro-life's Cheech and Chong. "Until I call you, I don't want either Dong or you on my ass. If you don't give me some space, the deal's off."

"You're not a man we can trust," Arcontius said. Funny, Judith Russet came to the opposite conclusion. No wonder the disk was being sold to *Quia Vita* and not this bony piece of trash.

"It's an island," I spat back. "I'm not going anywhere for the next four hours. Just don't crowd me. Makes me nervous."

"Here's what should make you nervous," Arcontius said and cocked his head at his .38. "I want you to remember another Latin phrase — *quod incepimus conficiemus*. It means, 'what we have begun, we will finish.'"

Chapter 25

Ellis Island. An hour ago, during the drive to Liberty State Park, Doc Waters had given me an unsolicited, ten-minute tutorial. The island was the immigration gateway to the U.S. for fifty-one years until it was converted to an immigration detention center in 1943. "One of the most romanticized sandbars in history," was how Doc described it, explaining that for many of the twelve million people looking for a welcome when they disembarked, it wasn't there. "It was a gauntlet," the professor contended. "Some made it through the turnstile, some didn't." The three-acre stretch of land once used by the British to hang pirates and criminals was where America turned back one in six immigrants. "History books call it the Isle of Hope," Doc said. "For a lot of people, it was the Isle of Tears."

The *Resolution* made a smooth approach to a landing a short distance from the entrance to Ellis Island's main building. Four tall towers jutted above the roofline looming into the now dusky sky like shadowy sentinels. The high-stakes crowd meandered onto a wide walkway that separated the harbor from the front of the building. I inserted myself into the thicket of handsomely dressed dignitaries, trying to make it difficult for Arcontius and Dong to keep me in sight. A column of male and female models sporting nineteenth- and early twentieth-century costumes directed the *Resolution*'s passengers toward the main building's baggage room—the same entryway used by immigrants decades ago when they first showed up on the island.

Before stepping inside, I saw Arthur Silverstein make his exit. Although I was at least a football field away from the yacht, I could see Arcontius, Dong, and a small group of other minions hustling the banker to a small vehicle about the size of a Mini Cooper. Cigar in hand, Silverstein waved to a contingent of guests who had been slow to leave the boat. Then he was whisked off toward the west side of the main building. Scurrying behind was one of Albert Martone's workers wearing a standard tux, perhaps a size too large for his frame. If it hadn't been for the thick white hair stuffed under his maritime cap, I probably wouldn't have recognized Doc.

Inside the baggage room, a young United Way employee dressed in a long, dark blue gown greeted me with a pasted-on smile. "Beautiful building, isn't it?"

"Very."

"It's French Renaissance made from brick and limestone." Her eyes darted to a cheat sheet on a skirted table covered with nametags.

"Quite a place."

"Your name?" The woman seemed to have a nose for money, and her suspicious look made it apparent I had the wrong scent. I told her who I was and she ran a polished fingernail down the list of invited guests.

"Oh, Mr. Bullock," she said when she found my name. Her smile reappeared. "You'll be at Sir Howard Stringer's table. Table twenty-six."

"Stringer?"

"Sony's CEO. Do you know him?"

"Not really. But I bet he put his pants on the same way you and I did this morning."

The woman blushed and glanced at her nether region. "Oh, well, welcome to Ellis Island."

"Could you tell me if Mr. Seleucus has arrived yet?"

"I'm sorry," the lady said. "What was his name again?"

"Osman Seleucus."

The woman eyeballed the printout. "I don't see a Mr. Seleucus on our list." Her edginess over my pants remark was replaced by a deeper concern. "Oh, God. Did we miss one of the guests? We don't have his name. Dr. Kool's going to have a conniption."

"No, no," I said. "Osman wasn't sure if he could make it tonight. I guess it didn't work out."

I mumbled a thank you and headed for a stairway that took me to the Registry Room, also known as the Great Hall, the cavernous belly of the main building and ground zero for Silverstein's testimonial dinner. Docents recruited as tour guides for the night towed small groups of guests through the room pointing out the hall's vaulted ceiling with its twenty-eight thousand interlocking terra-cotta tiles. Martone's models were stationed in different parts of the hall, showing off period clothing and antique jewelry.

Behind a cordoned-off section of prime floor space were linen-covered tables, floral centerpieces, and a stage backed by a twenty-by-twenty rear-screen audio-visual setup. For the next forty-five minutes, though, it was cocktail time with bars strategically stationed along the perimeter of the Registry Room. In deference to Arthur Silverstein, Doug Kool had, indeed, created an atmosphere fit for a billionaire.

The Registry Room was crowded and it took me five minutes to locate Doc. He and Maurice were clearing used glasses and hors d'oeuvres dishes from scores of small cocktail tables.

"Silverstein's in the research library," Doc said softly. He continued loading champagne glasses onto an oval tray and avoided eye contact. The collar on Doc's tux shirt was wet with sweat and his black bow tie looked as limp as a piece of cooked pasta.

"The research library—where is it?"

"West wing—third floor."

"A change of plans," I announced. "Before you two block and tackle Arcontius, there are a couple of other things we need to do."

Doc gave me a mistrustful look. "We? If we means Maurice and me, forget it. That fascist pig, Martone, has us busting our collective asses picking up after these upper-class dorks. Sorry, Bullet. Stopping Arcontius is enough."

I took a stab at his conscience. "Remember Zeus? You know—the guy canned up in some stink hole in Florida? Come on, Doc. Don't lose sight of what this is all about."

Doc hung his head. "All right, let's hear it."

Dodging the question, I looked at Maurice. "Yigal and Twyla—have you seen them?"

"Back of the buildin'," Maurice said. "In a trailer."

"What trailer?" I asked.

"Where the models get their costumes."

"Maurice, I want you to find them and tell them both to stay put. Give Yigal your cell phone."

"My cell?" Tyson protested. "I don't give nobody my cell."

"Do it for Zeus."

"Why can't Figgy use his own phone?" Waters asked.

"Broken," I answered without getting into Yigal's explanation as to why.

"Shit, man," Maurice sighed. He begrudgingly agreed to do what I had asked.

"Tell Yigal to stay where he is until I give him a call."

"Anythin' else?"

There was. A weird idea that had its roots in what Doug had told me about Silverstein's dementia. "Tell Twyla to look for a red dress. If she finds one, she should put it on."

I had piqued Doc's curiosity. "Red dress?"

I ducked around the question. "Ever hear of Lewy body disease? Some kind of dementia?"

"Yeah. Why?"

"Give me a ten-second explanation."

"LBD—Lewy body dementia. Common kind of neurological problem that hits older people. Lewy bodies are globs of protein in the brain that control memory and motor control. If you've got LBD, you're probably fluctuating between being sane and totally out to lunch, hallucinations included."

The Gateway's human encyclopedia was once again amazing. "Thanks."

"What's this about?"

"I'll explain later. Listen, I need you to track someone down—fast."

"Who?"

"A man named Osman Seleucus. Don't know what he looks like or anything about him. He's not on the guest list, so I'm thinking Albert Martone has him on his payroll. Or maybe he's one of the models. Is there a way you can find out?"

Doc thought for a moment. "Martone has a lieutenant who keeps track of personnel. Let me see what I can do."

"There's something else," I said. "Arcontius has a sidekick called Thaddeus Dong—a Chinese guy who sticks to him like Velcro. When it comes time to bump Arcontius out of the way, do the same to Dong."

"I don' know, man," Maurice said. I could read his mind. He and

Doc were planning to double team Arcontius. Adding Dong meant a change of strategy. "What's he look like?"

I opted not to make Tyson more uptight. "He's Asian," I said. "You'll know him when you see him."

The Registry Room was a sound chamber that squeezed the volume out of each note of music delivered by a nine-piece orchestra and turned civil conversations into shouting matches. The noise drove most of the United Way's elite into other parts of the building. But for seventy or eighty couples, the band's rendition of the Village People's "YMCA" elicited a primeval urge that drove them to the dance floor.

"Bizarre, isn't it?" Doug Kool asked. I bumped into my pal at one of the bars. He was nursing a Grey Goose martini.

"What?" I shouted.

"There's probably three billion dollars flapping around out there," Doug yelled back. He waved at the couples, most in their fifties and sixties, who were tracing the letters Y-M-C-A in the air. "Ninety-nine percent of the time, these people are so conservative they don't pass gas. Bring 'em to a black-tie dinner, play the "Do the Bunny Hop" or "The Chicken Dance" and you end up with a room full of complete idiots."

"Spoken like someone who can't say enough about United Way's most generous donors."

"Just because I schmooze 'em doesn't mean I have to love 'em." Doug led me by the arm to an anteroom where the noise was only half as loud. I still had trouble hearing Harris & Gilbarton's star performer. "You keeping an eye on your Get-Away boys?"

"Constantly," I fibbed. "I have a question. Who's Osman Seleucus?"

"What?"

"Osman Seleucus," I repeated.

"Never heard of him. Jesus, there she is."

"Who?"

"Paula Parsons. Over there in the Tom Ford gown." Doug pointed to a woman in her mid to late forties. "Looks terrific, doesn't she?"

"Who?"

"The woman you're sitting next to at dinner."

"What are you talking about?"

"Paula Parsons. You're widowed. She's divorced—three times. So, I put the two of you at table twenty-six."

Seventy-five linen-covered tables all encircled with ten chairs per table took up most of the Registry Room's floor space, with the lower numbered tables reserved for the more important guests. Since table twenty-six was on the cusp of being in the top third of the evening's Who's Who list, Doug probably thought I would be flattered. I wasn't.

"Dammit, Doug, I don't need—"

Doug put his mouth two inches from my left ear. "Don't screw this up. She's the top female hedge fund manager in the country. Money's coming out every orifice of her body. Paula. Got a second? I want to introduce you to your date!"

"For God sakes."

Doug drew the woman toward me. "Meet Rick Bullock. Rick, this is *Fortune*'s twenty-third most powerful woman in the country."

"Twenty-second," Paula Parsons snapped.

"And you'll be in the top ten by the end of the night," Doug promised. Watching Dr. Kool remove his Donald Pliner leather shoe from his mouth reminded me of just how slick my pal really was.

"What do you do?" Paula asked, giving me a vice-grip handshake. I had a feeling Ms. Parsons wasn't into polite preliminaries like "hello" or "nice to meet you."

"I run a shelter."

"What?" screamed Paula.

"Shelter." I shrieked.

"Jesus Christ," the woman squealed. "Perfect. I need help setting up a tax-shelter division. My traders don't know shit about shelters even though that's what my fat-ass clients want. Lucky we're sitting together."

"No, I—"

"What?"

"It's a different kind of shelter!"

"Must be! If you're at table twenty-six, you've got to know what you're doing. We need to talk."

"Yeah, we do," I cried. Doug had melted away. Fortunately, Doc Waters showed up and threw me a life line.

"Excuse me," the professor yelled as he stepped between my date and me.

"Can't find him," he announced.

"Who're you looking for?" Paula shouted.

"Somebody I thought would be here," I screamed back and pivoted to face Doc. "Maybe one of the waitstaff knows who he is."

"What's the name?" Paula demanded.

The deafening music must have clobbered my common sense because I blurted out, "Osman Seleucus."

Paula let out a horselaugh that rode over the band. "Hell, I haven't heard Seleucus since college."

What?"

"Seleucus," she screeched. "The king of Asia Minor." Paula was as bright as she was brash.

Doc had a habit of standing with a slight stoop. But when he heard Paula Parsons's words, the professor stood ramrod straight. "She's right."

"Pardon me, ma'am," Doc said to Paula. "Would you excuse Mr. Bullock and me for a few moments?"

Paula's glare told me she wasn't used to having the help get in the way. Nevertheless, Doc prevailed and tugged me back into the Registry Room.

"What is it?"

"I know where to find Seleucus."

Chapter 26

Doc opened the double glass doors of Ellis Island's Hearing Room and motioned me inside. The room was the last stop for prospective immigrants who didn't pass the medical, psychological, or morality requirements. They were given a final chance to persuade the island's gatekeepers to let them cross America's threshold. Historians like Doc had to be impressed by how carefully the room had been restored to its early-1900's look. For me, the room's best quality was the way it muted the racket coming from the Main Hall only a corridor away.

"Where's Seleucus?" I asked Doc.

"I think I know."

"What do you mean you think?"

"The hard-ass woman you were trying to pick up—"

"Whoa," I stopped him. "That wasn't what was happening."

"Whatever you say. Anyway, she's right. About Seleucus, I mean."

"Doc, she was talking about some king in Asia Minor. The man I'm looking for is walking around Ellis Island, probably carrying a small computer disk."

Doc removed his mandatory waitstaff maritime hat. "Don't think so."

What little music penetrated the Hearing Room stopped and I heard the first call for dinner. In five minutes, a rabbi from Yeshiva University would be intoning the invocation and Doug would be wondering why there was an empty seat next to Paula Parsons.

"I've got no time. Explain."

"The lady had it right—about Asia Minor. In Anatolia, Seleucus is a common last name."

"How did we get from Asia Minor to Anatolia?"

"Turkey took over a part of Asia Minor centuries ago. It's called Anatolia."

"So?"

"If you did a survey of given names of boys and men living in that part of Turkey during the early nineteen hundreds, Osman would pop up as one of the most popular."

I looked at my watch. "Where's this going?"

"To the Immigrant Wall of Honor."

"What?"

"That's where you'll find Osman Seleucus. He was an immigrant from Turkey. At least, I think he was."

Most of my Gateway clientele were not that hard to read. The professor, on the other hand, had an intellect that could spin you in circles. "What are you talking about, Doc?"

"An outdoor wall that runs around the back of this place. It's called the American Immigrant Wall of Honor. There are six hundred thousand immigrant names chiseled into it."

"And you're telling me Osman Seleucus is one of the names on that wall?"

"It's a good bet."

"Betting isn't your strong suit." Doc's mouth twitched, which might have had something to do with a gambling debt that had cost him a testicle.

"Even so, you should check it out."

"And I'm supposed to spend the rest of the night going through six hundred thousand names? I don't think so."

"It won't take long." Doc told me to go back to the reception desk in the Baggage Room and ask one of the Ellis Island staff members to do a computer search for Seleucus. "If he's in the database, they'll tell you where to find the name on the wall."

I was again impressed by the professor's brain. Even if he was wrong about Seleucus, which was unlikely, his memory was awesome. The fact that I so frequently Googled Doc's storehouse of information sharpened the pang of guilt I had been feeling since my meeting with Manny Maglio. I had yet to tell the professor that Twyla's uncle had quashed the mob contract that had been hanging around Doc's neck for years. He was a free man, but didn't know it. I was holding back the good news because I wanted the professor to stay on high alert; to catch the scent of anything suspicious. Admittedly, it was a selfish decision but until my "free Zeus" campaign was over, I didn't want Doc slipping into complacency.

I had a few more questions for Doc, but Albert Martone was cruising the second floor on one of his quality-control inspections. The professor was missing from his assigned post in the Registry Room. A split second before Martone barged into the Hearing Room, Doc disappeared.

I saluted the head of catering and retraced my steps to the Registry Room and table twenty-six. Paula Parsons gave me a smile. Or was that some kind of I-don't-like-to-be-left-standing-alone scowl? Impossible to tell.

"Sorry for the interruption," I said after pulling out Paula's chair and seating her at the Sony table. "I'm afraid I'm going to have to excuse myself again. Should be back soon."

"You're leaving again?"

Go to enough black-tie charity dinners, and you learn to pick up the social nuances. Like who's talking to whom, especially if it's a whispered conversation. Or who's not seated at a power table. Then there's the vacant chair. If it's next to someone like Paula Parsons, the chair becomes the Tyrannosaurus at the table. Somewhere in the room, talk was already starting about how Paula, whose beyond-bitch reputation was legendary, had just sent another poor bastard running for the door.

I was on the stairway heading to the ground floor when the United Way board chairman tapped the podium mike and welcomed seven hundred fifty wealthy and hungry guests to Ellis Island. In the Baggage Room, I literally bumped into the same young woman I had embarrassed earlier in the evening. It was a full frontal collision that jolted out a gasp from each of us.

"Sorry." I tried disentangling myself from the lady. "Can't seem to stay away from you," I chuckled but got nothing back. "Maybe you could help me."

She turned crimson. "I . . . I don't know if—"

I fabricated a story about my friend, Osman Seleucus, who cell phoned to apologize for missing the United Way dinner and to ask a favor. Would I check the immigrant wall and find his namesake—a great uncle who had made his way here from Turkey? The young woman waved to an eager-to-please docent in charge of "immigration records and information." A minute after keystroking a wireless laptop, the docent scribbled a few words on a slip of paper that validated what I already knew: that Doc Waters was a genius.

"Panel 561," the docent said, pointing to what she had written and giving me directions on how to get to the Wall of Honor. She plucked a pen-sized flashlight labeled BOEING: PROUD SUPPORTER OF UNITED WAY from one of hundreds of gift baskets to be handed out to guests when they left the island. "You're going to need this."

I thanked her and headed toward the *Peopling of America* exhibit that, I had been informed, was where I would find an exit to the back-side of the main building.

"Mr. Bullock—wait." the United Way staffer called after me. "They've started dinner."

I caught the hidden message. Get back to the Registry Room. Very likely, it was a Doug Kool order that had been ingrained in every United Way employee handpicked to work the crowd. All guests should be in their seats when the United Way messaging began. Anyone caught meandering the grounds at the wrong time should be herded to their assigned table.

"Yes, I know," I called back. "Won't be long."

Dusk was on its last legs. In a half hour, the island would be dark except for the well-lit main building and the sliver of a new moon. I should have suffered through the opening round of the dinner and waited for total darkness before playing detective, I thought. Too late. Instead of eating ginger salmon wontons with Napa cabbage and doing my best to tolerate Paula Parsons, I stuck with my plan. The five-course dinner with interruptions for music, dancing, and mini-speeches would stretch out another two hours before the audience was served coffee, dessert, and Arthur Silverstein. That gave me time to penetrate the banker's defenses ahead of his speech to the faithful.

Outside the main building, I followed a paved path that ran adja-cent to the wall, an extraordinary stainless steel circular border that rimmed a huge lawn and garden. It was a long, curved line of individual metal panels each inscribed with hundreds of names. According to the docent, it would take two or three minutes to walk to the section of the wall where I would find what I was looking for. On the way, I unfolded the slip of paper she had handed me and used the Boeing penlight to reread her note:

Osman Faruk Seleucus
Smyrna, Turkey, Asia Minor

I called Maurice to make sure he had made the ultimate sacrifice by turning over his phone to Yigal Rosenblatt. I got my answer when the lawyer answered.

"I don't have a lot of time, so listen up," I said. "I need you and Twyla to go to the Research Library on the third floor of the main building at eight fifteen. Wait by the library door, and I'll either meet you or call you."

"Why? What are we supposed to do?" Concern was working its way through Yigal's words.

"Agree with anything and everything I say."

"I should play along is what I should do," Yigal murmured.

"Exactly. If I say you graduated from rabbinical school in Brooklyn and run a temple in Poughkeepsie, then go with it. If I introduce Twyla as your wife of eight years, don't call me a liar."

"Oh, I won't," Yigal pledged enthusiastically.

"Here's the kicker. If I do bring you on stage, Arthur Silverstein is probably going to be your audience."

"Arthur Silverstein?"

"He didn't get to be a billionaire by being stupid. So just follow my lead. Can you do that?"

"I can do that," Yigal assured me. "But why?"

"I'll fill you in later. Is Twyla with you?"

"Yes. Yes, she is."

"Let me speak to her."

Yigal handed over the phone. "Hi, Bullet," she squeaked. "I found the most amazing gown. It's a real beautiful red and they have this lady who does adjustments right there in the trailer."

"You wearing the dress now?"

"I am," bubbled Twyla. "You won't believe how good it looks."

"Terrific," I said. "In about an hour, Yigal is going to take you to the third floor of the main building."

"Mr. Martone says I have to give the dress back by nine thirty."

An interesting picture—Albert Martone and Twyla Tharp discussing high fashion.

"Shouldn't be a problem. Just don't take the dress off until after we finish our business." Had there been more time, I would have said the same thing to Yigal.

"What business?" Twyla inquired.

Good question. "You're going to jog someone's memory."

"I am?" Twyla sounded genuinely pleased. "How, Bullet?"

"Just by being you."

I ended the conversation. A minute later I found Osman Faruk Seleucus at the bottom of the middle column on panel 561. Now what? I was staring at the name of a dead Turk wondering if this search was nothing more than a waste of time. There was, of course, the possibility that the disk might be hidden somewhere in the vicinity of the panel. But the metal wall and adjacent cement sidewalk didn't offer much in the way of a hiding place.

I searched for something, anything that would lead me to Henri Le Campion's CD. The Wall of Honor was a continuous lineup of metal teepees, each mounted on a concrete base with one plate facing the main building and the other the harbor. I ran my hand beneath the overhang where the panels met the base. Nothing. Stepping back, I made another scan of the walkway and everything within two or three yards of the panel. The more I looked, the more I was certain the only hiding place for a computer disk was underneath the overhang of the plate I had just inspected. I went flat on my back and peered upward into the narrow gulch that ran from one side of the plate to the other, using my fingers to do a second examination of the seam between steel and cement. This time, my effort paid off. A two-by-eight-inch plug popped free and clanked to the pavement. I pointed my penlight into the narrow opening.

Henri Le Campion's disk, if that's what it was, was wrapped in plastic and tape. The CD looked as commonplace as anything you would find in a music store except this one was labeled: *Bk. of Nath. Trnscpt.* I opened the case. The realization that I was holding what could be the key to freeing Miklos Zeusenoerdorf gave me a rush. At the same time, I couldn't shake the feeling that the disk had its own bad karma. I did my best to push aside the negative vibrations and congratulated myself for getting the best of *Quia Vita* and the Almira Society. They had paid millions to own what was lying in the palm of my hand. Next question—now that I had the disk, what was I going to do with it? Ten seconds later, someone else gave me the answer.

For a man the size of T Rex, Thaddeus Dong was remarkably agile. I hadn't seen or heard him maneuver along the opposite side of the wall while I was searching for Seleucus. And when he pulled himself up and over panel 561, I was too stunned to move.

"Stay where you are!" The index finger of Dong's left hand was aimed at my nose and his right hand locked on the grip of a Glock .45 jammed behind his waistband. When it was obvious I wasn't about to stand, he fished a cell phone from the pocket of his tux jacket. "He has it."

During the past few days, I had cheated serious injury or death twice. Maybe because each incident was unexpected, I'd had no time for fear. Tonight, the situation was different. Thaddeus Dong had the look and temperament of a ruthless killer. His phone call told me someone else would issue a live or die order. Not that it mattered. Whether acting on his own or following orders, Dong was the type who could pull a trigger and feel no remorse about sending a slug through my skull.

I made a quick scan of the walkway and lawn that had mostly been swallowed by darkness. There was no apparent means of escape. Dong's size and the likelihood he knew how to use a pistol made it pointless to consider a dash back to the main building. Maybe there was a way to dupe death a third time, but to figure that out I needed a better view of my options. I leaned to one side and shifted my body weight to my right knee.

"Stay down!" snarled Dong. He used one meaty hand to shove me hard. I landed back on my ass.

Dong loomed over me silently for a couple of minutes. A clack of footsteps broke the stillness, and it wasn't long after that Arcontius walked into view, his weird body a silhouette against the distant glow of lower Manhattan.

"Question, Mr. Bullock," Silverstein's right-hand man said. "Did you underestimate me? Or did I give you too much credit for being smarter than you really are?"

Smart is something one doesn't feel when parked on his butt looking up at two men who had caught me completely off guard.

"From the second you stepped off the yacht, my people have been watching you," Arcontius said. "You didn't make a move without our knowing where you were or what you were doing."

I was stuck on "my people." How much of an army did the Almiras Society have? The night had turned cool, but I couldn't stop sweating.

"By the way—ditto for the two imbeciles you brought with you."

Which imbeciles? I thought. Doc and Maurice or Twyla and Yigal?

Arcontius answered my unspoken question. "We convinced Albert Martone that both your men needed to be put in time out. They're getting some much-needed occupational retraining."

Doc and Maurice were now on the sidelines, which wasn't good news. At least they were safe—a few hours of hard labor under Martone's watchful eye was a lot better than floating facedown in New York Harbor.

"What's this about, Arcontius?" I asked, trying to mask my growing panic.

"It's about what you're holding," said Arcontius. "You're going to give us the disk, and then we're going to take a stroll."

Dong leaned forward, plucked the *Book of Nathan* CD from my hand and told me to get up. When I stood, Arcontius ordered me to surrender my cell phone and Boeing flashlight. I did what I was told. Dong gave me a fast body check to make sure there was nothing else worth confiscating.

"Just for the record," Arcontius said as he nudged me toward the east side of the island, "we were ready to pay the extra two million. Had you handled things differently, we wouldn't be having this conversation and you'd be a lot richer."

"The two point five million you already contributed will make life comfortable enough."

"Will it? Comfortable is not something you're going to be once we're done talking."

We continued walking toward a dark corner of the island. Arcontius pushed open an unlocked chain-link gate that led to a work area cluttered with building materials and construction equipment. Across the harbor, lower Manhattan was ablaze with lights. But the east end of Ellis Island was deserted and foreboding.

Arcontius jabbed Dong's arm with his free hand. "Let me have the disk."

Dong passed the CD to Arcontius then fell back several steps. Arcontius was too far ahead of Dong to hear him whisper a few words into a cell phone. Sandwiched between the two men, I was close enough to the Asian to overhear what he was saying.

"He's got it."

Pause.

"I'll take care of it."

That was the end of it. Dong glided past me, each catlike step so quiet that I was certain Arcontius had no idea what was about to happen. Dong gripped Arcontius's head with his huge hands, then with one sickening jerk, he yanked Arcontius's skull back and jammed it hard to the left. A snapping sound cut through the night. The effect was instantaneous. Arcontius was dead before Dong dropped him to the ground.

Chapter 27

Ellis Island's repository for rare books, unpublished manuscripts, periodicals, and old photos is its Research Library. On this night, the large room tucked into the third-floor corner of the main building was Arthur Silverstein's hideaway until nine p.m., when he would be escorted one floor below to deliver his brief message to the United Way audience.

Dong unlocked the library door and shoved me inside. Silverstein sat in a leather chair with a small circular glass table at his side. A floor lamp cast a cone-shaped glow of light over the small man.

"Ah, Mr. Bullock," Silverstein said. He rested his cigar on the lip of a brass and walnut ashtray. "I'd pretend to be surprised, but the fact is we thought we might see you tonight."

Running a men's shelter steels the nerves. You get hardened to misery, despair, brutality, and hopelessness. Acts of violence are no more the exception to everyday life than addicts speedballing themselves into oblivion. After twelve years, you think there's no aberration left that hasn't been thrown in your path. But then an Arthur Silverstein shows up to prove how wrong you can be.

Dong punched me to one side with his Glock, then placed the *Book of Nathan* disk between Silverstein's ashtray and a bottle of Glen Garioch Highland Scotch.

"Your boy just murdered Arcontius." I shot a quick look at Dong who looked as unperturbed as the man who gave him the order to break Abraham's neck.

Silverstein poured himself a glass of Scotch. "Murdered? I think you're mistaken. Abraham's body is at the foot of a stairway on the east side of the building. Terrible tragedy. Makes you think, doesn't it? Just a simple misstep and you're dead."

"It wasn't an accident."

Silverstein shrugged off my comment. "Abraham is—or, should I say, was—known to be a little too fond of this." The billionaire hiked his glass. "There'll be an autopsy, of course. The toxicology report is going to confirm Abraham had a high blood-alcohol level. Heavy drinking and a long flight of stairs. What a shame."

"Arcontius is lying face down in a construction site on the other side of the main building," I said warily. The muzzle of Dong's handgun pressed against the small of my back reminding me that the killer was only inches to my rear.

"No, he's not. You see, where Mr. Dong left off, other people moved in—people who are very skilled at making a misfortune look like an accident."

Ellis Island, it seemed, was overrun with other people. *Quia Vita* had at least two representatives waiting for the *Book of Nathan* handoff. Arcontius had claimed there were Almiras Society agents on deck ready to check the authenticity of Le Campion's disk. And now Silverstein was telling me he had his own team on the field.

Watching Arcontius get slaughtered like a barnyard chicken had sent me into temporary shock. But now I was face-to-face with a reality named Silverstein and his henchman Dong. I wondered why Dong hadn't left me with my nose in the mud next to Arcontius. I was still breathing, but given the look on Silverstein's face, maybe not for long.

"So you knew Arcontius was working for the other side," I said. The question sounded complimentary. *Wow, you clever old fart, you really are a smart bastard.* "When did you find out?"

"Quite some time ago," acknowledged Silverstein. "Several years, actually."

I wasn't surprised. "How much do you know about the Almiras Society?"

"Everything."

"What about Dong?"

I threw a sideways glance at the Asian, who stood like a fixture, his face void of emotion. Maybe there was a conscience inside that massive body. Another peek at those empty eyes and I dumped that idea.

"Thaddeus works for me," Silverstein announced. "He's a long-time employee, and I suspect he'll remain a loyal worker if I continue putting the right amount of money in his pocket. Like most everything else on earth, allegiance can be bought and paid for. Am I right, Thaddeus?"

Dong didn't respond. I took his silence to mean a fat paycheck more than offset having to put up with Silverstein's arrogance.

"Arcontius thought Dong belonged to him," I said.

Silverstein grinned. "So he did. But that was never the case. Dong kept me informed about all of Abraham's doings, including his work with the Almiras Society."

My brain was in a spin cycle, desperately looking for any way to escape. The only option that came to mind was figuring out how to stick a shard of distrust into the relationship between the old man and his Asian muscle.

"Did Dong mention how he let Arcontius steal millions from you? Did you know he said nothing while Arcontius sent truckloads of cash to the Almiras Society—probably the most radical pro-life movement in the country?"

Silverstein laughed. "Nice try, Mr. Bullock. I controlled the flow of any money Abraham removed from my accounts. Whatever he took was used for benign purposes—I made sure of that. True, Arcontius did siphon off a lot of cash. But the information I got in return made whatever he stole a good investment, considering what I was able to learn about Abraham's secret society as well as *Quia Vita*."

I could practically hear Arcontius screaming in hell. "You knew Arcontius worked for Judith Russet?"

"We used Abraham to feed *Quia Vita* information that took Russet's group on more than a few futile missions."

Silverstein's candor made me shiver. Whatever hope I had of surviving was going up in the billionaire's cigar smoke. The old man wouldn't be divulging this much information if he intended to keep me alive. I could practically feel Dong's fingers digging into my Adam's apple. I checked my watch. A minute or two after eight.

Concern cut across Silverstein's face. "Expecting someone?"

"Just the United Way team that's on its way to bring you downstairs."

"That's not how I operate. I set the timetable—not the other way around. We won't be interrupted for another fifty minutes. That's long enough for us to come to an understanding."

"What kind of understanding?"

"You'll recall that I paid you a ten thousand dollar retainer. Seems to me you still owe me some of your time. I have another job for you."

I tried to decipher what was being said. Arcontius's body wasn't even stiff, and the conversation had shifted to my living up to the terms of a one-sided contract.

Silverstein spoke through a billow of smoke. "You understand, I'm sure, that you're expendable. But eliminating you might not be necessary if you do what I ask."

I wiped a line of sweat that had beaded up on my forehead with my left hand. Silverstein didn't appear to notice that the maneuver gave me another quick check of my watch. Five after eight.

"I want you to deliver something to Judith Russet."

I thought about Doc's description of Lewy body dementia—about how someone with LBD could bounce back and forth between sanity and disorientation. The way Silverstein talked, the old man was sane. And yet what he was saying bordered on lunacy. What was this man like when he went over the edge?

"Deliver what?"

"The *Book of Nathan* disk."

The expression on my face delighted the old man. He hoisted his glass and gave me a wide smile. Give Russet the transcript of a Biblical book that might prove to be the pro-life movement's A-bomb? Silverstein hadn't killed Arcontius to get the disk, only to turn around and hand it to *Quia Vita*. The old man was as devious as he was rich, which meant there was a self-serving undercurrent running through his plan. "I don't understand," I said.

"*Quia Vita* won't be getting Le Campion's CD tonight. But in three or four days, we want you to tell Ms. Russet that you have it."

Which is what Judith Russet had suspected all along. That underneath a trumped-up crusade to free an innocent man, I was nothing more than a thief. I was beginning to make out the bleary edges of Silverstein's plot.

"My people need time to decipher the coded text," Silverstein went on. "And since Le Campion programmed the translation so it can't be copied, more time will be needed to re-create a facsimile of the original book. After we're done, you'll deliver the replacement disk to Russet, but not until she wires a second multimillion dollar payment to a Cayman Islands account I've set up."

Everything was now in full focus. "You get back the two point five million Arcontius paid for Le Campion's notes. On top of that, you edit the *Book of Nathan* so it says what you want it to say before I give it to *Quia Vita.*"

Silverstein released another cloud of smoke. "There's a possibility that no changes will be needed. The text might be in line with our point of view."

"Why me?" I asked. "Why not just drop the disk on Russet's doorstep or put the damn thing in the mail?"

"A CD worth another two point five million falls out of the sky?" replied Silverstein. "Judith Russet's far from stupid. If you walk into *Quia Vita* with an offer to sell the disk, that's a different story. It will simply shore up what Russet's been thinking since the beginning."

"There's a glitch in your plan," I said. "The person who took the disk is still out there and can blow your scheme apart with a phone call."

Silverstein emptied his glass, poured another. "We're not worried. Thanks to Arcontius, whoever that person might be happens to have two point million dollars of my money. *Quia Vita* probably matched what I paid."

"What about the payment due tonight?"

"Our thief will be disappointed," noted Silverstein. "But with so much tax-free money already in hand, disappointment doesn't tend to linger. He or she will go quietly into the night."

If anyone knew what kind of impact a large amount of money had on human behavior, it was Silverstein. I managed another surreptitious time check. Eight ten. Rows of book stacks blocked a view of the Research Library's entryway. I had no idea if Yigal and Twyla were on their way. My last hope was riding on the two of them. The thought made me shudder.

"What if I do what you want? What then?"

Silverstein shrugged. "Then our business dealings are over."

"And that's when Dong kills me."

Silverstein studied his Scotch. A slight palsy in his right hand sent ripples across the surface of the light brown liquid. "That shouldn't be necessary," the old man said, his words thick. "It's not that we couldn't explain away another accident; it's just that we needn't bother."

Silverstein's eyes began to drift. "You see, we have evidence that you masterminded the theft of the *Book of Nathan* disk—evidence that stays in my vault unless you force me to use it."

I felt my stomach knot. "What evidence?"

"For starters, the CD case that has your fingerprints all over it. The case and a fake *Book of Nathan* CD will be hidden in some location— possibly even here on Ellis Island. We'll tell anyone who's interested that you tried to sell us the disk but after giving you a front-end payment, we decided it would be unethical and possibly illegal to do business with you. But before we turned your offer down, you gave us a few hints about where you hid the disk."

"You never paid me—"

"I gave you a ten thousand dollar check—a check you cashed."

Silverstein had set me up from the start. He had tossed a few dollars my way and I had taken the bait without considering the consequences. Now I was on the old man's money hook, and I didn't like how it felt.

"Even if you were able to sell your story," I said, "it doesn't explain how I got the disk in the first place."

Silverstein tilted the bottle of Glen Garioch and splashed out another glass. His right hand was quivering badly and a puddle of single malt landed on the tabletop, coming dangerously close to the disk. Dong made a half step toward the table but pulled up when he realized the disk would stay dry. Which was more important to Dong—Le Campion's translation or Arthur Silverstein? I wasn't sure.

"Quite right," Silverstein said. "Of course, if pressed, we could put a theory on the table. That you learned from Dr. Douglas Kool or one of your other connections that Henri Le Campion sent Benjamin Kurios a valuable item. Miklos Zeusenoerdorf and perhaps a few others like him were dispatched to Orlando to get the disk and in the process Benjamin was killed."

"If you knew Zeusenoerdorf, you'd understand how ludicrous that story sounds," I said.

Both of Silverstein's hands were now trembling badly. "My legal team tells me Mr. Zeusenoerdorf is easily manipulated. Perhaps his story will end up like this: you paid Kurios's driver to make an unscheduled stop on a deserted roadway in Orlando. Zeusenoerdorf shows up and steals the *Book of Nathan* CD from Kurios. In the process your man beats Benjamin to death."

"Totally insane."

Silverstein reached for his cigar. His tremors scattered ash on the table and his tux before it reached his mouth. "Unexpectedly, the police make an appearance and arrest Zeusenoerdorf but not before he hides the disk and lets you know where to find it. You recruit someone to pick it up and soon after you're shopping the CD around looking for the highest bidder."

Eight fifteen. I wasn't sure what was going on inside Silverstein's head and even less certain about what was happening outside the Research Library door.

"There's not a prosecutor, judge, or jury who would buy that piece of fiction."

"My lawyers are very competent," Silverstein pushed on. "If this matter becomes an issue for a judge, jury, or the public to decide, a man who runs a homeless shelter isn't likely to prevail."

Just like Dong, jurisprudence wasn't immune to money, especially when it could be delivered by the truckload.

"If I do what you want, you let me live?"

"Precisely."

"And Miklos Zeusenoerdorf stays in jail."

"I'm afraid so. But we'll do what we can to keep him off death row. Instead of vegetating in your shelter, he'll do his time behind bars."

"I'm supposed to throw Zeusenoerdorf to the wolves for the sake of your cause?"

Silverstein shrugged. "Remember your visit to my home? I showed you a painting by Marc Chagall. *The Sacrifice of Isaac.*"

I remembered.

"Abraham was willing to take his son's life. He understood there are forces and causes more important than any one person, no matter who that person might be."

"Abraham may have said he would have killed his kid, but he didn't do it."

"He would have," Silverstein said, his voice soft. "Like Abraham, I consider anyone's life expendable if death serves the long-term interests of humanity."

"How does keeping Zeusenoerdorf locked up serve humanity?" I asked. "The man's innocent, for God sakes."

Silverstein reached again for his Scotch, his hand trembling badly. He managed to bring the tumbler to his chest, a shaky journey that sent a rivulet of liquor down the front of his jacket. "Your man is innocent?"

"He's not my man. And yes, he's innocent."

"What makes you think so?"

I was at one of those life-altering intersections. Turn one way and duck around Silverstein's question. That would have been the less hazardous route. But hell, I figured I didn't have a lot to lose. So I headed in a direction marked danger. "I know who's responsible for Kurios's murder and it isn't Zeusenoerdorf."

Silverstein's body stiffened. His eyes snapped back into focus. "Who?"

"You."

I got nothing. Not a word.

"Oh, you didn't actually get blood on your hands," I went on. "You paid someone to take care of business. You're good at delegating those kinds of duties. Am I right, Dong?"

Dong didn't respond and Silverstein remained silent. If it weren't for the old man's piercing eyes, I might have thought his dementia returned. But I knew better. My message was getting through. He was mute with rage.

"Here's how it happened. Arcontius paid a Venezuelan named Juan Perez to keep an eye on Kurios. You remember Perez—he was on your security payroll in Venezuela. Anyway, Perez was staking out Kurios's hotel and saw a thug beat Kurios with a tire iron and throw him into the back of a van. Kurios was carted off to parts unknown with Perez in his wake until the van reached a lonely stretch of road where it was forced into a bridge abutment. The crash sent Kurios out the back door of the van and onto the pavement. Then Perez and the driver of the van got into a winner-take-all wrestling match."

"How do you know all this?" asked Silverstein. The old man was attentive now. I disregarded his question.

"Zeusenoerdorf shows up and interrupts the fight. Perez panics and heads back to his car but not before the van driver finds a pistol and gets off a few shots. This has to be ancient history to you—but here's something you haven't heard."

I had to be sure that Silverstein was still in the real world before I continued. So I let a few seconds tick off until he finally muttered, "Go on." Then I hit him with a jackhammer of a lie.

"Zeusenoerdorf heard something before Perez and the van driver realized they had an audience."

"What?"

"Perez was beating the van driver bloody and the guy starts begging for mercy. You know what he said? That he was just a hired hand. That he worked for you. That it was you who paid him to get Henri Le Campion's disk even if it meant taking out Kurios in the process."

Silverstein glared at me. I kept talking before he had time to figure out I was bluffing. Almost eight twenty. "Here's what I don't understand."

If Yigal and Twyla were in position, there was a possibility they were catching some of the conversation going on in the back of the library. I turned up the volume. "How is it that you think cold-blooded murder is some kind of justifiable homicide?"

I didn't expect anything close to a confession. But the combination of Scotch and partial dementia shook out a revelation.

"It took a great deal of money and skill to turn Kurios into an icon," Silverstein said, his voice barely audible. "A few of us fortunate enough to have both the resources and the right beliefs were responsible for his success."

"You were also responsible for his death," I said, not lowering my voice. Silverstein didn't seem upset by my yelling, but when Dong pressed his pistol into my spine, I knew he wanted me to tone it down.

"It was never our intention that Benjamin be killed," Silverstein asserted. "The night he was taken from his hotel, we knew he had the disk with him. We sent someone to convince him to give us the CD. Unfortunately, he resisted and our man overreacted."

"Overreacted? He beat the shit out of Kurios."

"That wasn't supposed to happen. When we found out about Benjamin's head injuries, we made arrangements to have him treated at a private health clinic a few miles from where the van crashed."

"But Perez forced a change of plans and then Zeusenoerdorf showed up. I'm curious—what happened to the maniac driving the van?"

The way Silverstein's jaw tightened, I knew the question irked him. "He was an experienced professional. But his actions that night were— disappointing."

"So, he was sacrificed too?"

Silverstein nodded at the *Book of Nathan* disk. "We've paid a high price for this," he said. "Far beyond dollars, I mean. When something is so important to so many people, sacrifice—no matter how difficult—is justifiable."

"And just how difficult was it to sacrifice Benjamin Kurios?"

"Very difficult."

"Did you feel like Abraham?" I asked.

"What?" Clearly, he didn't get the reference.

"Did you know that I met with Roger Meseck?"

Judging by Silverstein's agitation, I guessed he knew nothing about my meeting with the doctor and his wife.

"Dr. Meseck?" Silverstein's tremors were coming in violent waves.

"Yes. Strange that your people didn't track me there. Or maybe they didn't bother to tell you." I paused to look at Dong. "Before I met with Meseck, I couldn't figure out what Kurios meant when he mumbled two words just before he died. 'Father' and 'Nathan' is what he said to Zeusenoerdorf. I spent a lot of time wondering how a priest named Father Nathan could be mixed up in all this. But once I talked to Meseck, I realized I'd been running in circles."

Silverstein's eyes widened.

"The 'father' Kurios was talking about was you. The 'Nathan' was the disk you stole from your own son."

"*Quiet!*" Silverstein shrieked.

"Benjamin Kurios was your best kept secret," I continued. "But when your daughter died, the truth came out. That was a terrible night, wasn't it? Ruth had a rare blood type, and the hospital couldn't find a match. She was bleeding to death. That's when you told the medical staff about your illegitimate infant son."

Anger contorted Silverstein's face. Anger and sadness.

"You sacrificed your own flesh and blood." I was back to shouting now. "You sacrificed your only son because you let a promise to your dead daughter turn into an obsession."

Chapter 28

I was there the night a sixteen-year-old kid shot Maurice Tyson's cousin, Roosevelt Mull, in the chest. When two .44 Magnum slugs shattered Roosevelt's rib cage, ripped open one lung, and pulverized his heart, I remember listening to the drawn-out moan of misery blow out of his body.

That wasn't a sound I wanted to hear again, but when Arthur Silverstein gave in to his dementia, I got a replay. The old man was being tortured, his conscience eviscerated by a painful realization of what he had done to Benjamin Kurios. Even Dong was shaken by the long howl of anguish that filled the Ellis Island Research Library.

Then the wail fell away to the murmur of a single word.

"Benjamin."

Then Silverstein's tremors returned full force and his speech clicked back in with a bellow. "Selfish, self-centered bastard. He was a stain on his sister's memory. *The Book of Nathan.* Only wanted it to glorify his own goddamned name. It had to be done. It had to be done."

Eight thirty.

I gave Dong a "what now?" look. For the first time, I saw a hint of expression in the Asian's eyes. Finding out about the bloodline between Benjamin Kurios and Silverstein surprised him. Something about a father having a role in the death of his son appeared to be nagging at Dong's miniscule moral core.

"Couldn't trust him," Silverstein continued. "My own son."

Hairline cracks cut through Dong's exterior. He ran his tongue over his thick lips.

"They'll be coming to get him," I told Dong, trying to capitalize on his uneasiness. "To bring him downstairs."

"Shut up," Dong growled.

Silverstein's mumbling disintegrated into a string of unintelligible sounds.

"Not much time," I warned Dong.

"I said, shut up. He'll come out of it. Five, maybe ten minutes, and it'll be finished."

Dong spoke like a man who had seen his boss disintegrate many times before. Apparently Silverstein's mental lapses were usually short, and if the old man kept to his usual schedule, he would snap back in just a matter of minutes. Which meant there would be time for Silverstein to collect himself before being put on stage.

Eight thirty five.

Silverstein had pumped out enough cigar smoke to permeate the Research Library with a light fog. Other than the well-lit corner where the old man was parked, the haze added to the murkiness of the rest of the library. We heard a weird clatter from some unseen part of the room, a bizarre thumping and clumping that edged toward us from behind a row of seven-foot-high bookshelves. Dong froze and stared into the semi-darkness. A lone figure darted into view.

"What the hell—" Dong wheezed.

"Heard talking is what I heard," said Yigal Rosenblatt. The lawyer wore a long black robe which I guessed came from Albert Martone's costume collection. He was a pulsating shadow—his black beard, hair, and robe turning him into a specter.

Dong repositioned himself so Yigal was unable to spot the pistol still attached to my back. "Nobody comes in this room," Dong shouted. "It's private. Get the hell outta here."

"Door wasn't locked," Yigal explained. "Just checking is all I was doing."

Dong's brain was not as well developed as his body. He'd apparently forgot to deadbolt the door. Even more surprising, Yigal had followed my instructions and had showed up at the library. I couldn't have asked for a better distraction. If there were a time to make a move, it was now. The library's maze of book stacks and shelving would make it difficult for Dong to do much damage with his Glock if Yigal and I could get lost in the labyrinth. I was about to try a fast break when Arthur Silverstein blew my plan to pieces.

"A *bekishe*," he squeaked, waving at Yigal. "Come closer. Closer."

Yigal inched his way forward until he was practically sitting in Silverstein's lap. The old man fingered Yigal's black silk robe.

"You're Hasidic!" said Silverstein. He was practically giddy.

"Not Hasidic," Yigal corrected. "Orthodox. Orthodox is what I am."

"But you're wearing a *bekishe*."

"For your dinner," Yigal explained. "They asked me to wear it just for tonight, is what they did. Put on a *bekishe*, they said, like the Jews who came to Ellis Island in the old days."

"I see, I see! Ah, those Hasidics—I'm Reform, you know."

Yigal sputtered something in English and Yiddish about how it was man, not God, who wrote the Torah, which apparently put him in the same reform camp as the billionaire.

Silverstein seemed to take an instant liking to Yigal. His shaking subsided and he smiled warmly. "But the *Halakhah* leaves room for our differences, doesn't it? At the end of the day, Hasidics, you, me—we're all Jews."

Yigal grinned.

"You should put on *Halb-Hoyzn*," the old man said gleefully. "You know—those knee pants that Hasidics used to wear."

"Don't look good in knee pants, no I don't."

"The past has so much to teach us," Silverstein mused without adding any explanation of what was whirling through his head. His eyes moved from Yigal to Henri Le Campion's disk parked on the side table. "Ahh," he whispered, making a valiant but failed attempt to return his glass to the side table. It shook out of his hands and what little Scotch was left in the glass sloshed on to his already liquor-soaked lap. Silverstein reached for the *Book of Nathan* disk, scraped it off the table, and fumbled the CD into the pocket of his tux.

"If we could only push replay and start again," he said to Yigal who was bounding from one foot to another looking as confounded as I was worried. "Would we make the same mistakes?"

"We might," Yigal replied. "But then again, we might not."

Silverstein shrugged. His unexpected partiality to Yigal was making Dong nervous. Silverstein tried retrieving his cigar that was perched on the edge of the Bugatti ashtray. It took three attempts, but he finally snagged the figurado, plugged it into his mouth, and astonishingly was able to relight it with the first snap of his lighter.

"If I could go back—" Silverstein began, but his fantasy slammed into a brick wall as he went wide-eyed and let out a high-pitched yelp. He was looking past Yigal, staring into the grey black haze that darkened everything outside the patch of light in the back corner of the library. Dong, Yigal, and I followed the old man's line of sight. Standing at the far end of an alley between two rows of steel bookshelves was a blonde woman dressed in a Venetian red floor-length gown. Distance, dim lighting, and polluted air made it impossible to get a clear view, but what we could see sent a jolt through the room. It was as if Ruth Silverstein had escaped from her life-sized portrait hanging behind Arthur Silverstein's desk and walked into the Ellis Island research library.

"Ohhh," Silverstein wailed.

He leapt out of the chair and kicked aside the ottoman. His quick movement jarred the cigar from his mouth and the stogie's lit end hit on the bottom of his tux jacket. The Glen Garioch Highland that had seeped into Arthur's clothing ignited. In a split second, flames were shooting up Silverstein's chest.

The fireball drove Dong back a step, and I felt the Glock detach from my vertebrae. I made a hard turn to the left and rammed Dong's right hand against one of the library's metal cantilever shelves. The Glock dropped to the floor just before I drove a shoulder into Dong's chest. Dong stumbled backward over the ottoman and landed with a floor-vibrating crash. Before Dong could recover, I lunged at a bookshelf loaded with archived materials and sent it hurtling toward him. Dong tried to roll to one side, but he wasn't fast enough. Most of the debris that hit him did little damage except for one heavy-duty metal plate that caught him on the side of his neck. Dong's body went slack.

I grabbed Dong's pistol and flew toward the library door. Yigal was a good twenty yards in back of Silverstein, who was about the same distance behind Twyla. She had kicked off her spiked heels and was running like hell trying to stay ahead of the firestorm.

"Ruth," Silverstein wheezed through the flames that were now licking his face. "Ruth." The old man's drunkenness, obsession, or a combination of the two seemed to block his pain. He kept moving forward.

Silverstein pursued Twyla through the main building's west wing corridor and onto a narrow third floor balcony. "Oh God," she screeched back at us. "What's happening? What's happening?"

Silverstein still had enough left to follow Twyla across the balcony to the main building's east wing stairway. I closed in on him, but he stumbled down the long staircase. Some unfathomable force kept him standing.

Twyla stopped, expecting Silverstein to fall. When the old man staggered ahead, she stepped into the Registry Room and shrieked—a piercing cry that brought most of the United Way table talk to a standstill. Some of the crowd stood, trying to catch a better view of the blonde in the red dress. When Silverstein lurched into the room, his tuxedo still a wick for the fire that engulfed him, curiosity turned to horror. Screams drowned out the orchestra, and those United Way guests anywhere near the night's guest of honor scrambled to distance themselves from the human torch cutting a path through the room.

The main hall was in chaos when I raced down the east wing stairway. I saw Twyla running to the head table desperately looking for help. But most of the crème de la crème, including Doug Kool, had already scattered, which left Twyla on her own. Silverstein drew closer.

"Ruthy—" the old man cried as he stumbled into table twenty-six and crumpled to the floor. "Keeping my promise. Keeping my promise."

Paula Parsons became Silverstein's first responder. She yanked a tablecloth from the ten-foot round table, sending dishes, silverware, and floral arrangements flying, then threw the fabric and herself on the billionaire who was now lying face up and motionless. There wasn't a lot left to burn on Silverstein's body so the fire was quickly extinguished.

I worked my way to Silverstein's side and knelt over him with Paula at my side. Yigal skidded past us and wrapped his *bekishe* around Twyla who was shuddering uncontrollably.

The scorched body on the floor had traumatized the Registry Room into silence. For a few seconds, there was no sound. No movement. Hundreds stood mute, gawking at what remained of one of the world's richest men. Then the room exploded.

Paula kept one hand pressed against Silverstein's charred neck. "I'll be damned," she said to me. "He's still alive!"

I leaned over the United Way's Man of the Year. Silverstein's eyes were thin, watery slits and his mouth nothing more than a lipless, dark hole.

"*Exitus acta probat*," the old man whispered. He was using what little life he had left to push out each word.

"I don't understand," I said.

"The outcome," the old man wheezed. He strained to draw in another breath. "The outcome . . . the outcome justifies the deed." Silverstein's body convulsed and he went silent.

One of several doctors in the room confirmed the obvious—the United Way's honoree was dead. The news cut through the crowd, turning shock and alarm into hysteria. A squad of uniformed security personnel added to the mayhem as they charged into the room and set up a perimeter around the lifeless body. Paula and I were pushed into a ring of horrified spectators who stood gaping at the remains of Arthur Silverstein.

"I couldn't make out what he was saying," Paula said.

"He said there are some ends that justify using any means—legal or otherwise."

"Which means?"

"Has to do with a promise Arthur made to his daughter. A promise that was more important than his or anyone else's life."

"Yeah?" Paula gave me an inquisitive look. "Must have been some promise."

"It had to do with coat hangers and back alleys. Silverstein was looking for something that would keep women from dying the way his daughter was butchered."

Paula turned her attention back to the charred body. "Did he find it? Whatever he was looking for?"

I stared at the puddle of plastic leaking out of Silverstein's tuxedo jacket. The liquefied remains of the *Book of Nathan* disk.

"We'll never know."

Chapter 29

Doug ordered the Colonel's extra crispy drumstick, one hot and spicy breast, two original-recipe wings, sides of coleslaw, fried potato wedges, and a hot biscuit.

"Which unlucky artery gets clogged today?" I asked. We were parked opposite each other at one of the few unoccupied tables inside a Kentucky Fried Chicken restaurant on the outskirts of New Brunswick.

"Don't hassle me, Bullet." Doug gave me a flip of his right hand as he talked. Mistake. His thumb caught the edge of his tray and sent it skidding over a thin layer of grease that coated the tabletop. Doug lunged and made a miraculous save.

"After everything I've done for you? I have a right to hassle."

"What are you talking about?"

"Manny Maglio put a lot of zeroes on his check to the United Way, didn't he? When you get your bonus this year from Harris & Gilbarton, buy me dinner. And forget about fast food."

"Give me a break." Doug dropped his chicken wing. "You roasted a billionaire who could have put the United Way on easy street for the next century."

"If Silverstein hadn't died, he'd have been slammed with all kinds of charges, including murder and attempted murder. After the justice system got through with him, the United Way would be looking at leftovers at best."

"Where are you from—Mars?" Doug asked. "Silverstein wouldn't have been found guilty of anything. Remember the O.J. equation? Put money in the mitt and you have to acquit. Silverstein could have bought his way out of any courtroom in America."

"You're forgetting about Thaddeus Dong. He would have taken his boss down with him."

"Nice theory," countered Doug, "but Dong isn't doing much talking, is he? And I doubt he ever will since nobody's been able to find the bastard."

How a man the size of a water tower could have gotten off Ellis Island the night Arcontius was murdered and Silverstein incinerated was a question that continued to be an embarrassment to police departments on either side of the Hudson River. A DNA check of the blood splattered on the floor of the main building's Research Library confirmed Dong had been injured. With or without outside assistance, the Asian had disentangled himself from the heavy steel shelving I had used to disable him and then did a disappearing act.

"You know, it's amazing how no one buys my story," I grumbled.

"They bought half of it," noted Doug.

He was right. Fifty percent of what I had to say was about Thaddeus Dong, and that information was considered credible mainly because it was backed by two Venezuelans who once worked for Silverstein. After their arrest on unrelated charges, they plea bargained for a reduced sentence by telling police when and how Dong wandered over to the dark side. That news prompted a second autopsy of Abraham Arcontius's remains and a conclusion that his neck injuries were not consistent with a fall down a flight of stairs. More importantly, the two men disclosed that it was Arcontius who hired a Caracas hit man to do damage to Benjamin Kurios for reasons unknown. A warrant was issued for Dong, but he was still among the missing. I wondered if he were playing basketball in Myanmar or pushing up daisies in Jersey. Either way, it wasn't likely he would be going to trial.

The other half of my story—the part about Arthur Silverstein— was tucked away in a "don't tarnish a great man's image" drawer. Seems nobody wanted to believe the billionaire was crazy enough to order Abraham Arcontius's execution. And the possibility that Arthur had something to do with Benjamin Kurios's murder was absurd. When I claimed that Kurios was actually Silverstein's son, there was a lot of laughter followed by a warning that libeling a deceased, wealthy man, not to mention the country's greatest evangelist, bordered on heresy.

"Arthur was a rich coot who had Lewy body dementia," Doug reminded me. "His problem was that he went a little haywire now and

then. Poor s.o.b. See, that's the kind of thing that gets you pitied not vil-
ified."

"So, Silverstein goes to his grave unscathed," I bitched.

"And you go back to running the Get-Away." Doug paused to attack
his chicken. "Does he know it was you who saved his weird-looking ass?"

"Who?"

"Zeuzamobroth."

"Zeusenoerdorf. And it was a team effort that got him out of jail, not
just me. Doc Waters, Yigal Rosenblatt, Maurice Tyson. Even Twyla
Tharp. They all did their thing."

"You hang with some strange people, Bullet," said Doug. "I'm curious—do you buy the FBI's theory? That a bad cop stole the *Book of
Nathan* disk and milked it for a few million?"

"Could have happened that way."

"Want to know what I think?"

"Not really."

Doug folded his arms. "I'm going to tell you anyway. I don't believe for a minute that there's a cop counting his chips in the Grand Cay-
mans."

"Really?"

"I understand Yigal Rosenblatt and Twyla Tharp are engaged."

"Change of subject?"

Doug cracked a half smile. "No—the subjects are interconnected."

"Hey, you should be jumping for joy. Twyla's getting married—to
a lawyer. That's got to be worth another mega-donation from Manny
Maglio."

"Word is that Yigal wants his little woman to quit Universal Studios
and play housewife."

"So I hear," I replied. "Mrs. Rosenblatt will be giving up her career."

Doug unwound his arms and returned to his fried chicken. "Which
one?"

"Any and all," I answered, hoping I was correct.

"I got word that Twyla's going to be a stay-at-home wife living in an
expensive neighborhood just outside of Orlando," Doug informed me.

"That right?" I pretended to be ignorant. Only two days ago, Twyla had sent me a photo of the million-dollar pad the Rosenblatts planned to purchase.

"Where do you think Yigal got the money to buy a pricey home? And how's he going to keep up his new lifestyle on what he makes?"

"Don't know," I said. "Maybe he signed a book deal. Could be Gafstein & Rosenblatt landed a bunch of new clients."

"Or, it could be Yigal understood perfectly well what Zeus said to him the first time the two met."

"Understood what?"

"Zeus told Yigal that he stuck the *Book of Nathan* CD under a rock not far from Kurios's body. Rosenblatt claimed he couldn't understand a word Zeus was saying. But supposing that wasn't true. Suppose Yigal knew exactly where to find the disk and got his hands on it. Then he decided to auction the disk off. Supposing it was Yigal Rosenblatt who got *Quia Vita* to fork over two point five million dollars and pulled another two point five million out of Abraham Arcontius's pocket?"

"That's conjecture gone wild," I said.

"Is it? Didn't you tell me that Yigal went to see some guy in Weehawken a while back?"

"So?"

"So, he takes a little side trip while he's in the neighborhood. Hops on the ferry at Liberty State Park and heads for Ellis Island. While he's there, he visits the Immigrant Wall of Honor and sticks the *Book of Nathan* disk under the panel that has Osman Seleucus's name on it. You and I both know the rest."

There were other chapters to the story that I was sure Doug knew nothing about. Like the $40,000 donation Rosenblatt pledged to the Gateway last week. Certain things are best left unspoken.

"We'll probably never figure out what happened," I said.

Doug gave me a how-stupid-do-you-think-I-am? look. "Something else I've been thinking about."

"Donating half your Harris & Gilbarton bonus to the Gateway Shelter?"

"You're hilarious. I've been thinking a lot about Henri Le Campion. After translating the *Book of Nathan*, Henri hid the original scrolls."

"So they say."

"Which means if they're discovered, we get an answer."

"To what?"

"Personhood, ensoulment, abortion. We'll find out who's right and who's not."

"It won't be that cut and dried," I predicted.

Doug tapped a half-eaten drumstick on his plate. "Why not? The book shows up, God speaks, and the world listens."

"I'm telling you—it's not going to happen."

"You're a cynic."

"Just a realist. Depending on your point of view, you'll either buy what the book has to say or write it off as bullshit. That's what Silverstein, Arcontius, and Russet intended to do."

Doug seemed disappointed. He was one of those people who longed for clarity. "You could be wrong. Maybe the book will get people thinking differently."

"Doubtful. Flexible thinking doesn't usually line up with topics like ensoulment and abortion."

Doug cocked his head. "I love your rosy outlook."

"It comes from studying the human condition. And I'm in class every day."

"Yeah, you are. Every day."

After lunch, I dropped Doug off at the New Brunswick train station, made a U-turn, and pointed my Buick toward the Gateway. The car began sputtering and bucking just as Doc had predicted it would. I didn't mind. I had a lot of practice being around things and people that didn't work quite right.

Miklos Zeusenoerdorf was where I had left him two hours ago—seated outside my office stuffing first-aid products and toiletries into gift boxes that Johnson & Johnson would be distributing at a dinner event later in the month. The Gateway and Goodwill Industries competed for pick-and-pack contracts that were big on repetition and light on intellect. We bid low on the J&J job mainly because I wanted to keep Zeus busy for another week.

"He owes you his life," Doc said, strolling into my office holding a shabby canvas duffel bag. "And not just because you kept him from being fried in Florida. It's how you help keep him going every day. Fact is, it's how you help a lot of people."

Doc wasn't the kind to hand out compliments. This had to be a warm-up to something else he wanted to say. He took another side trip before getting to the point.

"The way you still talk about her—" Doc said, looking at the framed photo of my wife that I kept on my desk. "Never met her, but I have this feeling I know the lady."

For the most part, I kept my personal life under wraps at the Gateway. But there were occasions when I'd field questions about Anne and my answers never failed to give away my feelings. "You two would have been good friends," I speculated.

"I think that's true," said Doc. "And I think that if she were around, you'd be getting high marks."

I glanced at Anne. A ray of afternoon sunlight leaked into my office, and her picture seemed to radiate. Doc was right—my wife would have been first in line to tell me that what I did for Zeus was worth a hundred times what Harris & Gilbarton paid Doug Kool. The professor studied my face as I looked at the picture of a woman who had literally changed my life. If he expected to see an expression of contentment that came from knowing how proud Anne might be, then I let him down. Contentment didn't come easy to someone haunted by a memory that left me with inconsolable loneliness.

I forced myself to look away from the photograph and turned to Doc. Then I motioned to the Gateway house rules posted outside the office entrance. "So, what's going on?" I asked, checking my watch. Two o'clock.

Doc knew the drill: all residents were to be out the door by nine in the morning with no reentry until after five in the afternoon. Exceptions: illness or special projects designated by the director. Doc wasn't sick, and I didn't need another pair of hands helping Zeus.

"I'm freeing up one of your beds," Doc explained. "Got a textbook publisher to hire me on as a fact checker."

I scrambled out of my chair and shook Doc's hand like he had just received another graduate degree. This had to be the perfect job for a man with a Wikipedia brain.

"More good news," the professor continued. "There's this lady I met who lives in Milltown. She has a spare room she's willing to rent out."

"That's fantastic," I said.

"Yeah, it is," Doc answered quietly. I wondered if his mixed feelings matched mine. I couldn't be happier that the professor was leaving the Gateway—but at the same time, I wasn't looking forward to the void when he was gone. "Can't recall if I told you before," Doc went on. "Most everybody who's been at the Gateway knows what a tough job you have."

"Hard work, but somebody has to do it," I laughed and put my hand on Doc's shoulder. The professor looked more at ease than I had ever seen him. Difficult to tell whether he was more pumped up by employment and a place to live or by the news I had passed along days ago— that Manny Maglio had erased his name from the mob's hit list

"No—it's not work somebody has to do," Doc said. "Truth is, you do your job because you want to do it. You belong to a very small club, Bullet."

I shrugged off the compliment. Seeing Doc walk out the Gateway door for the last time was thanks enough for me.

"Question is—will you keep doing what you're doing?" Doc asked. "Or are you on to bigger and better things?" Doc nodded to a Post-It note near my phone. I recognized his handwriting.

"What's this?" I asked.

"A call from FEMA at Homeland Security in Washington. I took the message just before you got back to the office."

I was constantly fielding calls from different private and public agencies around the country, usually about homeless policies and strategies. This could have been more of the same. Except Doc's demeanor made it apparent that it wasn't.

"The guy from FEMA thought I was your assistant," Doc said. "Told me he wanted to talk to you about a job in DC. Seems the Kurios case has turned you into a star."

The three-by-three-inch note suddenly took on the proportions of a billboard.

"Washington's looking for a celebrity," Doc went on. "The feds think they need a tsar who can link up government and nonprofit programs so they're more efficient. Somebody who can kick ass when things have to get done."

I stared at the 202 area code and phone number.

"Interesting, isn't it?" asked Doc. "You could be a big-picture honcho. Like Kurios, Silverstein, Arcontius, and Russet. People who fight at the top of the pile where it's about ideas and ideals. No more trench work where things get messy and bloody. No more saving the world one man at a time."

Doc hoisted the duffel bag to his shoulder and walked to the Gateway front door. "So what's it going to be, Bullet?"

I glanced at the note another time, then looked up. Doc Waters was gone.